Brother Kakzim pinched the pulsing left-side artery of Cerk's neck. "Questions can kill," Brother Kakzim warned calmly as his fingers began to squeeze the artery shut.

Cerk had less than a heartbeat to concoct a question that wouldn't. "I—I do not understand why the cavern-folk must die tonight," he whispered with just enough sincere terror to make Brother Kakzim unbend his fingers.

"When the water dies, all Urik will die. All Urik must die. All that exists in the Tablelands must die before the BlackTree triumphs. That is our goal, little brother, our hearts' desire!"

Other DARK SUN® Books

CHRONICLES OF ATHAS

CINNABAR SHADOWS

LYNN ABBEY

CINNABAR SHADOWS

Cover art by Brom.

First Printing: July 1995

Printed in the United States of America

Library of Congress Catalog Card Number: 94-61678

9 8 7 6 5 4 3 2 1

ISBN: 0-7869-0181-0

TSR, Inc.
201 Sheridan Springs Road
Lake Geneva, WI 53147
United States of America

TSR Ltd.
120 Church End, Cherry Hinton
Cambridge CB1 3LB
United Kingdom

This book is dedicated to

Lonnie Loy
my accountant

A good accountant is like a good magician:
There are lots of places you just won't survive
without one on your side.

ONE

Urik.

Viewed through the eye of a soaring kes'trekel, the walled city was a vast sulphur carbuncle rising slowly out of a green plain. Towers, walls, and roofs shimmered red, gold, and amber, as if the city-state itself were afire in the steeply slanted light of a dying afternoon. But the flames were only the reflections of the sun's bloody disk as it sank in the west: an everyday miracle, little noticed by the creatures great and small, soaring or crawling, that dwelt in Urik's purview.

Roads like veins of gold traced from city walls to smaller eruptions in the fertile plain. Silver arteries wove through the patchwork fields that depended on that burden of water as Urik depended on the fields themselves. Beyond the ancient network of irrigation channels, the green plain faded rapidly to dusty, barren badlands that stretched endlessly in all directions except the northwest, where the dirty haze of the Smoking Crown Volcano put a premature end to the vision of man and kes'trekel alike.

Drifting away from the haze, toward the city, a kes'trekel's eye soon enough discerned the monumental murals decorating the mighty walls. One figure dominated every scene: a powerful man with the head of a lion. Sometimes inscribed in profile, other times full-face, but never without a potent weapon grasped in his fist, the man's skin was burnished bronze, his flowing hair a leonine black, and his eyes

1

a fierce, glassy yellow that shone with blinding brilliance when struck by the sun.

The kes'trekel swerved when Urik's walls flashed gold. Through uncounted generations, the scaled birds had adapted to the harsh landscapes of the Athasian Tablelands. They knew nothing natural, nothing worthwhile, nothing safe or edible shone with such a brief yet powerful light. Given their instincts and wings, they sought other, less ominous night roosts. The men and woman trudging along the dusty ocher roads of Urik's plain possessed the same instincts but, bereft of wings, could only flinch when the blinding light whipped their eyes, then swallow a hard lump and keep going.

Unlike the kes'trekels, men and women knew whose portrait was repeated on Urik's walls: Lord Hamanu, the Lion of Urik, King of Mountain and Plain, the Great King, the Sorcerer-King.

Their king.

And their king was watching them.

No Urikite doubted Lord Hamanu's power to look through any wall, any darkness to find the secrets written on even a child's heart. Lord Hamanu's word was Law in Urik, his whim Justice. In the Tablelands where death was never more than a handful of unfortunate days away, Lord Hamanu gave Urik peace and stability: *his* peace, *his* stability— so long as his laws were obeyed, his taxes paid, his templars bribed, and he himself worshiped as a living, immortal god.

Lord Hamanu's bargain with Urik had withstood a millennium's testing. There was, despite the cringing, a measure of pride in the minds of those roadway travelers: their king had not fallen in the Dragon's wake. Their city had prospered because their king was as wily and farsighted as he was rapacious and cruel. The mass of them felt no urge to follow the road into the badlands, to the other city-states where opportunity consorted openly with anarchy. Wherever they lived—on a noble estate, in a market village, or within the mighty walls—most Urikites willingly hurried home each evening to their suppers and their families.

They had to hurry: Lord Hamanu's domain extended as far as his flashing eyes could be seen, and farther. Early on in his career as sorcerer-king, he'd decreed a curfew for law-abiding folk that began with the appearance of the tenth star in the heavens. And, unlike some of his other law-making whims, that curfew stood unchanged. Law-abiding folk knew better to linger where the king or his minions could find them after sunset.

Except in the market villages.

In another longstanding whim, Lord Hamanu did not permit anyone to enter his city unannounced, and he levied a hefty tax on anyone who stayed overnight at a public house within its walls. In consequence of this whim—and the city's daily need for food that no whim could eliminate—ten market villages studded Urik's circular plain. In a rotation as old as the reign of King of the Plain himself, the ten villages relayed produce from nearby free-farms and outlying noble estates into the city. They also gave their names to the days of Urik's week. On the evening before its nameday, each village swelled with noisy confusion as farmers and slaves gathered to gossip, trade, and—most importantly—register with the templars before the next morning's trek to the massive gates of Urik.

Nine of the villages were sprawling, almost friendly settlements with walls and gatehouses that could scarcely be distinguished from animal pens. Registrators from the civil bureau of Lord Hamanu's templarate had become as much a part of the community as templars could, considering their loyalties and the medallions hung around their necks, symbols of Hamanu and the terrible power a true sorcerer-king could channel to and through his chosen minions.

In many cases, the registrators had been born and raised in their village, as had their parents, grandparents, and so on back through the generations. In their inmost thoughts, they considered themselves Modekaners, Todekites,

Khelons, and such. Villagers rather than city-dwellers, they
had no ambition to brave the dangers of Urik's greater hier-
archy. To protect their sinecures, the rural yellow-robes had
learned the arts of negotiation. They compromised when
compromise would resolve a village problem without
attracting the attention of their superiors in the civil bureau—much less that of their overlord, Mighty Hamanu.

Long after curfew on market-day eve and market-day
night, there was usually music in the village streets and rau-
cous laughter in its inns.

Except in the market village of Codesh.

The first day of Urik's week and the first of its villages,
Codesh was as old as the city itself. In the beginning, before
conquering Hamanu laid claim to this corner of the Tablelands, it was also larger than Urik—or so the village elders
proclaimed at every opportunity. Codeshites feared Hamanu
more than their compatriots in the other villages because
they challenged him more than his other subjects would
dare. When there was trouble outside Urik's walls, Codesh
was the first place the templars came. Not templars from
the tame civil bureau, but hardened veterans from the war
bureau, armed with dark magic and the will to use it.

There was no camaraderie between templars and villagers in Codesh.

Wicker walls and rickety towers weren't sufficient for the
fractious village. Both Codeshite and Urikite templars
wanted stalwart towers and fortress walls that might give
them the advantage if push ever came to shove. Codesh's
walls were only a third as high as Urik's, but that was more
than enough to separate the stiff-necked Codeshites from the
more congenial market-farmers who congregated outside the
village walls on Codesh eve and Codesh night each week.

There were murals on the Codesh walls: the obligatory
portraits of the Lion of Urik, without the sunset flashing
eyes, and invariably armed with a butcher's poleaxe, which
explained what the village was and why its insolence was
tolerated generation after generation. Codesh was Urik's

sanctioned abattoir: the place where beasts of every kind were brought for slaughter in the open-roofed, slope-floored killing ground and processed into meat and other necessities.

Nothing valuable was wasted by the butchery clans of Codesh. Each beast that came into their hands was slain, gutted and carefully flensed into layers of rawhide and fat that were consigned to subclans of tanners and renderers, all of whom maintained reeking establishments elsewhere within the Codesh walls. The renderers took the small bones and offal, as well, adding them to the seething brews of their giant-sized kettles. Long bones went to bonemen who excised the marrow with special drills, then sold the best of what remained to joiners for the building of houses, and the scraps to farmers for their fields.

Honeymen collected the blood that ran into the pits at the rear of each killing floor. They dried the blood in the sun and sold it underhand to mages and priests of every stripe. They also sold their rusty powder overhand to the farmers who dribbled it like water on their most precious crops. Gleaners collected their particular prizes—jewel-like gallstones, misshaped organs, bright green inix eyes, polished pebbles from erdlu gizzards—and sold them, no questions asked, to the highest bidder. Gluemakers took the last: hooves, talons, beaks, and the occasional sentient miscreant whose body must never be found.

And if some bloody bit did fall from a clansman's cart, sharp-eyed kes'trekels flocked continuously overhead. With an eerie scream, the luckiest bird would fold its wings and plummet from the sky. A score of others might follow. A kes'trekel orgy was no place for the fainthearted. The birds brawled as they fed, sometimes on each other, until nothing remained. Even a strong-stomached man might wisely turn away.

The mind-bender who'd claimed the mind of a soaring kes'trekel from boredom hours earlier let it go when it became part of that descending column of hungry scavengers. He settled into his own body, his thoughts returning to their familiar byways through his mind, sensation coming back to arms, not wings, to feet, not talons. The constant, overwhelming stench of Codesh struck the back of his nose. He breathed out heavily, a conscious reflex, expelling the poisons in his lungs, then breathed in again, accepting the Codesh air as punishment.

"Brother Kakzim?"

The urgent, anxious whisper in Kakzim's ear completed his return. He opened his eyes and beheld the killing floor of Codesh's largest slaughterhouse. His kes'trekel was one of a score of birds fighting over a length of shiny silver gut. Before Kakzim could avert his eyes, the largest kes'trekel plunged its sharp beak into the breast of the bird whose mind he had lately haunted. Echoes of its death gripped his own heart; he'd been wise, very wise, to separate himself from the creature when he did.

He steadied himself on the polished bone railing that framed the balcony where he stood, waiting for the pangs to end. It was a somewhat awkward reach. Everything in Codesh was built to accommodate the needs of adults of the human race, who were by far the most numerous and, indeed, the most average of the sentient races throughout the Tablelands. Elves and dwarves made do without much difficulty, half-giants were cramped and clumsy, and halflings like himself were always reaching, climbing, or standing on their toes.

"Brother? Brother Kakzim, is there—? Is there a *problem*, Brother Kakzim?"

Kakzim gave a second sigh, wondering how long his companion had been standing behind him. A moment? A watch? Since he snared the now-dead kes'trekel? Respect was a useful quality in an apprentice, but Cerk carried it too far.

"I don't know," he said without looking at the younger halfling. "Tell me why you're standing here like a singed jozhal, and I'll tell you if there's a problem."

The senior halfling lowered his hands. The sleeves of his dark robe flowed past his wrists to conceal hands covered with scars from flames, knives, and other more obscure sources. The robe's cowl had fallen back while his mind had wandered. He adjusted that, as well, tugging the cloth forward until his face was in shadow. Wispy fibers brushed against his cheeks, each feeling like a tiny, acid-tipped claw. Kakzim made another quick adjustment and let his breath out again.

The bloody sun had risen and set two-hundred fifty-four times since Kakzim had brushed a steaming paste of corrosive acid over his own face, exchanging one set of scars for another. That was two-thirds of a year, from highsun to half ascentsun, by the old reckoning; ten quinths by the current Urik reckoning, which divided the year into fifteen equal segments; or twenty-five weeks, as the Codeshites measured time. For a halfling born in the verdant forests beyond the Ringing Mountains, weeks, quinths, and years had no intrinsic meaning. A halfling measured time by days, and there had been enough days to heal the acid wound into twisted knots of flesh that still burned when touched or moved. But the acid scars were more honorable than the ones they replaced, and constant pain was a fitting reminder of his failures.

When he was no older than Cerk—almost twenty years ago—Kakzim had emerged from the forests full of fire and purpose. The scars from the life-oath he'd sworn to the BlackTree Brethren were still fresh on his heart. *The silty sea must be made blue again, the parched land returned to green. What was done must be undone; what was lost must be returned. No sacrifice is too great.* The BlackTree had drunk his blood, and the elder brothers had given him his life's mission: to do whatever he could to end the life-destroying tyranny of the Dragon and its minions.

The BlackTree Brethren prepared their disciples well. Kakzim had sat at the elders' feet until he'd memorized everything they knew, then they'd shown him the vast chamber below the BlackTree where lore no halfling alive understood was carved into living roots. He'd dwelt underground, absorbing ancient, forgotten lore. He knew secrets that had been forgotten for a millennium or more and the elders, recognizing his accomplishments, sent him to Urik, where the Dragon's tyranny was disguised as the Lion-King's law.

Kakzim made plans—his genius included not merely memory, but foresight and creativity—he watched and waited, and when the time was ripe, he surrendered himself into the hands of a Urikite high templar. They made promises to each other, he and Elabon Escrissar, that day when the half-elf interrogator took a knife, carved his family's crest into Kakzim's flesh, then permanently stained the scars with soot. Both of them had given false promises, but Kakzim's lies went deeper than the templar's. He'd been lying from the moment he selected Escrissar as a suitable partner in his life's work.

No halfling could tolerate the restraints of forced slavery; it was beyond their nature. They sickened and died, as Escrissar should have known . . . *would* have known, if Kakzim hadn't clouded the templar's already warped judgment with pleas, promises and temptations. Escrissar had ambitions. He had wealth and power as a high templar, but he wanted more than the Lion-King would concede to any favorite. In time, with Kakzim's careful prompting, Escrissar came to want Lord Hamanu's throne and Urik itself. Failing that—and Kakzim had known from the start that the Lion-King could not be deposed—it had been possible to convince Escrissar that what he couldn't have should be destroyed.

Reflecting on the long years of their association, Kakzim could see that they'd both been deluded by their ambitions. But then, without warning from the BlackTree or anything Kakzim could recognize as their assistance, Sorcerer-King Kalak of Tyr was brought down. Less than a decade later

Borys the Dragon and the ancient sorcerer Rajaat—whom the BlackTree Brethren called the Deceiver—were vanquished as well.

For the first time in a millennium there was reason for a BlackTree brother to expect success in his life's work.

Kakzim sent a message back across the Ringing Mountains—his first in fifteen years. It was not a request for instructions, but an announcement: The time had come to unlock the ancient halfling pharmacopoeia, the lore Kakzim had memorized while he dwelt among the BlackTree's roots. The time had, in fact, come and passed.

Kakzim informed the elders that he and the man who thought he was Kakzim's master were making *Laq*—an ancient, dangerous elixir that restored those on exhaustion's brink, but enslaved and destroyed those who took it too often. Their source was innocuous zarneeka powder they'd found in Urik's cavernous warehouses. The supply, for their needs and purposes, was virtually unlimited.

The seductive poison spread quickly through the ranks of the desperate or despondent, sowing death. He and Escrissar planned to expand their trade to include the city-state of Nibenay. When both cities were contaminated, their sorcerer-kings would blame each other. There'd be war. There'd be annihilation and, thanks to him, Brother Kakzim, the BlackTree Brethren would see their cause victorious.

Kakzim promised on his life. He'd opened the old scars above his heart and signed his message with his own blood.

He'd had no doubts. Escrissar was the perfect dupe: cruel, avaricious, enthralled by his own importance, blind to his flaws, easily exploited, yet blessed with vast wealth and indulged by Lord Hamanu, the very enemy they both hoped to bring down. The plans Kakzim had made were elegant, and everything was going their way until a templar of the lowest sort blundered across their path.

Paddle, Puddle, Pickle . . . Kakzim couldn't remember

the ugly human's name. He'd seen him once only, at night in the city warehouse when catastrophe had been the furthest thought from his mind. The yellow-robed dolt was boneheaded stupid, throwing himself into battles he couldn't hope to win. It beggared halfling imagination to think that templar Pickle could stand in their way at all, much less bring them down. But the bonehead had done just that, with a motley collection of allies and the kind of luck that didn't come by chance.

Kakzim had abandoned Escrissar the moment he saw disaster looming. Halflings weren't slaves; BlackTree Brethren weren't martyrs, not for the likes of Elabon Escrissar. Kakzim raided Escrissar's treasury and went to ground while the high templar marched to his doom on the salt wastes.

Ever dutiful to the elder brothers of the BlackTree, Kakzim had sent another message across the Ringing Mountains. He admitted his failure and promised to forfeit his now-worthless life. Kakzim used all the right words, but his admissions and promises were lies. He knew he'd made mistakes; he'd been bested, but not, absolutely not, defeated. He'd learned hard lessons and was ready to try again. The cause was more important than any one brother's life, especially his.

Brother Kakzim wasn't any sort of martyr. He told the elder brothers what they'd want to hear and fervently hoped they'd believe his promise of self-annihilation and never bother him again. He was deep in his next plotting, here in the market-village of Codesh, when his new apprentice arrived fresh out of the forest and with no more sense than a leaf in the wind.

He'd wanted to send Cerk back. Bloody leaves of the bloody BlackTree! He'd wanted to kill the youngster on the spot. But without the resources of House Escrissar behind him, Kakzim discovered he could use an extra set of hands, eyes, and feet—so long as he didn't delude himself that those appendages were attached to a sentient mind.

"Brother Kakzim? Brother Kakzim—did you—? Have you—? Are you having one of your fits? Should I guide you to your bed?"

Fits! Fits of boredom! Fits of frustration! He was surrounded by fools and personally served by the greatest fool of all!

"Don't be ridiculous. Stop wasting my time. Tonight's an important night, you know. Tell me whatever it is you think I must know, then leave me alone and stop this infernal chatter about fits! You're the one with fits."

"Yes, Brother Kakzim. Of course. I merely wanted to tell you that the men have begun to assemble. They're ready—armed exactly as you requested—but, Brother, they wish to be paid."

"Then *pay* them, Brother Cerk!" Kakzim's voice rose into a shrill shout as he spun around on his companion. The cowl slid back, dusting his flesh with excruciation as it did. "We're so close. So close. And you torment me!" He grabbed the youngster's robe and shook it violently. "If we fail, it will be *your* fault!"

*   *   *   *   *

Cerk staggered backward, lucky to keep his balance—lucky to be alive at all.

The elders of the BlackTree had warned him Brother Kakzim would not be an easy master, but that he should be grateful for the opportunity. They said Brother Kakzim was a genius in the alchemic arts. There was no halfling alive who knew what Brother Kakzim knew about the old ways of manipulation and transformation. Brother Kakzim had decrypted the ancient knowledge the Brethren guarded at the BlackTree. He knew what the ancestors knew, and he'd begun to use it. The elders wanted to know more about *how* Brother Kakzim was applying his knowledge. They wanted Cerk to be their eyes and ears in Urik.

An apprentice should be grateful for such an opportunity,

for such trust, and Cerk supposed he was. Brother Kakzim *was* a master beyond reckoning where alchemy was concerned; Cerk had learned things in this foul-smelling village he could never have learned in the BlackTree Forest. But Cerk wished the elder brothers had mentioned that Brother Kakzim was completely mad. Those white-rimmed eyes above the ruined cheeks looked out from another plane and had the power to cloud another man's thoughts, even another halfling's thoughts.

Cerk was careful not to look straight at Brother Kakzim when the madness was on him, as it was now. He kept his head down and filled his mind with thoughts of home: lush green trees dripping water day and night, an endless chorus of birds and insects, the warm, sweet taste of ripe bellberries fresh off the vine. Then Cerk waited for the danger to pass. He judged it had when Brother Kakzim adjusted his robe's sleeves and cowl again, but he was careful to stay out of reach.

"It is not just the men who want to be paid, Brother Kakzim. The dwarves who own this place want to be paid for its use tonight, and for the rooms where we've lived. And the joiners say we owe them for the scaffolding they've already constructed. We owe the knackers and the elven gleaner, Rosu. She says she's found an inix fistula with the abscess still attached, but she won't sell it—"

"Pay them!" Brother Kakzim repeated, though without the raving intensity of a few moments past. "You have the coins. I've given you all our coins."

"Yes," Cerk agreed, thinking of the sack he kept under his bed. Money had no place in the BlackTree Forest. The notion that a broken ceramic disk could be exchanged for food, goods, or a man's service—indeed, that such bits, disks, or the far rarer metal coins *must* be exchanged—was still difficult for him to understand. He grappled with the sack nightly, arranging its contents in similar piles, watching as the piles grew steadily smaller. "I keep careful count of them, Brother Kakzim, but if I give these folk all that they claim is theirs, we ourselves will have very little left."

"Is *that* the problem, Brother Cerk?"

Reluctantly, Cerk bobbed his head.

"Pay them," Brother Kakzim said calmly. "Look at me, Brother Cerk—"

Cerk did, knowing it was a mistake, but Brother Kakzim's voice was so reassuring at times. Disobedience became impossible.

"You don't doubt me, do you?"

Cerk's lower lip trembled. He couldn't lie, didn't want to tell the truth.

"Is it the money, Brother Cerk? Haven't I always given you more money when you needed it? Money is nothing to worry about, Brother Cerk. Pay the insects. Pay them generously. Money grows like rope-vine in shadowed places. It's always ready for harvest. Don't worry about money, Brother Cerk."

He wasn't such a fool as that. The Brethren elders hadn't sent him out completely unprepared. It was the precision of money that eluded him: the how and why that equated a day of a man's life with a broken chip from a ceramic disk, while the rooms he and Brother Kakzim occupied above the slaughterhouse equated an entire ceramic disk each week, and Rosu's festering fistula was the same as an entire shiny silver coin.

Cerk knew where money came from generally and Brother Kakzim's specifically. Whenever the need to refill the sack arose, he sneaked into Urik following the brother through the maze of sharp-angled intersections and identical buildings. Brother Kakzim's money came from a blind alley hoard-hole in the templar quarter of the city, and it was much diminished compared to what it had been when Cerk first saw it.

No doubt Brother Kakzim could harvest ceramic disks and metal coins from other trees. Brother Kakzim didn't risk his fingers when he picked a pocket. All Brother Kakzim had to do was touch a rich man's thoughts with mind-bending power—as Brother Kakzim was doing to Cerk at this very moment—and that man would shed his wealth on the spot.

As Cerk should have shed his doubts beneath the seductive pressures of Brother Kakzim's Unseen urging. And maybe the Urikites *were* as simple as lumbering mekillots. Maybe their minds could be touched again and again with them never recognizing that their thoughts were no longer wholly their own. But the BlackTree elders had taught Cerk how to defend himself from Unseen attack without the attacker becoming aware of the defense. They'd also taught him never to underestimate the enemy.

Cerk shaped himself simple and befuddled. He made his thoughts transparent and his mind seem empty. Brother Kakzim accepted the illusion, then molded it further to his own liking while Cerk watched and learned and quelled waves of nausea.

"You see, little brother, there's nothing to worry about."

Brother Kakzim came close enough that their robes were touching. They embraced as elder to apprentice, with Cerk on the verge of panic as he forced himself to remain calm and pliant. His companion *was* mad. That made him more, not less, dangerous.

Cerk didn't flinch when Brother Kakzim pinched his cheek hard enough to pierce skin, then nearly undid everything with a relieved gasp when the hand withdrew. Brother Kakzim pinched Cerk again, not on the cheek, but over the pulsing left-side artery of his neck.

"Questions can kill," Brother Kakzim warned calmly as his fingers began to squeeze the artery shut.

Cerk has less than a heartbeat to concoct a question that wouldn't. "I—I do not understand why the cavern-folk must die tonight," he whispered with just enough sincere terror to make Brother Kakzim unbend his fingers.

"When the water dies, all Urik will die. All Urik must die. All that exists in the Tablelands must die before the Black-Tree triumphs. That is our goal, little brother, our hearts' desire."

Cerk swallowed hard, but inwardly, he'd begun to relax. When Brother Kakzim talked about the BlackTree, his mind was focused on larger things than a solitary halfling apprentice. Still, he tread carefully; Brother Kakzim had not answered his question, which was an honest question, one to which he dearly wanted an answer.

"Why start with the cavern-folk, Brother Kakzim? Won't they die with the rest of Urik once we've putrefied their water? Why do we have to kill the cavern-folk ourselves? Why can't we let the contagion kill them for us?"

A tactical mistake: Brother Kakzim backhanded him against the nearest wall. Cerk feared that worse was to come, but his Unseen defenses hadn't broken. There were no further assaults, physical or otherwise, just Brother Kakzim, hissing at him in Halfling.

"Cut out your tongue lest you tell all our secrets! The cavern-folk must die because our contagion cannot be spat into the reservoir by the thimbleful. The ingredients must seethe and settle for many days before they'll be potent enough to destroy first Urik, then all the cities of the Tablelands. Our contagions must be incubated . . . " The white-rimmed eyes wandered, and Cerk held his breath. Kakzim was on the verge of inspiration, and that always meant something more for Cerk to do without thanks or assistance. "They must be incubated in alabaster bowls—ten of them, little brother, eight feet across and deep. You'll find such bowls and have them set up in the cavern."

Cerk blinked, trying to imagine ten alabaster bowls big enough to drown in and completely unable to imagine where he might find such objects, or how to transport them to the reservoir cavern. For once, his slack-jawed confusion was unfeigned, but Brother Kakzim mistook his bewilderment for insight.

"Ah, little brother, *now* you understand. This is not Laq to be measured by the powder packet. This is a contagion of poison and disease on a far grander scale. Once we've simmered it and stirred it to perfection, we'll spill the bowls into the reservoir and Urik will begin to die. Whoever draws water from a city wellhead or drinks from a city fountain will sicken and die. Whatever fool nurses the dying, he'll die, too as the plague spreads. In a week, Brother Cerk, no more than two, all the lands of Urik will be filled with the dead and dying. Can you see it, Brother Cerk? *Can you see it?*"

Brother Kakzim seized Cerk's robe again and assailed him with Unseen visions of bloated corpses strewn through the streets and houses of the city, on the roads and in the fields, even here on the killing floors of Codesh. In Brother Kakzim's envisioning, only the Urikites were slain, but Cerk knew that all living things needed water, and anything living that drank Urik's water after Brother Kakzim tainted it would die. The useful beasts, the wild beasts, birds, insects, and plants that drank water through their roots, they all would die.

Even halflings would die.

Cerk could see Brother Kakzim's vision more clearly than Brother Kakzim, and he was sickened by the sight. He nodded without enthusiasm. The poor wretches living in darkness on the shores of Urik's underground reservoir were actually the luckiest folk alive. They'd be the first Urikites to die.

A chill ran through Cerk's body. He clasped his arms tight over his chest for warmth and told himself it was nothing more than the coming of night now that purple twilight had replaced the garish hues of the sunset. But that was a lie. His shivers had nothing to do with the cooling air. An inner voice counseled him to run away from Brother Kakzim, Codesh, and the whole mad idea. Cerk swallowed that inner voice. There was no escape. The Brethren had made Brother Kakzim his master; he couldn't leave without breaking the oath he'd sworn beneath the BlackTree.

The choice between dying with Brother Kakzim in the Tablelands and returning to BlackTree Forest with his sacred oath forsworn was no choice at all.

"Can you see it, Brother Cerk?"

"I see it all," Cerk agreed, then squaring his shoulders within his dark robe, he grimly followed his companion and master down from the balcony to the killing floor where a silent, surly crowd was already gathered. "I see everything."

That evening was like a dream—a living nightmare.

At sundown, Cerk took a seat behind a table, beside the abattoir door. He methodically and mindlessly put a broken ceramic bit onto the palm of every thuggish hand that reached toward him once its owner had crossed the abattoir threshold. A decent wage for a decent night's work: that's what Brother Kakzim said, as though what these men—the thugs were all males, mostly dwarves, because their eyes saw more than human eyes in the dark—were going to do tonight was decent.

And perhaps it was. The killing that went on in the abattoirs and would go on in the reservoir cavern wasn't like the hunting Cerk had done as a boy in the forest, and it wasn't sacrifice as the Brethren made sacrificial feasts beneath the branches of the BlackTree. In Codesh they practiced slaughter, and the slaughter of men was no different.

When the doors were shut and barred and a ceramic bit had been placed in every waiting hand, Cerk had done everything that Brother Kakzim had asked of him. He rolled up his mat, intending to slip quietly upstairs to his room, but got no farther than the middle steps before Brother Kakzim began his harangue.

Brother Kakzim was no orator. His voice was shrill, and he had a tendency to gasp and stutter when he got excited. The burly thugs of Codesh exchanged snickering leers and for a moment Cerk thought—hoped—they'd all walk out of the abattoir. But Brother Kakzim didn't harangue with words. Like a sorcerer-king, Kakzim used the Unseen Way to focus his audience and forge them into a lethal weapon. Brother Kakzim worked on a smaller scale than Lord Hamanu: forty hired men rather than an army, but the effect was the same.

The mat slipped out of Cerk's hands. It bounced down the stairs and rolled unnoticed against the wall.

Cerk returned to the killing floor in an open-eyed trance. His inner voice frantically warned him that his thoughts were no longer his own, that Brother Kakzim was bending and twisting his will with every step he took. His inner voice spoke the truth, but truth couldn't overcome the images of hatred and disgust that swirled up out of Cerk's deepest consciousness. The dark-dwellers were vermin; they deserved to die. Their death now, for the cause of cleansing Urik, was the sacrifice that redeemed their worthless lives.

With his final mote of free thought, Cerk looked directly at Brother Kakzim and tried to give his whipped-up hatred its proper focus, but he was no mind-bending match for an elder brother of the BlackTree brethren. His images were overwhelmed.

The last thing Cerk clearly remembered was grabbing a torch and a stone-headed poleaxe that was as long and heavy as he was. Then the mob surged toward a squat tower at the abattoir's rear, and he went with them. Brother Kakzim stood by the tower's door. His face shone silver, like a skull in moonlight.

Delusion! Cerk's inner voice screamed when Brother Kakzim's eyes shot fire and one of the thugs fell to the ground. *Mind-bending madness! Go back!*

But Cerk didn't go back. Wailing like a dwarven banshee, he kept pace with the mob as it made its noisy way to the cavern.

Later, much later, when he'd shed his bloodstained clothes, Cerk consoled himself with the thought that he wasn't strong, even for a halfling. He had no skill with heavy weapons. It was possible—probable—that he hadn't killed anyone. But he didn't know; he couldn't remember anything after picking up the torch and axe.

He didn't know how his clothes had become bloodstained.

He was afraid to go to sleep.

TWO

All residents of Urik knew precisely when Lord Hamanu's curfew began, but few knew exactly when it ended. Those who could afford to laugh at the Lion-King's laws said curfew ended one moment after it began. Templars said curfew ended at sunrise and they'd arrest or fine anyone they caught on the streets before the sun appeared above the city walls, but usually they left the city alone once the sky began to brighten. Someone had to have breakfast waiting when the high and mighty woke up. Someone had to entertain the nightwatch templars before they went on duty and again when they left their posts. Someone had to sweep the streets, collect the honey jars, kindle the fires; someone had to make breakfast for the entertainers, sweepers, honeymen, and cooks. And since those someones would never be the yellow-robed templars of the nightwatch, compromises as old as the curfew itself governed Urik's dark streets.

Law-abiding folk—the good and honest folk of Urik who greatly outnumbered all others and whom the Lion-King cherished as any herder cherished his passive flock—were wise to shut themselves behind doors with locks, if they could afford them. But the other folk of Urik—the folk who were above the law, beneath its notice, outside it, or whose lives simply could not be lived within its limits—went about their business throughout the night. The templars, in their

watchtowers along the city's outer walls and the inner walls
where neighborhood quarters abutted each other, knew
them all by type, if not by face. So long as nightwatch palms
were liberally greased, those with business could go about
it. Urik's nights were more dangerous than its days, but no
less orderly.

Nowhere were the nighttime rituals more regular than in
the templar quarter itself, especially the double-walled
neighborhood that the high templars called home. Even
war bureau templars, each with a wealth of colored threads
woven into their yellow sleeves, knew better than to question the comings and goings of their superiors. They challenged no one, least of all the thieves and murderers, who'd
undoubtedly been hired by a dignitary with the clout to
execute an overly attentive watchman on the spot, no questions asked. And if the watch would not challenge the crim-
inals in their own quarter, they certainly left the high templars and their guests alone as well.

The sky above the eastern wall was glowing amber when
an alley door swung open and a rectangle of light briefly
illuminated the austere red-striped yellow wall of a high
templar residence. The dwarven sergeant leaned heavily on
the rail of her watchtower, taking note of the flash, the distinctive *clunk* of a heavy bolt thrown home again, and a
momentary silhouette, tall and unnaturally slender, against
the red-striped yellow wall. She snorted once, having recognized the silhouette and thereby knowing all she needed
to know.

Folk had to live, to eat, to clothe themselves against the
light of day and the cold of night. It wasn't any templar's
place to judge another poor wretch's life, but it seemed to
the sergeant that sometimes it might be better to lie down
and die. Short of the gilded bedchambers of Hamanu's
palace, which she had never seen, there wasn't a more
nefarious place in all Urik than the private rooms of a high
templar's residence. And the slender one who slipped
quietly through the lightening shadows below her post

spent nearly every night in one disreputable residence or another.

"Great Hamanu's infinitesimal mercy strike you down, child," the sergeant whispered as the footsteps faded.

It was not a curse.

*   *   *   *   *

Mahtra felt anonymous eyes at her back as she walked through the templar quarter. She didn't fear those who stared at her. There was very little that Mahtra feared. Before they drove her out onto the barren wastes, her makers had given her the means to take care of herself, and what her innate gifts could not deflect, her high templar patrons could. She had not developed the sensitivities of born-folk. Fear, hate, love, friendship were words Mahtra knew but didn't use often. It wasn't fear that made her pause every little while to adjust the folds of the long, black shawl she clutched tightly around her thin shoulders.

It wasn't because of cold, either, though there was a potent chill to the predawn air. Cold was a sensitivity, just like fear, that Mahtra lacked, though she understood cold better than she understood fear. Mahtra could hear cold moving through the nearest buildings: tiny hisses and cracklings as if the long-dead bones that supported them still sought to warm themselves with shrinking or shivering. Soon, as sunrise gave way to morning, the walls would warm, then grow hot, and the hidden bones would strive to shed the heat, stretching with sighs and groans, like any overworked slave.

No one else could hear the bones as Mahtra could, not even the high templars with their various and mighty talents, or the other nightfolk she encountered in their company. That had puzzled Mahtra when she was new to her life in Urik. Her sensitivities were different; she was *different*. Mahtra saw her differences in the precious silver mirrors high templars hung on their walls. They said mirrors could not lie. Of course, everyone was different in a mirror's magical reflection. Some of those she met nightly in these identically striped residences were more different than she was. That was hardly surprising: the high templars who commanded the gatherings Mahtra attended were collectors of the exotic, the new, and the different of the city.

But Mahtra's difference was inside, too, like the bones hiding inside the walls, as if she were made of old bones herself. Father said no, that she was flesh and blood and living bone, for all that she'd been made, not born. He was very wise, Father was, and as old as she was new, but he couldn't explain the difference between *made* and *born*. Mahtra listened carefully to all that Father said. He'd taught her left from right, right from wrong, and many other things about this world in which she'd found herself new and grown; made, not born. She was grateful and could neither imagine nor remember her life without Father's welcome each morning when she returned to their hide-and-bone hut beside the underground water, but where she herself was concerned, Mahtra believed the differences she saw in high templar mirrors and those she heard in the walls.

Mahtra's skin was white, that was one difference—not pale like that of a house-bound courtesan who never saw the light of day, but white like chalk or salt or bones that the sun had bleached dry. Her skin was cool to the touch, harder and lightly scaled, as if she'd been partly made from snakes or lizards. Her body grew no hair to cover her stark skin, but there were burnished, sharp-angled scars on her shoulders and around her wide-set turquoise eyes, scars that were like gold-leaf set into her flesh. The makers had put those scars on her, though Mahtra could not remember when or how. They were what the makers had given her to protect her, as born-folk had teeth and knives. Mahtra knew she could protect herself against any threat, but she could not explain how she did it, not to Father, not to herself.

The dignitaries she met at the high templar gatherings were fascinated by her skin—as they were fascinated by anything exotic. They handled her constantly, sometimes with ardent gentleness, sometimes not.

The reasons for their fascination were unimportant to Mahtra, so long as they gave her something when they were finished. Coins were best; coins had so many uses. She could take them to the market and exchange them for food, fuel, clothing, or anything else Father and the other waterside dwellers needed. Jewels were almost as useful; they could be turned into coins in the elven market. Sometimes, though, her nighttime consorts gave Mahtra things she kept for herself, like the long, black shawl she wore this chilly morning.

A human merchant had given Mahtra the shawl at one of the first high templar gatherings she'd attended. He said the forest-weavers of Gulg had woven it from song-spider silk. He said she should wear it to conceal her delicate white-white skin—and the dark mottled blotches he'd made on it. She obeyed without argument. Obedience was so much easier than argument when she was still so new and the world, so old.

Father had sucked on his teeth when she handed him the shawl. Burn it or sell it, he said, throwing it on the damp, stony shores of the water; there were better ways to live above ground, if that was where she was determined to live. But Father couldn't tell her how to live those better ways, any more than he could explain the difference between made and born.

So Mahtra disobeyed him, then, and kept the shawl as a treasure. It warmed her as she walked between the hut and the high templar residences and it was softer than anything she'd felt before or since. She didn't think about the merchant; neither he nor the mottled blotches mattered enough to remember. Her skin always turned white again, no matter how dark a night's handling left it.

And the shawl would hide her no matter what color her skin was.

Hiding; hiding was why Mahtra kept the shawl pulled tight

around her. The stares of folk who were only slightly different from each other hurt far more than the hands that touched her at the high templar gatherings. Children who looked up from their street games to shout "Freak," or "Spook," or "Show us your face!" hurt most of all, because they were as new as she was. But children were born; they could hate, despise, and scorn. She was made; she was different.

Mahtra clung to her shawl and the shadows until she reached yesterday's market. Early-rising folk and nightfolk like herself were dependent on the enterprising merchants of yesterday's markets: collections of carts that appeared each sunrise near Urik's most heavily trafficked intersections. Yesterday's markets served those who couldn't wait until the city gates opened and the daily flood of farmers and artisans surged through the streets to the square plazas where they set up their stalls and sold their wares. The vendors of yesterday's markets lived in the twilight and dawn, buying the dregs of one day's market to sell before the next day's got under way.

Yesterday's markets were very informal, completely illegal, and tolerated by Lord Hamanu because they were absolutely necessary to his city's welfare. And as with all other things that endured in Urik, yesterday's markets had become traditional. The half-elf vendor who laid claim to the choice northwestern corner where the Lion's Way crossed Joiners' Row sold only yesterday's fruit, as his father had sold only such fruit from the cart he wheeled each dawn to that precise location, and as his children would when their turn came. His customers, sleepy-headed at either the start or finish of their day's work, relied on his constancy and he, in turn, knew them, as well as strangers dared to know each other in Urik.

Mahtra was much too new to Urik and the world to appreciate the grand traditions that brought her favorite fruitseller to his corner each morning. He was simply there the first time she'd thought to bring fruit to Father, and there every morning since.

"Cabras, eleganta," he said with a smile and a gesture toward four of the husky, dun-colored spheres. "Almost fresh from the Dolphiles estate. First of this year's crop, and the best. A bit each, two bits for the lot."

The fruitseller talked constantly, without expecting an answer, which Mahtra appreciated, and he called her *eleganta*, which Father said was a polite word for improper activities, but she liked the sound of it. Mahtra liked cabras, too, though she had almost forgotten them. Seeing them now on the fruitseller's cart, she remembered that she hadn't seen them for a great many mornings. For a year's worth of mornings, according to the half-elf.

Years and crops confused Mahtra. Her life was made up of days and nights, strings of dark beads following light beads, with no other variations. Others spoke of weeks and years, of growing up and growing old. They spoke of growing crops, of planting and harvesting. She'd been clever enough to piece together the notion that food wasn't made in the carts of yesterday's market; food was born somewhere outside the city walls. But growing was a more difficult concept for someone who hadn't been born, hadn't been a child, couldn't remember being anything except exactly what she was.

Staring at the cabras, Mahtra felt her differences—her made-ness and her newness—as if she were standing in an empty cavern and her life were a meager collection of memories strewn in a spiral at her feet.

When she concentrated, Mahtra found six cabra-places among her memories. Six cabra-years, then, since wherever cabras were born, wherever they grew, they appeared on the fruitseller's cart just once a year. That made six years since she'd found herself in Urik and memories began, because the sixth cabra-place, all bright red and cool, sweet nectar flowing down her throat, was very near the beginning of the spiral. She'd have to make a new cabra-place in her memory today, the seventh cabra-place. She'd been in Urik, living in a hide-and-bone hut beside underground water, for seven years.

Changing her hold on her shawl, Mahtra thrust her hand into the morning. She extended one long, slender finger tipped with a dark-red, long, sharp fingernail.

"Only one, eleganta? What about the rest? Share them with your sisters—"

Mahtra shook her head vigorously. She had no sisters, no family at all, except for Father, who said the sweet cabra nectar hurt his old teeth. There was the dwarf, Mika, who shared the hide-and-bone hut. Like her, Mika had no family, but Mika's family had died in a fire and Father had taken Mika in, because he'd been born. He was "young," Father said, not new, and without family he couldn't take care of himself.

Mika had arrived since the last cabra-place. Mahtra didn't know if he liked sweet fruit.

She extended a second slender finger.

"Wise, eleganta, very wise. Let me have your sack—"

She retrieved a wad of knotted string from the sleeve of her gown. The fruitseller shook it out while Mahtra sorted two ceramic bits out of her coin-pouch. By the time she had them, the half-elf was stuffing the fourth cabra into the back. Mahtra didn't want the other fruits, but he didn't notice when she shook her head. She considered reaching across the cart to get his attention by touching his hand; Father said strangers didn't touch each other, unless they were children, and she—despite her newness—wasn't a child. Grown folk got each other's attention with words.

With one hand deathgripped on her shawl and the other clutching her two ceramic bits, Mahtra used her voice to say: "Not four, only two."

"Eh, eleganta? I don't understand you. Take off your mask."

Mahtra recoiled. She let go of the ceramic bits and snatched her string-sack, four cabra fruits and all.

"Eleganta . . . ?"

But Mahtra was gone, running toward the elven market with her chin tucked down and the shawl pulled forward.

She took off the mask only in the hide-and-bone hut, where Father knew all her secrets, and in the high templar residences, but no where else. Though the mask wasn't a part of her, like the burnished marks on her face and shoulders, she'd been wearing it when her awareness began. Her makers had made the mask to hide their mistakes. That was what Father said when he examined its carefully wrought parts of leather and metal . . . when he'd looked at the face her makers had wanted to keep hidden.

It wasn't the mask that made Mahtra's words difficult to understand; it was the makers. She'd collapsed the first time she saw her face in a silver mirror—the only time she'd lost her consciousness. Then she smashed the mirror and cursed her nameless, faceless makers: they'd forgotten her nose. Two red-rimmed counter-curving slashes reached down from the bony ridge between her eyes. The slashes ended above a mouth that was equally malformed. Mahtra's lips were thin and scarcely flexible. Her jaw was too narrow for the soft, flexible tongue that other sentient races used to shape their words. The tongue the makers had given her, like the fine scales on her white skin, might have come from a lizard.

No matter how hard she tried, how much she practiced, the words Mahtra heard so clearly in her head were badly mangled by the time they emerged from her mouth. Father could understand her, but Father could hear the words in her head whether she spoke them or not. Some of the high templars and their guests had that gift, too. Of all the rest, only Mika seemed to understand what she said.

The elven market was a world unto itself inside Lord Hamanu's city. It had its own walls built against the city walls and its own gate opening into Urik-proper. A gang of templars stood watch at the gate where the doors were thick and tall and their hinges were corroded from disuse. Why the templars watched and what they were looking for was a mystery. They challenged folk sometimes as they entered or left, letting the lucky pass and leading the unlucky away, unless they executed them on the spot, but they never challenged her, even when she approached the gate at a panicky run.

Maybe they knew who she was—or where she spent her nights. Maybe she was too different, even for them. They let her pass between them and through the gaping gates without comment this morning as they had every other morning.

Unlike the other markets of Urik, the elven market wasn't a gathering of farmers and vendors who arrived in an empty plaza, hawked their wares, and then disappeared. The elven market wasn't a market at all, but a separate city, the original Urik, older than the Dragon or the sorcerer-kings, older than the barren Tablelands that now surrounded the much larger city. Lord Hamanu's power was rightly feared in the elven market, but his laws were largely ignored and could be ignored because the unwritten laws of this ancient quarter were every bit as brutally efficient.

Enforcers had carved the mazelike market into a precinct patchwork through which strangers might wander unaware that every step they took, every bargain, every sidelong glance or snicker was watched and, if necessary, remembered. The market residents were watched by the same network, and paid dearly for the privilege. In return, those who dwelt within the old walls of the elven market, where the Lion-King's yellow-robed templars feared to travel in gangs of less than six, were assured of protection from everyone except their protector.

Mahtra was neither a stranger nor a resident. She paid several enforcers for the privilege of walking through the precinct maze early each morning when the market was as close to quiet as it ever got. Having paid for her safe passage, Mahtra was careful never to deviate from her permitted path, lest the eyes that always watched from rooftops, alleyways, and shadowed, half-open doors report her missteps to the enforcers.

Once, when she was much newer than she was now, curiosity had lured Mahtra off the paid-for path. She meant no harm, but the enforcers didn't believe—or couldn't understand—her mute protestations. They'd sent their bully-boy runners after her, and they'd learned the hard way that Mahtra would protect herself. She couldn't be harmed, except at great cost in lives and the greater risk of drawing Lord Hamanu's attention down to their little domains.

That long-ago morning, when she was very new and didn't understand what was important, Mahtra said nothing to Father when she returned to the cavern, nor anything when she went out at dusk. But when she returned the next morning, five corpses, all tortured and mutilated, lay in the chamber at the head of the elven market passage to the cavern. The enforcers had decided that others—born-folk without her ability to take care of themselves—would pay the price of her indiscretions.

Men and women with weapons in hand were waiting for her in the cavern, demanding justice, demanding retribution. Mahtra prepared to defend herself, but Father told her no, and faced the angry mob himself. She heard herself called terrible things that day, but Father prevailed, and the mob dispersed.

When they returned to the hide-and-bone hut, Father took her wrists firmly in his hands and said cavern children were allowed one mistake, no matter how serious, and that he'd persuaded the others that she should be granted the same grace, because being new was like being a child. Then, holding her wrists tight enough to hurt, Father said she must concern herself with the born-folk who were their neighbors along the shore of the underground water. She must not endanger the whole community with her curiosity; she must stick to the path she'd paid for, else he himself would be the one to banish her and nothing her makers had given her would protect her from his wrath.

Father had come into Mahtra's mind then, as a warning, not as her mentor. His face was more terrible than her own and there was a horror he named *death* burning in his eyes. She was powerless before him. She learned a meaning of fear and had stayed on the paid-for path.

After more than six years, the early-risers of the elven market knew her by name and sometimes hailed her as she hurried on her way.

"Mahtra! Mahtra!" a woman called from behind, a dwarf by the deep pitch of her voice and, considering where Mahtra was on her path, most likely Gomer, a trader who specialized in beads and amulets.

Mahtra stopped and turned. Gomer flashed a smile and beckoned her. With a glance at the rooftops, alleys and the other places where her invisible escort might be lurking, Mahtra backtracked to the dwarf. Gomer sold her goods from the inside a boxlike stall along Mahtra's paid-for path. The enforcers wouldn't object—not if she saved a bit or two for the runner who'd surely show up, demanding a share of Gomer's trade, before Mahtra left this precinct.

"What've you got in your sack? Got yourself some cabras, eh?" Gomer knew Mahtra didn't talk much; she didn't waste precious time pausing between questions. "So they're starting to show up in the markets? Have to go out and get me some, maybe. Unless we could make a bargain, you and I. That's a lot of fruit you've got there. Make you sick, it would—even you. But I've got something here you'd like better than cabra—cinnabar!"

Gomer's meaty, powerful hand wove delicately over the compartmented trays set out on her selling board. She plucked up a carved bead about the size of her thumb's knuckle and the same color as Mahtra's fingernails. The sight of it made Mahtra's mouth water. She liked cabra fruit, but she craved the bitter-tasting beads carved from red cinnabar.

"Thought you'd want it, dearie," Gomer chuckled.

She closed her fingers over the bead, shook her hand and blew across it, as if she were casting dice in a high-stakes game, and then opened her fist one finger at a time. To

Mahtra's dismay, the bead had vanished.

"You do want it, don't you?"

Mahtra nodded vigorously. The dwarf chuckled again. She made extravagant motions with her hand, and when she showed her palm again, there were three red beads nestled among the calluses.

"I should charge you a silver, that's what they're worth, you know—especially since you won't resell them—but give me two of your cabras and I'll let you have them for a half-disk."

Mahtra would have made a bad bargain to acquire the beads, but Gomer's offer was ideal. She fished the extra fruits out of her sack and five ceramic bits out of her coin-pouch. Gomer dribbled the beads into her hand. They were pretty little things, with leaves and flowers carved all over two of them and a strange animal she'd never seen before carved in the third. But it was the cinnabar itself that excited her. Her hand began to warm as soon as the red beads touched it.

"Have fun, dearie," Gomer said.

The dwarf balanced one of the husky fruits against her thigh and smashed it open with a blow from her fist. Red juice sprayed her tunic, looking for a heartbeat like blood. Mahtra didn't like blood; it was something old and deep within her, from beyond the spirals of her memory. An inner voice told her to run, and she did, though she knew the splatters were only sweet cabra juice.

A runner appeared a bit farther on. He was a human youth, sleek and well-muscled, typical of the well-fed bullies who worked for the market enforcers. He stopped her. There was an obsidian knife in his hand and an arrogant jut to his jaw, but he kept his distance as he said:

"For luck, Mahtra," and held out his hand. "Give me some of what you bought."

She'd have paid him however many ceramic bits he wanted, or gone off with him to whatever bolthole he called home, but she wouldn't surrender her cinnabar beads. She tried to make her refusal plain, but the youth couldn't understand her gestures—or perhaps that was only his own stubborn refusal.

"Give me half," he demanded, "or I'll tell Map."

Another sturdy human, Map was the local enforcer and a man with a temper to be avoided. Mahtra thought of the butchered corpses in the antechamber years ago and of the three beads in her hand right now. Three wasn't a number that could be easily divided in half. Although she and the runner stood in an intersection, Mahtra felt as if she were trapped in a corner. Juggling the loose beads and the heavy string sack with one hand, she fumbled through her coin-pouch with the other and fished out a shiny silver coin.

The bully frowned. "I want what you bought from Gomer. She's making special bargains for you. Map's gonna want to know about it."

That was too much threat, too much confusion, for Mahtra to bear. She felt trapped, she felt angry, and the burnished scars on her shoulders began to grow warm beneath her shawl. Stiffness spread down her arms, down her spine all the way to her feet; she couldn't move. The scars around her eyes burned as well, and a cloudy membrane slipped across her vision while the makers' precautions protected her.

"Hey! No need to get hotted up, Mahtra," the bully-boy protested. "Give me the coin, and we'll call it quits."

Mahtra's scars were burning; her vision was blurred. She felt the silver coin yanked out of her fingertips and heard hard pounding as the bully ran away, but it was several more heartbeats before the membranes withdrew, her limbs relaxed and she could move again.

She hadn't actually done anything wrong, but Father would be angry—very angry. He might not believe it wasn't her fault, even when he could look inside her mind where the truth was marked into her memory. Fear emerged from its lonely corner, haunting her thoughts as she continued through the market maze.

Her destination was a plaza built around a broad, circular fountain that was scarcely different from the tens of other fountains scattered through Urik. Women of every race scrubbed and pounded their laundry on its curbstones while a steady parade of men and children filled water jugs from the four spouts. An old elf with a crippled leg and a sullen demeanor kept watch from an awning-crowned, tall, wheeled chair. He was the enforcer, and the fountain plaza was his entire precinct. Mahtra didn't approach him, or the squat stone building in the northwest corner of the plaza until he recognized her with the ivory-tipped walking stick he balanced across his thighs.

Usually he spotted her a heartbeat after she appeared on the plaza verge, but today he stared at the sky and a rippling stripe of clouds that were much too high to threaten rain. When he did lower his head and command his minions to swivel his chair about, there was still no sign of recognition, no invitation to cross the plaza. Mahtra feared Map and the runner had gotten here first, and feared something deeper, too, to which she could not put a name—except that it was dark and cold, and it smothered the cinnabar warmth she clutched in her hand.

A half-elf child came running toward her. Mahtra juggled her beads and fruit once again, expecting another demand, but the child stopped short and delivered a message:

"Henthoren," she said, the crippled-elf enforcer's name, "wishes you to know you are the first to approach the well since the nightwatch rang its first bells. He keeps the peace. He wishes you to remember that."

The child bowed low and retreated. Mahtra looked toward the enthroned Henthoren, who leveled his stick at her, giving her leave to traverse his little domain. Then the old elf went back to staring at the sky. She raised her eyes as well, half-expecting that the clouds had fallen and darkened, so palpable had the sense of chill darkness become within her mind. But the clouds remained distant white streaks in the cerulean vault.

Mahtra longed to ask the enforcer what he meant, why this morning he sent a child to tell her what was always true: she was the first walker from the cavern to return home since the midnight bells. But asking was talking and talking to the enforcer was more daunting than his message had been, more daunting than the unease she felt striding past the fountain to the little stone building with its metal-grate door.

There were eyes on her back as she opened the door. She hesitated before crossing the threshold into the unlit antechamber, but nothing flew from the shadows or darted past her feet. There were no sounds—no smells, as there had been when the corpses were laid out as examples. Bornfolk had an expression: quiet as a tomb. Mahtra had never seen a tomb, but it could not have been quieter than the windowless antechamber and its stone carved stairway leading into the ground. She stepped inside and pulled the door shut behind her.

Father said she had human eyes, meaning that she didn't see well in the dark, though she knew the passageway from the antechamber down to the cavern well enough that she didn't need one of the torches that were kept ready by the door. She did pause long enough to loosen the gauze-pleated sidepieces of her mask and slip one of the cinnabar beads into her mouth. Her narrow jaw, so ill-suited to ordinary speech, was strong enough to shatter the bead with a single effort. Her tongue carried the fragments to the back of her mouth where they began to dissolve, along with her unease.

A shimmering drapery of blue-green light, the hallmark of the Lion-King's personal warding, shone at the top of the stairway where torchlight would have revealed the maw of a passage high enough to admit a full-grown elf. Templars with their medallions could pass safely through the light. Anyone else died. The cavern-dwellers had another way, which could not have been entirely unknown to either the market enforcers or the yellow-robe templars of the larger city. Using the boundary of Lord Hamanu's spell as a reference, Mahtra stepped sideways, one, twice, three times and felt the opening of a passage no torch would reveal, no elf or dwarf could see.

Ten tight, twisting steps later, the two passages became one again. Mahtra slipped the second bead into her mouth and continued with confidence down the lightless slope. A faint aroma of charcoal and charred meat lingered in the air, a bit unusual, but accidents happened in the darkness beside the water. People got careless, lamps overturned, cookfires leapt out of their hearths. Mika had lost his family that way, but Father was careful, and Mahtra's fear did not return.

Not until she rounded the last curve that opened into a gallery above the water.

From here she should see the whole community: thirty-odd huts and homesteads beside thirty-odd hearths burning bright in the cavern's eternal night. But there were only a handful of fires, and all of them were wildfires, outside the hearths. The charred scent was thick in the air; Mahtra could taste it through her mask, feel it on her skin through the shawl. The only sounds came from the crackling fires. There was no laughter, no shouts, none of the ordinary buzz that should have greeted her ears here.

"Father?" Mahtra whispered. "Mika?"

She started to run, but hadn't gone ten paces before she tripped and stumbled hard to her knees. The cabras went flying. Mahtra groped for them, for the cause of her tumble. She wasn't the only cavern dweller with human eyes. Most of the community didn't see in the dark. There were penalties for cluttering the paths; there'd be a reckoning when Father and the other elders found out.

Mahtra's hands touched something round, but it wasn't a cabra fruit. It was hair . . . a head . . . a lifeless head. Her hands dripped blood when she sprang back.

"Father! Father!"

She couldn't run. There were other bodies in the gallery.

There were bodies everywhere, all lifeless and bloody.

"Father!"

Mahtra staggered to the gallery's end and the first of the homesteads where flames consumed the last of a hide-and-bone hut like her own and a human woman she recognized lay on her back, staring up.

"Dalya!"

Dalya had never understood Mahtra's clumsy speech, but she didn't blink at the sound. Dalya didn't move at all. Dalya was as lifeless as the rest, and suddenly Mahtra couldn't get air into her lungs no matter how hard she breathed. Warmth kindled in her burnished scars again. The protective membrane twitched in the corners of her eyes.

"No!" she gasped, ordering her body to behave, as if it belonged to someone else.

She couldn't lose her vision. She had to see. She had to find Father, and trembling so badly that she had to crawl, she made her way down once-familiar lanes to another burning hut.

Mahtra sat on her knees a few paces short of the destruction. The makers had given her human eyes where light and darkness were concerned, but they hadn't given her the ability to cry as humans and all the other sentient races did. It had never been a hardship before, but now—looking at Mika's body, partly seared by fire, and his face, split by a gouge that reached from his forehead across his right eye, nose, and cheek before it ended on his neck—now, Mahtra could only make sad, little noises deep in her throat. The sounds hurt worse than any mottled skin she'd acquired in the high templar residences.

But the makers had made Mahtra strong. She rose to her feet and stepped around Mika's corpse. Father lay a few steps farther. Fire hadn't touched him; a club had: his skull was crushed. Mahtra couldn't see his face for the gore. Kneeling again, she slid her slender arms beneath him and lifted him carefully, easily. She carried him to the water's edge where she washed the worst away.

The keening sounds still trilled in the base of Mahtra's throat. Sharp pains from no visible source lashed her heart. Grief, she told herself, remembering how Mika's cheeks had glistened the night his family died. Grief and cold and dark: Death, suddenly more real than anything else around her. Crouched and cowering over Father, Mahtra peered into the darkness, expecting Death to appear.

Death *was* here in the cavern. She could feel it. Death *would* take her, too; she couldn't stay. But as she lowered Father to the stony shore, he opened his remaining eye.

Mahtra—

His voice sounded in her mind; his lips had not moved.

"Father? Father—what's happened? What has happened? Mika . . . You . . . Father, tell me—What do I do now?"

You must leave, Mahtra. They will come back, and they will overwhelm even you—

"Who? Why? You did no wrong, Father; this should not have happened. You did no wrong."

It doesn't take wrong for killing to start, Father explained, patient with her newness even now.

"Killing," Mahtra felt the word in her thoughts, on her malformed tongue. It wasn't a new word, but it had a new meaning. "Have you been killed, Father?"

Yes—

"Then I will *kill*. I will kill whoever killed you. I will take wrong against wrong and make it right again."

Mahtra felt Father's sadness. He would chastise her, she thought, as he had chastised her for keeping the black shawl. She knew wrong couldn't be made right—she knew that from looking in the high templar mirrors.

Father surprised her. *You have powerful patrons, Mahtra. They will help you. This must not happen again. You must make certain of it.*

Father made an image grow in Mahtra's mind then, the last image of his life: a stone-head club, an arm descending, and a wild-eyed, burn-scarred face beyond it. After the image, there was nothing more; but the image was enough.

It was a stranger's face for a heartbeat, then in her mind's closer inspection, Mahtra saw a halfling's distinctive old-young features. A single black line emerged from the scars. It made two angles and disappeared into raw flesh again. That was enough, along with the wild eyes. She knew him.

"Kakzim," she whispered as she rose and walked away without a backward glance.

THREE

Death was loose in the cavern, in the clubs and flame. Death would take Father and Mika—if she didn't find them first.

Mahtra stood at the junction of the antechamber corridor and the sloping gallery ramp that led to the water. The community was in flames that soared and crackled and threw countless shadows of sweeping arms and dripping stone-headed clubs onto the rock walls. Screams reverberated off the hard rock all around her and echoed between her ears, as well. Mahtra couldn't distinguish Father's screams, or Mika's, from all the others, but they were down there among the flames and the carnage.

Mahtra ran as fast as she could, leaping lightly over those whom Death had already claimed. She'd gone faster and farther than she'd gone before. Hope swelled in her pounding heart, but hands rose out of the darkness at the base of the ramp. They grabbed her wrists and her ankles. They pulled her down, held her down. Faces that were only eyes and voices hovered over her, muttering a two-word chorus: mistake and failure.

She fought free of them, sprang to her feet and ran onto the stony shore where flames and screams made everything seem unfamiliar. Dodging arms and clubs, Mahtra looked for the path that would take her to the hide-and-bone hut where Father and Mika were waiting. There were paths she'd never seen before, and all of them blocked by the same five mutilated corpses who rose up when she approached them, blaming her, not Death, for their dying.

She was frantic with despair when a wild-eyed halfling ran toward her. His cheeks were on fire and his bloody club was the most terrible of all Death's weapons. While Mahtra cowered, he found the familiar path that wound between the reproachful corpses and led to the hide-and-bone hut where little Mika stood bravely before the door.

The burnished marks on Mahtra's face and shoulders grew warm. Her vision blurred and her limbs stiffened, but it wasn't herself she wanted to protect; it was Father and Mika, and they were too far away. In agony, she forced her eyes to see, her legs to move. One stride, two strides . . . gaining on Death with every stride, but still too late.

The club fell and the only scream she heard was Father and Mika screaming as halfling-Death battered the hut with his club. Mahtra threw herself at Death and was repelled, simply repelled. Death did not want her; Death wouldn't threaten a made creature like her, who'd never been born—and without threat, Mahtra's flesh wouldn't kindle, her vision wouldn't blur.

Gouts of Mika's blood flew off the club as Death whirled it overhead. The sticky clots adhered to Mahtra's face. She fell to her knees, clawing at her hard, white skin, unable to breathe, unwilling to see. Her vision finally blurred, now—when it was too late and there was blood already on her hand, but she didn't give up, not completely. Lunging blindly, Mahtra aimed herself where her mind's vision said Death last stood. She felt the hem of Death's robe in her hands, but Death didn't fall. Death pulled free, and she fell instead.

Crawling again, she sought Death by the sound of his club as it fell, again and again. Warm, sticky fluid pelted her. She wanted to curl into a tight ball, but forced her back to straighten, her head to rise. She opened her eyes—

—And saw sunlight. The nightmare images of fear, rage, helplessness, and defeat faded quickly in the bright light of morning. Since escaping the cavern, Mahtra had had this same nightmare, with its hopeless ending, whenever she'd fallen asleep. Its terrors were at least familiar, which was not true of her surroundings.

With her heart pounding as if the nightmare had not ended, Mahtra swiveled on her hips and sat cross-legged in the center of linen-covered mattress beneath the silken canopy. Night curtains had been drawn down from the canopy, but they were sheer, like spiderwebs, and she could see through them. . . .

And be *seen* through them.

Mahtra felt her nakedness as an afterthought, but reacted swiftly, tucking the coverlet tightly around her lest she be seen by someone *uninvited*. There was no one watching. She was alone, as far as she could tell, in this bright bedchamber, and there was no one in the next chamber, which she could see through an open doorway.

Her gown was neatly folded on a chest at the foot of the bed. Her belt and coin pouch were on top of the dress; her sandals had been cleaned, oiled, and set beside them. And her mask—her mask wasn't on the chest. Mahtra's hands leapt to her face. The mask wasn't there, either. She kept her fingers pressed over what the makers had given her for a mouth and nose and racked her memory for the places she had been last night.

Not this room. Not any room. Not since she'd staggered out of the cavern many days ago.

As soon as she'd felt the sun on her face, Mahtra had made her way to the high templar quarter, but she hadn't gone back to her old eleganta life. She hadn't been inside any residence. She'd hied herself to House Escrissar and sat herself down on the alleyway doorsill. House Escrissar was locked up, boarded up. It had been that way for a long time—not a year, but still a long time. Before it was locked and boarded, Mahtra had been a frequent visitor, entering at sunset through this alleyway door, leaving again at dawn.

Mahtra had met Lord Escrissar when her life in Urik was very new. He had noticed her admiring cinnabar beads in a market plaza. He'd bought her a bulging handful and then

invited her to visit him at his residence. And because Lord
Escrissar had worn a mask and because he'd made her feel
welcome, she'd accepted his invitation that night and every
night for all the years thereafter, until he had vanished and
his residence had been sealed.

She'd been comfortable in House Escrissar, where everyone wore masks. Everyone except Kakzim. The halfling was
a slave, and slaves did not wear masks. Their scarred
cheeks, etched in black with a house crest, were masks
enough.

Mahtra didn't understand slavery. She had little contact
with the scarred drudges who hovered silently in the shadows of every high templar residence. There were drudge
slaves in House Escrissar, but Kakzim was not one of them.
Kakzim mingled with his master's guests and offered her
gifts of gold and silver.

By then she knew that the high templars and their guests
found her fascinating. She knew what to expect when she
led them to the little room Lord Escrissar had set aside for
her, deep within his residence, but Kakzim did not ask her
to remove the mask, nor any of the other things to which
she'd grown accustomed. He wanted to study the burnished
marks on her shoulders, and she permitted that until he
tried to study them with a tiny, razor-sharp knife. She protected herself so fast that when her vision cleared again,
almost everything in the room was broken and Kakzim was
slumped unconscious in the farthest corner.

Mahtra expected Lord Escrissar to chastise her, as Father
would have if she'd wrought such damage underground, but
the high templar apologized and gave her a purse with
twenty gold coins in it. She went back to House Escrissar
many, many times after that; she didn't started visiting the
other residences in the quarter until after House Escrissar
was boarded up. She saw Kakzim almost every time, but
he'd learned his lesson and kept his distance.

When Lord Escrissar first disappeared, there had been
new rumors every night, whichever high templar residence

she had visited. Lord Escrissar, she had learned, had had no friends among his peers and wasn't missed; his guests wore masks when they had come to his entertainments because they had not wished their faces to be noticed. Eventually the rumors had stopped flowing.

No one came back to House Escrissar; none came to find Mahtra sitting there, clutching that same purse he had given her.

Mahtra had no friends left, not even Lord Escrissar, who'd never shown her his true face. With both Father and Mika dead, there was no one to miss her, either. She sat on the sill of Lord Escrissar's residence, hoping he'd know she was waiting for him, hoping he'd come back from wherever he was, hoping he'd help her find Kakzim.

Hope was all Mahtra had as one day became the next and another without anyone coming to the door. She was hungry, but after so much waiting, she was afraid to leave the alley, for surely Lord Escrissar would return the moment she turned her back in the next intersection. The nightwatch, which had a post on the rooftop at the back of the alley, tossed her their bread crusts when they went off duty. Between those mouthfuls of dry bread and water in the residence cistern, which had not been tapped since the last Tyr storm, Mahtra survived and waited.

There'd been no novelty in the alleyway, nothing but the angle of the shadows by day and the movement of the stars overhead by night to distinguish one hour from another. The days and nights themselves fell on top of each other in Mahtra's memory rather than stringing themselves out in a row. She wasn't sure how many days and nights she'd been waiting, but it seemed certain that she'd done nothing else. Leaving the alley, coming to this place with its bright walls, spiderweb curtain, and her own nakedness should have left a mark in her mind—if she'd done it of her own will.

And Mahtra didn't do things not of her own will. Kakzim and the enforcers of the elven market had learned that lesson. She could not have been forced here. She must have entered willingly, and removed her mask the same way. But she remembered nothing between the alley and the bed-chamber except her nightmare.

The cold, hard presence of fear, which had become Mah-tra's most constant companion since the cavern, reasserted itself around her. She curled inward until her forehead touched her toes and her face was completely hidden. The coverlet couldn't warm her, nor could her own hands chaf-ing her skin. Her body shivered from an inner chill and tears her eyes couldn't shed.

"Ah—you are awake, child. There is water here for wash-ing, then you must dress yourself, yes? The august emerita waits for you in the atrium."

Mahtra raised her head cautiously, with her fingers splayed over her malformed face, leaving gaps for her eyes. A human youth stood in the doorway with a bundle of linen in his arm. He was well fed and well groomed, with only a few faint lines on his tanned cheeks to proclaim his status in this place. She knew in an instant she'd never seen him before. Except for Kakzim, she'd encountered no slaves who'd stare so boldly at a freewoman.

She wanted to tell him to go away, or to ask where she was and who the august emerita might be, since she knew no one by that name or title. But, that was talking and, especially without her mask, she didn't talk to strangers. So, she glowered at him instead, and without thinking stuck her tongue at him, as Mika had done whenever she told him to do something he didn't want to do. The slave yelped and jumped backward, nearly dropping his bundle of cloth. He turned and fled the room without another glance at her. For several heartbeats, Mahtra listened to his sandals slapping; the august emerita lived in a very large residence.

Her mask could be anywhere. It could be in the next room, but more likely it was in the atrium, with the august emerita. If she could face Death every night in her dreams, she could face the august emerita. The sooner she did, the sooner she could get out of here and back to her vigil outside House Escrissar. Mahtra made good use of the washstand first. Life by the underground water had spoiled her for the city's scarcity. Even here, in what was plainly an important place, the basin was barely large enough for her hands and the water was used up before she felt completely clean.

It was better than nothing, much better than the grit and grime she'd accumulated sitting in the alleyway. Her skin was white again, a stark contrast with her midnight gown, which had been brushed and shaken with sweet leaves before it was folded. She found her shawl beneath her gown. It, too, had been handled carefully by the august emerita—or her slaves. In lieu of her mask, Mahtra wrapped the shawl over her head, the way the wild elves did when they visited Henthoren in the elven market.

The youthful slave had not returned; Mahtra set out alone to find the august emerita in her atrium. It wasn't difficult. An examination of the roofs and walls revealed by the bedchamber window had convinced her that she was, indeed, still in the high templar quarter where all the residences were laid out in squares and the atrium was the square at the center of everything else. She made mistakes—the residences weren't identical, except on the outside—but she saw no one and no one saw her. Aside from the vanished slave and the august emerita for whom she was searching, Mahtra seemed to be the only person wherever she went.

She thought she was still alone when she reached the atrium. At the heart of the august emerita's residence was a wonder of trees and vines, leaves and flowers in such profusion that, suddenly, Mahtra understood *growing* as she hadn't understood it before. The atrium was filled with sounds as well, sounds she had never heard before. Most of the sounds came from birds and insects in brightly colored wicker cages, but the most fascinating sound came from the atrium fountain.

Lord Escrissar's residence had an atrium and a fountain, of course, but his fountain was nothing like the august emerita's fountain where water sprayed and spilled from one shallow, pebble-filled bowl to another, dulling the background noise of Urik so much that it could scarcely be heard. And the pebbles themselves sparkled in many colors —and some of them were the rusty-red of cinnabar! One cinnabar pebble from the fountain's largest bottom bowl surely wouldn't be missed.

Squatting down, Mahtra stuck her fingers into the cool, clear pool, but before she'd claimed a pebble, something brightly golden and sinuous streaked through the water. It struck her fingertip with raspy sharp teeth. She jerked her hand back so quickly that she lost her balance and wound up sitting ungracefully on the leonine mosaic of the floor. A bead of blood, not cinnabar, glistened on her forefinger.

She heard laughter then, from two places: to her right, where the slave held his sides as he giggled, and behind, where a human woman—the august emerita—sat behind a wicker table and laughed without moving her lips.

"Ver guards his treasure well, child," the emerita said. "Take your cinnabar pebble from another bowl."

Mahtra was wary—how could the woman have known she wanted a *cinnabar* pebble?—but she was clever enough about the ways of high templars to know she should take what had been granted without delay. And the august emerita was a high templar. Though she wrapped her ancient body in layers of sheer silk just like a courtesan, there was a heavy gold medallion hanging around her withered neck. Mahtra snatched the biggest red pebble she could see, then, while it was still dripping, stuffed it in her mouth.

"Good. Now, come, sit down and have something more nourishing to eat."

There was a plate of *things* on the wicker table . . . pinkish-orange things with too many legs and wispy eyestalks that were still moving and were nothing that Mahtra wanted to eat.

"Bettin, go to the pantry and fetch up a plate of fruit and dainties. Our guest has a delicate palate."

She didn't want fruit, Mahtra thought as the slave departed. She wanted her mask; she wanted to leave, she wanted to return to her vigil outside House Escrissar.

"Sit down, child," the woman said with a sigh.

Despite the sigh—or possibly because of it—Mahtra hied herself to a chair and sat.

"How many days and nights have you been waiting, child?"

Mahtra considered the layers in her memory: More than two, she was sure of that. Three or four?

"Three or four, child—try ten. You'd been sitting there for ten days and nights!"

Ten—that was more than she'd imagined, but what truly jolted Mahtra was the realization that, like Father, the august emerita could skim the words of her thoughts from her mind's surface. So she thought about her mask, and how badly she wanted it.

The woman smiled a high templar's knowing smile. She looked a little like Father, with creases across her face and streaks in her hair that were as white as Mahtra's own skin. Her eyes, though, were nothing like Father's. They were dark and hard, like Lord Escrissar's eyes, which she'd seen through the holes of his mask. All the high templars had eyes like that.

"All of us have been tempered like the finest steel, child. Tell me your name—ah, it's Mahtra. I thought so. Now, Mahtra—"

But she hadn't thought the word of her name. The august emerita had plunged deep into her mind to pluck out her name. That roused fear and, more than fear, a sense that she was unprotected, and that made the marks on her shoulders tingle.

I mean you no harm, Mahtra. I'm no threat to you.

Mahtra felt the makers' protection subside as it had never done before, except in her nightmares when Death ignored her. This was no dream. The woman had done something to her, Mahtra was sure of that. She couldn't protect herself, and learned yet another expression for fear.

"No harm, Mahtra. Your powers will return, but were I you, child, I'd learn more about them. I'm long past the days when helplessness excited me, but—as you've noticed—I'm an old woman, and you won't find many like me. I want only to know why you've sat on the doorsill of House Escrissar these last ten days. Don't you know Elabon's dead?"

Dead? Dead like Father, like Mika, and all the others in the cavern? What hope had she of finding Kakzim if Lord Escrissar was dead?

Mahtra lowered her head. She was cold and, worse than shivering, she felt alone, without the powerful patrons Father mentioned in his last words to her. Blinding pressure throbbed behind her eyes and strange high-pitched sounds brewed in her throat. She couldn't cry, but she couldn't stop trying, any more than she could bring back the makers' protection.

Suddenly, there was warmth, but not from within. The high templar had left her chair. She stood behind Mahtra, massaging her neck.

"How witless of me," the august emerita said.

Lord Escrissar had used the same words in his apology after he'd left her alone with Kakzim. There was more pressure behind her eyes, more sound brewing in her sore throat. The coincidence had been too great; Mahtra couldn't bear the pain any longer. She slumped sideways, and only the considerable strength in the old templar's arm kept her from falling to the floor.

"You are just a child. I've been too long without children in this house; I've forgotten what they're like. Tell me from the beginning. Use words—your thoughts are troubled, confused. I'll help you, if I can, but I don't want to make a mistake. Not with what you've let leak already. Why were you sitting on Elabon's doorsill? What has that slave alchemist of his done now?"

Mahtra was ready to tell someone—anyone—what had happened, but it was very difficult to keep her thoughts clear enough for the august emerita to understand without saying the words, however poorly, as they formed in her mind. And without her mask, Mahtra was too self-conscious to speak. So, when Bettin returned to the atrium with a plate of sliced fruits and other appetizing morsels, the high templar sent him off after the mask.

"You'll eat everything on that plate first, child."

Eating, like talking, made Mahtra uncomfortable, but the sight of food had awakened her stomach and the august emerita was not a person to be disobeyed. Mahtra ate with her fingers, ignoring the sharp-edged knife and sharp-tined fork the slave, Bettin, had laid beside the plate. She'd seen such devices before, in other high templar residences, and knew they were more polite, more elegant, than fingertips. She was eleganta, though, not elegant, and she made do with sticking her fingers under the concealing folds of her shawl. The august emerita didn't say anything about Mahtra's manners; the august emerita seemed to have forgotten she had a guest.

Clutching an ornate walking-stick as if it were a weapon rather than a crutch, the old woman paced circles around her fountain and her trees. She wasn't the tallest human woman Mahtra had ever seen, but she was just about the straightest: her shoulders stayed square above her hips as she took her measured steps, and her nose pointed forward only, never to either side, even when Mahtra accidently nudged her unused fork, and it skidded and clattered loudly to the mosaic floor.

Yet the august emerita was paying attention to her. She returned to her own chair on the opposite side of the table as soon as Mahtra had swallowed the last morsel of the last sweet-meat pastry. Bettin appeared, suddenly and silently, out of nowhere and disappeared the same way once he'd deposited Mahtra's mask on the table beside his master. Like her clothes and sandals, the mask had been carefully tended. Its leather parts had been oiled, the metal parts, polished, and the cinnabar-colored suede that would touch her skin once she fastened the mask on had been brushed until it was soft and fragrant again. The august emerita looked aside while Mahtra adjusted the clasps that held the mask in place.

"Now, child, from the beginning."

The beginning was a hot, barren wasteland, with the makers behind her and the unknown in front of her. It was running until she couldn't run anymore. It was falling onto her hands and knees, resting, then rising and running some more—

"The cavern, Mahtra. Begin again with the cavern however many days ago it was. You lived by the reservoir. You were going home. What happened? What did you see? What did this Father-person say to you?"

Perhaps it was only the sun moving overhead, but the creases in the august emerita's face seemed to have gotten deeper and her eyes even harder than they'd been before. She sat on the edge of her chair, as arrow-straight as she'd paced, with her palms resting lightly on the pommel of the walking stick. The pommel was carved in the likeness of a hooded snake with yellow gemstones for its eyes. Mahtra couldn't decide if the snake or the august emerita herself unnerved her more.

She went back to that not-so-long-ago morning and retraced her steps: cabra fruits, cinnabar beads, and Henthoren's eerie message. The snake's eyes didn't blink, and neither—or so it seemed—had the high templar's. Indeed, there was no reaction from the far side of the table until Mahtra came to the very end of her tale.

". . . Father said he'd been killed with Mika and the others. He gave me an image of the man who'd killed them. He said . . . He said I had patrons who could make certain no one else was killed. I knew the man in Father's last image, Lord Escrissar's halfling slave, Kakzim. So I went to Lord Escrissar—to House Escrissar—to wait for him."

The august emerita was on her feet again, and pacing, holding her snake-stick but not using it. Her free hand rose to the medallion she wore, then fell to her side.

"You had no right to live there. The reservoir is a proscribed place; you saw King Hamanu's wards and circumvented them. The one you call 'Father,' broke the king's law living there and taking you there. Urik has places for those who cannot work or have no kin. They'd all be alive if they lived within the law where the templarate could protect them."

Her stick clacked emphatically on the mosaic, and Mahtra felt no need to tell her that the folk who lived beside the underground water were wary of their king's law and twice wary of his templars. Father said he'd sooner live underground in total darkness than live in slavery in the light, and even new-made Mahtra knew that slavery was the lot of those whose work or family could not keep them out of debt. She wondered, though, if the lithe and laughing Bettin would agree.

The august emerita's stick struck the mosaic a second time. "Ask him," she said, thereby reminding Mahtra that her thoughts were not private here.

She took her thoughts back to the cavern, then, and Father's last image.

"Yes, yes—" the old woman said wearily. "The wheels of fortune's chariot turn fair and strange, child. None of you should have been living beside the reservoir, and you should have been among them when catastrophe struck. Had the wheel turned as it should have turned, there'd be no tale to tell or no one to tell it. But Kakzim . . . Damn Elabon!" She struck her stick loud enough to disturb her caged birds and insects. "He was warned."

Not knowing whether "he" was Kakzim or Lord Escrissar, Mahtra closed her eyes and tried very hard to think of neither man. It must have worked; the august emerita started pacing again.

"This is more than I can know: Elabon's mad slave and

Urik's reservoir. I have been too long behind my own walls, do you understand me, Mahtra?"

Mahtra didn't, but she nodded, and the woman did not skim her thoughts to know she'd lied.

"I do not go to the bureau. I do not go to the court. I am *emerita*; I've put such things behind me. I cannot pick them up again. I mistook your purpose on his doorstep, child. I thought you were his, or carrying his, that's all. In my dreams I saw nothing like this. *Damn* Elabon!"

The old woman strode to a wall where hung several knotted silk ropes that Mahtra had not noticed before. She yanked on one that was twisted black and gold and another that was plain blue, then turned to Mahtra.

"Follow me. I will write a message for you. That is all I dare do. There would be too many questions, too much risk. There is only one who can look and listen and act."

A message for her, and written, too. Mahtra shivered as she rose from the table. Writing was forbidden. Lord Escrissar and Father both had warned her that she must never try to master its secrets; Lord Escrissar and Father had almost never given her the same advice. But the august emerita was going to write a message for her. Surely this was what Father meant when he said her powerful patrons would help her.

Mahtra snatched another cinnabar pebble from Ver's fountain, then hurried to keep up with the fast-striding woman. They wound up in a smaller room where the only furnishings were another table, another chair, and shelf upon shelf of identical chests, each with a green-glowing lock. On the wall behind the table someone had painted a fresco-portrait of Lord Hamanu. The Lion-King glowered at Mahtra through gemstone eyes while the august emerita snipped a corner off a fresh sheet of parchment and covered it with bold, red lines of ink.

Two more human slaves, neither of whom was Bettin but who were like him in all other ways—lithe, tanned, and lightly scarred—joined them. Mahtra guessed that one of them was the blue rope while the other was the black-and-gold, but she had no way of knowing for certain, and the august emerita did not address them by name.

"You will accompany Mahtra to the palace. Show this to the sergeant at the gate, and the instigator, too—but don't give it to them, and don't let Mahtra out of your sight until you reach the golden doors. Stay with her. Show my words to anyone who challenges you."

She folded the parchment, struck a tinder stick with flint and steel, and then lit a shiny black candle. She sealed the parchment with a glistening blob of wax. One of the two slaves took the candle from her hand and extinguished it. The other handed her a stone rod as long as her forearm and topped with the carving of a skull. Black wax and a skull. The symbols and their meanings were inescapable: the august emerita was—or had been—a deadheart, a necromancer at the very least; but considering the way this necromancer plucked the thoughts of the living, more likely, an interrogator, like Lord Escrissar himself, and one of the Lion's cubs.

Mahtra cried out when the august emerita hammered the rod against the wax. She felt foolish immediately, but these two slaves were not the laughing, teasing sort that Bettin was. Or perhaps they, like her, were overwhelmed by the old woman's intentions.

"This should be sufficient." She handed the sealed parchment to the slave who'd held the rod. "It shouldn't be opened at all until you reach the golden doors. But if it is, remember the face well. Remember all their faces, their masks, their names, if you hear them."

The young men weren't overwhelmed by King Hamanu; they were overwhelmed by their master, whose orders they were expected to obey to death's door and beyond. Their scarred cheeks were their protection, as the marks around her eyes were Mahtra's. No one would tamper with the slave of an interrogator, not knowing what an interrogator could do, to whom an interrogator could turn.

No one had dared tamper with Kakzim.
Not even the august emerita.

*   *   *   *   *

Sobered and chastened, Mahtra accompanied the two
slaves from the templar quarter and through the wide-open
gates of Hamanu's palace. The courtyard was as vast as the
cavern, but open to the sky and dazzling in the midday sun.
Here and there clots of templars, nobles, and wealthy merchants conducted their business. She recognized some of
them. They recognized her by pretending not to. And
though the air was dead still and the heat oppressive, Mahtra hid herself within her shawl.

They were hailed at the inner gate by a war bureau
sergeant and a civil bureau instigator, each in a yellow robe
with the distinctive and appropriate sleeve banding. The
war bureau sergeant wanted to carry the message himself to
the next post. He told the two slaves that they were dismissed, but he withdrew his order when the taller slave said:

"I will remember your face."

After that they traveled through a smaller courtyard
where trees grew and fountains squandered their water.
Threads of gold and copper were woven in the sleeves of the
templars they encountered next, and more metal still in the
sleeves of the third pair who stood at the mighty doors of
the palace proper. Mighty doors, but not golden ones—
Mahtra and her two companions were passed to a fourth
and finally a fifth pair of templars—high templars, with
masks and other-colored robes—before they came to a
closed but unguarded pair of golden doors.

"You've done well," one of the masked templars said to
the slaves. "Remember us to the august emerita. We wish
her continued peace." He took the black-sealed parchment, then opened one of the golden doors. "Wait in here,"
he said, and as quickly as that, Mahtra was completely
alone.

She found herself in an austere chamber no larger than the august emerita's atrium, but empty, save for a single black marble bench; and quiet, save for the gentle cascade of water flowing over the great black boulder in front of the bench. There was no source for the water. Its presence, its endless movement, had to be the manifestation of powerful magic.

Mahtra had learned a few useful things in House Escrissar, like where to sit when she didn't know what to expect next. She headed for that part of the wall that was farthest from the rock and yet afforded a clear view of the now-shut golden doors. It was no different than sitting on Lord Escrissar's doorsill, except the door was in front of her, not behind.

"Have you been waiting long?"

The doors hadn't opened, the young man hadn't come through them, and she nearly leapt out of her skin at the sound of his voice.

"Did I frighten you?"

She shook her head. Surprise was one thing, fright another, and she knew the difference well enough. He'd surprised her, but he wasn't frightening. With his lithe limbs and radiant tan, he could have been one of the august emerita's slaves, if his cheeks hadn't been as flawless as the rest of him. As he was, with those unmarked cheeks and wearing little more than his long, dark hair and a length of bleached linen wound around his body, she took him for eleganta, like herself.

"Who are you waiting for?" he asked, standing in front of her and offering his hand.

Without answering the question, she accepted help she didn't need. He was stronger than Mahtra expected, leaving her with the sense of being set down on her feet rather than lifted up to them. Indeed, there seemed something subtly amiss in all his aspects, not a disguise, but not quite natural either. He was like no one she'd known, as different as she was, herself.

In the space of a heartbeat, Mahtra decided that the eleganta was made, not born. That he was what the makers meant when they called her a mistake.

"I am waiting for your lord, King Hamanu," she answered slowly and with all her courage.

"Ah, everybody waits for Hamanu. You may wait a long time."

He led her toward the bench where she sat down again, though he did not sit beside her.

"What will you tell him when he gets here? —*If* he gets here."

"If I tell you, will you tell me about the makers?"

The young man cocked his head, staring at her through crooked amber eyes, but Mahtra wasn't fooled. She'd been right to bargain; he could answer her questions. He was the makers' perfect creation, not chased across the barrens, but sent to Urik's king instead.

"*Those* makers," he said after a moment, confirming her suspicions and her hopes. "It's been a very long time, but I can tell you a little about them . . . after you tell me what you're going to tell Hamanu."

What he'd just told her was enough: a very long time. Made folk didn't grow up. She hadn't changed in the seven years she could remember. He hadn't changed in a very long time. They weren't like Father or the august emerita; they didn't grow old.

Mahtra began her story at the august emerita's beginning and this seemed to satisfy her made companion, though he interrupted, not because he hadn't understood, but with questions: How long had Gomer been selling her cinnabar beads? What did Henthoren look like and had she ever met any other elven market enforcers? Did she know the punishment for evading Hamanu's wards was death by evisceration?

She hadn't, and decided not to ask what evisceration was. He didn't tell her, either, and that convinced her that he wasn't skimming words from her mind, but understood her as Mika had.

When she had finished, he told her that the water-filled cavern was Urik's most precious treasure. "All Hamanu's might and power would blow away with the sand if anything fouled that water-hoard. He will reward you well for this warning."

Reward? What did Mahtra want with a reward? Father and Mika were gone. She had only herself to take care of, and she didn't need a reward for that. "I want to *kill* them," she said, surprising herself with the venom and anger in her voice. "I want to kill Kakzim."

A dark eyebrow arched gracefully, giving Mahtra a clearer view of a dark amber eye. His face was, if anything, more expressive than a born-human face, which told her what the makers could have done, if they hadn't made mistakes with her.

"Would you? Hamanu's infinitesimal mercy takes many forms. If you wish vengeance, Hamanu can arrange that, too."

The eleganta smiled then, a perfect, full-lipped smile that sent a chill down Mahtra's spine, and she thought she would take whatever reward the Lion-King offered, leaving the vengeance to others. His smile faded, and she asked for his side of their bargain.

"Tell me about the makers—you promised."

"They are very old; they were old when the Dragon was born, older still when he was *made*—"

Behind her mask, Mahtra gasped with surprise: one life, both born *and* made!

"Yes," he said, with a quick, almost angry, twitch of his chin. "They do not make life, they make changes, and their mistakes cannot be undone." He touched the leather of the mask. "But there are masks that cannot be seen. You could speak clearly through such a glamour. Hamanu would grant you that. But I must leave now. He will come, and I cannot be seen beside him."

And he was gone, before Mahtra could ask him his name or what he meant by masks that couldn't be seen. She didn't see him leave, any more than she'd seen him arrive. There was only a wind waft from the place where he'd been standing and a second against her back, which had been toward the golden doors.

Mahtra remained on the bench until she heard a commotion beyond the doors: the tramp of hard-soled sandals, the thump of spear-butts striking the stone floor at every other step, the deep-pitched bark of men issuing orders that were themselves muffled. A few words did penetrate the golden doors: "The Lion-King bestrides the world. Bow down! Bow down!" And though, at that moment, she would have preferred to hide behind the black boulder, Mahtra prostrated herself before the doors.

The doors opened, templars arrayed themselves with much foot-stamping and spear-pounding. They saluted their absolute ruler with a wordless shout and by striking the ribs over their hearts with closed fists. Mahtra heard every step, every salute, every slap of their leather armor against their bodies, but she kept her forehead against the floor, especially when a cold shadow fell over her back.

"I have read the message of Xerake, august emerita of the highest rank. I have heard the testimony of the woman, Mahtra—made of the Pristine Tower, and find it full of fear and truth, which pleases me and satisfies me in every way. My mercy flows. Rise, Mahtra, and ask for anything."

The first thing Mahtra noticed when she rose nervously to her feet was that King Hamanu was taller than the tallest elf and as brawny as the strongest mul. The second thing was that although he resembled his ubiquitous portraits in most ways, his face was less of a lion's and more of a man's. The third thing Mahtra noticed, and the thing that made her gasp aloud, was a pair of dark amber eyes beneath amusement-arched eyebrows.

Vengeance? A mask that could not be seen? Or nothing at all, which she could hear Father's voice telling was the wisest course. That smile—full-lipped, perfect, and cruel— appeared on King Hamanu's face. For a heartbeat she felt hot and stiff as her innate protection responded to perceived threat, then she was cold as the cavern's water. The king brought his hands together over her head. She heard a sound like an egg cracking. Magic softer than her shawl spread over her head and down her body. It had no effect that she could see or feel, but when she tried to speak, even though she could not join two coherent thoughts together, the sounds themselves were soft-lipped and pleasant.

"A mask that cannot be seen," the king said with a slight nod. "An everlasting glamour, so you can do what I need you to do. As you brought me a message from Xerake, you'll take another across the sand and salt for me. There is a man there—an ugly, human man, a high templar who owes me service. You will give him my message, and together you shall have your vengeance on Kakzim."

FOUR

Pavek leaned on the handle of his hoe and appraised his morning's work with a heavy sigh. He'd shed his yellow robe over a year ago. Exactly how much over a year had become blurred in his memory. The isolated community of Quraite that had become Pavek's home had no use for Urik's ten-day market weeks or its administrative quinths. By the angle of the sun beating down on his shoulders, he guessed high-sun was upon the Tablelands and another year had begun, but he wasn't sure, and he no longer cared. He was farther from his birthplace than any street-scum civil bureau templar ever expected to find himself; he'd been reborn as a novice druid.

These days he measured time with plants, by how long they took to grow and how long they took to die. Elsewhere in Quraite, the plants he had spent all morning setting out in not-quite-straight rows would have been called weeds and not worthy of growth. The children of the community's farmers hacked weeds apart before throwing them into cess pits where they rotted with the rest of the garbage until the next planting phase when they'd be returned to the fields as useful fertilizer.

Farmers treated weeds the way templars treated Urik's street-scum, but druids weren't farmers or templars. Druids tended groves. They nurtured their plants not with fertilizer but with magic—usually in the form of stubbornness and sweat. Telhami's stubbornness and Pavek's sweat. Right now, his sweaty hide was rank enough to draw bugs from every grove and field in Quraite. He wanted nothing more than to retreat to the cool, inner sanctum of the grove where a stream-fed pool could sluice him clean and ease his aches.

Armor-plated mekillots would fly to the moons before Telhami let him off with half a day's labor in her grove. Telhami's grove—Pavek never thought of it as his, even though she'd bequeathed it to him with her dying wishes—was Quraite's largest, oldest, and least natural grove. It required endless nurturing.

Pavek suspected Telhami's grove reached backward through time. Not only was it much larger within than without, but the air felt different beneath its oldest trees. And how else to explain the variety of clouds that were visible only through these branches and the gentle, regular rains that fell here, but nowhere else?

It was unnatural in less magical ways, too. Druids weren't content to guard their groves or enlarge them. No, druids seemed compelled to furbish and refurbish; their groves were never finished. They transplanted rocks as readily as they transplanted vegetation and meddled constantly with the water-flow, pursuing some arcane notion of 'perfect wilderness' that a street-scum man couldn't comprehend. In his less charitable moments, Pavek believed Telhami had chosen him to succeed her simply because she needed someone with big hands and a strong back to rearrange every rock, every stream, every half-grown plant.

Not that Pavek was inclined to complaint. Compared to the mul taskmaster who'd taught him the rudiments of the five templar weapons—the sword, the spear, the sickles, the mace, and a man-high staff—while he was still a boy in the orphanage, Telhami's spirit was both good-humored and easygoing in her nagging. More important, at the end of a day's labor, she became his mentor, guiding him through the maze of druid magic.

For all the twenty-odd years of his remembered life,
Pavek had longed for magic—not the borrowed spellcraft
that Urik's Lion-King granted his templars, but a magic of
his own command. While he wore a regulator's yellow robe,
he'd spent his off-duty hours in the archives, hunting down
every lore-scroll he could find and committing it to his
memory. When fate's chariot carried Pavek to Quraite, he'd
seized the opportunity to learn whatever the druids would
teach him. Under Telhami's guidance, he'd learned the
names of everything that lived in the grove and the many,
many names for water. He could call water from the ground
and from the air. He could summon lesser creatures, and
they'd eat tamely from his hand. Soon, Telhami promised,
they'd unravel the mysteries of fire.

How could Pavek dare complain? If he suffered frustration or despair, it wasn't his mentor's fault, but his own.

The hoe clattered to the ground as Pavek sank to his
knees beside the transplanted weeds. He mounded the
freshly broken dirt around the stem of each scraggly plant,
willing roots toward water and water toward roots—but not
with magic. Telhami swore that magic in any form was forbidden here on the grove's verge where lush greenery gave
way to the hardscrabble yellow of the sand barrens, and she
swore it in a way that allowed no argument.

The permitted process was straight-forward enough: Dig
up the weeds from an established part of the grove. Bring
the bare-root stalks to the verge, and plant them here with
all the hope a man could summon. If a weed established
itself, then the grove would become one plant larger, one
plant stronger, and the balance of the Tablelands would tilt
one mote away from barrenness, toward fertility.

Day after day since Telhami died, Pavek weeded and
planted little plots along the verge of her grove. In all that
time, from all those hundreds and thousands of weeds,
Pavek had tilted the balance by exactly one surviving plant:
a hairy-leafed dustweed looming like the departed Dragon
over the slips he had just planted. The dustweed was waist

high now and in full, foul-smelling bloom. Pavek's eyes and nose watered when he got close to it, but he cherished the ugly plant as if it were his firstborn child. Still on his knees, he brushed each fuzzy leaf, pinching off the wilted ones lest they pass their weakness to the stem. With the tip of his little finger, he collected sticky, pale pollen from a fresh blossom and carefully poked it into the flower's heart.

"Leave that for the bugs, my ham-handed friend. You haven't got any talent for such sensitive things."

Pavek looked around to see a luminously green Telhami shimmering in her own light some twenty paces behind him, where the verge became the lush grove. He looked at his dustweed again without acknowledging her, giving all his attention to the next blossom.

Telhami wouldn't come closer. Her spirit was bound by the magic of the grove and the grove didn't extend to the dustweed. . . .

Not yet.

"You're a sentimental fool, Just-Plain Pavek. You'll be talking to them next, and giving them names."

He chuckled and kept working. Other than Telhami, only the half-elf, Ruari, and the human boy, Zvain, treated him anything like the man he'd always been. And Telhami was the only person, living or dead, who still used the name he claimed when he first sought refuge here. To the rest of Quraite he was *Pavek,* the glorious hero of the community's desperate fight against High Templar Elabon Escrissar. In the moment of Quraite's greatest need, when the community's defenses were nearly overrun, when druid and farmer alike had conceded defeat in their hearts, *Pavek* had called on Hamanu the Lion-King of Urik. He surrendered his spirit to become the living instrument of a sorcerer-king's deadly magic. Then, in a turn of events that seemed even more miraculous in the minds of the surviving Quraiters, *Pavek* had delivered the community from its deliverer.

Pavek hadn't done any such thing, of course. King Hamanu came to Quraite for his own reasons and departed the same way. The Lion-King had ignored them since, which made a one-time templar's heart skip a beat whenever he thought about it.

But there was no point in denying his heroism among the Quraiters or expecting them to call him Just-Plain Pavek again. He'd tried and they'd attributed his requests and denials to modesty, which had never been a templar's virtue, or—worse—to holiness, pointing out that Telhami had, after all, bequeathed the high druid's grove to him, not Akashia.

Until that fateful day when Hamanu walked into Quraite and out again, every farmer and druid would have sworn that Akashia was destined to be their next high druid. Pavek had expected it himself. Like Pavek, Akashia was an orphan, but she'd been born in Quraite and raised by Telhami. At eighteen, Kashi knew more about druidry than Pavek hoped to learn with the rest of his life, and though beauty was not important to druids or to Kashi herself, Pavek judged her the most beautiful woman he'd ever seen.

And as for how Akashia judged him . . .

"You're wasting time, Just-Plain Pavek. There's work to be done. There'll be no time for lessons if you stay there mooning over your triumphs."

Pavek wanted his lessons, but he stayed where he was, staring at the dustweed and getting himself under control before he faced Telhami again. He didn't know how much privacy his thoughts had from the grove's manifest spirit; he didn't ask. Telhami never mentioned Akashia directly, only needled him this way when he wandered down morose and hopeless paths.

If Pavek couldn't deny that he'd become a hero to the Quraiters, then he shouldn't deny, at least to himself, that right after the battle he'd hoped Kashi would accept him as her partner and lover. She had turned to him for solace while Telhami lay dying, and he'd laid his heart bare for her, as he'd never done—never been tempted to do—with anyone. Then, when Telhami made her decision, Kashi turned away from him completely. She wouldn't speak with him privately or meet his eyes. If he approached, she retreated, until Pavek retreated as well, nursing a pain worse than any bleeding wound.

Pavek didn't understand what he'd done wrong—except that it was probably his lack of understanding in the first place. Street-scum templars knew as much about solace as they knew about weeds.

These days, Kashi kept counsel and company strictly with herself. Quraite's reconstruction had become her life, and for that she needed workers, not partners. As for love, well, if Akashia needed any man's love, she kept her needs well hidden, and Pavek stayed out of her way. He spent one afternoon in four drilling the Quraiters in the martial skills Kashi wanted them to have; otherwise Pavek came to the village at supper, then returned to the grove to sleep with starlight falling on his face.

It was easier for them both.

Easier. Better. Wiser. Or so Pavek told himself whenever he thought about it, which was as seldom as possible. But the truth was that he'd give up Telhami's grove in a heart-beat if Kashi would invite him to hers.

A wind-gust swirled out of the grove. It slapped Pavek smartly across the cheek—Telhami was annoyed with his dawdling and guessed, he hoped, at the reasons. He dusted off the pollen and retrieved his hoe. A stone-pocked path led from the verge to the heart of the grove—Telhami's magic from his first days here when he'd spent most of his time getting lost. This one path would take him anywhere in the grove, anywhere that Telhami wanted him to go. He veered off it at his own risk, even now. Telhami's grove abounded with bogs and sumps as dank as any Urik midden hole. Such places were home to nameless creatures that regarded the grove's current, under-talented druid as Just-Another Meal.

There was a black-rock chasm somewhere near the grove's heart—he'd come upon it from both sides without

ever finding a way across. And a rainbow-shrouded waterfall
that he'd like to visit again, except that it had taken him
three days to find the path out.

Stick to the path, Akashia had snarled when he'd finally
returned to Quraite, tired and hungry after that misadven-
ture. *Do what she tells you. Don't make trouble for me.*

He'd told her about the misty colors and the exhilaration
he'd felt when he stood on a rock with the breathtakingly
cold water plummeting around him. Foolishly and without
asking, he'd taken her hand, wanting to show her the way
while it was still fresh in his memory.

Do what you want in Telhami's *grove,* she'd said, as hateful
and bitter as any Urik templar. *Wander where you will. Sit
under your waterfall and never come back, if you think there's
nothing more important to be done. But don't drag me after you.
I don't care.*

Pavek couldn't remember the waterfall without also
remembering Kashi's face contorted with scorn. He'd tried
to find his way back, to restore himself in the pure beauty of
the place, but he couldn't remember the way. She'd seared
the landmarks from his mind.

It wasn't right. His old adversaries in the templarate
could have a man's eyes gouged out if he looked at them
wrong, but, except for the deadheart interrogators, they left
his memories alone.

Another gust of wind struck Pavek's cheek.

"Work, that's what you need, Just-Plain Pavek. Escrissar's
havoc isn't all mended yet, not by a long shot. There's a
stream not too far from here. He knocked down the trees
along its banks; now it's dammed and stagnant. Can't count
on anything natural to set it flowing again, not here in the
Tablelands. The channel needs to be cleared and the banks
need to be shored up."

With one last thought for the waterfall, Pavek followed
today's path into the grove. He'd never been one for rebellion. Following orders had kept him alive in Urik; it would
keep him alive in Quraite as well.

A little walking on Telhami's path and Pavek came to a place where a mote of Elabon Escrissar's wrath had come to ground beside what been a stand of sweet-nut trees beside a brook. The trees were all down, black with mold, and crawling with maggots. Their trunks had dammed the brook, turning it into a choked, scummy pond. An insect haze hovered above the mottled green water and the stench of rotting meat weighed down the air.

Compared to the other places where Escrissar's malice had struck the grove, this place was healthy and almost serene. There was no danger here, only the hard work of getting the water to flow again. Evidently, Telhami had been saving this particular mess for a day when she thought he needed the kind of distraction only exhaustion could bring. Pavek wondered how many such places she held in reserve, how many he'd need before he could think of Kashi without sinking into his own mire.

Telhami shimmered into sight atop one of the decaying trees. "Get the water flowing. Work with the land rather than against it."

Time was that Pavek wouldn't have known what to look for and she would have fed him clues. Now she expected him to resolve messes·on his own. He dropped to one knee and surveyed the land with his own squinted eyes. There was nothing he could do for the fallen trees, but he could see the way the stream used to flow and he could get it flowing again.

The insects had Pavek's scent and his heat. They swarmed around him in a noisy, stinging cloud. Without thinking, he slapped at his neck. There was blood on his fingers when he glanced at them.

"Brilliant, Just-Plain Pavek, just-plain brilliant," the shimmering sprite mocked him from her perch. "You'll run out of blood before you run out of bugs!"

Much as Pavek loved the sensations of druid magic flowing through him, druidry might never be the first thought in his mind when he confronted a problem. Feeling foolish, he closed his eyes and pressed his palms into the mud. Quraite's guardian was there, waiting for him.

Elsewhere, Pavek thought, adding the image of another scummy pond that might, or might not, exist somewhere in the grove. The guardian's power rose into Pavek and out of him. It stirred the bugs, gathering them into a buzzing, blurred ribbon of life that abandoned Pavek without resistance or hesitation. Flushed with his own success, Pavek sat down on his heel, sighing as residual power drained back into the land.

Every place had a guardian; that was the foundation of druidry. Every tree, every stone had its spirit. When the Tablelands had teemed with life, the guardians of the land had been lively, too. In the current age of sun-battered and lifeless barrens, druids could still draw upon the land for their power, but except in places like Quraite, where the groves retained a memory of ancient vigor, the guardians they touched were shattered. Those guardians that weren't weak were mad and apt to pass that madness to a druid who associated too closely with them.

Quraite's guardian had no personality of its own that Pavek had been able to discover. Telhami, by her own admission, was only a small aspect of its power and sanity. Pavek suspected that every druid who died in Quraite became part of the guardian, and a few Quraiters who weren't druids as well. He'd sensed another aspect from time to time: Yohan, the dwarven veteran who'd died that day when Escrissar attacked. In life, Akashia had been Yohan's focus, the core of loyalty and purpose all dwarves needed. In death, he still protected her, not as a banshee, but as an aspect of the guardian.

"On your feet, Just-Plain Pavek, or the bugs'll be back before you've moved a stick!"

Pavek got to his feet. Telhami was right, as she usually was. There was nothing to be gained by thinking of the dead who protected Quraite—or Akashia, whom he would personally protect, if she'd let him. After shedding his belt and weapons, Pavek waded into the pond. One afternoon wasn't enough to get the stream flowing swiftly again, but before the sun was sinking into the trees, he'd hauled away enough debris to get water seeping through the dam in several places.

"A little luck," he told the green-skinned spirit on an overhead branch, "and the stream will do the rest of the work for us."

"You're a lazy, lazy man," she replied with approving pride.

The path took an easy route back to the clearing Pavek called home. There was a stream-fed pool for water, a sandy hearth, and a rickety lean-to where he stored the hoe beside his sword. He'd thrown his sweated clothes into the pool and was about to follow them when the leaves on the nearby trees began to shiver and the grass bent low.

"Someone's coming," Telhami said from the rocky rim of the pool.

Pavek bent down and swept his hands through the grass. He cocked his head, listening to the leaves. Telhami knew who was coming and, after another moment of listening, he did as well. "Not someone," he corrected. "Zvain and Ruari."

"Running or walking?"

He touched the grass a second time and answered: "Running."

Ruari had his own grove, as befitted a novice druid. He had trees and shrubs, the familiar wildlife that half-elves always attracted, and a pool of water not much bigger than he was. It certainly wasn't large enough to entertain two energetic youths, since Zvain spent most of his time in Ruari's shadow, having no gift for druid magic.

Pavek wasn't surprised that they were coming to visit him. Half the time they were already in Telhami's pool by the time he returned from the grove's depths. But he was surprised that they were running. The druid groves were only a small part of Quraite, and between the groves the land was blasted by the bloody sun, just like every other place in the Tablelands. Usually, Quraiters walked, like everyone else, unless they had good reason to run. He snagged his shirt before it drifted downstream and started to follow the bending grass toward the verge.

He hadn't taken ten steps before Ruari burst through the underbrush, running easily right past Pavek to leap fully clothed into the pool. Zvain came along a few heartbeats later—a few of Pavek's heartbeats. The boy was red-faced and panting from the chase. Ruari might never be able to run with his mother's elven Moonracer tribe, but no mere human was going to catch him in a fair race: an inescapable fact that Zvain had failed to grasp. Extending an arm, Pavek caught the boy before he flung himself into the chilly water.

"Slow down. Catch your breath. You'll make yourself sick."

Somewhere between Urik and the grove, between then and now, Pavek had become the closest thing to a father any of the three of them had ever known, though only the same handful of years separated him and Ruari as separated Ruari and Zvain. The transformation mystified Pavek more than any demonstration of druidry, especially on those rare occasions when one of them actually listened to anything he said. Zvain leaned against him and would have collapsed if Pavek hadn't kept an arm hooked around his ribs.

"He said it wasn't a race—" Zvain muttered miserably between gasps.

"And you believed him? He's a known liar, and you're a known fool!"

"He gave me a twenty-count lead. I thought—I thought I could beat him."

"I know," Pavek consoled, thumping Zvain gently on the top of his sweaty head.

It wasn't so long ago that he'd been having pretty much the same conversation with Ruari, who'd nurtured the same futile hope of besting his elven cousins at their games. Life was better for the half-elf now. Like Pavek, Ruari had become a hero. He'd rallied the Quraiters to defend Pavek while Pavek summoned the Lion-King. Then, when Escrissar's mercenaries had been annihilated, he'd gone to Akashia's aid, helping her to direct the guardian's power against Escrissar himself after Telhami had collapsed.

The past two sun phases had been kind to Ruari in other ways, also. The half-elf could no longer be mistaken for a gangly erdlu in its first molt. He'd stopped growing and was putting some human flesh on his spindly elven bones. His hair, skin, and eyes were a study in shades of copper. There wasn't a woman in Quraite—young or old, daughter or wife—who hadn't tried to capture his attention, and the Moonracer women were almost as eager. Ruari had grown into one of those rare individuals who could quiet a crowd by walking through it.

No wonder Zvain ached with envy; Pavek felt that way himself sometimes. The two of them were both typical of Urik's human stock: solid and swarthy, good for moving rocks rather than the hearts of women. Zvain had an ordinary face that could blend into any crowd, which, by Pavek's judgment, was an advantage he himself had lost before he escaped the templar orphanage. The stupidest fight of a brawl-prone youth had left him with a gash that wandered from the outside corner of his right eye and across the bridge of an oft-broken nose before it came to an end at his upper lip. Years later, the scar hurt when the wind blew a storm down from the north, and his smile would never be more than a lopsided sneer. He'd put that sneer to good use when he wore a yellow robe, but here among the gentler folk of Quraite he was embarrassed and ashamed.

Ruari surfaced with a swirl and a splash of water that pelted Pavek and Zvain where they stood.

"Cowards!" he taunted, which was enough to get Zvain moving.

Pavek hung back, waiting for the other pair to become engrossed in their bravado games before he stepped down into the pool. A stream-fed pool still unnerved a man who'd grown up never seeing water except in calf-deep fountains, sealed cisterns, or hide buckets hauled out of ancient, bottomless wells. Zvain loved water; he'd learned to splash and swim as if water were a natural part of his world. Pavek *liked* water well enough, provided it didn't rise higher than his knees. And at that depth, of course, he couldn't learn to swim.

Early on, Pavek had hauled a rock into the shallows where, left to his own preferences, he'd sit and enjoy the current flowing around him. Sometimes—about one time in three—his companions would leave him alone. Today was not one of Pavek's lucky times. They double-teamed him, sweeping their arms through the cold water, inundating him repeatedly until he struck back. Then, Zvain wrapped his arms like twin water-snakes around Pavek's ankle and pulled him into the deep, dark water of the pool's center.

He roared, fought, and splashed his way back to the shallows, which merely signalled the start of another round of boisterous fun. Pavek trusted them to keep him from drowning—the first time in his life that he'd trusted anyone with his life. He trusted Telhami as well. The other two couldn't perceive the old druid's spirit, but Pavek could hear her sparkling laughter circling the pool. She wasn't above lending the youths an extra slap of water to keep him off-balance, but she'd help him, too, by making the deep water feel solid beneath his feet, if he breathed wrong and began to panic.

The fun lasted until they were all too exhausted to stand and sat dripping instead on the rocks.

"You should learn to swim," Ruari advised.

Pavek shook his head, then raked his rough-cut black hair away from his face. "I keep things the way they are so you'll stand a chance against me. If I could swim, you'd drown—you know that."

Snorting laughter, Ruari jabbed an elbow between Pavek's ribs. "Try me. You talk big, Pavek, but that's all you do.

Pavek returned the gesture, knocking the lighter half-elf off the rock, into the water. Ruari replied with a wall of water that was a bit less good-natured than his earlier pranks, as was the arm that Pavek swung at him. For all the time they spent together, despite the fact that they'd saved each other's lives, Pavek didn't know if they were friends. Friendship wasn't something Pavek had learned in the templar orphanage where he'd grown up or in the civil bureau's lower ranks. And it wasn't something the half-elf understood particularly well either. Sometimes they couldn't get two breaths into a conversation before they were snarling at each other.

Yet when Ruari slipped and started to fall, Pavek's hand was there to catch him before any damage could be done.

"You two are kank-head fools," Zvain announced when the three of them were sitting again. "Can't you do *anything* without going after each other?"

Zvain wasn't the first youth, human or otherwise, whose need for attention got in the way of his good sense. Needing neither words nor any other form of communication, Pavek and Ruari demonstrated that they didn't need to fight with each other, not when they could join forces to torment their younger, smaller companion. It was a thoughtless, spontaneous reaction, and although Pavek reserved his full strength from the physical teasing, Zvain was no match for him or Ruari alone, much less together. After a few moments, Zvain was in full, sulking retreat to the pool's far side where he sat with his knees drawn up and his forehead resting between them.

The youngster didn't have a secure niche in the close-knit community. Unlike Pavek and Ruari, he hadn't been a hero during Quraite's dark hours. Following a path of disaster and deceit, Zvain had become Elabon Escrissar's pawn before Ruari, Pavek, and Yohan spirited him out of Urik. He'd opened his mind to his master as soon as he arrived in the village. Although Zvain was as much victim as villain, in her wrath and judgment, Telhami had shown him no mercy.

Young as he was, she'd imprisoned Zvain here, in her grove.

He'd lived through nights of the guardian's anger and Escrissar's day-long assault. Ruari said he was afraid of the dark still and had screaming nightmares that woke the whole village. Akashia still wanted to drive the boy out to certain death on the salt flats they called the Fist of the Sun. Kashi had her own nightmares and Zvain was a part of them, however duped and unwitting he'd been at the time. But the heroes of Quraite said no, especially Pavek whom she'd once accused of having no conscience.

So Zvain stayed on charity and sufferance. He couldn't learn druidry—even if he hadn't been scared spitless of the guardian, his nights in this grove had burned any talent out of him. The farmers made bent-finger luck signs when the boy's shadow fell on them; they refused to let him set foot in the fields. That left Ruari, who had his own problems, and Pavek, who spent most of his time in this grove, avoiding Akashia.

A vagrant breeze rippled across the pool and Zvain's shoulders. The boy cringed; Pavek did, too. There was only one good reason for Pavek to return to Urik and the Lion-King's offer of wealth and power in the high bureau: Zvain's misery here in Quraite. It wasn't noticeable when the boy was whooping and hightailing after Ruari, but watching that lump of humanity shrink deeper into the grass was almost more than Pavek could bear.

"Let's go," he said, rising to his feet and retrieving the shirt he'd thrown on the grass. Ruari hauled himself out of the pool, but Zvain stayed where he was. "Talk to him, will you?" he asked the half-elf as he wrung the shirt out before pulling it over his head.

Ruari grumbled but did as he was asked, crouching down in the grass beside Zvain, exchanging urgent whispers that ignited Pavek's own doubts as he bent down to lace his sandals. Those doubts seemed suddenly justified when he looked up again and saw them standing together with a single guilty expression shared across their two faces.

"Give it up," he snarled and started toward the verge.

There was another frantic exchange of whispers, then Ruari cleared his throat vigorously. "You should maybe bring your sword. . . ."

Pavek stopped short. "What for?" But he headed for the lean-to without waiting for an answer. "I'm not teaching you swordplay, Ru. I've told you that a thousand times already."

"I know. It's not for me," Ruari admitted softly. "Kashi wants you to bring it. There might be trouble. There's something out on the Sun's Fist."

"Hamanu's infinitesimal mercy!" Pavek swore, adding other, more colorful oaths he hadn't used much since coming to Quraite. He glanced into the nearest trees where there was no sign of Telhami. She was a part of the guardian; she could sense what was happening out on the brutal salt plain as easily as she had sensed Ruari and Zvain approaching earlier. He thought she would have told him if there was any danger. "When? Where? Riders? How many?" he asked when he had the sword buckled around his waist and neither of his glum companions had volunteered more information. "Moonracers?"

The elven tribe were Quraite's only regular visitors. They usually came from the south, across the Sun's Fist, but they crossed the salt at night, when it was cooler and safer. They weren't due back for another quinth and when they arrived, Quraite greeted them with a festival, not a sword.

"Who, Ruari? Who does Akashia say is out on the Fist? Damn it, Ruari—answer me! Did she send you out here with that message? that warning? and *you* decided to ignore it?"

"I forgot, that's all. Wind and fire, Pavek—whoever it is, they're on the salt; they won't be here until after sundown, if they don't melt and die first."

"She wasn't really worried or nothing," Zvain added in his friend's defense. "She just said there's someone on the Fist, coming straight toward us like an arrow, and that we—"

He gulped and corrected himself; Akashia never talked to him. "That Ru should come out here and get you. There's lots of time."

"In your dreams, Zvain! Lots of time for her to decide where she's going to hang our heads. Don't you two ever learn?"

It wasn't a fair question. Zvain couldn't sink any lower in Akashia's estimation. Likely as not, the boy wouldn't complain if things came to a head and Akashia exiled the three of them together. And as for Ruari . . .

Ruari and Akashia had grown up together, and though it had always seemed to Pavek that she treated the half-elf more like a brother than a prospective suitor, Ruari had made no secret of his infatuation. Before they became heroes, they'd been rivals, in Ruari's mind at least. The half-elf's hopes had soared once Kashi turned her back on Pavek. He'd courted her with flowers and helpfulness. Pavek thought he'd won her, but something had gone wrong, and now Akashia treated Ruari no better than she treated him. Ruari had every woman in the village swooning at his feet. Every woman except the one that mattered.

"Never mind," Pavek concluded. "Let's just get moving."

They did, covering the barrens at a steady trot with the sword slapping, unfamiliar and uncomfortable, against Pavek's thigh. He kept an eye on the horizon where dust plumes would betray travelers approaching Quraite in a group. But the air there was quiet, and so was the village as they approached through the manicured, green fields. Folk paused in their work to greet Pavek and Ruari, ignoring Zvain, which made the boy understandably sullen.

Maybe it was time to go back to Urik—not forever, not to accept the Lion-King's offer, but for Zvain. The boy would be better off returning to his old life, scrounging under Gold Street, than surrounded by scorn in Quraite. Pavek knew he was telling himself a lie, a choice between scorn and scrounging was no choice at all. He'd have to come up with something better, or convince himself that Zvain's fate was no concern of his.

He swung an arm around Zvain's shoulders, trying to reel him in for a reassuring hug and wound up wrestling with him instead. Ruari joined in, and they were fully absorbed in their own noisy games as they came into the village-proper.

"It's taken you long enough to get here!"

A woman's voice brought them all to a shame-faced halt.

"We came as soon as I heard the message. I was deep in the grove," Pavek lied quickly. "They had to wait for me to get back to the pool."

"Quraite could have been destroyed by now," Akashia countered, believing the lie, Pavek guessed, but unpersuaded by it.

He guessed, as well, that Quraite's destruction would take more than an afternoon. Rather than pull down or fill in barricades and ditches they'd thrown up before their battle against Escrissar, Akashia had given orders to expand. Quraite had surrendered fertile fields to permanent fortifications. By the time she was satisfied, finished, there'd be two concentric elf-high berms around the village with a palisade atop the inner one and a barrier of sharpened stakes lining the ditch between them.

"You're supposed to set an example, Pavek," she continued. "Your grove is the very center of Quraite. If you don't care, why should anyone else? They follow your example. Not just Ruari and—"

But Akashia wouldn't say Zvain's name, not even during a tirade. The boy hid behind Pavek.

"Not just these two, but all the rest. You should be wary all the time."

"Telhami wasn't worried," Pavek snapped quickly, thinking more about Zvain than the effect his words were going to have on Akashia.

He might have gut-punched her for the look of shock and pain that came down over her face.

"Oh," she said softly, cryptically, and "Oh," again. "I

didn't know. Grandmother doesn't visit my grove or come here to the village. I *was* worried. I should have known with *him*"—she waggled her fingers in Zvain's general direction—"with Escrissar's little pawn laughing and leaping about, that nothing could possibly be wrong. We have nothing to worry about while *he's* happy."

"Sorry I said anything," Pavek apologized, ignoring the fist Zvain thumped against his spine. "I know it's hard for you, not having Telhami's grove, or her to talk to. If there's anything you need to ask, I can—"

Once again he'd said precisely the wrong thing.

"I don't need your help, high templar of Urik!"

His jaw dropped; she'd never called him that before.

"Well, that is you, isn't it? There's a woman coming across the Sun's Fist, bound straight for Quraite as if she knows exactly where it lies, and there's only one thought in her head: Find Pavek, high templar of Urik! Not the erstwhile templar, not the just-plain civil bureau templar, but *high* templar. Why not make yourself useful: Go out there and welcome her."

Pavek was speechless. His hands rose and fell in futile gestures of confusion. He certainly didn't know who was coming. If there was any substance to Telhami's shimmering green body, he was going to grab her and shake her until her teeth rattled, but until then, all he could do was mutter something incoherent in Akashia's direction and start walking toward the Fist, with Ruari and Zvain clinging to his shadow.

FIVE

Salt sprites still danced on the Sun's Fist—short-lived spirals of sparkling powder that swirled up from the flats and glowed like flames in the dying light of sunset. In the east, golden Guthay had already climbed above the horizon. Pavek spread his arms, stopping his young companions before they strode from the hard, dun-colored dirt of the barrens onto the dead-white salt. With the moon rising, there'd be ample light for finding their visitor and no need to risk themselves on the Fist until the sun was well set.

"Who do you think it is?" Ruari asked while they waited.

Pavek shook his head. He hadn't left any women behind who would come looking for him; none at all who might know him as a high templar. *That* was an unwelcome title that Lord Hamanu had bestowed upon him, which implied—to Pavek's great discomfort—that Lord Hamanu had sent the messenger, too.

He strained his eyes staring Urik-ward. There was nothing there to be seen, not yet. He consoled himself with the knowledge that Telhami must have known and that while she would tease and test him relentlessly, her mischievousness didn't include exposing Quraite to danger.

"Maybe she's dead," Zvain suggested, adding a melodramatic cough to indicate the way her death might have occurred.

Ruari countered with: "Maybe she got lost, or maybe she

will get lost. The guardian reaches this far, Pavek. It could cloud her mind, if you don't want to meet her, and she'd wander till her bones baked."

"Thanks for the thought, but I doubt it," Pavek said with a bitter laugh. "If not wanting to meet her were enough, Akashia would have done it already."

If Just-Plain Pavek had been a wagering man—which he wasn't—he'd have wagered everything he owned that Akashia had done her best to direct the guardian's power against their visitor. That power was formidable, but it wasn't infallible or insurmountable. Elabon Escrissar wouldn't have been able to find Quraite, much less attack it, if he hadn't been able to pawn Zvain off on him, Ruari, and Yohan while they were distracted rescuing Akashia from Escrissar. But once Zvain was in Quraite he opened his mind to his master. From that moment forward, Escrissar had known exactly where to bring his mercenary force, and there was nothing Quraite's guardian could do to cloud his mind.

Likewise, Lord Hamanu had apparently known of Quraite's existence. He'd asked after Telhami by name immediately after he'd disposed of Escrissar and chided her gently about the village's sorry condition. But even the Lion of Urik hadn't known *where* Quraite was until Pavek had unslung his medallion and shown the way. The mind of a sorcerer-king was, perhaps, the most unnatural, incomprehensible entity Pavek could imagine, but he was certain Lord Hamanu hadn't forgotten any of them, or where they lived.

The sun was gone. The last salt sprites dissolved into powder that would sleep until dawn. Countless shades of lavender and purple dyed the heavens as the evening stars awakened. Pavek recognized their patterns, but he took his bearings from the land itself before he started across the Fist.

There were two places in this world whose location Pavek believed he would always know. Quraite, behind him, was

one. He could see green-skinned Telhami in his mind's eye
and calm his own pounding heart in the slow, steady
rhythms of life that had endured longer than the Dragon.
The other place was Urik, but then, Pavek had roused a
guardian spirit in Urik, too, much to Telhami's surprise.

Druid tradition held that guardians were rooted in
places—forests, streams, rocks, and other phenomena of the
land, not in man-built cities. Pavek wasn't about to argue
with tradition, but Urik stood on a hill that was no less a
place than Telhami's grove, and the force that distinguished
Quraite's guardian from the lesser spirits of the barrens was
born in the generations of druids who'd lived and died
above it. Pavek wasn't bold enough to equate the street-
scum of Urik with the druids of Quraite, but he had roused
a guardian there, and ever since he'd known without thinking where the city lay over the horizon.

The path between Urik and Quraite was a sword-edge in
Pavek's mind: straight, sharp, and unwavering. As far as he
knew, he was the only one walking it, but if there were a
woman coming the other way, they'd meet soon enough.

Heat abandoned the salt as quickly as the sun's light.
They hadn't walked far before the ground was cool beneath
their feet and they were grateful for the shirts on their backs.
A little bit farther, when the sky had dimmed to deep indigo
and the stars were as bright as the moon, Pavek heard the
sounds he'd dreaded. Zvain heard them, too, and as he'd
done in the face of Akashia's scorn, he tucked himself into
Pavek's midnight shadow.

"The Lion's bells," the boy whispered.

Pavek grunted his agreement. Most folk who dared the
Tableland barrens did so discreetly, striving not to attract
the attention of predatory men and beasts. It was otherwise
with Lord Hamanu's personal minions. They carried
bells—tens, even hundreds of ceramic bells, stone bells, and
bells made from rare metals—that announced their passage,
and their patron, across the empty land. During Pavek's ten
years in the orphanage and ten subsequent years in the civil

bureau, he knew of only one time that Urik's official messengers had been waylaid.

Lord Hamanu had hunted the outlaws personally and brought the lot of them—a clutch of escaped slaves: men, women, and their children—back to Urik in wicker cages. With his infinitesimal mercy, the Lion-King could have slain the outlaws in a thousand different and horrible ways, but Urik's king had no mercy where his minion-messengers were concerned. He ordered the cages slung above the south gate. The captives had all the water they wanted, but no protection from the sun or the Urikites, and no food, except each other as they starved, one by one. As Pavek recalled, it was two quinths before the last of them died, but the cages had dangled for at least a year, a warning to every would-be miscreant, before the ropes rotted through and the gnawed bones finally spilled to the ground.

Quraite would deal fairly with its uninvited visitor, or suffer the consequences. Pavek swallowed hard and kept walking.

Ruari saw them first, his elven inheritance giving him better night vision and an advantage in height over his human companions.

"What are they?" he asked, adding an under-breath oath of disbelief. "They can't be kanks."

But they were; seven of them spread out in an arrowhead formation. Seven, and all of them bearing travel-swathed riders. And Kashi had sensed only one mind, blaring its intentions as it moved closer to Quraite. That implied magic, either mind-benders who could conceal their thoughts and presence, or templars drawing the Lion-King's power through their medallions, or defilers who transformed plant-life into sterile ash in order to cast their spells. Then again, Urik's king had a well-deserved reputation for thoroughness; he might have sent two of each.

Hamanu had definitely spared nothing to make certain his messenger reached her destination. His kanks were the giants of their kind, and laden with supply bundles in addition to their riders. Their chitin was painted over with bright enamels that glistened in the moonlight and, of course, hung with clattering bells.

When they needed transportation, the druids of Quraite bartered for or bought kanks from the Moonracer tribe. The elven herders were justly proud of their shiny black kanks, selectively bred for endurance and adaptivity. Lord Hamanu, however, wasn't interested in a bug that could run for days on end with nothing but last-year's dried scrub grass to sustain it. The Lion-King of Urik wanted big bugs, powerful bugs, bugs that made a man think twice before he approached them. And what the Lion wanted, the Lion got.

And Pavek would get, too, if he returned to Urik, because these were the bugs that the high templars and the ranking officers of the war bureau rode. The thought made Pavek's knees wobbly as he stood his ground in front of the advancing formation.

The kanks chittered among themselves, a high-pitched drone louder than all the bells combined. They clashed their crescent-hooked mandibles, a gesture made more menacing by the yellow phosphorescence that oozed out of their mouths to cover them. There were worse poisons in the Tablelands, but dead was dead, and kank drool was potent enough to kill.

Pavek loosened his sword in its scabbard and wrapped his right hand around its hilt. "In the name of all Quraite, who goes?" he demanded.

The dark silhouettes atop five of the kanks failed to twitch or prod their beasts to a halt. The kanks kept coming. Pavek drew his sword partway. "Halt now, or be run through."

"I can't see their faces," Ruari advised with his better nightvision. "They're all slumped over. I don't like this—"

The lead kank—the biggest one, naturally, with mandibles that could slice through a man's neck or thigh with equal ease—took exception to Pavek's weapon. With its antennae flailing, it emitted an ear-piercing drone and sank its weight over its four hindmost legs.

"It's going to charge," Ruari shouted in unnecessary warning.

"You've entered the guarded lands of Quraite! Hospitality is offered. Stand down," Pavek shouted with less authority than he would have liked to hear in his voice. He had the sword drawn, but he and the other two with him were doomed if he had to use it. "Stand down, now!"

The kank reared, brandishing the pincer claws on its front legs. Pavek's breath froze in his throat, then, to his complete astonishment, the kank's hitherto silent, motionless rider hove sideways and tumbled helplessly to the ground, like a sack of grain. That was all the signal Ruari needed. He wasn't fool enough to use druidry in competition with a rider's prod, but if the riders weren't in control, he knew the spells.

Pavek felt his heart skip a beat as Ruari drew upon the guardian's power. He muttered a few words—mnemonics shaping the power and directing it—to create rapport between himself and the bugs. The now-riderless kank dropped to all six feet with a clatter of chitin and bells as Ruari began weaving his arms about. One by one the kanks began to echo his movements with their antennae. Their clashing mandibles slowed, then stopped, and high-pitched chittering faded into silence.

"Good work!" Pavek exclaimed, pounding Ruari on the shoulder hard enough to send him sprawling, but there was a grin on the half-elf's face when he stood up. Pavek was as pleased with himself for remembering the niceties of friendship as he was that Ruari had saved their lives.

With the danger past and the niceties disposed of, there were questions to be answered. Keeping a wary eye on the huge, drowsy kank, Pavek scabbarded his sword and knelt down beside the fallen rider. He got his first answer when, as he rolled the body over, the rider's heavy robe opened. There was a handspan's worth of dark thread intricately woven into a light-colored right-side sleeve. The war bureau wore its ranks on the right and though the patterns were difficult to read, Pavek guessed he was looking at a militant templar, if he was lucky, a pursuivant, if he wasn't—and he usually wasn't lucky.

The robe slipped through his suddenly stiff fingers: old habits getting the better of him. Third-rank regulators of the civil bureau didn't lay hands on war bureau officers. Chiding himself that he was neither in Urik nor a third-rank regulator, Pavek got his hands under the templar's body to finish rolling it over. From the inert weight, he was prepared to see a man's face, even prepared to look down at a corpse. He wasn't prepared for the dark, foul liquid that spilled from the corpse's mouth and nose. It had already soaked the front of his robe and shirt. Pavek's hands holding the robe became damp and sticky.

Men died from the bright, brutal heat on the Sun's Fist— Pavek had nearly died there himself the first time he came across it—but he didn't think anything nearly so natural had killed this man.

"Is he—?" Zvain asked and Pavek, who hadn't known the boy was so close, leapt to his feet from the shock.

"Very," he replied, trying to sound calm.

"May I—May I search him?"

Pavek started to rake his hair, then remembered his fingers and looked for something to wipe them on instead. "Search, not steal, you understand? Everything you find has got to go back to Urik, or we'll have the war bureau hunting our hides as well." He left a dark smear on the kank's enameled chitin.

The boy pursed his lips and jutted his chin, instantly defensive, instantly belligerent. "I'm not *stupid*."

"Yeah, well—see that you stay that way."

He headed for the next kank and another bloody, much-decorated templar: a dwarf whose lifeless body, all fifteen stones of it, started to fall the moment he touched it. Cursing and shoving for all he was worth, Pavek kept the corpse on top of the kank, but only after he'd gotten himself drenched in stinking blood.

"This one's dead, too," Ruari shouted from the far end of the kank formation.

"Is it a woman?" Pavek wiped his forearms on the trailing hem of the dwarf's robe. "Akashia said a woman was coming."

"No, a man, a templar, and, Pavek, he's got a damned fancy yellow shirt. You think, maybe, there's someone else out here?"

"Not a chance. The Lion's the one who changed my rank. These are his kanks, his militants. He's the one who's sending Quraite a messenger. Keep looking."

So they did, with Pavek turning his attention to an empty-backed kank. When the druids traveled, they often fitted their biggest bugs with cargo harnesses, but the bug Pavek examined had been saddled for an ordinary rider, who'd met an unpleasant death: his charred hands, clinging to an equally charred pommel, were all that remained. Pavek assumed the rider had been male. He couldn't actually be certain. The hands looked to be as large as his own but he wasn't about to pry them free for closer examination.

The saddle had been burnt down to its inix bone frame, although the chitin on which it sat was unharmed, suggesting that the incineration had been very fast, very precise. A leather sack protruded slightly from a hollowed-out place below the pommel, a stowaway of some sort that had been exposed when the padding burned. A few iridescent markings lingered on the sack. Pavek couldn't decipher them, but with the rest, he was fairly certain Lord Hamanu had sent a defiler along with the templars. The defiler's apparent fate confirmed his suspicion that nothing natural had befallen these travelers.

There was another, larger sack attached to the rear of the saddle. The high bureau's seven interlocking circles were stamped in gold on its side. Usually such message satchels were sealed with magic, but there was no magical glamour hovering about the leather, and thinking its contents might tell them something about Lord Hamanu's message, Pavek looked around for a stick with which to prod it open.

He'd just found one when Ruari erupted with a streak of panicky oaths. Casting the stick aside and drawing his sword in its place, Pavek raced to the half-elf's side.

"Pyreen preserve and protect!" Ruari sputtered, invoking the aid of legendary druid paladins. "What is she . . . it?" he asked, retreating from the rider he'd hauled down from the bug's back.

Pavek caught Ruari at the elbows from behind and steered him to one side. For all his sullenness and swagger, for all his hatred of Urik and the human templar who, in raping his elven mother, had become his father, Ruari was an innocent raised in the clean, free air of Quraite. He knew elves and dwarves and humans and their mixed-blood off-spring, but nothing of the more exotic races or the impulses that might drive a woman to mark her body, or wrap it in a gown tight enough to be a second skin and cut with holes to display what the women of Quraite kept discreetly covered.

A templar, though, had seen everything the underside of Urik had to offer—or Pavek thought he had until he squatted down for a better look at what Ruari had found. She was beyond doubt a woman: leaner than Ruari or a full-blooded elf, but not an elf, not at all. Her skin wasn't painted; white-as-salt was its natural color, despite the punishment it must have taken on the journey. Pavek couldn't say whether the marks around her eyes were paint or not, but the eyes themselves were wide-spaced and the mask that ran the length of her face between them covered no recognizable profile. He'd never seen anyone like her before, but he knew what she was—

"New Race."

"What?" Ruari asked, his curiosity calming him already.

"Rotters," Zvain interrupted. He left off searching, but didn't come all the way over to join them. "Better be careful, they're beasts for the arena. Things that got made, not born. Claws and teeth and other things they shouldn't have. Rotters."

"Most of 'em," Pavek agreed, sounding wiser than he felt and wondering if the boy knew something that he didn't. The white-skinned woman with her mask and torn gown appeared more fragile than ferocious. As the wheels of fate's chariot spun, he knew that appearances meant nothing, but if this was the woman Akashia had sensed, he wanted to preserve the peace as long as he could. "They stay beasts, if they start out beasts. If they start as men and women, that's what they come out as, but different. And they don't all choose to go to the Tower. Some do; they've got their reasons, I guess. Mostly it's slavers that take a coffle chain south and bring back the few that come out again." Time and time again during Pavek's years as a templar, the civil bureau had swept through the slave markets in search of the lowest of the low who supplied the mysterious Tower. Maybe they saved a few slaves from transformation, but they did nothing for the ones who'd been transformed.

"Come from where? Come out how? What Tower?" Ruari pressed. "I *know* elves and half-elves; she's neither. Wind and fire, Pavek, her skin—She's got *scales!* I felt them. What race of man and woman has scales?"

Pavek shook his head. "Just her, I imagine. Haven't seen many of them, but I never saw two that were alike—"

"But you said 'New Race'."

"They're New Race because, man, woman, or beast, they all come from the same place, 'way to the south. Somewhere south there's a place—the Tower—that takes what it finds and changes it into something else—"

"Made, not born," Zvain echoed.

Pavek sighed. They were young. One of them had seen too much; the other, not enough. All men were made, women, too. Talk to any templar. "Made, not born. All by themselves, no mothers or fathers, sisters or brothers. They die, though. Just like the rest of us."

Ruari shuddered. "She's not dead. I heard her—felt her—breathing." He shuddered a second time and wrapped his arms over his chest.

Her eyes were closed and she lay with her arms and legs so twisted that Pavek had taken the worst for granted. His mastery of druid spellcraft didn't extend this far from the grove and didn't include the healing arts, but Ruari was a competent druid; he knew enough about healing to keep her alive until they found Akashia.

Kneeling beside the fallen New Race woman, he held his hands palms out above her breasts and looked Ruari in his moonlit eyes. "Help me." The words weren't phrased as a request. Ruari shrugged and twisted until their eyes no longer met. "You're wrong, Ru," Pavek chided coldly. He loosened the length of fine, dark cloth the woman had wound around her head and shoulders, then he laid his big, callused hands on her cheek to turn her head and expose the fastenings of her mask.

"Don't!" Zvain shouted.

The boy had finally come closer and taken Pavek's place beside the manifestly uncomfortable Ruari. Had his arms been long enough, Pavek would have grabbed both of them by their ears and smashed their stubborn, cowardly skulls together. He might do it anyway, once he'd taken care of the matters at hand.

"Don't touch her!"

He'd be damned first, if he wasn't already. Pavek touched her cold, white skin and found it scaled, exactly as Ruari had warned, but before he could turn her head, a Zvain-sized force struck his flank, knocking him backward. Blind rage clouded Pavek's eyes and judgment; he seized the boy's neck and with trembling fingers began to squeeze.

"*She'll blast you, Pavek!*" Zvain said desperately. He was a tough, wiry youth, but his hands barely wrapped around Pavek's brawl-thickened wrists and couldn't loosen them at all. "She'll blast you. I've seen her do it. I've *seen* her, Pavek! I've seen her do it."

With a gasp of horror, Pavek heard the boy's words, saw what he, himself, had been doing. His strength vanished with his rage. Limp hands at the end of limp arms fell against his thighs. Zvain scampered away, rubbing his neck, but otherwise no worse for the assault. Pavek was too shamed to speak, so Ruari asked the obvious question:

"Where did you see her?"

Shame was, apparently, contagious. Zvain tucked his chin against his breastbone. "I told you she was a rotter. I *told* you. She'd come to—you know—*that* house, almost every night."

Pavek let the last of his breath out with a sigh. "Escrissar? You saw her while you were living with Escrissar?" He swore a heartfelt oath as the boy nodded.

"She's got a power, even *he* couldn't get around it, and she doesn't like anyone to touch that mask."

"What was she doing at House Escrissar?" Ruari demanded, his teeth were clenched and his hands were drawn up into compact fists. He'd never forgive or forget what had happened to Akashia in House Escrissar; none of them would. Lord Hamanu had exacted a fatal price from his high templar pet without slacking Quraite's thirst for vengeance.

Zvain didn't answer the question. He didn't willingly answer any questions about Elabon Escrissar or his household. Akashia remembered him from her own nightmare interrogations. That was enough for her, but Pavek, who knew the deadhearts better and despised them no less, suspected Zvain had endured his own torments as well as Akashia's.

"What was she doing there?" Ruari repeated; Zvain withdrew deeper into himself.

"He doesn't know," Pavek shouted. "Let it lie, Ru! He doesn't know. She can tell us herself when we get her to the village—"

"You're not taking her where Kashi'll see her?"

Pavek didn't need the half-elf's indignation to tell him that it was a bad idea. He knew enough about women to know there were some you didn't put together unless you wanted to witness a tooth-and-nail fight. If he had half the wit of a stone-struck baazrag, he'd haul himself into one of the empty saddles and head south with Lord Hamanu's message and the New Race woman in tow behind him, but having only the wit of a man, he lifted the woman and started toward Quraite instead.

"What about the kanks and the corpses?" Zvain and Ruari asked together.

"What about them?" Pavek replied and kept walking.

They caught up soon enough, amid a chorus of bells that alerted the village and brought everyone out to the verge. Akashia stood in front of the other farmers and druids. Between Guthay's reflection and a handful of blazing torches, there was enough light for Pavek to read her expression as he drew closer; it was worried and full of doubt. There was silence until the two of them were close enough to talk in normal voices.

"I sensed only one traveler."

"The rest are dead. This one's the one you heard. She's unconscious." Pavek glanced over his shoulder, where Ruari stood with seven kank-leads wound around his wrist. "We thought it would be best if you roused her. She's New Race."

It was going to be as bad as Pavek feared, maybe worse. Akashia's eyes widened and her nostrils flared as if she'd gotten whiff of something rotten, but she retreated toward the reed-wall hut where she lived alone and slightly apart from the others.

"What about all this?" Ruari demanded, shaking the ropes he held and making a few of the bells clatter.

Akashia gave no sign that she had a preference, so Pavek gave the orders: "Pen the kanks. Feed them and water them well. Strip the corpses before they're buried. Bundle their clothes, their possessions—everything you find—carefully. Don't get tempted to keep anything. We'll take the bundles back with us."

" 'We'll take them back'? You've already decided? Who's 'we'?" Akashia asked, walking beside him now without looking at him or what he carried.

"We: she and I, if she survives. Lord Hamanu sent her and the escort—"

" 'Lord Hamanu?' The Lion's your lord, again?"

"Have mercy, Kashi," Pavek pleaded, using her nickname as he did only when he was flustered. "He knows where Quraite is: He's proved that, and he's proved he can send a messenger safely across the Fist—"

"Safely? Is that what you call this?"

Akashia waved a hand past Pavek's elbow. Her sleeve brushed against the dark cloth in his arms, loosening it and giving her a clear view of the New Race woman's masked face. Pavek held his breath: the woman was unforgettable, if there would be recognition, it would come now, along with an explosion.

There was no explosion, only a tiny gasp as Akashia pressed her knuckles against her lips. "What manner of foul magic has the Lion shaped and sent?"

They'd reached the flimsy, but shut, door of Akashia's hut. Pavek's arms were numb, his back burned with fatigue. He was in no mood to bargain with her outrage. "I told you: she's one of the New Races. They come from the desert, days south of Urik. The Lion has nothing to do with their making and neither did Elabon Escrissar."

Pavek waited for her to open the door, but no such gesture was forthcoming—and no surprise there, he'd been the blundering baazrag who'd dropped Escrissar's name between them.

"What's *he* got to do with this?"

Pavek put a foot against the door and kicked it open. "I don't"—he began as he carried the woman across the threshold—"know."

"She's a rotter," Ruari interrupted, adopting Zvain's insults as his own. Heroes didn't have to pen kanks or dig graves. He did unfold a blanket and spread it across Akashia's cot, but that was probably less courtesy than a desire to prevent contamination.

Zvain slipped through the open door behind Akashia. Timid and defiant at the same time, he found a shadow and stood in it with his back against the wall. Scorned boys didn't have chores, either. "I saw her there," he announced, then cringed when Akashia spun around to glower at him.

But there remained no recognition in her eyes when she looked down at the woman Pavek had laid on her cot.

"What did she do there?"

"She came at night. The house was full at night. All the rooms were full—"

The boy's voice grew dreamy. His eyes glazed with memories Pavek didn't want to share. "She was—" he groped for the word. "They're called the eleganta. They *entertain* behind closed doors."

"A freewoman?" There were gold marks on the woman's skin. Pavek hadn't seen anything like them before, but he knew they weren't slave scars, and Akashia knew it, too.

"I would die first."

Pavek smiled, as he rarely did, and let his own scar twist his lips into a sneer. "Not everyone is as determined as you, Kashi. Some of us have to stay alive, and while we live, we do what we have to do to keep on living."

Ruari spat out a word that belonged in the rankest gutters of the city and implied that the New Race woman belonged there as well. Without a sound or changing his expression, Pavek spun on his heels. Before he left the city, there were those in the bureaus who said Pavek had a future as an eighth-rank intimidator, if he'd ingratiate himself sufficiently with a willing patron. He was a head shorter than the half-elf, and there was a clear path to the open door, but Ruari stayed right where he was. Once learned, the nasty tricks of the templar trade couldn't be forgotten. Pavek subjected his friend to withering scrutiny before saying:

"You're too pretty. You'd last a morning on the streets, maybe less. You wouldn't even make it as far as the slave market. No one would want to carve up your pretty face." Although that face wasn't very pretty just then, with ashen cheeks and a cold sweat blooming on his forehead, as if the half-elf were about to get violently ill. Pavek repeated the malediction Ruari himself had used.

Akashia placed her hands on his arm and tried, futilely, to turn him around. "Stop, please! You've made your point: we don't understand the city the way you do . . . she does. Stop. Please?"

He let himself be persuaded. The scar throbbed the way it did when he let his expression pull on it, but pain wasn't the reason he'd never have made intimidator—and not because he couldn't have found a patron, precisely as the New Race woman had found one in Escrissar. . . . *Pavek* was the one—the only one in the hut—who truly felt ill. He wanted to leave at a dead run, but couldn't because the woman had awaked.

She sat up with slow, studied and graceful movements, like those of a feral cat. After examining herself, she looked up. Her open eyes were as astonishing as the rest of her: palest blue-green, like gemstones, they showed none of the differentiation between outer white and inner color of the established races. There were only shiny black pupils that swelled dramatically as her vision adjusted to the light of a single, tiny lamp.

"Who are you? What do you want from us?" Akashia spoke first.

"I am Mahtra." Her voice was strange, too, with little expression and a deep pitch. It seemed to come from somewhere other than behind her mask. "I have a message for the high templar called Pavek."

Pavek stepped away from the others and drew her attention. "I am Pavek."

Bald brows arched beneath flesh of living gold. Her pupils grew inhumanly large, inhumanly bright, as she stared him up and down, but mostly at his scarred face. "My lord said I would find an ugly, ugly man."

He almost laughed aloud, but swallowed the sound when he saw Akashia's face darkening. "Your lord?" he asked instead. "King Hamanu? The lord of Urik is your lord?"

"Yes, he is my lord. He is lord of everything." Mahtra rose confidently to her feet, displaying no sign that she'd been unconscious rather than asleep. Extending a wickedly pointed red fingernail, she reached for Pavek's face. He flinched and dodged. "Will it always look like that? Is it painful?"

New Race, he reminded himself: not a mark on her scaly skin other than those metallic patches. Not a scratch or a scar, nor a sun blister. He recalled Zvain's warnings about the mask and didn't want to imagine what scars it might conceal. She was as tall as Ruari; her slight, strong body was almost certainly full-grown, but what of her mind?

"It aches sometimes. I would rather you didn't touch it. You can understand that, can't you?" He met the pale blue stare and held it until she blinked. He hoped that was understanding. "You have a message for me?"

"My lord says he's given you more time than a mortal man deserves. He says you've dawdled in your garden long enough. He says it's time for you to return and finish what you started."

Aware that everyone—Mahtra, Akashia, Ruari, and Zvain —was staring at him intently, Pavek asked, "Did the Lion tell you what that might be?" in an almost-normal voice.

"He said you and I would hunt the halfling called Kakzim, and I would have vengeance for the deaths of Father and Mika."

"Kakzim!" Zvain exclaimed. "Kakzim! Do you hear that, Pavek? We've got to go back now."

"Father! *What* Father? You said she was made, not born. She's lying—!"

Pavek watched those jewel-like eyes brighten as the New Race taunt came out of Ruari's mouth. "Shut up—both of you!" he shouted.

All along, while Escrissar was his enemy and Laq the scourge Pavek sought to eliminate, Escrissar's halfling slave had lurked in the background. The Lion-King had come to

Quraite to destroy Escrissar, but the Lion didn't know
about the slave. Among the last things the living Telhami
had said to him was that Hamanu didn't notice a problem
until it scratched him in the eye. Kakzim—whose name
Pavek had gotten from Zvain that same day when Telhami
died—had finally caught the Lion's attention. Pavek wondered how and, though he didn't truly want to know the
answer, asked the necessary questions:

"How do you know of Kakzim? What has he done?"

Bright eyes studied Ruari first, then Zvain before returning to Pavek. "He is a murderer. His face was the last face
Father saw before he was killed. . . ." Mahtra's composure
failed. She looked down at her hands and contorted her fingers into tangles that had to hurt her knuckles. "I turned to
Lord Escrissar, but he never returned. Another high templar
sent me to Lord Hamanu, and he sent me here to you. Aren't
you also a high templar? Don't you already know Kakzim?"

Pavek was speechless. This Mahtra had elegant phrases
and elegant hands, but she was a child in her heart, a child
in her mind, and he didn't know how to answer her questions. He paid dearly for his hesitation, though, when Akashia said:

"Escrissar." Her loathing made a curse of the name. "You
turned to that foul nightmare disguised as a man? What was
he—your friend, your lover? Is that why you wear a mask?
Rotter. Is it your face that's rotten, or your spirit?"

He'd never heard such venom in Akashia's voice. It
rocked Pavek back a step and made him wonder if he knew
Akashia at all. Were a handful of days, however tortured and
terrible, enough to sour *Kashi's* spirit? What did she see
when she looked at Mahtra? A mask, long and menacing
fingernails, black cloth wrapped tightly around a slender
body. Were those similarities enough to summon Escrissar's
memory to her eyes?

Without warning, Akashia lunged toward Mahtra. She
wanted vengeance, and failed to get a taste of it when Pavek
and Zvain together seized her and held her back. The

golden patches around Mahtra's eyes and on her shoulders glistened in the lamplight, distorting the air around them as sunlight distorts the air above the salt flats.

"Kakzim was Escrissar's slave," Pavek shouted, wanting to avert disaster but pushing closer to the brink instead. "His house would be the first place anyone would look."

"Get her out of here," Akashia warned, wresting free from them, no longer out of control but angrier and colder than she'd been ten heartbeats before. "Get out of here!" she snarled at Mahtra.

"I go with High Templar Pavek," the New Race woman replied without flinching. She was eleganta. She made her life in the darkest shadows of the high templar quarter. There was nothing Akashia could do to frighten her. "With him alone or with any others who desire vengeance. Do you desire vengeance, green-eyed woman?"

Confronted by an honesty she couldn't deny and a coldness equal to her own, it was Akashia who retreated, shaking her head as she went. Pavek thought they'd gotten through the narrows, but he hadn't reckoned on Ruari, who'd come to Akashia's defense no matter how badly she treated him—or how little she needed it.

"She can't talk to Kashi that way. Take her to the grove, Pavek!" he demanded—the same demand he'd made when Pavek had arrived here, and for roughly the same reason. "Let the guardian judge her, *and* her Father *and* her vengeance."

"No," he replied simply.

"No? It's the way of Quraite, Pavek. You don't have a choice: the guardian judges strangers."

"No," he repeated. "No—for the same reason we'll bury the templars and return their belongings. The Lion will know what we do to his messengers, and he knows how to find us. And, more than that, this isn't about Quraite or the guardian of Quraite. This is about Urik and Kakzim. I saw Kakzim making Laq, but I didn't go back to find him because I thought when he couldn't make Laq anymore, he couldn't harm anyone either. I was wrong; he's become a murderer with his own hands. Hamanu's right, it's time for me to go back. We'll leave as soon as the kanks and Mahtra are rested—"

"Now," Mahtra interrupted. "I need no rest."

And maybe she didn't. There was nothing weary in her strange eyes or weak in the hand she wrapped around Pavek's forearm.

"The bugs need rest," he said, and met her stare. "The day after tomorrow or the day after that."

She released her grip.

"I'm going with you," Zvain said, which wasn't a surprise.

"Me, too," Ruari added, which was.

Akashia looked at each of them in turn, her expression unreadable, until she said: "You can't. You can't leave Quraite. I need you here," which was a larger surprise than he could have imagined.

"Come with us," he said quickly, hopefully. "Put an end to the past."

"Quraite needs me. Quraite needs you. Quraite needs *you*, Pavek."

If Akashia had said that she needed him, possibly he would have reconsidered, but probably not, not with Hamanu's threat hanging over them. That, and the knowledge that Kakzim was wreaking havoc once again. He started for the door, then paused and asked a question that had been bothering him since Mahtra spoke her first words.

"How old are you, Mahtra?" He deliberately asked it where Akashia could hear the answer.

She blinked and seemed flustered. "I'm new, not old. The cabras have ripened seven times since I came to Urik."

"And before Urik, how many times had they ripened?"

"There is no before Urik."

As Pavek had hoped, Akashia's eyes widened and the rest of her face softened. "Seven years? Escrissar—"

He cut her off. "Escrissar's dead. Kakzim. Kakzim's the reason to go back."

Pavek left the hut. Mahtra followed him, a child who didn't look like a child and didn't particularly act like one, either. She slipped her arm through his and stroked his inner forearm with a long fingernail. He wrested free.

"Not with me, eleganta. I'm not your type."

"Where do I go, if not with you?"

It was a very good question, for which Pavek hadn't an answer until he spotted a farmer couple peering out their cracked-open door. Their hut was good-sized, their children were grown and gone. He took Mahtra to stay with them until morning, and wouldn't hear no for an answer. Still this was one night Pavek wasn't going back to Telhami's grove. He stretched out in a corner of the bachelor hut.

Tomorrow was certain to be worse than tonight. He'd get some sleep while he could.

SIX

How old are you?

A voice, a question, and the face of an ugly man haunted the bleak landscape of Mahtra's dreams.

Seven ripe cabras. A whirling spiral with herself at the center and seven expanding revolutions stretching away from her. The spiraling line was punctuated with juicy, sweet fruit and the other events of the life she remembered. Seven years—more days than she could count—and all but the last several of them spent inside the yellow walls of Urik. She hadn't known the city's true shape until she looked back as the huge, painted bug carried her away to this far-off place.

Mahtra hadn't remembered a horizon other than roof-tops, cobbled streets, and guarded walls. She had known the world was larger than Urik; the distant horizon itself wasn't a surprise, but she'd forgotten what empty and open looked like.

What else had she forgotten?

There is no before Urik.

Another voice. Her own voice, the voice she wished she had, echoed through her dreams. Did it tell the truth? Had she forgotten what came before Urik, as she had forgotten what stretched beyond it?

Turn around. Step beyond the spiral. Find the path. What came before Urik? Remember, Mahtra. Remember. . . .

The spiral of Mahtra's life blurred in her dream-vision. Her limbs became stiff and heavy. She was tempted to lie down where she was, at the center of her life, and ignore the beautiful voice. What would happen if she fell asleep while she was dreaming? Would she wake up in her life or in the dream, or somewhere that was neither living nor dreaming?

Somewhere that was neither living nor dreaming . . .

Mahtra knew of such a nowhere place. She had forgotten it, the way she'd forgotten the colors and shapes on the other side of Urik's walled horizon. It was the outside place, beyond the memories of the cabra-marked spiral.

A place before Urik.

* * * * *

A place of drifting, neither dark nor bright, hot nor cool. A place without bottom or top, or any direction at all, until there was a voice and a name:

Mahtra.

Her name.

Walking, running, swimming, crawling, and flying—all those ways she'd used to move toward her name. At the very end, she fought, because the place before Urik had not wanted her to leave. It grew thick and dark and clung to her arms, her ankles. But once Mahtra had heard her name, she knew she could no longer drift; she must break free.

There were hands, like her own, awaiting her when she burst through the surface, strong arms that lifted her up while water—

Mahtra put a word to the substance of her earliest memories: the place before Urik was water and the hands were the hands of the makers, lifting her out of a deep well, holding her while she took her first unsteady steps. Her memory still would not show her the makers' faces, but it did show Mahtra her arms, her legs, her naked, white-white flesh.

Made, not born. Called out of the water fully-grown, exactly the person she was in her dream, in her life:

Mahtra.

The hands wrapped her in soft cloth. They covered her nakedness. They covered her face.

Who did this? The first words that were not her name touched her ears. *What went wrong? Who is responsible? Who's to blame for this—for this error, this oversight, this mistake? Whose fault?*

Not mine. Not mine. Not mine!

Accusing questions and vehement denials pierced the cloth that blinded her. The steadying hands withdrew. The safe, drifting place was already sinking into memory. This was the true nature of the world. This was the enduring, unchanging nature of Mahtra's life: she was alone, unsupported in darkness, in emptiness; she was an error, an oversight, a mistake.

That face! How will she talk? How will she eat? How will she survive? Not here—she can't stay here. *Send her away. There are places where she can survive.*

The makers had sent her away, but not immediately. They dealt honorably with their errors. Honorably—a dream-word from Urik, not her memory. They taught her what she absolutely needed to know and gave her a place while she learned: a dark place with hard, cool surfaces. A cave, a safe and comforting place . . . or a cell where mistakes were hidden away. Cave and cell were words from Urik. In her memory there was only the place itself.

Mahtra wasn't helpless. She could learn. She could talk—if she had to—she could eat, and she could protect herself. The makers showed her little red beads that no one else would eat. The beads were cinnabar, the essences of quicksilver and brimstone bound together. They were the reason she'd been made, and, though she herself was a mistake, cinnabar would still protect her through ways and means her memory had not retained.

When Mahtra had learned all she could—all that the makers taught her—then they sent her away with a shapeless gown, sandals, a handful of cinnabar beads, and a mask to hide their mistake from the world.

Follow the path. Stay on the path and you won't get lost.

And with those words the makers disappeared forever, without her ever having seen their faces. In her dream, Mahtra wondered if they had known what awaited her on the path that led away from their isolated tower. Did they know about the predators that stalked the eerie, tangled wilderness around their tower? Were those ghastly creatures mistakes like herself? Had they strayed from the path and become forever lost in the wilderness? Were they the lucky mistakes?

Mahtra had followed the makers' instructions until the shadowy wilderness ended and the path broadened into the hard ground of the barrens. She wasn't lost. There were men waiting for her. Odd—her memory hadn't held the words for water or cave or any of the beasts she'd avoided in the wilderness, but she'd known mankind from the start, and gone toward them, as she had not gone toward the beasts.

In the dream, a shadow loomed between Mahtra and the men. She veered away from the memories it contained.

Stay on the path.

Again, she heard the voice that might be her own and watched in wonder as a glistening path sliced through the shadow, a path that had not existed on that day she did not want to remember.

Follow the path.

The voice pulled her into the shadow where rough hands seized her, tearing her gown and mask. Her vision blurred, her limbs grew heavy, but she was not in the drifting place. A flash of light and sound radiated from her body. When her senses were restored, she stood free.

This was what the makers meant when they said she could protect herself. This was what happened to the cinnabar after she ate the red beads. The men who'd held her lay on the ground, some writhing, others very still. Mahtra ran with her freedom, clutching the corners of her torn gown against her breasts. She ran until she could run no farther and darkness had replaced the light: not the pure darkness of a cave or cell, but the shadowy darkness of her first moonless night.

Her cinnabar beads could protect her, but they couldn't nourish her flesh nor slake her thirst. She rested and ran again, not as far as she'd run the first time, not as far as she had to. The men followed her. They knew where she was. She could hear them approach. The cinnabar protected her again, but the men were wily: they knew the range of her power and harried her from a safe distance throughout the night.

Time after time, she tried to escape from the dream and from memory, but the voice held her fast.

Fear, Mahtra. Fear. There is no escape.

The men caught her at dawn, when she was too exhausted to crawl and the cinnabar flash was no more potent than a flickering candle. They bound her wrists behind her back and hobbled her ankles before they confined her in a cart. She had nothing but her mask to hide behind, because even these cruel and predatory creatures—

No mask. Nothing. Nothing at all. There is no escape from your memory.

Mahtra's mask vanished. She was truly, completely naked in the midst of men who both feared her and tormented her. There were other carts, each pulled by a dull-witted lizard and carrying one of the makers' unique creations. She called to them, but they were not like her; they were nameless beasts and answered with wails and roars she couldn't understand. Her voice made the men laugh. Mahtra vowed never to speak where men could listen.

Crouched in the corner of the cart as it began to move, she heard the word Urik for the first time.

Urik! the voice of her dream howled. *Remember Urik! Remember the fear. Remember shame and despair. There is no escape!*

She shook her head and struggled against her bonds.

There was no escape from the voice in her dream, but the dream was wrong. Memory was wrong. She still had the makers' mask; it had not been taken from her. It had not vanished. Urik was on the path the makers had told her to follow. It was the place where she belonged, where the makers said she could, and would, survive.

Remember Urik. Remember Elabon Escrissar of Urik!

In a heartbeat, Mahtra did remember. A torrent of images etched with bitter emotion and pain fell into her memory. Consistent with her nakedness and helplessness, the images expanded her memories, transforming everything she'd known. The shame she'd felt for her face spread to cover her entire body, her entire existence, and fear extended its icy fingers into the vital parts of her being.

Fear and shame and despair. They are a part of you because you were a part of them. Remember!

Mahtra fought out of the dream. The cruel men of memory disappeared, along with the bonds around her wrists and ankles. Her mask returned, comfortable and reassuring around her face, but the last victory—waking up—eluded her. She found herself on a gray plain, more dreary and bleak than anything she'd imagined, assaulted by an invisible wind that blew against her face no matter where she looked. While Mahtra tried to understand, the wind strengthened. It drove her slowly backward, back to the dream and memories of shame.

"*Enough!*" A voice that was not Mahtra's or the dream's thundered across the gray plain. It set an invisible wall against the wind and, a moment later, dealt Mahtra a blow that left her senseless.

*   *   *   *   *

"*Enough!*"

Akashia inhaled her mind-bending intentions from the subtle realm where the Unseen influenced reality. She feared she recognized that voice, hoped she was wrong, and took no chances. As soon as she was settled in her physical self, she swept a leafy frond through the loose dirt and dust on the ground in front of her, destroying the touchstone patterns she'd drawn there. In another moment she would have erased them from her memory as well, replacing them with innocent diversions.

But Akashia didn't have another moment.

A wind from nowhere whisked through her Quraite hut. It took a familiar shape: frail-limbed and hunched with age, a broad-brimmed hat with a gauze veil obscuring eyes that shone with their own light.

Not a friendly light. Akashia didn't expect friendship from her one-time mentor. She knew what she'd been doing. There were fewer rules along the Unseen Way than there were in druidry. Still, it didn't take rules to know that Telhami wouldn't approve of her meddling in the white-skinned woman's dreams.

"Grandmother."

A statement, nothing more or less, a paltry acknowledgment of Telhami's presence in this hut, their first meeting since Telhami's death a year ago. For in all that time, no matter what entreaties Akashia offered, Telhami hadn't left her grove, hadn't strayed from the *man* to whom she'd bequeathed that grove.

Even now, after all that silence, Telhami said nothing, only lifted her hand. Wind fell from her outstretched arm, an invisible gust that scoured the ground between them. When it had finished, the touchstone pattern had reappeared.

"Is this what I taught you?" Telhami's first words. Grandmother's voice, exactly as Akashia remembered it, but heavy with disappointment. While Telhami lived, Kashi had never heard that tone directed at her.

She drew a veil of her own around her thoughts, preserving her privacy. While Telhami might have the mind-bending strength to pierce Akashia's defenses, Akashia had survived more fearsome assaults than Grandmother was likely to throw at her, no matter how great her disappointment. Courtesy of Elabon Escrissar, Akashia knew what dwelt in every murky corner of her being, and she'd learned to transform that darkness into a weapon.

If Telhami wanted to do battle with those nightmares, Akashia was ready.

"Is this judgment?" Telhami's spirit demanded, adding its own judgment to its disappointment.

Akashia offered neither answer nor apology to the woman who'd raised her, mentored her, ignored her and now presumed to challenge her.

"I asked you a question, Kashi."

"Yes, it's judgment," she said, defying the hard bright eyes that glowed within the veil. "It had to be done. She came from *him!*" she snarled, then shuddered as defiance shattered. Escrissar's black mask appeared in her mind's eye. And with the mask, bright unnatural talons fastened to the fingers of his dark-gloved hands appeared also. Talons that caressed her skin, leaving a trail of blood.

The New Race woman's mask was quite, quite different. Her long red fingernails seemed impractical; nevertheless a rope had been thrown and pulled tight. Akashia couldn't think of one without thinking of the other.

"It had to be done," she repeated obstinately. "I told Pavek to take her to his grove—to the grove *you* bequeathed to him—but the Hero of Quraite refused. So I judged her myself."

"Ignoring his advice?"

"She'd already blinded his common sense. I'm not afraid, Grandmother; I'm not weak. There was no reason for you to turn to him instead of me. Pavek will never understand Quraite the way I do, even without your grove to guide me. He doesn't care the way I care."

"The white-skinned woman came from Hamanu, not his high templar," Telhami corrected her, ignoring everything else. "The Lion-King sent her. She alone traveled under his protection, she alone survived the Sun's Fist. It's not for druids to judge the Lion-King, or his messengers. If you will not believe the woman herself, if you refuse to listen to Pavek, believe *me*."

Why? Akashia wanted to scream. Why should she believe? All the while she'd been growing up, learning the druid secrets under Grandmother's tutelage, Urik and its sorcerer-king had been Quraite's enemy. Everything she learned was designed to nurture the ancient oasis community and hide it from the Lion-King's rapacious sulphur eyes. The only exception was zarneeka, which the druids grew in their groves and which Quraite sent to Urik to compound into an analgesic for the poor who couldn't afford to visit a healer. And then, they learned that Escrissar and his halfling alchemist were compounding their zarneeka not into Ral's Breath, but into the maddening poison Laq.

They'd made a mistake, she and Telhami; Escrissar's deadly ambitions had taken them by surprise. They'd paid dearly for that mistake. *Quraite* had paid dearly. Telhami had died to keep Escrissar from conquering zarneeka's source, villagers and other druids had died too, and they'd be years repairing the damage to the groves and field.

But they would have won—*had* won—before the sorcerer-king's intervention—Akashia believed that with all her heart. What she couldn't believe was Urik's ruler on his knees beside Grandmother's deathbed, caressing Grandmother's cheek with a wicked claw that was surely the inspiration for the talons Escrissar had used on her.

The sense of betrayal souring Akashia's gut was as potent now as it had been that night. Clenching a fist, relaxing it, then clenching it again, she waited for the spasms to subside. When they had, she calmly dragged a foot through the touchstone patterns—defying Telhami to restore them again.

"Mahtra went to House Escrissar frequently and willingly, she said so herself. She was *there*, Grandmother. She was there when Escrissar interrogated me, when he laid me to waste—just like the boy was! They witnessed . . . *everything!*"

She was, to her disgust, shaking again, and Telhami stood there, head drawn back and tilted slightly, glowing eyes narrowed, taking everything in, coldly judgmental—as Grandmother had never been.

"And what is it that you expected to accomplish?"

"Justice! I want justice. I want judgment for what was done to me. They should all die. They should endure what I endured, and then they should die of shame."

"Who?"

"*Them!*"

The unnatural eyes blinked and were dimmer when they reappeared. "You didn't," Grandmother whispered. "That's the root, isn't it. You wanted to die of your shame, but you survived instead, and now you're angry. You can't forgive yourself for being alive."

"No," Akashia insisted. "I need no forgiving. *They* need judgment."

"Destroying Mahtra won't change your past or the future. Destroying Zvain won't, either. Born or made, life wants to go on living, Kashi. The stronger you are, the harder it is to choose death."

Not everyone is as determined as you, Kashi. Some of us have to stay alive, and while we live, we do what we have to do to keep on living. Pavek's sneering face surfaced in Akashia's memory, echoing Telhami.

"You were assailed by corruption, you were reduced to nothing, you wanted to die, but you survived instead. Now you want to punish Mahtra for your own failure and call it justice. What judgment for you, then, if Mahtra's only crime were the same as yours: She survived the unsurvivable?"

It was a bitter mirror that Pavek and Telhami raised. Akashia raked her hair and, for the first time, averted her eyes.

"Where *is* my justice? Awake or asleep, I'm trapped in that room with *him*. I can't forget. I *won't* forgive. It's not right that I have all the scars, all the shame."

"Right has little to do with it, Kashi—"

"Right is all that remains!" Akashia shouted with loud anguish that surprised her and surely awoke the entire village. Embarrassment jangled every nerve, tightened every muscle. For a moment, she was frozen, then: "Everything's dark now. I see the sun, but not the light. I sleep, but I don't rest. I swallowed his evil and spat it back at him," she whispered bitterly. "I turned myself inside out, but he got nothing from me. *Nothing!* Every day I have to look at that boy and remember. And, *she's* come to put salt on my wounds. They *know*. They must know what *he* did to me. And yet *they* sleep sound and safe."

"Do they?"

She set her jaw, refusing to answer.

"Do they?" Telhami repeated, her voice a wind that ripped through Akashia's memory.

According to Ruari, Zvain at least did not sleep any better than she. And for that insight, she'd turned against her oldest friend, her little brother.

Something long-stressed within Akashia finally collapsed. "I'm weary, Grandmother," she said quietly. "I devote myself to Quraite. I live for them, but they don't seem to care. They do what I tell them to do, but they complain all the while. They complain about using their tools in weapons-practice. I have to remind them that they weren't ready when Escrissar came. They complain about the wall I've told them to build. They say it's too much work and that it's ugly—"

"It is."

"It's for their protection! I won't let anything harm them. I've put a stop to our trade with Urik. No one goes to the city; no one goes at all, not while I live. I'd put an end to the Moonracer trade, too . . . if I could convince them that we have everything that we need right here."

Akashia thought of the arguments she'd had trying to convince the Quraiters, farmers and druids alike. They didn't understand—couldn't understand without living through the horror of those days and nights inside House Escrissar.

"Alone," she said, more to herself than to Telhami. "I'm all alone."

"Alone!" Telhami snorted, and the sound cut Akashia's spirit like a honed knife. "Of course you're alone, silly bug. You've turned your back to everyone. Life didn't end in House Escrissar, not yours nor anyone else's. Walls won't keep out the past or the future. You're alive, so live. You've been pleading for my advice—yes, I've heard you; everything *hears* you—well, that's it. That, and let them go, Kashi. Let Pavek go, let Ruari go. Let them go with your blessing, or go with them yourself—"

"No," Akashia interrupted, chafing her arms against a sudden chill. "I can't. They can't. Pavek's the Hero of Quraite. The village believes in him. They'll lose heart if he goes—especially if he goes to stinking Urik—and doesn't come back. I had to judge that woman. If I could make her reveal what she truly was, he wouldn't follow her. He'd stay here, where he belongs. They'd all stay here."

The sleeping platform creaked as Telhami sat down beside Akashia. She had neither pulse nor breath, but her hands were warm enough to drive away the chill.

"At last we get down to the root: Pavek. Pavek and Ruari. They *do* know what happened. You can scarcely bear the sight of either of them—or the thought that they might leave you. It would be so much easier, wouldn't it, if all the heroes of Quraite were dead: Yohan, Pavek, Ruari, and Telhami—all of us buried deep in the ground where we could be remembered, but not seen."

Despite her best intentions, Akashia nodded once, and a demeaning tear escaped from her eyes. She clenched her fists hard enough to hurt, hard enough to obscure the scarred face she saw in her mind's eye. "He—They chose the boy. He's the one they pity," she muttered. "And now they're choosing Mahtra."

She swiped tears with back of her hand, but more followed.

"Pity?" The bloodless hands were warm, but the voice

was still cold and ruthlessly honest. "What pity? None was asked for, none was given. Outside this hut, I've seen life go on. I've seen compassion. I've seen love and friendship grow where nothing grew before. But I see no pity, no clinging to a past that's best forgotten."

"I don't want to forget. I want my life back. I wish life to be as it was before."

It was a foolish wish—life didn't go backward—but an honest one, and Akashia hoped Telhami would say something. She hoped Grandmother would reveal the words that would prevent Pavek and Ruari from leaving Quraite.

"Let them go, Kashi," Grandmother said instead. "Tear down the wall."

"It won't ever be the same as it was."

"It won't ever be different, either, unless you let go of what happened."

"I can't."

"Have you tried?"

She shook her head and released a stream of tears, not because she'd tried and failed but because it was so easy to forget, to live and laugh as if nothing had changed—until a word or gesture or a half-glimpsed shadow jarred her memory and she was staring at Escrissar's mask again.

"Laugh at him," Grandmother advised after the old spirit unwound her thoughts. "Run through your fields and flowers and if he appears—laugh at him. Show him that he has no more power over you. He'll go away, too."

More tears. Kashi took a deep breath and asked the most painful question of all: "Why, Grandmother—why did you give your grove to him?"

"It was not mine to give," Telhami's spirit confessed. "Quraite chose its hero. And a wise choice it was, in the end. I'd made a mess of it, Kashi. Can you imagine the two of us grappling with all those toppled trees? We'd be at it forever—but Pavek! The man was born to move wood and rock through mud. You should see him!"

And for a moment, Kashi did, hip-deep in muck, cursing,

swearing and earnestly setting the grove to rights again. She had to laugh, and the tears stopped.

"You're not alone," Grandmother said suddenly, which Akashia mistook for philosophy, then she heard footsteps outside the hut.

Telhami disappeared before Akashia could tell her midnight visitor to go away. Feeling betrayed and abandoned once again, Akashia plodded to her door where two of Quraite's farmers greeted her. One held a pottery lamp, the other, Mahtra's hand.

"She had a dream," the lampbearer said. "A nightmare. It scared us, too. Pavek said he'd be in the bachelor hut, but we thought . . ."

Some folk needed neither spellcraft nor mind-bending to convey their notions silently. The farmer's hollow-eyed, slack-jawed expression said everything that needed to be said.

"Yes, I understand." She made space in the doorway for Mahtra to pass. With her strange coloring and wide-set eyes—not to mention whatever the mask concealed—the white-skinned woman's face was almost unreadable. When Mahtra squeezed herself against the door jamb rather than brush against her, Akashia had the sense that they were equally uncomfortable with the situation. "She can stay here with me for the rest of the night. Pavek shouldn't have troubled you in the first place."

" 'Tweren't no trouble," the farmer insisted, though he was already retreating with his wife and his face belied every word.

Akashia stood in the doorway, watching them walk back to their hut, and all the while conscious of the stranger at her back. As soon as was polite, she shut the door and braced it with her body. She didn't know what to say. Mahtra solved her problem by speaking first.

"It was only a dream. I didn't know my dreams could frighten someone else. That has never happened before. You said I should go to the grove. What is a grove? Would my dreams frighten anyone there?"

"No." Akashia pushed herself away from the door with a sigh. "Not tonight. It's too late."

It was too late for the grove under any circumstance. Mahtra's voice wasn't natural. Her jaw scarcely moved as she formed the words and the tone was too deep and deliberate to come from her slender throat, yet listening to her now, Akashia believed Mahtra had lived in the world for only seven years. As much as she craved justice, Akashia couldn't send a seven-year-old to the grove.

"Sit down," she suggested. She would have liked to accuse Grandmother of masterminding this encounter, but she had only herself and her own meddling to blame. "Are you hungry? Thirsty. We eat in common, but I could—"

"No, nothing, thank you."

Of course not, Akashia realized, feeling like a fool. Eating or drinking would have meant removing the mask. While ransacking Mahtra's memory, Akashia had found the white-skinned woman's self-image—what she thought she looked like. If it was halfway accurate, there was good reason for that mask, though appearances alone would not have bothered Akashia.

One thing that did bother her was the way that Mahtra chose to stand a step away from the touchstone patterns on the dirt floor. Grandmother had known what they were: mind-benders' mnemonics, makeshift symbols Akashia had used to push and poke her way through Mahtra's dreams. Akashia was the only one who could have deciphered their meaning, yet Mahtra stared at them as if they were a public text on a Urik wall.

Akashia strode across her hut. She stood in the center of the pattern, scuffing it thoroughly—she hoped—with her bare feet before she took Mahtra by a white wrist. "Please sit down." Akashia tugged her guest toward a wicker stool. "Tell me about your dream," she urged, as if she didn't already know.

Mahtra's narrow shoulders rose and fell, but she went

where Akashia led her and sat down on the stool. "It was a dream I would not want to have again. I knew I was dreaming, but I couldn't wake up."

"Were you frightened?" Akashia sat cross-legged on her sleeping platform. It was wrong to ask these questions, but the damage was already done, and she was curious. Mindbenders rarely got a chance to study the results of their efforts.

The pale blue-green bird's-egg eyes blinked slowly. "Yes, *frightened,* but I don't know why. It was not the worst dream."

"You've had other dreams that frightened you more?"

"Worse memories make worse dreams, but they're still dreams. Father told me that dreams can't hurt me, so I shouldn't be frightened by them. Sometimes memories get worse while I'm dreaming about them. That happened tonight, but that wasn't what frightened me."

"What did frighten you?" Akashia found herself speaking in a small voice, as if she were talking to a child.

Mahtra stared at her with guileless but unreadable eyes.

"Near the end, when I couldn't stop dreaming, I remembered memories that weren't mine. They frightened me."

Akashia's blood ran cold. She thought of the touchstone pattern and the possibility that she was not as skilled with the Unseen Way as she believed, at least not with the mind of a child-woman who'd been made, not born. "What kind of memories?" she asked, curiosity getting the better of her again. "How do you *know* they weren't your own?"

For a long moment Mahtra stared at the ground, as she'd stared at the patterns. Perhaps she was simply searching for words.

"Father was killed in the cavern below Urik, but Father didn't die until after I found him and after he'd given me the memories that held his killer's face—Kakzim's face—so I could recognize it. Father was very wise and he was right to save his memories, but now I remember Kakzim and I remember being killed. In my dreams the memories are all confused. I want to save Father and the others, but I never can. It's only a dream, but it makes me sad, and frightened."

"And your dream earlier tonight—it was like that?"

Mahtra's head bobbed once, but her eyes never left the dirt. "I remember what never happened, not to me, but to someone like Father. Someone who's been killed and holding on to memories, waiting to die. I don't think I'll go to sleep again while I'm here."

Akashia was grateful that Mahtra wasn't looking at her. "There's no reason for you to stay awake." Not anymore. Akashia swore to herself that she wouldn't tamper with Mahtra's mind again.

"No one's been killed in Quraite," she continued, "not in a long time. There's no one dying here either."

"You are," Mahtra said as she raised her head and her odd eyes bore into Akashia's. "It was your voice I heard in my dream. I recognize it. You told me to remember what came before Urik. You told me to feel shame and fear, because you felt shame and fear. I felt what you felt, and then, I remembered what you remember."

"No," Akashia whispered. For one moment, one heartbeat moment, the loathing she'd been trying to awaken in Mahtra had been awakened in her instead. She thought the touchstone pattern had protected her. She certainly hadn't acquired any of Mahtra's memories but, in her narrow drive for judgment, it seemed that her own had escaped. "No, that can't be."

"I recognize you. I recognize my lord Escrissar; I remember him as you remember him—isn't that what you wanted? The makers gave me protection. I couldn't be hurt as you were hurt. Now I remember your pain, but what the makers gave me won't protect you, no more than it protected Father. I think Father would tell me that I've made a bad trade. He would tell me to learn from my mistakes, but I don't know what there is for me to learn. The august emerita told me that my lord Escrissar is dead. I believe her. If you believe her, then he can't hurt you again and it doesn't matter that what the makers gave me won't help you. Is that an even trade? Do you believe what the august emerita told me?"

Mahtra was a child of Urik's darkest nights, its murkiest shadows, but mostly she was a child, with a child's cold sense of right and wrong. Akashia nodded. "Yes," she said quickly, swallowing a guilty sob. "Yes, I believe he's dead. It's an even trade."

"Good. I'm glad. Without Father, there's no one to ask and I can't be sure if I've done the right thing. Your memories will sleep quietly now, and I can leave here with the ugly man and not look back. Kakzim killed Father. The ugly man and I will hunt Kakzim and kill him, too. For Father. Then all my memories will sleep quiet."

Akashia rose and faced a corner so she didn't have to face Mahtra. The white-skinned woman's world was so fiercely simple, so enviably simple. Mahtra's memories would sleep quietly, as perhaps Akashia's own memories would grow quieter, if she could truly believe in Mahtra's simple justice.

"Pavek," she said after a moment, still staring at the corner, still thinking about justice. "You should call him Pavek, if you're going to take him away. He's not an ugly man; you shouldn't call him that. He'll tell you when you've done the right thing. You should listen to him."

"Do you?"

It was a question Akashia could not find the strength to answer aloud.

"Father said the best lessons were the hardest lessons," Mahtra said after a long silence, then—to Akashia's heartfelt relief—walked softly out the door.

No need to worry: Mahtra could take care of herself wherever she went.

Reclaiming her bed, but not for sleeping, Akashia extinguished her lamp. She sat in the dark, thinking of what she'd done, what Telhami had said, and all because of the extraordinary individual the Lion-King had sent from Urik. Mahtra was like a Tyr-storm, rearranging everything she touched before disappearing. Akashia had taken a battering since sundown. She wouldn't be sorry to see the white-skinned woman leave, but she wasn't sorry Mahtra had come to Quraite, either. There was a bit of distance between herself now and the yesterday of Elabon Escrissar.

Akashia still found it difficult to think of Ruari or Pavek. Ruari was the past of hot, bright, carefree days that would never come again. Pavek was a future she wasn't ready to face. She didn't want either of them to leave with Mahtra, but she could admit that now, at least silently to herself, and with the admission came the strength to say good-bye before dawn, two days later.

She was proud of herself, that there were no tears, no demands for promises that they would return, only embraces that didn't last long enough and, from Pavek, something that might have been a kiss on her forehead just before he let go. Standing on the verge of the salt, Akashia watched and listened until the bells were silent and the Lion-King's kanks were bright dots against the rising sun. Then she turned away and, avoiding the village, walked to her own grove.

There were wildflowers in bloom and birds singing in the trees—all the beautiful things she'd neglected since her return from Urik. There was a path, too, which she'd never noticed before and which she followed . . . to a waterfall shrouded in rainbows.

SEVEN

A trek across the Athasian Tablelands was never pleasant. Pavek and his three young companions were grateful that this one was at least uneventful. They encountered neither storms nor brigands, and all the creatures who crossed their path appeared content to leave them alone.

Pavek was suspicious of their good fortune, but that was, he supposed, his street-scum nature coming to the fore as he headed back to the urban cauldron where he'd been born, raised, and tempered. That and the ceramic medallion he'd worn beneath his home-spun shirt since leaving Quraite.

The closer they came to Urik, the heavier that medallion—which he had not worn nor even touched since Lord Hamanu strode out of Quraite—hung about both his neck and his spirit. The medallion's front carried a bas-relief portrait of the Lion-King in full stride. The reverse bore the marks that were Pavek's name and his rank of third-level regulator in the civil bureau, marks now bearing a lengthwise gouge where the sorcerer-king had raked his claw through the yellow glaze. Ordinarily, high templar medallions were cast in gold, but it was that gouge, not the precious metal, that declared a templar had risen through the ranks of his bureau to the unranked high bureau.

High Templar Pavek. Pavek of the high bureau. *Lord* Pavek. He could call himself whatever he chose now, although Just-Plain Pavek still felt like his name.

Still, with nothing but the relentless sun, the clanging kank bells that limited conversation among the travelers, and the mesmerizing sway of the saddle to distract him, Pavek let his imagination run wilder each day of the ten-day journey from Quraite to Urik.

There were no more than fifty high templars in Urik— men and women; interrogators, scholars, or commandants—whose power was second only to Lord Hamanu's. Pavek considered paying a visit to his old barracks, the training fields, or the customs house where he'd worked nine days out of ten. Not that he'd left any friends behind who might congratulate him; he simply wanted to witness the reaction when he unslung the medallion and made the gouge visible.

There'd be laughter, at first. No one in his right mind would believe any templar could rise from third rank to the top, especially not within the civil bureau where the ranks weren't regularly thinned by war.

But that laughter would cease as soon as someone dared touch his medallion. That lengthwise gouge couldn't be forged. Even now, quinths after the Lion-King had touched it, the medallion was still slightly warm against Pavek's chest. Anyone else would feel a sharp prickling: high templars had an open call on their patron's power and protection.

Once convinced of the mark's authenticity, he'd have more friends than he knew what to do with. In his mind's eye, Pavek watched the taskmasters, administrators, and procurers who'd run his life since his mother bought him a pallet in the templar orphanage trample each other in their eagerness to curry his favor.

Pavek had countless fantasies beneath the scorching sun, but he indulged them only because he knew that many of those whose comeuppance he most wished to witness were already dead, and that he'd never act on the rest. He'd had too much personal acquaintance with humiliation to enjoy it in any form.

Besides, in his calmer moments Pavek wasn't certain he wanted to *be* a high templar. He certainly didn't want to have regular encounters with Urik's sorcerer-king. On the other hand, the more he learned from Mahtra, frequent encounters of any kind were a decreasing possibility. First he had to survive this, his first high-templar assignment. Night after night as they sat around a small fire, Pavek quizzed the white-skinned woman about the disaster that had eventually brought her to Quraite.

Mahtra had told him about a huge cavern beneath the city and the huge water reservoir it supposedly contained. When he gave the matter thought, it seemed reasonable enough. The fountains and wells that slaked Urik's daily thirst never ran dry, and although the creation of water from air was one of the most elementary feats of magic—he'd mastered the spell himself—it was unlikely that the city's water had an unnatural origin. That a community of misfits dwelt on the shores of this underground lake also seemed reasonable. For many people, life anywhere in the city, even in the total darkness beneath it, was preferable to life anywhere else.

Not much more than a year ago, Pavek would have thought the same thing.

And he could imagine a mob of thugs descending on that community with extermination on their minds. It wasn't a pleasant image, but riots happened in Urik, despite King Hamanu's iron fist and the readiness of templars to enforce their king's justice. While he wore the yellow, Pavek had swept through many an erupting market plaza, side-by-side with his fellow templars, bashing heads and restoring order with brutal efficiency that kept the bureaus more feared than hated.

It was the sort of work that drove *him* to a melancholy two-day drunk, but there were a good many templars who enjoyed it, even volunteered for it.

Templars were certainly capable of causing the carnage in Mahtra's cavern, but it seemed this was one civic outrage for which they weren't responsible. With all the time she'd spent in the templar quarter, Mahtra would know a templar if she'd gleaned one from the dying memories of the mind-bender she called Father. But there wasn't a snatch of yellow in the images she'd received from Father's dying mind and, even off-duty, the kind of templars who might have ravaged the cavern wore their robes as a sort of armor.

What Mahtra had gleaned from inherited memories was the face of a slave-scarred halfling who she insisted was Escrissar's alchemist. Pavek had seen Kakzim just once, when he stood beside his master, Escrissar, in the customs-house warrens. It had struck Pavek then that the alchemist had enough hate in his eyes to destroy the world. He could believe that the mad halfling was the force behind the rampage. What he couldn't figure was Kakzim's purpose in slaughtering a community Lord Hamanu would have executed anyway.

It didn't make sense to a thick-skulled man like himself, any more than it made sense that the Lion-King would send across the Tablelands for him to resolve the problem. True, he'd been concerned that Kakzim hadn't been caught and killed along with Escrissar in the battle for Quraite, but not concerned enough to pack up his few possessions and head back to the city. He'd seen no pressing need. Urik belonged to Lord Hamanu, as children belonged to their parents, and over the millennia the king had demonstrated that he could take good care of what belonged to him.

If Lord Hamanu wanted Kakzim dead, Kakzim would be dead. Simply and efficiently.

Try as he might, Pavek could find only one satisfactory explanation for the summons Mahtra carried to Quraite: Lord Hamanu was bored. That was the usual explanation when sudden, strange orders filtered down through the bureau hierarchies; orders that once put an adolescent orphan on the outer walls repainting the images of the Lion-King for a twenty-five day quinth, changing all the kilts to a different color.

Lord Hamanu made war to alleviate his boredom and indulged his high templar pets for the same reason. He'd turned Pavek into a high templar, and now it was Pavek's turn to provide a day's amusement before Lord Hamanu hunted down the halfling himself.

Pavek dreamt of sulphur eyes among the stars, eyes narrowing with laughter, and razor claws descending through the night to rip out his heart. The heavens were naturally dark each time he awoke, but the gouged medallion was hot against his ribs, and Pavek was not completely reassured.

In contrast to his own nightmare anxiety, Zvain and Ruari seemed to think they'd embarked on the great adventure of their young lives. They chattered endlessly about cleverness, courage, and the victory that would be theirs. Zvain imagined throwing Kakzim's bloody head at the Lion-King's feet and being rewarded with his weight in gold. Ruari, to his credit, thought he could assure Quraite's isolation. Even Mahtra got swept up in vainglory, though her expectations were more modest: an inexhaustible supply of cabra melons and red beads.

The trio tried to infect him with their enthusiasm, calling him an old man when he resisted. They had a point. Pavek could remember himself at Ruari's age—it wasn't more than a handful of years ago—and he'd been a cautious old man even then.

After dealing with the sorcerer-king's boredom, Pavek feared his greatest challenge was going to be riding herd on his rambunctious allies.

Ruari had matured in the past year. He had moments of blind, adolescent stubbornness, but overall Pavek trusted the half-elf to act sensibly and hold up under pressure. Zvain was still very young, in the midst of his most willful and rebellious years, and nursing childhood wounds. He was inclined at times to crumble, to curl in on himself—especially when Pavek and Ruari lapsed into one of their vigorous but ultimately inconsequential arguments. The boy craved affection that Pavek could barely provide and then frequently rejected it just as fast, which only made life more difficult.

As for Mahtra . . . the made-woman was an enigma. Younger than Zvain by several years, she wasn't so much a child—though she had a child's notion of cause and effect— as a wild creature, full-grown and unpredictable. She was much stronger than she appeared, and, or so she claimed, had the capacity to 'protect herself'.

Mahtra said she'd ridden out of Khelo, the market village most nearly aligned with Quraite's true location and the one where Lord Hamanu maintained his kank stables. But Pavek held to the Quraite tradition of entering Urik from a deceptive direction.

They circled the city, camping one final night on the barrens, and joined the city's southern road shortly after dawn the next morning.

That was the limit of caution or discretion. Once the bright, belled kanks were on the road, rumor traveled with them through the irrigated fields. Pavek spotted the isolated dust plumes as runners spread the word, and before long there were gawkers on the byways. They kept their distance, of course, even the noble ladies in their distinctive gauze-curtained howdahs, but curiosity was the strongest mortal emotion and a parade of the Lion-King's decorated bugs was almost as fascinating as the Lion himself. Pavek, Ruari, and Zvain were nothing to look at, but Mahtra, the eleganta with her stark white skin and unusually masked features, captured the onlookers' attention. She certainly did when they reached Modekan, the village where, in the past, Quraiters had registered their intent to bring zarneeka into Urik the following day.

Pavek had no idea what day it was as they approached Modekan, but the village was quiet. The Modekan registrators weren't expecting visitors, at least not visitors riding the sorcerer-king's kanks. Pavek began to regret his decision to pass through Modekan, where their impending arrival had all the earmarks of the event of the year, if not the decade.

He counted nineteen frantic clangs of the village gong before they arrived; within the city walls, even the appearance of Lord Hamanu only warranted ten.

Every village templar was lined up at the gate, wearing tattered, wrinkled yellow robes that would never pass muster at Pavek's old barracks. The rest of Modekan mobbed behind the line, necks craning and heads bobbing for a good look. Three strides through the gate, and every pair of eyes was fastened tight on Mahtra. A burly human woman with a bit more weaving in her yellow sleeve than the others hurried forward to crouch beside Mahtra's kank, offering her own back as a dismounting platform. Mahtra's bird's-egg eyes fairly bulged with surprise, and rather than dismounting, she pulled her feet up onto the saddle.

It was an insult, a breach of tradition. Pavek didn't imagine that registrators liked being treated as kank-furniture—regulators certainly didn't—but having humiliated oneself, no low-rank templar like to be refused. Confusion reigned and threatened to turn ugly with the village's ranking templar groveling in the dust and Mahtra trying to keep her balance. Pavek had his eye particularly focused on another templar in the crowd, young enough and angry enough to be the crouched woman's son, who'd turned a dangerous shade of red.

When the furious templar began to move, Pavek moved as well, dismounting in the war bureau style—off leg swinging forward over the pommel, rather than backward over the cantle, so the rider landed with the kank at his back and eyes on his enemy. He'd seen the method, but never tried it before. Success made him bold.

"Who's in charge here?" he demanded with his arms folded over his chest. No one answered. Mahtra looked like someone important; he looked like a farmer. Pavek hooked the leather thong around his neck and brought the gouged medallion into the light. "Who is in charge?" he repeated.

Audacity often succeeded in the Tablelands because the price of failure was so high that few would dare it. Templar and villager alike knew the punishment for impersonating a high templar. They stared at Pavek brandishing his ceramic medallion as if it were made of gold. After a long moment during which his heart did not beat at all, the crouching woman got to her feet. There was a smile on her face as she came toward him. The earlier insult was forgotten; now she expected to have the honor of turning an imposter over to higher authorities.

Then she saw the gouge in the medallion he held out to her, and her smile wavered. Pavek didn't need magic or mind-bending to hear the doubts contending in her mind as she extended her arm. They were, however, equally shocked when crimson sparks leapt from the gouge to her fingertips, sparks bright enough to make them both blink.

"Great One!" she cried, nursing burnt fingers as she dropped to her knees. "Great One, Lord, forgive me. I meant no disrespect."

All the others followed her example, parents grabbing their children as they knelt and holding them close. The children cried protest at the rough handling, but there were adult sobs, also. Pavek could slay them all with his own hands, no questions asked nor quarter given. He could enslave them on the spot, selling them or keeping them without regard for kinship. Such were the ingrained powers of the Lion-King's high templars.

Pavek chewed his lower lip, sickened by what he'd done, uncertain how to rectify it. The only high templar he'd met in the flesh was Elabon Escrissar, whose example he'd sooner die than follow.

"Mistakes happen," he muttered. Mistakes did, of course, and people died for them. "You weren't expecting us." They should have gone to Khelo. "There's been no harm done, to us or you. No reason to sweat blood."

Slipshod and undisciplined as the registrators were, they *were* templars, and they knew about sweating blood. Here and there, a head came up to stare at him. If mekillots would fly before a high templar showed mercy to fools, then Pavek had just sprouted wings.

"We'd like water to drink and to wash off the dust, and a hand-cart for our baggage. Then we'll be on our way. We have business in Urik."

More heads had come up, more folk questioning fortune. The burly registrator got to her feet, still cradling her hand against her breast. She looked at the medallion, then at Pavek's face.

"Whatever you wish, Great One, Lord. Whatever your dreams desire. Please, Great One, Lord, tell us who are you or—?"

"Pavek," he replied, almost as uncomfortable as she was.

Judging by the lack of reaction, his name, which had been associated with a forty-gold-piece reward less than a year ago, had been forgotten. The registrator's lips worked, summoning up the fortitude for another question:

"Forgive me, Great One, Lord Pavek, we are so isolated here. We know only peasants, slaves, and farmers, but what is your house-name, so we may honor you, Great One, Lord Pavek, with the proper respect."

Of course. Like the nobility living on their estates, high templars had a second name engraved on their medallions. Pavek could have made one up out of whole cloth to satisfy these nervous registrators, and he would have, for their sakes and his, but his mind had gone completely blank.

"By decree of Hamanu, Lord of the Mountains and the Plains, King of the World—"

They'd all forgotten Mahtra, still sitting cross-legged atop her kank. Lord Hamanu must have prepared her for this moment, at least Pavek hoped the sorcerer-king had taught her the words when he gave her the message she brought to Quraite. The alternative was that Lord Hamanu was bending Mahtra's thoughts at this very moment. Pavek noticed he wasn't the only one looking for sulphur eyes in the skies over her head. He didn't find any.

"—Lord Pavek is sole inheritor of House Escrissar. You may call him Lord Escrissar."

There was a name everyone recognized, feared and rightly despised, Pavek included. The Modekaners looked at him, more uncertain than before, and even Ruari and Zvain seemed taken aback. It shouldn't have been such a gut-numbing surprise—the Lion-King had all but told him he was replacing the half-elf—but it was. Pavek felt as if he'd been stained with a foul dye that would never wash off.

The woman registrator retreated a full stride. "We will send to Khelo for sedan chairs, Lord Escrissar." She flashed a hand-sign and two elven templars took off running. "There are none here."

Another reason they should have gone to Khelo. Draft and riding animals were outlawed in Urik and in the belt of land between the city and its market villages. High templars and nobles got around that law with slave-labor sedan chairs, which could be hired at Khelo.

"There's no time for that," Pavek protested, finding his voice too late to recall the elves. "Water and a hand-cart, that's all we want; then we'll be on our way."

They got their water, and all the succulent fruit they could eat, but not the hand-cart. There was no way Modekan's chief registrator was going to let a high templar, especially a high templar calling himself Lord Escrissar, leave her village pulling his own baggage in a rickety two-wheeled bone-and-leather cart. The village had twenty hale men who'd be honored to pull their cart. Her very own son would be especially honored to pull a second cart for the eleganta, whose rank they'd mistaken earlier.

"Surely, Lord Escrissar, you can't expect her to *walk?*"

Pavek knew Mahtra wasn't nearly as frail as she appeared to be, but her sandals weren't suited for the long walk to the city. After a futile grumble, he bowed his head, accepting the registrator's advice. The bloody sun hadn't moved twice its breadth across the cloudless sky, and already he was being told what to do again, respectfully and correctly, but told, nonetheless.

By the time the Modekaners had piled what appeared to

be every pillow in the village into Mahtra's cart, there wasn't a yellow-robed elf to be seen. The templars at the city gate weren't going to be surprised by an unexpected high templar and his entourage. And Pavek wasn't going to get an opportunity to talk tactics with his companions on the final leg of their journey, as—fool that he was—he'd intended.

Pavek didn't get a chance to talk with them at all. In addition to the two men pulling the carts, half the able-bodied folk of Modekan marched along with them, each of them taking advantage of the opportunity to ply a cause or air their favorite grievance with, wonder-of-wonders, an approachable high templar. They made varied promises and offered their service for quinths, phases, or all the years of their lives, if only he would take them into his presumably vast patronage. One nubile young woman offered to become his wife, guaranteeing him strong, healthy sons to carry on his lineage; she already had three by the man she was leaving, the man who, moments earlier, had offered to become his water-servant for ten years and a day.

He said he'd think about it and tucked the little sealstone with her name on it into his bulging belt-pouch. An older fellow, a dwarf with a mangled ear and a gimpy leg, took aim at him next, but not before Pavek got a glimpse of Mahtra, Ruari, and even Zvain under similar assault, the three of them looking similarly overwhelmed. He cursed himself for a fool and was glad Telhami wasn't around to see what a mess he'd made of things, then the dwarf caught up with him.

The dwarf knew of a place, deep in the barrens, where a sandstorm had overtaken a rich caravan, leaving everyone dead but him. For twenty years, he'd kept the caravan's lost treasure a secret, but now, if Lord Escrissar would put up twenty gold pieces—for men, supplies, and inixes to haul the treasure back to Urik—the dwarf would split the treasure evenly with him.

Hamanu's infinitesimal mercy! Did they all take him for that great a fool?

Pavek grew more irritated with himself and the smarmy dwarf until the walls and roofs of the city hove into view. He hadn't realized how much he'd missed Urik—he hadn't thought he'd missed it at all, but the sunlight flash of the Lion-King's yellow-glass eyes embedded in the majestic walls sent a chill down his spine. His body tightened. He walked lighter, feeling Urik's vitality through the balls of his feet, the chaotic rhythms of sentient life different from the slow regularity of Quraite's groves. The dwarf fell behind as Pavek picked up the pace. Cruel, perhaps, to take advantage of a dwarf's shorter stride, but not unjust, not unlike the Lion-King whose wall-bound portraits beckoned him home.

His former peers in the civil bureau were waiting for Pavek at the southern gate. They remembered his name. At least a few of them would have cheerfully sold him to Escrissar, had the opportunity presented itself, to collect that forty-gold-piece reward. Now they claimed him as one of their own, bullying the Modekaners in ways both subtle and physical, until the four visitors were secure inside the city walls.

"The Mighty Lord expects you, Great One," the instigator in charge of the southern gatehouse informed Pavek. "We sent word to the palace after the Modekan messengers arrived. Manip"—the instigator indicated a tow-headed youth wearing the regulator's bands that Pavek knew best— "lingered in the corridor. He saw messengers dispatched to the quarter with the keys to your house."

The instigator paused, as if he had more to say, as if it were pure happenstance that his hand was palm-up between them. Gatekeeping templars couldn't *demand* anything from a high templar, but Manip had taken no small risk eavesdropping in the palace. Pavek fished carefully through his cluttered belt-pouch; it was useful to know that they had a place to sleep, albeit an ill-omened one. He put an uncut ceramic coin in the instigator's hand. It disappeared immediately into the instigator's sleeve, but no more information was forthcoming, and Pavek had no assurance that Manip would receive a fair share of the reward.

"Shall I escort you to the palace, Great One?" the instigator asked.

Pavek understood that the man would expect another gratuity when they reached the palace gate. He needed another moment to remember that he was a high templar now and that there was no need for him to reward this man, or anyone. Nor was he compelled to accept services he didn't want.

"I know the way, Instigator," he said firmly, liking the sound. "Your place is here. I would not take you from it. Let Manip, there, haul our cart to my house." That was a way to reward the templar who'd actually taken the eavesdropping risk, and rid themselves of a bulky pile in the bargain. The other cart, Mahtra's cart with the abundance of pillows, was already on its way back to Modekan.

"Great One, the palace?" The instigator's tone was less bold. "The Mighty Lord was informed of your imminent arrival, Great One. He expects you and your companions."

"That is not your concern, Instigator." Pavek made his voice cold. He smiled his practiced templar smile and felt his scar twitch.

The tricks of a high templar's trade came easily. He could grow accustomed to the power, if he weren't careful. Corruption grew out of the bribes he was offered, the bribes he accepted, which was no surprise, but also out of those he refused, and that was a surprise.

He set Manip, the cart, and three ceramic bits on their way toward the templar quarter, then herded his companions deeper into the city, where they could almost disappear into the afternoon crowds.

"Didn't you hear what he said?" Zvain demanded when they were sheltered in the courtyard of an empty shop. "Wheels of fate, Pavek—King Hamanu's got his eye out for us. We're goners if we don't hie ourselves to the palace!"

"And do what when we get there?" Pavek countered. "Slide across the floor on our bellies until he tells us what to do next?"

Zvain said nothing, but his expression hinted that he had expected to slither.

"Mahtra, can you take us to the reservoir now?" Pavek turned to her. "I want to see it with my own eyes before we go to the palace."

She pulled back, shaking her head like a startled animal.

"If we're going to hunt for Kakzim, we have to start where he was last seen."

"My Lord Hamanu—" Mahtra began to protest.

But Pavek cut her off. "Doesn't know everything there is to know in Urik." The words were heresy, but also the truth, or Laq would never have gotten loose in the city. "Can you lead us there? I don't want to go to the palace with an empty head."

"There was death everywhere. Blood and bodies. I didn't want to go back. I didn't go back. Father, Mika, they're still there."

A child, Pavek reminded himself. A seven-year-old who'd come home one morning and found her family slaughtered. "You don't have to go all the way, Mahtra. Just far enough so we know where we're going. Zvain will stay with you—"

"No way!" the boy protested. "I'm going with you. I'm not afraid of a few corpses."

But he was afraid of Mahtra. That had been simmering since the Sun's Fist and had finally reached a boil now that they were both back in Urik, where they knew each other from House Escrissar and shared memories Pavek didn't want to imagine. He shot a glance at Ruari. Of all of them, the half-elf was the most anxious. Ruari didn't know much about cities, and what he did know wasn't pleasant. He'd reclaimed his staff from the baggage cart and clung to it with both hands. The rest of his body was in constant motion, affected by every sound he heard. It was time to test his belief that the half-elf was reliable.

"You'll stay with her, won't you, Ru?"

"Aye," Ruari replied, but he was staring at the roofs across the street where something had just gone *thump*.

"There—you lead us as far as you can, and Ruari will stay with you until Zvain and I get back." Never mind that *he'd* trust Mahtra's street-sense before he'd trust Ruari's; Mahtra was reassured.

"We have to get to the elven market. There'll be enforcers to pay, and runners. I haven't paid them since—" Mahtra's voice faltered. Pavek began to worry that the return to Urik had overwhelmed her, but she cleared her throat and continued. "There's Henthoren. I don't know if he'll let me bring someone new across his plaza. . . ."

"We'll worry about that when we get there," Pavek said with a shrug.

He might have known the passage would be in the elven market—the one place in Urik where a high templar's medallion wouldn't cut air. They'd be better off if no market enforcer or runner suspected who he was, what he was. Tucking the medallion inside his shirt, he started walking toward the market. He had three companions, each of whom wanted to walk beside him, but only two sides.

Ruari staked a claim to Pavek's right side. He held it with dire glowers and few expert prods from his staff, which Pavek decided diplomatically to ignore.

"What do I do with these?" the half-elf asked plaintively.

Pavek looked down on a handful of colorful seal-stones sitting in Ruari's outstretched hand. "Did anyone tell you a story that you believed?"

"No. They all wanted something from me."

"Throw them away."

"But—?"

The stones went tumbling when Pavek jostled the half-elf's arm.

"But—?" he repeated. "The stones themselves—shouldn't I try to return them, if I don't want them?"

"Forget the stones. Potters sell them at twenty for a ceramic bit, forty after a rain. Forget the Modekaners. If you'd believed them, it might be different—*might be*. But you didn't believe them. Trust yourself, Ru. You for damn sure can't trust anyone else."

Ruari wiped the lingering dust onto his breeches. The great adventure had lost its glow for him and was further dimmed when they passed through the gates into the elven market. Ruari had been conceived somewhere in the dense maze of tents, shanties, and stalls. His Moonracer mother had fallen afoul of a human templar. The templar was long dead, but Ruari still held a grudge.

The market was quiet, at least as far as enforcers and runners were concerned. Mahtra led them confidently from one shamble-way to the next. Keeping an eye out for authority, Pavek spotted several vendors who seemed to recognize her—hardly surprising given her memorably exotic features—but no one called to her. And that wasn't surprising either. Folk in the market minded their own business, but they had a good memory for strangers, an excellent memory for the three strangers traveling in Mahtra's wake.

They stopped short on the verge of a plaza not greatly different from a handful of others they'd crossed without hesitation.

"He's not here. Henthoren's not here," Mahtra mumbled through her mask. She pointed at an odd but empty construction, an awning-chair atop a man-high tower and the tower mounted on wheels. Henthoren—a tribal elf by the sound of his name—presumably sat in the chair, but there were no elves to be seen today, not even among the women pounding laundry in the fountain. "He's gone."

"He can't stop you from leading us across then, can he?" Pavek chided gently. "Let's go."

She led them to a squat stone building northwest of the fountain. The stone was gray, contrasting with the ubiquitous yellow of Urik's streets and walls. There were rows of angular marks above a leather-hinged grating. Writing, Pavek guessed, but none that he was familiar with. After spending all his free time breathing dust and copying scrolls in the city archive, he thought he'd deciphered every variant script in the Tablelands cities. He'd have liked a few moments to study the marks, but Mahtra had opened a grate.

"Wind and *fire*," Ruari exclaimed as he crossed the threshold. "We're flat out of luck, Pavek."

Zvain used more inventive language to say the same thing. Mahtra said nothing until Pavek was inside the stone building.

"It has changed," she whispered, staring at a potent blue-green warding that cut the space inside the building in half. "Grown bigger and brighter. There is no way. That is why Henthoren is gone."

That was possible. The warding was as thick and bright as any Pavek had seen before; thicker by far than the wardings the civil bureau maintained on the various postern passages through the city walls. He'd guess a high templar had hung the shimmering curtain.

"There was some light before, but there was a passage here, too." Mahtra indicated a place now hidden by the warding. "We'd use the passage. Now—They showed me what would happen if I touched the light."

"It must be twice as powerful as the one under the walls," Ruari said, making a pensive face. He remembered warding from when Pavek had led them through a postern passage on their way to rescue Akashia from House Escrissar. "At least twice as powerful. I can feel it; it makes my teeth hurt and my hair stand up. The other one didn't. Don't think your medallion trick's going to work like it did last year."

Pavek shouldered his way to the front. He took his medallion from his neck and grasped it carefully by the edges, with the striding lion to the front. "You forget: I'm at least twice the templar I was then."

A cascade of blue-green sparks leapt to the medallion, leaving a black, wardless space in the curtain. Pavek moved the ceramic in an outward-growing spiral, collecting more sparks, making a bigger hole. His arm was numb and faintly blue-green by the time he had a hole large enough to let them through. He went last; it closed behind him, leaving them in darkness. Pavek sucked his teeth and swore under his breath.

"What's the matter?" Ruari asked.

"One-sided warding."

"So? Then we've got no problem getting out—"

The half-elf would have walked headlong into oblivion if Pavek hadn't seized his arm and shoved him against the rough stone wall.

"Death-trap, fool! Warding to keep curious folk out, but a blind trap for anyone who was already inside when the wards were set."

Ruari went limp against Pavek's grip on his shirt. "Can we get out?"

"Same way we got in—just have to make certain I'm in front and my medallion's in front of me," Pavek said with more good-humor and optimism than he felt. "Wish I had a bit of chalk to mark the walls. Wish I had a torch to see the walls . . ."

"There're torches on the other side," Mahtra volunteered, then added: "There used to be."

"I can see," Ruari informed them, relying on the night-vision he'd inherited from his elven mother. "I've marked these rocks in my mind. I'll know this place when we're here again. Swear it."

"See that you do," Pavek said, and Zvain tittered nervously somewhere on his left. "Still wish I had a torch."

"The path's not hard," Mahtra assured them. "I never carried a torch, and I can't see in the dark. Hold hands; I'll lead."

And she did, without a hint of her earlier trepidations. Her grip was cool and dry around Pavek's fingers, while Zvain, behind Pavek, had a sweaty hand that threatened to slip away with every hesitant step the boy took. Ruari brought up the rear, or Pavek assumed he did. Between his druid training and his innate talents, the half-elf could be utterly silent when he chose.

The air in the passage was nighttime cool and heavy with moisture, like the air in Telhami's grove. It had a faintly musty scent, but nothing approaching the stench Pavek would have expected from the carnage Mahtra had described. He'd believed her since she appeared on the salt flats. He'd trusted her unquestioningly, as he trusted no one else, certainly not the Lion-King who'd sent her. A thousand ominous thoughts broke his mind's surface.

"There's light ahead," Ruari announced in an excited whisper.

Light meant magic or fire. Pavek took a deep breath through his nose. He couldn't smell anything, but he couldn't see anything, either.

"Let me go first," he said to Mahtra, striding past her.

The passage was wide enough for two good-sized humans and high enough that he hadn't bumped his head. They'd come through a few narrower spots, but none that made Pavek feel as if the ground had swallowed him whole. He didn't suggest that Mahtra stay behind or that Ruari stay behind with her. He didn't sense danger ahead, not in that almost-magical way a man could sometimes sense a trap or ambush before it was too late, but if things did go bad, he wanted Ruari and his staff where they could be of some use—not to mention the 'protection' Mahtra claimed to possess but hadn't ever described or demonstrated.

He thumbed the guard that held his steel sword—scavenged from the battlefield after the battle with Escrissar's mercenaries for Quraite—in its scabbard. "Stay close. Stay quiet," he ordered his troops. "Keep balanced. If I stop short, I don't want to hear you grunting and stumbling."

They whispered obedience, and he led them forward. The light grew bright enough that he could see it: a dimly glowing blue-white splotch in the distance, not any kind of firelight Pavek knew. It grew larger, but remained dim, even when they approached the end of the passage. Pavek left his companions behind, then, even though they'd be trapped without him to brandish his medallion at the upper warding. He saw the decision as a question of risk against responsibility: he'd be responsible for them, no matter what, but at that moment the greatest risk lay in the light he could see, not in the warding.

The enclosed passage ended at the top of a curving ramp. Overhead, there was open air filled with the dim light, solid rock on his left, and a slowly diminishing wall on his right. Pavek edged along the wall, keeping his head down, until the wall was low enough for him to see over while still providing him with something to hide behind. After taking a deep breath for courage, he peeked over the top—

And was so amazed by what he saw that he forgot to hunker down again.

Urik's reservoir was larger than any druid's pool, larger than anything Pavek could have imagined on his own. It was a dark mirror reflecting the glow from its far shore, flawless, except for circular ripples that appeared and faded as he gazed across it. The glow came from five huge bowls that seemed at first to hover in the still air, though when he squinted, Pavek could make out a faint, silvery scaffolding beneath them.

Other than the bowls, there was nothing: no corpses, no burnt-out huts, none of the debris a veteran templar expected to find in the aftermath of carnage.

But the bowls themselves . . .

Pavek didn't have the words to describe their delicate, subtly shifting color or the aura that shone steadily around them. They were beautiful, identical, perfect in every imaginable way, and now that he'd seen them, the foreboding he hadn't felt when Ruari first saw light ahead fell on him like burning oil.

Mahtra wasn't a liar. Lord Hamanu was trustworthy. And someone—Kakzim—had contrived the deaths of countless innocents and misfits so these bowls could be set in their places above the water.

Set there and left alone.

By everything Pavek could see or hear, there wasn't

another living creature in the cavern. He gave the agreed-upon signal, and Ruari brought the other two down the ramp.

Mahtra gasped.

Zvain began a curse: "Hamanu's great, greasy—" which he didn't finish because Pavek clouted him hard on the floating ribs. Notwithstanding an eleganta's trade or the things Mahtra must have seen in House Escrissar, there were some things honest men did not say in the presence of women. The boy folded himself around the ache. Tears ran from his eyes, but he kept his lips sealed and soundless.

"What do you think?" Pavek gave his attention to Ruari, who was his superior where magic was concerned.

The half-elf rolled his lower lip out. "I don't like it. Doesn't feel . . ." He closed his eyes and opened them again. "Doesn't feel *healthy*."

Pavek sighed. He'd had the same sensation. He'd hoped Ruari could be more specific.

They stayed where they were, waiting for a sound, a flicker of movement to tell them they weren't alone. There was nothing—unless the most disciplined ambushers on the Tablelands were waiting for them. When Pavek's instincts said walk or scream, he started down the ramp, slow and quiet, but convinced that they were in no immediate danger. The cavern was too vast for the sort of one-sided warding they'd encountered earlier; it was too vast for any warding at all. Ruari prodded the reservoir's gravelly shore with his staff, searching for more traditional traps. He overturned a few charred lumps that might have been parts of huts or humans, but nothing that would tell anyone what had happened here less than two quinths ago, if Mahtra hadn't told them.

When they got to the far shore, they found each bowl mounted on its own platform that leaned over the water. The silvery scaffolds shone with light as well as reflecting the greater light of the bowls they held. Caution said, look, don't touch, but Pavek was a high templar who'd painted the Lion-King's kilts. He wasn't afraid of a bit of glamour, and he recognized a ladder in the scaffold's regular cross-pieces. With his medallion against his palm, he touched a glowing strut.

"I'll be—" he began, then caught himself. "It's made of bones!"

Pavek ran the medallion from one lashing to the next, absorbing the silver glow. The scaffolding that emerged from the glamour was constructed from bones of every description. It was thoroughly ingenious, but except for the glamour—which was a simple deception and not much of one at that—it was completely nonmagical. He tested the built-in ladder and, finding it strong enough to bear his weight, scrambled up to the platform. Ruari came after him, but the other two stayed on the ground.

Pavek scrubbed the bowl's side with Lord Hamanu's medallion, hoping to dispel the glowing, shifting colors. The glamour here was stronger. His arm ached before he could see the bowl's true substance: not stone, as he'd first thought, but a patchwork of leather set on top of a patchwork of bones.

There was a pattern: leather and bones, a lot of leather, a lot of bones. Pavek felt a word rising through his own thick thoughts, but without breaking the surface, the word was gone when the bowl suddenly shuddered.

Hand on his sword, he turned around in time to see Ruari tottering on the bowl's rim. Demonstrating a singular lack of foresight, the half-elf had apparently tried to leap up there from the scaffold, but all those losing contests with his elven cousins finally yielded a victory. Ruari thrust his staff forward and down into the bowl. The move acted as a counterbalance, and he stood steady a moment before leaping lightly back to the scaffold platform beside Pavek.

Slop from the tip of Ruari's staff struck Pavek's leg. It was warm, slimy, and unspeakably foul. Pavek swiped it off with his fingers, then shook his hand frantically. Ruari reversed the staff to get his own closer view of the remaining gook.

He touched it, sniffed it, and would have touched it a second time with the tip of his tongue—if Pavek hadn't swung at the staff and sent it flying.

"Have you lost what little wit you were born with, scum?"

Ruari drew himself up to his full height, a good head-and-a-half taller than Pavek. "I was going to find out whether it was wholesome or not. Druids can do that, you know. Not bumble-thumbs like you, but *real* druids."

"Idiots can do it, too, the same way you were going to do it! Hamanu's infinitesimal mercy—the stuff's poison!"

"Poison?"

Ruari stared at the dark slime on his fingers, and, judging by his puzzled expression, saw something entirely different. So Pavek grabbed Ruari's hand and smeared the sludge clinging to the half-elf's hand across the medallion, where it hissed and steamed with a frightful stench. Ruari was properly appalled

"Laq?" he whispered.

"Damned if I know."

"Laq?" Zvain shouted from the ground where he brandished Ruari's staff.

"You keep your hands away from that tip—understand!" Pavek shouted, which only drew the boy's attention to that exact part of the staff, which he promptly touched.

Pavek leapt to the ground, twisting his ankle on the landing. By the time things were sorted out, both he and Zvain were limping and Ruari had joined them.

"This time, Kakzim's trying to poison Urik's water," the half-elf said, proud that he'd deciphered the purpose of the bowls.

"Looks like it," Pavek agreed, putting weight gingerly on his sore ankle. "Had to get rid of the folk living here so he could build these damn bone scaffolds and skin bowls!" Which, while true, were not the wisest words he'd ever uttered.

Mahtra raised her head to stare wide-eyed at the bowls. It didn't take mind-bending to guess what kind of skin she thought Kakzim had used to make them.

Mahtra shrieked, "Father!" She took off at a run for the nearest scaffold.

Ruari grabbed her as she ran past him, and let go just as quickly shouting: "What are you!"

She fell to the shore with her head tilted so they could see that a milky membrane covered her eyes. The gold patches on her skin gave off bright fumes that smelled a bit of sulphur.

Zvain dropped to the ground as well. "Don't fight!" he shouted, then curled up with his knees against his forehead. "Don't fight," he repeated, sobbing this time. "She'll blast you if you fight."

Pavek stood beside Ruari, one hand on his sword, the other on his medallion, waiting for Mahtra to be herself again. The fumes subsided, the membranes withdrew. She sat up slowly, stretching her arms.

"You want to tell us what that was about?" Pavek demanded.

"The makers—" Mahtra began, and Pavek rolled his eyes.

She began to cry—at least that's what Pavek thought she was doing. The sound she made was like nothing he'd heard before, but she was starting to curl up the same way as Zvain. Ignoring his ankle, he squatted down beside her.

"I didn't mean to frighten you."

"Father—"

"I don't know what happened to your father's body, but those aren't his bones. Those are bones from animals. The bowls, too. The bowls are made from animal hides, inix maybe. I was a cruel, dung-skulled fool to say what I did."

"Bones and hides," Ruari commented. "House Escrissar wasn't bloody enough for him, so Kakzim's moved into a slaughterhouse—"

A slaughterhouse. Pavek got to his feet. "Codesh!" The word that had escaped before all the excitement began. "Codesh! Kakzim's in Codesh! He's in the butchers' village—" His enthusiasm faded as quickly as it had arisen.

"But the passage's in the elven market. Someone would have noticed, not the hides, maybe, but the bones for sure. There's no way to get those bones here without *someone* noticing."

Mahtra stood up slowly, using Pavek's arm for balance. "Henthoren sent a runner across the plaza to me that morning. He said he'd let no one into the cavern since sundown, when I left. I think—I think he knew what had happened, and was trying to tell me it wasn't his fault—"

"Because there's another passage to the cavern . . . in Codesh," Pavek concluded.

Zvain raised his head. "No," he pleaded. "Not Codesh. I don't want to go to Codesh. I don't want to go anywhere."

"Don't worry. Codesh can wait until morning," Pavek assured the boy. He'd had enough adventure for one day himself. His ankle throbbed when he took an aching step toward the distant ramp to Urik. The sprain wasn't as serious as it was painful. "Food," he said to himself and his companions. "A good night's sleep. That's what we all need. We'll worry about Codesh—about *Hamanu*—in the morning."

Ruari, Mahtra and Zvain fell in step behind him.

EIGHT

Civil bureau administrators were waiting outside the door of House Escrissar when Pavek, still hobbling on a game ankle, led his companions through the templar quarter a bit before sunset. The administrators were drowsy with boredom and leaning against the loaded hand-cart Manip had dragged up from the gate. Exercising his high templar privileges, Pavek rewarded Manip and sent him on his way before he said a word to the higher ranking administrators.

With proper deference, one of the administrators gave him a key ring large enough to hang a man. The other handed him a pristine seal, carved from porphyry and bearing his exalted rank, his common name, and his inherited house. He tried to give Pavek a gold medallion, too, but Pavek refused, saying his old ceramic medallion was sufficient. That confused the administrator, giving Pavek a momentary sense of triumph before he etched his name—Just-Plain Pavek—through the smooth, white clay surface of the deed, revealing the coarse obsidian beneath it.

The administrators wrapped the deedstone in parchment that was duly secured with the Lion-King's sulphurous wax by them and by Pavek, using his porphyry seal for the first time. The administrators departed, and Pavek tried five keys before he found the one that worked in the door. He dragged the hand-cart over the threshold himself.

House Escrissar had been sealed quinths ago. It was quiet

as a tomb beneath a thick blanket of yellow dust. Otherwise both Zvain and Mahtra assured its new master that the house was precisely as they remembered it—which sent a chill down Pavek's spine. There was nothing in the simple furniture, the floor mosaics, or the wall frescoes to proclaim that a monster had lived here. He'd expected obscenity, torture, and cruelty of all kinds, but with their depictions of bright gardens and green forests, the frescoes could have been commissioned by a druid . . . by Akashia herself.

"It was like this," Zvain repeated when curiosity drove Pavek to touch a painted orange flower. "That was the *worst—*"

The boy's words stopped abruptly. Pavek turned around. They'd been joined by the oldest, most frail half-elf he'd ever seen, a woman whose crinkled skin hung loose from every bone and whose back was so crippled by age that she gazed most naturally at her own feet. She raised her head with evident discomfort and difficulty. Her cheeks were scarred with black lines in a pattern Pavek promised himself would never be cut into flesh again.

"Who has come?" she asked with a trembling voice.

Pavek caught Zvain and Mahtra exchanging anxious glances before they shied away from the old woman's shadow. Ruari was transfixed by the sight of what he, himself, might become. Pavek swallowed hard and jangled the key ring he held in his weapon hand.

"I've come," he said. "Pavek. Just-Plain Pavek. I am—I am the master here, now." He couldn't help but notice the way she stared at the key ring.

Her name, she said, was Initri. She had chosen to remain inside the house with her husband after all the other slaves were dispersed and the administrators had come to lock the doors for the last time. Her husband tended the house gardens.

Lulled by the bucolic frescoes, Pavek had let down his guard. He wanted to meet another Urik gardener, the man who made flowers bloom in House Escrissar. Initri led them all to the center of the residence where lush vines turned the yellow walls green and a carpet of wax-flower creepers covered the ground. Kneeling beside a clear-water fountain, another ancient half-elf in faded, threadbare clothes, went about his weeding, oblivious to their arrival.

"He doesn't hear anymore," Initri explained and made her way with small, halting steps along the cobbled garden path.

Initri got her husband's attention with a gentle touch. He read silent words from her lips, then set aside his tools with the slow precision of the venerably aged before he took her hand. While Pavek and his companions watched from the atrium arch, the old man took his wife's arm, for balance, as he stood. They both tottered as he rose from his knees. Pavek strode toward them, but they leaned against each other and were steady again without his help. Pavek expected scars and saw them before he saw the metal collar around the gardener's neck and the stone-link chain descending from it. Each link was as thick as the half-elf's thigh. The chain had to weigh as much as the old man did himself.

They stood side-by-side in the twilight, the loyal gardener and his loyal wife, she with one hand on his flank, the other clutching the chain. No wonder Initri had stared so intently at the keys he held in his hand—keys that the administrators had kept secure under magical wards in King Hamanu's palace. Overcome by shame and awe, Pavek looked away, looked at the flowers in their profuse blooming.

If ever a man had the right to destroy the life of Athas, this old man had had that right, but he'd nurtured life instead.

"How?" Pavek stammered, forcing himself to face the couple again. "How have you survived? The house was locked."

Initri met his gaze and held it. "The larders were full," she said without a trace of emotion. "Some nights the watch threw us their crusts and scraps. It depended on who had the duty." She indicated the crenelated platform visible above the garden's rear wall.

Pavek whispered, "Hamanu's infinitesimal mercy."

He heard long-striding footfalls behind him: Ruari disappearing. Ruari making certain Pavek knew he was angry about something; the half-elf didn't have to make noise when he ran. Zvain and Mahtra showed no more emotion than Initri did. Compassion was a wasted virtue in Urik; Pavek knew they were better off without it, but he sympathized more with Ruari. The elderly couple said nothing. They stared at him, the new high templar master of House Escrissar—their new master—without reproach or expectation on their faces.

The keys.

One of the keys must belong to the lock that bound the chain and collar together. Pavek fumbled with the ring, dropping it twice. He tried the first two keys he touched; neither fit the lock, much less opened it. Locks were nothing a man without property had ever needed to understand. Pavek resolved to work his way around the ring, a key at a time, and had tried two more when Initri's withered fingers reached toward him. Her motion stopped before their hands touched; the fears and habits of slavery were not easily shed.

"Which one?" Pavek asked her gently. "Do you know which one?"

She pointed toward a metal key that had been shaped to resemble a thighbone. Pavek slipped it into the socket and twisted it. The mechanism was stiff; he was afraid to apply his full strength. The key might break and Pavek had no notion where he'd find a smith after sunset—though he knew he wouldn't be able to rest until he had.

Once again, Initri came to Pavek's rescue, her parchment fingers resting lightly over his, guiding them through tiny jerks and jiggles. The lock's innards released themselves with an audible *click*. The thick shaft pulled loose, then the first link of the chain. Finally Pavek could take the ends of the metal collar and force the sweat-rusted hinge to yield.

The gardener examined the collar after Pavek had removed it. His hands trembled. Tears fell from his eyes to the corroded metal. Initri showed no such sentiment.

"Lord Pavek, your larder holds dried beans, a cask of flour, and some sausage a jozhal wouldn't steal," she said in a slave's habitual monotone. "Does that please my lord for his supper?"

Pavek twisted the collar until the hinge broke. He would have hurled it at the wall, but it would have struck the vines and loosened a few leaves, which seemed a poor way to acknowledge the gardener's extraordinary devotion to his plants. So, he let the pieces fall atop the stone links and raked his stiff, filthy hair. He wanted a steam bath, and a hot supper, and could have gotten both, if he'd gone to a city inn instead of coming here, instead of coming home.

His home—not a narrow cot in the low-ranks' barracks where he planted two of the cot's legs on the soles of his sandals each night to be sure that he'd still have shoes to wear come morning, but this place, a high templar residence, where there were more rooms than people. People who looked at him. Slaves who hid their thoughts behind wrinkled masks and friends who expected him to take care of them. Zvain's stomach growled loud enough to make Pavek turn his head; the boy hadn't eaten anything since the bowl of fruit in Modekan, and for a boy that might just as well have been a year ago. Looking past Zvain, Pavek saw Ruari skulking behind the vine-covered lattice of the atrium's colonnade, not wanting to be seen, but almost certainly as hungry as Zvain.

Pavek's own gut growled, reminding him that he, too, was hungry and that on occasion he could eat more than his two younger friends combined.

Except for a quinth or two before he left Urik, throughout Pavek's life, whether in the orphanage, the barracks, or Quraite, he hadn't had to worry about his next hot meal. That had all changed. Whatever else he'd done, Elabon

Escrissar had at least kept his larder filled with beans, flour, and vile sausage. The larder was Pavek's responsibility now, along with who-knew-what-else, except that it would all require gold and silver coins in greater quantities than he possessed.

"A treasury?" he inquired. "Is there a treasury in the house?"

Initri shook her head. "Gone, Lord Pavek. Gone before the administrators came. Gone while Lord Elabon still lived. Will beans serve, my lord?"

The deaf gardener picked up the metal pieces Pavek had dropped and slowly carried them out of his domain, as if they were no more significant than wind-fallen branches, as if he'd been able to leave whenever he chose. Pavek watched until the man and his shadow had disappeared through a side archway.

"Lord Pavek—will beans serve for your supper?"

Pavek's hand went to the familiar medallion hanging from his neck. He needed money. Not the pittance of ceramic bits and silver that had sufficed in his regulator's past, nor the plump belt-pouch he'd worn out of Quraite; he needed *gold*, by the handful.

Leaping through the bureau ranks as he had, he'd missed all the intervening opportunities to enrich himself. He needed a prebend, that regular gift from Lord Hamanu himself that kept high templars loyal to the throne. A gift Pavek imagined the Lion-King would grant him in an instant, once he made the request. Why else had he been brought back to Urik? But he'd give up any claim to freedom once he accepted it. Once he asked Lord Hamanu for money, he might as well pick up the gardener's chain and fasten it around his own neck.

That slave's fate, however, was tomorrow's worry. Tonight's worry was beans, and they would not serve.

"Zvain, unload our baggage and take our food to the kitchen. Initri, follow him—no, wait for him in the kitchen. See what you can make up for all of us."

"Yes, Lord Pavek," she said, as passionless as before. She obediently started for the door, where Zvain stood between Mahtra and Ruari, who had crept out of the shadows. The half-elf wouldn't meet his eyes, a sure sign of anger waiting to erupt.

"Mahtra you go with Zvain. Help him unload the baggage. Wait in the kitchen."

Two of them went. Ruari sulked silently for about two heartbeats, then the eruption began.

"Initri, make my dinner. Unpack my baggage! Go to the kitchen! Wind and fire! You should have freed them, *Lord Pavek*. Or doesn't *owning* your parents' parents bother you?"

Pavek should have known not merely that Ruari was angry, but why. There weren't any slaves in Quraite, certainly no half-elven ones. He should have had an explanation sitting on his tongue, but he didn't. At that moment, with Ruari glaring at him, Pavek didn't know himself why he hadn't freed the old couple immediately, and he expressed shame or embarrassment with no better grace than Ruari expressed his anger or confusion.

"They aren't my kin or yours," Pavek replied, adopting Ruari's outraged sarcasm for himself. "They're just two people who've lived here a long time."

"*Slaved* here, you mean. Lord Pavek, your templar blood is showing. You should have set them free. Those were the words that should have come out of your mouth, not orders to cook your supper!"

"Set them free and then what? Turned them out of this house? Where would they go? Would you send them across the wastes to Quraite? Would you send every slave in Urik to Quraite? How many would die on the Fist? How many could Quraite feed before everyone was starving?"

Ruari pulled his head back. His chin jutted defiantly, but Pavek knew those questions struck the half-elf solidly. "I didn't say that," Ru insisted. "I didn't say send them across the Fist to Quraite. They could stay here in Urik. There're free folk in Urik. Zvain's free. Mahtra is. You—when we met you."

"You're blind," Pavek retorted and turned away. "Freedom's a hard road in Urik, a hard road anywhere. You won't find many venerable parents walking it. Freedom costs money, Ru." And Pavek thought about the gold he didn't have and the bits of his life he'd have to forfeit to get it. He gained some insight into himself and whatever mixed feelings he still had about not freeing the old couple, those feelings didn't include shame or embarrassment.

"He could work for someone else, tending their garden."

"No one hires gardeners, Ru. They buy them. Besides— this is *his* garden. Didn't you understand that? He was chained here, but he didn't have to make this place bloom. He's a veritable druid. Should I banish him from his grove?"

"Free him, then hire him yourself."

"Make him a slave to coins instead of men? Is that such an improvement? What if he gets sick? He's old, it could happen. If he's a slave, I'm obligated to take care of him, whether he can garden or not, but if I'm paying him to tend my garden, what's to stop me from simply hiring another man. Why should I care? He doesn't belong to me anymore."

"Slavery's wrong, Pavek. It's just plain wrong."

"I didn't say it was right."

"You didn't free them!"

"Because that wouldn't be right, either!" Pavek's voice rose to a shout. "Life's not simple, not my life, anyway. I wouldn't want to be a slave—I think I'd kill myself first. Hamanu's infinitesimal mercy, I swear I'll never buy a slave, but by the wheels of fate's chariot, that *is* a small mercy. There's not enough gold in all Urik for both freedom and food."

"You'll keep slaves, but you won't buy them," Ruari shouted back. "What a convenient conscience you have, Lord Pavek."

Lord Pavek kicked the stone links coiled at his feet and jammed his toe. "All right," he snarled, grinding his teeth against a fool's pain. "Whatever you say, Ruari: I've got a convenient conscience. I'm not a good man; never pretended that I was. I've never known a thoroughly good man, woman, or child and, yes, that includes you, Kashi, *and* Telhami. I don't have good answers. Slavery's a mistake, a terrible mistake, but I can't fix a mistake by setting it free and tossing it out to the streets. Once a mistake's made, it stays made and someone's got to be responsible for it."

"There's got to be a better way."

That was Ruari's way of ending their arguments and making peace, but Pavek's toe still throbbed and the half-elf had scratched too many scars for a truce.

"If you're so sure, go out and find it. We'll both become better men. But until you do have something better to offer, get out of my sight."

"I only said—"

"*Get!*"

Pavek threw a wild punch in the half-elf's direction. It fell short by several handspans, but Ruari got the idea and ran for cover.

Twilight had become an evening that was not as dark as in Quraite. Pavek could see the wall where the gardener lined up his tools: shovel, rake, hoe, and a rock-headed maul. Testing its heft and balance as if it were a weapon, Pavek gave the maul a few practice swings. The knotted muscles in his shoulders crackled. He wasn't the sort of man who handled tension well; he'd rather work himself to exhaustion than think his way out of a puzzle.

One end of the stone-link chain remained where the gardener had dropped it. The other end was fastened to a ring at the center of the garden. Pavek coiled all the links around the ring and started hammering. The links slid against each other; Pavek never hit the same place twice. Stone against shifting stone was as futile labor as Urik had to offer, but Pavek found his rhythm and once he'd broken a sweat, his conscience was clearer—emptier—than it had been in days.

Swinging and striking, he lost track of time and place, or

almost lost track. He'd no notion how much time had passed when he became aware that he wasn't alone. Ruari, he thought. Ruari had returned for the final word. He swung the maul with extra vigor, missed the links altogether, but raised sparks from the ring. The gasp he heard next didn't come from a half-elf or a human boy.

"Mahtra?"

He saw her in the doorway, a study in moonlit pallor and seamless shadows. Their eyes met and she receded into the dark. A child, Pavek reminded himself; he'd frightened her with his hammering. He set the maul aside.

"Mahtra? Come back. Has Initri got supper ready?"

She shook her head. The shawl slid down her neck. With the mask dividing her head, it was like looking at two incomplete faces—which was probably not an inaccurate way to describe her.

"Does this place make you uneasy? Do you want to talk to me about it?" He'd already failed miserably with Ruari, but the night was young and filled with opportunity.

"No, I like it here. I remember Akashia, but my own memories are different."

"You used to come to this garden?"

"No, never. No one came here, except Agan. He was always here. Agan and Initri, they were special."

Their conversation was assuming its familiar pattern: Pavek asking what he assumed were simple questions and Mahtra replying with answers he didn't quite understand. "How?" he asked, dreading her answer.

"Sometimes Lord Elabon, he called Agan 'my thrice-damned-father'."

The maul handle stood beside Pavek, in easy reach. He could swing it and imagine the link it struck was Elabon Escrissar's skull. He'd been wise to dread anything Mahtra could tell him about his inherited home. How had Escrissar—even Escrissar—enslaved his own parents? What was he, Just-Plain Pavek, supposed to do to correct *that* mistake? What could he do?

"It might not mean anything," Mahtra continued. "Father wasn't my father. I don't have a father or mother; I was made, not born. I just called Father that because it felt good. Maybe Lord Escrissar did the same."

Pavek said, "I hope not," and Mahtra receded into the shadows again. He called her back saying, "It's all right for you feel good about calling someone Father—" Mahtra had a clear sense of justice and honor; he assumed she'd gotten it from the man she called Father who had, therefore, been worthy of a child's respect. She certainly hadn't gotten anything honorable from Elabon Escrissar. "But it wouldn't be right if you'd put scars on his face and a chain around his neck, and then you felt good about calling him Father."

"It would feel good to call you Father. You truly wouldn't set your mistakes free, would you?"

She'd been eavesdropping on his argument with Ruari, if it could be called eavesdropping when they'd been screaming at each other.

"I wouldn't—not deliberately, but Mahtra, you can't call me Father. I'm Pavek, Just-Plain Pavek. Leave it at that."

She blinked, and pulled her arms tight around her slender torso as if Pavek had struck her, which only made him feel worse. But he couldn't have her calling him Father; that was a responsibility he couldn't take.

"Mahtra—"

"I need someone to talk to and I don't think I should talk to Lord Hamanu. I think he'd listen, but I don't think I should. I think he's made, too, or born so long ago he's forgotten."

"You can talk to me," Pavek assured her quickly, determined to put an end to any thought of confiding in the Lion-King. "You can't call me Father, but you can talk to me about anything." He felt like a man walking open-eyed off a cliff.

Mahtra came closer. Her bird's-egg eyes sparkled—actually sparkled—with excitement. "I can protect myself now!"

"Haven't you always been able to do that?" he asked,

hoping for a comprehensible answer. She'd talked about the protection her makers had given her before, but she'd never been able to explain it.

"Before, it just happened. I got stiff and blurry, and *it* happened. But today, by the water, when I got angry at Ruari, I didn't want him to stop me, so I made myself afraid that he'd hurt me, and made it happen."

Pavek recalled the moment easily. "You made it stop, too. Didn't you?"

"Almost."

That was not the answer he'd hoped for. "Almost?"

"Angry-afraid makes the protection happen. When Ruari pushed me down, I wasn't angry-afraid anymore, I was sad-afraid, and sad-afraid makes the protection go away. I'm glad it went away without happening; I didn't want to hurt Ruari, not truly. But I didn't make it not-happen."

Pavek looked up into her strange, trusting eyes. He scratched his itchy scalp, hoping to kindle inspiration and failing in that endeavor, too. "I don't know, Mahtra, maybe you did learn how to control what your makers gave you: angry-fear makes it start; sad-fear makes it stop. If you could make yourself angry, you can make yourself sad."

"Is that good—? Making myself feel differently, to control what the makers gave me?"

"It's better than hurting Ruari—however you would've hurt him. It's better than making a mistake."

Mistake was an important word to her, and she reacted to it by nodding vigorously.

"If I made a mistake, then I'd be responsible for it, like you? I want to be like you, Pavek. I want to learn from you, even if you're not Father."

He turned away, not knowing what to say or do next. It was bad enough when Zvain or Ruari put their trust in him, but there always came a point in those conversations where he could poke them in the ribs and break the somber mood with a little roughhousing. A poke in the ribs wouldn't be the same with Mahtra. With Mahtra, he could only say:

"Thank you. I'll try to teach you well."
And pray desperately for Initri to ring the supper bell.

Ruari came back during supper. Pavek didn't ask where
he'd been, but he had a turquoise and aqua house-lizard the
size of his forearm clinging contentedly to his shoulder, its
whiplike tail looped around his neck. In itself that was a
good sign. The brightly beautiful lizards had innate mind-
bending defenses: they could sense a distressed or aggres-
sive mind at a considerable distance and make themselves
scarce before trouble arrived. Even Ruari, who turned to
animals for solace when he was upset, couldn't have gotten
close to the creature while he was angry.

Ruari unwound the lizard from his neck and offered it to
Pavek. "My Moonracer cousins say that in the cities a house
where one of these lizards lives is a house where friends can
be found."

Friendship—the greatest gift an elf could give, and a gift
Ruari had never gotten from those Moonracer cousins of
his. Or offered, and that's what Ruari was offering. Pavek
held out his hands with a heart-felt wish that the damn
thing found him acceptable and didn't take a chunk out of
his finger. It probed him with a bright red tongue, then
slowly climbed his arm.

"I'll keep it in the garden," he said once it had settled on
his shoulder.

They ate quietly, quickly, grateful for the food rather than
the cooking. The question of baths and laundry came up.
House Escrissar had a hypocaust where both clothes and
bodies could be soaked clean in hot water, but it required a
cadre of slaves to stoke the furnace and run the pumps.
Mahtra said she'd take care of herself. Pavek and Ruari
sluiced themselves as best they could at the kitchen cistern.
They cornered Zvain and subjected him to the same treat-
ment. Fresh clothing came out of the packs they'd brought
from Quraite: homespun shirts and breeches, not really suitable for a high templar, but what remained of Elabon Escris-

sar's clothes wouldn't go around Pavek's brawny, human shoulders and Ruari would have nothing to do with them.

Ruari refused to sleep in a bed where Elabon Escrissar might have slept. Late evening found the half-elf spreading his blankets in the garden under the watchful, independent eyes of their new house lizard. Pavek considered telling the youth that he was a fool, that Urik was noisier than Quraite and the sounds would keep him awake, but those were the precise sounds Pavek was spreading his own blankets to hear throughout the night.

Midnight brought an echoing chorus of gongs and bells as watchtowers throughout the city signalled to one another: all's well, all's quiet. Pavek listened to every note, and all the other sounds Urik made while it slept—even Ruari's soft, regular breathing an arm's length away on the other side of the fountain. As the stars spun slowly through the roof-edged sky, Pavek tried to appreciate the irony: much as he enjoyed the cacophony of city life, he was the one who couldn't sleep.

Pavek's thoughts drifted, as a man's thoughts tended to do when he was alone in the dark. They took a sudden jog back to the cavern with its glamourous bowls and deceptive scaffolds, the noxious sludge clinging to Ruari's staff; oozing down his own leg. He imagined he could feel the slime again, and without thinking further, swiped his thigh beneath the blankets. His fingers brushed the soft, clean cloth of his breeches. For a heartbeat, Pavek was reassured, then panic struck.

Wide-awake and chilled from the marrow out to his skin, Pavek threw his blankets aside. Stumbling and cursing in unfamiliar surroundings he made his way from the garden and through the residence. He found his filthy clothes where he'd left them: in a heap beside the cistern. Viewed by starlight, one stain looked like another and there was no safe guessing which, if any, came from the cavern sludge.

There were bright embers in the hearth and an oil lamp

on the masonry above it. Pavek lit the lamp and went searching for Ruari's staff, which he found against a wall, just inside the main door. Stains mottled the wooden tip. Lamp in hand, Pavek got down on his knees to examine its stains more closely.

"What are you doing?"

Ruari's unexpected question scared a year from Pavek's natural life—assuming he'd be lucky enough to have one.

"Looking for proof that we saw what we saw in the cavern."

Pavek probed the largest of the stains with a jagged thumbnail. The wood crumbled as if it were rotten. Ruari swore and yanked his most prized possession out of Pavek's hands. He probed the stain and another bit of soggy, ruined wood came away on his fingertip.

"Careful!" Pavek chided. "That's all we've got between us and Hamanu tomorrow!"

The half-elf was sulky, stubborn, and quick to anger, but he wasn't stupid. He glowered a moment, thinking things through, then handed the staff back to Pavek.

"The Lion—he'd believe us, wouldn't he? I mean, you're the one he sent for, why wouldn't he believe you? He wouldn't have to ravel your memories. He wouldn't leave you an empty-headed idiot. That's just talk, isn't it?"

Pavek shook his head. "I've seen it done."

"Telhami could get the truth out of anyone, too, but she'd just look at you, she didn't *do* anything. No one ever lied to her; she knew the truth when she heard it."

"Aye," Pavek agreed, tearing off the hem of his dirty shirt and beginning to wind it around the stained part of the staff like a bandage. "Heard or saw or tasted. Hamanu can do that, too, or he can spin your memories out, floss into thread, and leave you as empty as the day you were born. That's what I've seen. Should've let you collect a great dollop of that swill."

"I was glad I hadn't—until now. Will this be enough?" Ruari asked, taking his staff and checking the knot Pavek had made for fastness.

"Slaves would tell you to pray to Great Hamanu; they think he's a god."

"And we know better. What else can we do?"

"Except pray? Nothing. It's me he'll come after, Ru; you shouldn't worry too much. When he killed Escrissar, he decided I'd make a good replacement. That's what this is about. He wants me for a pet."

Pavek didn't think he'd made a stunning revelation; the look on Ruari's face said otherwise.

"There're always a few Hamanu favors. Some called them the Lion's Cubs; we called them his pets in the barracks. He gives them free rein and they dull his boredom. Escrissar was one." Telhami was another, but Pavek didn't say that aloud; he'd given Ruari a big enough mouthful to chew on already.

"We can go back to the cavern. . . . We can go back right now with a bucket!"

"Don't be foolish. It's the middle of the night."

"That won't make any difference in a cavern! We can do it, Pavek. That messed-up medallion of yours will get us past anyone who challenges us *and* the warding in the elven market. We could be back by dawn, if we hurry."

Pavek's heart was touched to see Ruari so eager, so blind to danger on his behalf. Friendship, he supposed. But it was too foolish to consider. "Maybe tomorrow morning—if there's no one from the palace hammering on the door before them."

"Wind and fire, Pavek. If we're going to wait until tomorrow morning, we might just as well go to this Codesh-place, too, and see if we can find the other end of the passageway."

It would be a long shot, and Pavek had never been a gambler, but Ruari was right. If they walked into the palace with the a bucket of sludge in their hands and a Codesh passageway to the cavern on the surface of their minds, they'd be in as good a bargaining position as mortals could attain in the Lion-King's court.

"I'm right, aren't I?" Ruari asked, cracking a grin. "I'm right!"

Ruari didn't let that smile out too often, but when he did, it was contagious. Pavek took a deep breath and clamped his lips tight. Nothing helped. Laughter burst out anyway.

"Nobody's perfect, Ru. It had to happen sometime."

"We'll go now—"

"The gates are locked until sunrise—and we may be escorted to the palace before then."

"But, if we're not—we're on our way to Codesh!"

NINE

Pavek considered modifying Ruari's plan from *we* to *me*.
Codesh had a vicious reputation. There was no need to risk
his unscarred companions exploring its alleys, looking for a
hole that might lead to the reservoir cavern. No need to
have them underfoot while he explored, either. But Lord
Hamanu's enforcers from the palace would come calling
soon enough, and compared to the Lion-King, Codesh was
no risk at all.

Dawn's first light found the four of them tying their sandals by the front door.

"Leave that behind," he told Ruari and pointed to the
bandaged staff the half-elf had in his hand. "In case something goes wrong, that's all we've got."

"Anything goes wrong, I'm going to need it with me, not
here."

Pavek disagreed, but they didn't have time for arguments.
It was Farl's day, and the best time to slip out Urik's west
gate would be the moment when it opened up to let the
farmers and artisans of that western village into the city.
The branch of the west road that led to Codesh would be
nearly empty, but they'd be well out of Urik's sight before
they started walking along it.

The templar quarter was the busiest quarter of Urik at
this early hour as bleary-eyed men and women got themselves to their assigned duties. White-skinned Mahtra stood

out in any crowd, and any clothing that wasn't dyed yellow was glaringly obvious on the streets nearest House Escrissar. Pavek recognized a fair number of the faces pointed their way. Surely he was remembered and recognized, too, but throughout the Tablelands, no creatures were more adept at not-seeing what was directly in front of them than a sorcerer-king's templars. In their own quarter, templars were very nearly blind.

They were more attentive outside their quarter. Pavek told his companions to keep heads down and eyes aimed at the ground. He knew how information flowed through the bureaus. By sundown it would be a rare templar who didn't know Just-Plain Pavek, the renegade regulator, had taken up residence in House Escrissar. This time tomorrow, he'd have a slew of friends and enemies lining up to see what they could gain or he could lose. Even now, hurrying toward the western gate, Pavek caught the occasional measuring gaze from a face that had recognized him. In a very real sense, his troubles wouldn't begin until and unless he successfully hunted Kakzim down.

The western gate was still closed when they arrived, but it had swung open by the time Pavek had fed everyone a breakfast of fresh bread and hot sausage. Between them, Zvain and Ruari could eat their way through a gold coin every day. The stash Pavek had brought from Quraite was shrinking at an alarming rate. Grimly, he calculated they'd be bit-less in six or seven days. Even more grimly, he calculated that, one way or another, by then money would be the least of his worries. He bought more food for later in the day and struck a path for the crowded gate.

The regulators and inspectors on morning gate duty were busy taking bribes and confiscating whatever caught their fancy. They didn't notice four plainly dressed Urikites going the other way. If they had, Pavek's gouged medallion would have cleared their path, but by not using it, there was less chance of some enterprising regulator sending a messenger back to the palace. Before he left the residence, Pavek had written their plan on parchment and secured it with his porphyry seal. He told Initri to give the parchment to anyone who came looking for them. Until she did, no one else knew where they were going or what they planned to do.

Getting into Codesh several hours later was easier than Pavek dared hope. Registrators handled the affairs of the weekly influx of market folk, but guarding the Codesh gate was a serious matter, entrusted to civil bureau templars on loan from the city, none of whom stayed very long. Through sheer luck, Pavek knew the man in charge, an eighth rank instigator named Nunk, and Nunk recognized him.

"I'll be a gith's thumb fool," Nunk grinned, baring the two rows of rotten broken teeth that spoiled his chances with the ladies, as Pavek's twisted scar spoiled his. "The rumors must be true." He held out his hand.

"What rumors?" Pavek asked, taking Nunk's hand as if it had been offered in friendship rather than in hope of a bribe. Although, in fairness to Nunk, if five bureau ranks weren't layered between regulators and instigators, they might have been as friendly as templars got with one another. Neither one of them had ever been tied to the numerous corrupt cadres that dominated the civil bureau's lower ranks. They both kept to themselves, which, given the hidden structure of the bureau, meant their paths had crossed before. The biggest obstacle between them would always be rank. It ran the other way now, with far more than five levels separating an instigator from Hamanu's favorites. Pavek couldn't blame Nunk for currying a bit of favor when he had a chance.

"Rumors that you're the one who brought down a high bureau interrogator. Rumors that you're the one who made Laq disappear. Rumors that you've got yourself a medallion made of beaten gold."

Pavek stopped pumping the instigator's hand and fished out his regulators' ceramic with the gouged reverse. "Rumors lie."

"Right," Nunk replied with a fading smile. He led the way to the small, dusty room that served as his command chamber. He closed the door before asking: "What brings you and yours to this cesspit, Great One? Remember, I helped you before."

Pavek didn't remember any help, just another templar prudently deciding to mind his own business at a moment when Pavek impulsively decided to get involved. Still, he'd have no trouble putting in a good word or two on Nunk's behalf, if the opportunity arose, as it probably would. "I remember," he agreed, and Nunk's jagged grin returned, full strength. "I want to go inside and look around, maybe ask a few questions."

"Why not ask me first? You'll know where your gold's going."

"No gold, not yet. Got things to finish first."

"Laq?"

"Seen any around?"

"Not since the deadheart disappeared and everyone connected to him went to the obsidian pits. Lord, you should have seen it—the Lion Himself marching through the quarter calling out the names. I'll tell you something: the city's cleaner than it's been since my grandfather got whelped. Rumor is we'll be at war with Nibenay this time next year, and the Lion always cleans house before a war, but this time it's different. The scum he sent to the pits wasn't just Escrissar's cadre. He cast a wide net and the ones that got away left Urik."

"Not all of them. I'm looking for a halfling, Escrissar's slave—"

Nunk's eyebrows rose. It was common knowledge halfling slaves withered fast.

"When I saw him, he had Escrissar's scars on his cheeks. He's the one who cooked up the Laq poison, but he didn't go down with his master. I think he's gone to ground in Codesh. You keeping watch on any halfling troublemakers? Name's Kakzim. Even if the scars were just a mask, like Escrissar's, you'd know him if you'd seen him. You'd never forget his eyes."

"Don't know the name, but we've got a halfling lune living in rented rooms along the abattoir gallery—he'd have to be a lune to live there. He's a regular doomsayer—there seem to be more of them all the time, what with all the changes now that the Dragon's gone. He gets up on his box a couple times a day, preaching the great conflagration, but this is Codesh, and they've been preaching the downfall of Urik since Hamanu arrived a thousand years ago. A faker's got to deliver a miracle or two if he wants to keep drawing a crowd in Codesh. Can't speak about this halfling's eyes, but from what I hear, he's got a face more like yours than a slave's—no offense, Great One."

"No offense," Pavek agreed. "I'd like to get a look at him. Which way to this abattoir?"

Nunk shrugged. "Don't go inside, that's what regulators are for—or have you forgotten that?" He stuck two fingers between his teeth and whistled. An elf with very familiar patterns woven into her sleeve answered the summons. "These folk want to take a look-see through the village and abattoir."

She looked them over with narrowed, lethargic eyes. Pavek had stuffed his medallion back inside his shirt when the door opened. He left it there, letting her draw her own conclusions, letting her make her own mistakes.

"Four bits," she said. "And the ghost wears a cloak."

It was a fair price, a fair request: Kakzim might spot Mahtra long before they spotted him. Pavek dug the money out of his belt-pouch.

Her name was Giola, not a tribal name, but elves who wound up wearing yellow had little in common with their nomadic cousins. She armed herself with an obsidian mace from a rack beside the watchtower door before leading them to the village gate, which, unlike the gates of the Lion-King's city, was never wide open.

"You know how to use that sticker?" she asked and pointed at Pavek's sword.

"I won't cut off my hand."

"That's a lot of metal for a badlands boy to carry around on his hip. There're folk inside who'd slit your throat for it. Sure you wouldn't rather I carried it for you? Push comes to shove, the best weapon should be in the best hands."

"In your dreams, Great One," Pavek replied, using a phrase only templars used. Between friends, it was commiseration; between enemies, an insult. When Pavek smiled, it became a challenge Giola wisely declined.

"Have it your way," she said with a shrug. "But don't expect me to risk my neck for four lousy bits. Anything goes wrong, you're on your own."

"Fair enough," Pavek agreed. "Anything goes wrong, you're on your own." He'd never been skilled in the subtle art of extortion, which was probably why he was always skirting poverty. He didn't begrudge Giola for shaking him down, but he didn't intend to give her any more money, either. "Let's go. We're looking for a way underground, a cave, a stream, something big enough for a human—"

"A halfling," Ruari corrected, speaking up for the first time since they entered the watchtower and earning one of Pavek's sourest sneers for his unwelcome words.

"Halflings, humans, dwarves, the whole gamut," Pavek continued, barely acknowledging the half-elf's interruption. "Maybe a warehouse or catacombs—if Codesh has any."

"Not a chance, not even a public cesspit," Giola replied. "The place is built on rock. They burn what they can—" she wrinkled her nose and gestured toward the several smoky plumes that fouled Codesh's air. "The rest they either sell to the farmers or cart clear around to Modekan."

Not a chance. The only thing Pavek heard after that was the sound of his heart thudding. He'd been so certain when he saw those glamourous bone scaffolds and stitched-together bowls. Usually he knew better than to trust his own judgment . . . or Ruari's. He watched a boy about Zvain's age lead a string of animals through the gate. They were bound for slaughter, and Pavek saw his own hapless face on each of them.

Giola led them through the gate after the boy and his animals.

Codesh was a tangled place, squeezed tight against its outer walls. Its streets were scarcely wide enough for two men to pass without touching. Greedy buildings angled off their foundations, reaching for the sun, condemning the narrow streets to perpetual, stifling twilight. When one of the slops carts Giola had described rumbled past, bystanders scrambled for safety, shrinking into a doorway, if they were lucky; grabbing the overhanging eaves and lifting themselves out of harm's way, if they had the strength; or racing ahead of the cart to the next intersection, which was rarely more than twenty paces away.

Every cobblestone and wall was stained to the color of dried blood. The dust was dark red, the garments the Codeshites wore were dark red, their skin, too. The smell of death and decay was a tangible presence, made worse by the occasional whiff of roasting sausage. The sounds of death mingled with the sights and smells. There was no place were they didn't hear the bleats, wails, and whines of the beasts waiting for slaughter, the truncated screams as the axe came down.

Pavek thought of the sausage he'd paid good money for at Urik's west gate and felt his gut sour. For a moment he believed that he'd never eat meat again, but that was nonsense. In parched Athas, food was survival. A man ate what he could get his hands on; he ate it raw and kicking, if he had to. The fastidious or delicate died young. Pavek swallowed his nausea, and with it his despair.

He gave greater attention to the places Giola showed them—he was paying for the tour after all. They came to a Codesh plaza: an intersection where five streets came together and a man-high fountain provided water to the neighborhood. For all its bloody gloom and squalor, Codesh was a community like any other. Women came to the fountain with their empty water jugs and dirty laundry. They knelt beside the curb stones, scrubbing stains with bone-bleach and pounding wet cloth with curving rib bones. Water splashed and dripped all around the women. It puddled around their knees and flowed between the street cobblestones until it disappeared.

"The water. Where does the water come from? Where does it go?" Pavek asked.

Giola stared at him with thinly disguised contempt. "It comes from the fountain."

"Where does it come from *before* the fountain? How is the fountain filled? Where does it drain?"

"How in the bloody, bright sun should I know? Do I look like a scholar to you? Go to the Urik archive, hire yourself a bug-eyed scribe if you want to know where water comes from or where it goes!"

Several cutting replies leapt to the front of Pavek's mind. With difficulty he rejected them all, reminding himself that most people—certainly most templars—didn't have his demanding curiosity. Things were what they appeared to be, without why or how, before or after. Giola's life was not measured in questions and doubts, as his was.

But without questions, there wasn't much to say except, "Keep moving, then. We're still looking for a way underground. Some sort of passage—"

"Or a building," Mahtra interrupted. Her strangely emotionless voice was well-suited to dealing with low-rank templars. "A very old building. Its walls are as tall as they are wide. The roof is flat. There's only one door and inside, there's a hole in the floor that goes all the way underground."

Pavek cursed himself for a fool. He'd been so clever looking for his second passage into the reservoir cavern that he'd never thought to ask if there was another building like the one Mahtra had led them to in Urik's elven market.

Giola scratched her shaggy blond hair. "Aye," she said slowly. "A little building, smack in the middle of the abattoir. A building inside a building. No use I could ever guess. I never noticed a door, but I never looked."

"The abattoir," Pavek mused aloud. The abattoir, where Nunk said the halfling lune lived. He flashed Mahtra a grin and took her by the arm. "That's it! That's the place."

Mahtra shied away from his grip, her eyes so wide-open they seemed likely to fall to the ground. "What's an abattoir? I do not know this word."

He relaxed his hold on Mahtra's arm. Like eleganta, abattoir was a word that concealed more than it revealed. And, knowing she was still a child in many ways, Pavek was instinctively reluctant to destroy its mystery with a precise definition. "It is—it is—" he groped for a phrase that would be the truth, but not too much of it. "It is the place where the animals die," then added quickly, "the place where we'll find the man we're looking for."

Mahtra looked up at the roofs. As always, the sounds of fear, torment, and dying were in the air. She cocked her head one way and another, fixing the primary source of the sound. When she had it, she nodded her masked face once and said: "I understand. The killing ground. We will find him on the killing ground."

* * * * *

The abattoir was the heart of Codesh. It was an old building, similar in style to the little building they hoped to find inside it, and etched with the same angular, indecipherable script Pavek had noticed at the elven market. Shadowed patches on its time- and grime-darkened walls led the eye to believe that there had once been murals, but whatever grandeur the abattoir might have possessed in the past, it was a dismal place now.

Another templar watchtower rose beside a gaping archway carved through thick limestone walls. There were as many yellow-robed men and women watching over the abattoir as Nunk kept with him at the outer gate. A rack of hook-bill spears stood on one side of the watchroom door while a stack of shields made from erdlu scales lashed to flexible rattan sat on the other. Inside the watchroom, each templar wore a sword and boiled leather armor; that was very unusual for civil bureau templars and a measure of Codesh's reputation as a thorn in Urik's foot. They greeted Giola as if hers were the first friendly—as in not belonging to the enemy—face they'd seen in a stormy quinth.

"Instigator Nunk says I'm to take these rubes onto the floor," Giola informed Nunk's counterpart, a dwarf with a bit less decoration woven through his sleeve.

The dwarf swiped the oily sweat from his bald scalp before sauntering over to greet Pavek and his companions.

"Who in blazes are you that I should let you and yours stir up trouble I don't need?"

He grabbed the front of Pavek's shirt, a gesture well within his templar's right to harass any ordinary citizen, but he caught Pavek's medallion as well, and the shock knocked him back a step or two.

"Be damned," he swore, partly fear and partly curse.

Pavek could watch the thoughts—questions, doubts and possibilities—march between the dwarf's narrowed eyes. He judged the moment had come for revelation and pulled his medallion into view, gouge and all.

"Be damned," the dwarf repeated.

This time the oath was definitely a curse and definitely directed on himself. Pavek felt a measure of sympathy; he had the same sort of rotten luck.

"Who I am is Pavek, Lord Pavek, and what I want on the killing ground is no concern of yours."

Standing behind the dwarf, and half again as tall, elven Giola had a good view of the ceramic lump Pavek held in his hand. She turned pale enough to be Mahtra's sister.

"A thousand pardons, Great One. Forgive my insolence, Great One," she humbled herself, dropping to one knee and striking her breast with her fist. But for all Giola's humility, there was one flash of fire when her eyes skewed in the direction of the outer gate watchtower where Nunk, who'd gotten her into this, was waiting.

"Forgive me, also, Great One," the dwarf said quickly. "May I ask if you're Pavek . . . Lord Pavek who was once exiled from Urik?"

Pavek truly got no exhilaration from the embarrassment of others. "I'm the Pavek who lit out of Urik with a forty-gold piece bounty riding on my head," he said, trying to break the grim mood.

Giola stood erect. She straightened her robe and said, "Great One, it is good to see you are alive," which surprised Pavek as much as the sight of his medallion had surprised her. "There's never been a regulator dead or alive who was worth forty pieces of gold. I don't know what you did, but your name was whispered in all the shadows. You were not without friends. Luck sat on your shoulder."

She took a long-limbed stride around the dwarf and extended her open hand, which held the four ceramic bits Pavek had given her earlier. Everyone said Athas had changed in the few years since the Tyrians slew the Dragon. Nunk said the bureaus had changed since Pavek left, and partly because of him. There could be no greater symbol of those changes than a regulator offering to return money. Or telling him, in the plain presence of other templars, that she'd gone to a fortune-seller and bought him a bit of luck.

A human could study the elves of Athas all his life without truly learning what an elf meant when he—or she— called someone a friend. Now two elves had called Pavek friend in as many days—if he considered Ruari an elf. There was always a gesture involved, be it a bright-colored lizard or four broken bits. Last night Pavek had known to take the lizard. Today he knew he'd spoil everything if he touched those rough-edged bits.

He said, "Friends need all the luck they can get," instead and, clasping her hand, gently folded her fingers back to her palm.

Giola cocked her head, pondering a moment before she decided the sentiment was acceptable. Then she touched her right-hand's index finger first to her own breast then to his. Judging by Ruari's slack-jawed astonishment, he could rely on his assumption: he'd been accorded a rare honor. The dwarf, the highest rank templar in the watchtower, save for Pavek himself, must have sensed the same thing.

He got in front of Giola. "Great One, it would be an honor to help you. Let me escort you personally."

There were some traditions that were more resistant to change than others. Giola retreated, and the dwarf led them downstairs.

The abattoir wasn't so much a building as an open space surrounded by walls and a two-tier gallery, open to the brutal sun, and filled from back to front, side to side, with the trades of death. Pavek judged the killing floor to be as large as any Urik market plaza, at least sixty parade paces square. Carcasses outnumbered people many times over. Finding Kakzim would be a challenge, but finding the twin of the building Mahtra had used to come and go from the reservoir cavern was as simple as looking at the middle of the killing floor.

Getting there was another matter. The abattoir didn't fall silent the moment one yellow-robed templar and four strangers appeared on the watchtower balcony, but their presence was noted everywhere, and not welcomed. Pavek's quick scan of the killing floor didn't reveal any scarred halflings among the faces pointed their way. And although Mahtra wore her long, black shawl and a borrowed cloak, her white-white face divided by its mask was a distinct as the silvery moon, Ral, on a clear night.

"Stay close together," Pavek whispered to his companions as they started across the floor. "Keep an eye out for Kakzim—you two especially." He indicated Mahtra and Zvain. "You know what to look for. But he's not what we're here for, not today. We'll go inside that little building, go down to the reservoir and come back up in Urik." The last was a spur-of-the-moment decision. Pavek liked the mood on the killing floor less with every step he took across it.

Mahtra reached down and took Zvain's hand in her own.

Whether that was to reassure him or her, Pavek couldn't guess; he let the gesture pass without comment. The dwarf hadn't drawn his sword, but he kept his hand on the hilt as he stomped forward with that head-down, single-minded determination that got dwarves in a world of trouble when things didn't go according to their plan.

Giola hadn't noticed a door in the little building because at first glance there wasn't one, just four plain stone walls. Then Pavek noticed the weathered remains of the indecipherable script carved into one of the walls. He thumped the seemingly solid stone below the inscription with his fist and felt it give.

The dwarf said, "False front, Great One," and added an oath. It didn't really matter what lay behind the door or who'd hung the false front. The discovery had been made on his watch, and he was the one who'd answer for it. That was another Urik tradition that wasn't likely to change. "Is it trapped, Great One?"

Pavek caught himself before he said something foolish. He was the high templar; he was supposed to have open call on the Lion-King's power. A little borrowed spellcraft and any magical devices associated with the door would be sprung and any warding behind it would be dissolved. The problem was, Pavek didn't want to use his high templar's privilege. Like as not, he'd forfeit his hard-earned druidry if he went back to templar ways. He'd have to make the choice eventually, but eventually wasn't now.

Their halfling enemy was an alchemist who, as far as any of them knew, had no use for magic. He could have bought a scroll or hired someone to cast a spell—Codesh looked like the sort of place where illicit magic was available for the right price. But halflings, as a rule, had no use for money and didn't buy things, either. Probably they were dealing with nothing more dangerous than a hidden latch.

Probably.

He hammered the door several times, getting a feel for its movement and the likely position of its latch and hinges.

He'd decided that it swung from the top and was tackling the latch problem when he felt the mood change behind him.

"There he is!" Mahtra shouted, pointing over everyone's head and toward a section of the two-story high wall.

The distance was too great and the shadows on the second-story balcony were too deep for Pavek to recognize a halfling's face, but the silhouette was right for one of the diminutive forest people. He had the sense that the halfling was looking at them, a sense that was confirmed when a slender arm was extended in their direction. One instant Pavek wondered what the movement meant; the next instant he knew.

Kakzim had given a signal to his partisans on the killing floor. Well-fed and well-armed butchers were coming for them.

Pavek drew his sword and said his farewell prayers.

"Magic!" the dwarf cried. "Magic, Great One. The Lion-King!"

"No time!" Pavek shouted back, which was the truth and not an excuse.

He needed both hands on his sword hilt and all his concentration to parry the deadly axes massed against them. Their backs were to the false-front door; that would be an advantage for a moment, then it would become disaster as Kakzim's partisans gained the roof. They'd be under attack from all directions, including above. The slaughter would be over in a matter of heartbeats, and they'd be gone without a trace or memory left behind.

While the Lion-King could raise the dead and make them talk, not even he could interrogate sausage.

Civil bureau templars received the same five-weapons instruction that war bureau templars did. The dwarf drilled three-times a week. Pavek had kept himself in shape and in practice while he was in Quraite. If the brawl were fought one-against-one, or even two-against-one, he and the dwarf could have cleared a path to the gate where—one hoped, one prayed—they'd be met by yellow-robed reinforcements from the watchtower.

If they could have picked a single target and attacked rather than being confined to a desperate, futile defense. They had no time for tactics, no time for thought, just parry high, parry low, parry, parry, parry.

And a flicker of consciousness at the very end telling Pavek that the final blow had come from behind.

* * * * *

Mahtra felt the makers' protection radiate from her body: a hollow sphere of sound and light that felled everyone around her. She saw them fall—Pavek, Ruari, and the dwarf among them. Her vision hadn't blurred, her limbs were heavy, but not paralyzed. Maybe that was because, even though the danger was real enough, she'd made the decision to protect herself. Or, maybe her tight grip on Zvain's trembling hand had made the difference. Either way, she and Zvain were the only folk standing in a good sized circle that centered itself around them.

She and Zvain weren't the only folk standing on the killing ground. The makers' protection—*her* protection—didn't extend to the walls. Men and women cursed her from beyond the circle. Those who'd fallen near the circle's edge were beginning to rise unsteadily to their feet. The balcony where she'd seen Kakzim was empty. Mahtra wanted to believe the halfling had fallen, but she knew he'd simply escaped.

"You better be able to do that again," Zvain whispered, squeezing her hand as tightly as he could, but not tight enough to hurt.

She'd never protected herself twice in quick succession, but as Mahtra's mind formed the question, her body gave the answer. "I can," she assured Zvain. "When they come closer."

"We can't wait that long. We got to start moving toward

the door. We got to get out of here." Zvain pulled toward the door.

She pulled him back. "We can't leave our friends behind."

The young human didn't say anything, but there was a change in the way he held her hand. A change Mahtra didn't like.

"What?" she demanded, trying to look at him and keep an eye on the simmering crowd also.

"There's no use worrying about them. They're dead, Mahtra. You killed them."

"No." Her whole body swayed side to side, denying what Zvain said had happened. Yet the folk nearest to them, friend and enemy alike, lay as they'd fallen, their arms and legs tangled in uncomfortable positions that they made no effort to change. "No," she repeated softly. "No."

Kakzim hadn't died in House Escrissar all that time ago, and he'd held a knife against her skin. Ruari had been an arm's length away when she loosed her protection's power. He couldn't have died.

Couldn't have.

Yet he didn't move.

"Too late now," Zvain said grimly. "They're coming again."

But the Codesh butchers weren't coming. The noise and movement came from the yellow-robed templars charging through the crowd with pikes lowered and shields up. Without Kakzim to command them, the butchers weren't interested in a brawl. They fell back, retreating into the circle of Mahtra's power, but dispersing before they got close. Elsewhere, the brawlers quickly faded into the throng of bystanders.

A few voices still cursed Mahtra from the safety of the crowd. They called her freak and evil. Someone called her a dragon. They all wanted her dead, and when the templars broke through the crowd and got their first look at the circle she'd made with her protection, Mahtra feared they might heed her accusers. They stared at her, weapons ready, faces hidden by their shields. Mahtra stared back, fear and anger brewing beneath her skin. She didn't know what to do next and neither did they.

Zvain released her hand. "Wind and fire, what took you so long? We were starting to get worried."

The templar phalanx heaved a visible sigh. Spears went up, shields came down, and the elf named Giola strode out of the formation.

"What happened?" she demanded with a quavering voice. "We took up arms as soon as the mob moved. We were at the gate when we heard the noise—it was like Tyr-storm thunder."

"Mahtra didn't think you'd get here in time. She took matters into her own hands."

"A spell? You're no defiler. Do you wear the veil?"

Defiler? Veil? These words meant nothing to Mahtra, only that she was under close scrutiny and there was no one to speak for her, except a human boy who spoke fast enough for both of them.

"No way! Mahtra's no wizard, no priest, neither. Where she comes from, they do this all the time. No swords or spears or spellcraft, just *boom, boom, boom*. Thunder and lightning all the time!"

Zvain sounded so sincere that Mahtra almost believed him herself. The elf seemed equally uncertain for a moment then, shaking her head, Giola picked her way through the bodies.

"Never mind. It doesn't matter, does it? What about the rest of them. Lord Pavek, Towd—?"

"D-Dead," Zvain muttered, losing all his brash confidence in a single word.

His tears started to flow, and Mahtra reached out to him, but he scampered away. Mahtra's arm fell to her side, heavier than it had ever been, even in the grip of the makers' protection. She would have sobbed herself, if her eyes had been made that way. Instead, she stood silent and outcast as

Giola knelt and pressed her fingers against the necks of Pavek and the dwarf.

"Their hearts are still beating," the elf proclaimed.

Zvain sniffed up his tears. "They're alive?" he asked incredulously. "She didn't kill them?" He skidded to his knees beside Pavek. "Wake up!" He started shaking Pavek's arm.

Giola got to her feet without making the same determination for Ruari. She rejoined the templars, and they split into two groups. One group stood with their backs to the little stone building, keeping watch over the Codeshites, who seemed to have gone back to their work as if the brawl had never erupted. The other group stripped off their yellow robes. They tied their robes together and shoved spears the length of the sleeves to make two stretchers, one for Pavek, a second for the dwarf.

When they were traveling from Quraite, Ruari had told her that his mother's folk wouldn't lift a finger to save his life. Mahtra hadn't believed him—her own makers weren't that cruel. Now she saw the truth and was ashamed of her doubts. She was emboldened by them, too, seizing Giola's arm and meeting the elf's disdainful stare when it focused on her mask.

Mahtra told Giola, "You must carry Ruari to safety," then gave silent thanks to Lord Hamanu, whose magic had given her a voice anyone could understand.

"She means it," Zvain added. He was kneeling beside Ruari now that the templars had lifted Pavek. "Remember: *boom, boom, boom!*"

A shiver ran down Mahtra's spine, down her arm as well, which made Giola's eyes widen. The elf tried to free herself. Mahtra let her get away. While listening to Zvain's boasting, Mahtra realized she did have the wherewithal to use her protection when she wasn't afraid. She didn't want to; she didn't know how to limit its effects to one specific person, but the power itself belonged to her, not the makers, and when she fastened her gaze on Giola, the elf knew where the power lay, too.

Pavek and the others revived somewhat in the abattoir watchroom. They could sit up and sip water when Nunk arrived from the outer gate, but none of them could stand or speak. The Codesh instigator looked at the high templar's glazed, unfocused eyes and his seedy face and decided the situation had deteriorated too far for him to handle.

"They're going to the city, to the *palace!*" He gave a spate of orders for handcarts and runners. "Hamanu's infinitesimal mercy, we'll all be gutted if Pavek—*Lord* Pavek dies here."

Zvain started to object, but the instigator's plan seemed excellent to Mahtra. She gave Zvain the same look she'd given Giola, and, like the elf, the boy did what she wanted him to.

* * * * *

Pavek began stringing coherent thoughts together as the handcart bounced along the Urik road. He pieced together what had happened to him from the disconnected, dreamlike images cluttering his mind: Mahtra had saved him from certain death in the abattoir. She was with him still; he could see her head and shoulders as she ran beside the cart, easily keeping pace with the elves who were pulling it. Fate knew what had happened to Ruari and Zvain, but Pavek could hear another cart rumbling nearby and hoped his companions were in it. He hoped they were alive, and hoped most of all that he'd think of something to say to Lord Hamanu that would keep them alive.

Inspiration didn't strike along the Urik road. It wasn't waiting at the western gate where Pavek insisted he was ready to walk on his own two feet. And it didn't cross his path at any of the intersections between there and the palace where another high templar, who introduced herself as Lord Bhoma, had instructions to bring them to the audience chamber without delay.

Lord Bhoma let Pavek keep his sword, which might be a

sign that the sorcerer-king wasn't going to execute them—
or it might mean that Hamanu would order him to perform
the executions himself, including his own. Ruari still had his
staff, but both the staff and Ruari were sporting bandages.
Lord Bhoma might have dismissed them as a threat to anyone but themselves. Zvain was plainly terrified; they all were
terrified—except Mahtra who'd been here before.

Hamanu, King of Mountains and Plains, was already in
his audience chamber when Lord Bhoma commanded
palace slaves to open the doors. He'd been sitting on a black
marble bench, contemplating water as it flowed over a black
boulder, and rose to meet them. Urik's sorcerer-king was as
Pavek remembered him: a golden presence in armor of
beaten gold, taller than the tallest elf, a glorious mane sur-
mounting a cruelly perfect human face.

"Just-Plain Pavek, so you've come home at last."

The king smiled and held out his hand. Somehow Pavek
found the strength to stride forward and clasp that hand
without flinching—even when the Lion's claws rasped
against his skin. The air was always hot around Hamanu,
and sulphurous, like his eyes. Pavek found it difficult to
breathe, impossible to talk, and was absurdly grateful when
the king let him go.

"Mahtra, my child, your quest was successful."

Pavek's heart skipped a beat when she accepted Hamanu's embrace without fear or ill-effects. The king patted the
top of Mahtra's white head and somehow Pavek knew she
was smiling within her mask. Then Hamanu fixed those
glowing yellow eyes on Ruari.

"You—I remember: You were curled up on the floor
beside Telhami when I wanted to speak with her that night
in Quraite. You were afraid then, when the danger had
passed. Are you still afraid?"

The Lion-King curled his lips in a smile that revealed
fearsome ivory fangs. The poor half-elf trembled so badly
he needed his staff for balance. That left Zvain, who was
paralyzed with wide-eyed terror until Hamanu touched his

cheek. His eyes closed and remained that way after the king withdrew.

"Zvain, that's a Balican name, but you've never been to Balic, have you?"

"No-o-o-o," the boy whispered, a sound that seemed drawn from the bottom of his soul.

"The truth is best, Zvain, always remember that. There are worse things than dying, aren't there, Lord Pavek?" The king looked at Pavek, and Pavek knew his ordeal was about to begin. "Recount."

Words flowed out of Pavek's mouth as fast as he could shape them, but they were his own words. He didn't feel his life slipping away; Hamanu wasn't unreeling his memory on a mind-bender's spindle, like silk from a worm's cocoon. He told the truth, all of it, from Quraite to Modekan, Modekan to the elven market and the warded passage underground. When he got to the cavern, the pressure on his thoughts relented. He described how the bowls and their scaffolds had first appeared: magically shimmering and glorious from the far side of the cavern. And how, when he pierced their glamour, he learned that they actually were made from lashed-together bones and pitch-patched hide and filled with sludge he believed was poison.

"I thought of Codesh, O Mighty King. But I wanted proof, not my own guesses, before I came here."

"You wanted a measure of that sludge, because you'd forgotten to collect it the first time and you believed your own words would not be enough."

Pavek gulped air. The king *had* used the Unseen Way. His memories *had* been unreeled, and he had not died, he had not even known it was happening. . . .

"Tell me the rest, Lord Pavek. Tell me your conclusions, which are not part of your memories. What do you *think?*"

"I think Kakzim has found a way to poison Urik's water, but I have no proof—except for a few stains on Ruari's staff—"

Hamanu moved swiftly, more swiftly than Pavek could

measure with his eyes, to Ruari's side, and when the half-elf did not immediately relinquish his staff, the Lion-King roared loud enough to deafen them all. His arm swept forward, claws bared, and took the wood out of Ruari's hands. Ruari collapsed on his hands and knees with a groan. Pavek didn't twitch to help his friend, couldn't: he was transfixed by Lord Hamanu's rage.

The Lion-King's human features had all but vanished. His jaw thrust forward, supporting a score or more of identical, sharp teeth. His leonine mane vanished, too, replaced by a dark, scaly crest. He seemed not so much taller as longer, with an angled spine rather than an erect one, and a sinuously flexible neck. Dark, nonretractable talons slashed through the linen bound over the stains on Ruari's staff. A slender, forked tongue slashed once and touched the stains, then with another roar, Lord Hamanu hurled the staff over their heads. It exploded when it hit the wall and fell to the floor in pieces.

"Why have you taken so long?"

The words echoed inside Pavek's skull. He was not certain he'd heard them with his ears and didn't try to answer with his fear-thickened tongue. Instead, Pavek threw up images a mind-bender could absorb: He'd tried. He'd done his best to solve problems he didn't understand. He was merely a human man. If they had failed, it was because he had failed, and he alone should bear the blame. But his failure was not deliberate—merely mortal.

Pavek stared into the eyes of a creature who was everything he was not. He willed himself not to blink or flinch, and after an eternity it was the creature who turned away. With the tension broken and their lives saved for another heartbeat, Pavek let his head hang as he tried, gasp by painful gasp, to draw air into his burning lungs.

"It is enough. I am satisfied. I am satisfied with you, Lord High Templar, and with what you have done. But you are not finished."

A shadow fell across Pavek's back. He could see the Lion-

King's feet without raising his head. They were ordinary human feet shod in plain leather sandals. For one fleeting moment he thought he'd rather die than raise his head— then shuddered, waiting for the fatal blow, which did not fall, though Pavek was certain he had no secrets from his king. It seemed Lord Hamanu wanted him to live a little longer.

Sighing, Pavek straightened his neck and looked upon a king once again transformed, this time into a man no taller than he. A hard-faced man, no longer young, but human, very human with weary human eyes and graying human hair.

"What else must I do, O Mighty King?"

"I will give you a cadre from the war bureau. Lead them into the cavern. Destroy the scaffolds. Destroy the bowls and their contents. Then, find the passage to Codesh. Another cadre will await you. With two cadres, *find* Kakzim, *find* those who assist him. Destroy them, if you feel merciful; bring them to me, if you don't."

"Now?"

"Tomorrow . . . after dawn. This sludge, as you call it, is no simple poison; it must be destroyed with the same precision that has been used in its creation. Kakzim has breached the mists of time and brewed a contagion that could despoil every drop of our water, if it fully ripened. It's dangerous enough now: spill a drop of it into our water by accident as you destroy the bowls, and someone surely will sicken and die. But in a handful of days . . ." Hamanu paused and drew a hand through his gray-streaked hair, transforming it into the Lion-King's mane, and himself as well. "Of course! Ral occludes Guthay in exactly thirteen days! Release the contagion then and it would spread not only through water, but through air and the other elements. All Athas would sicken and die. We must take no chances, Pavek, you and I. I will decoct Kakzim's horror, reagent by reagent, until I know its secrets, and you will follow my orders precisely when you destroy it—"

"My Lord—" Pavek squandered all his courage interrupting Urik's king. "My Great and Mighty King—all Athas is too much for one man. I beg of you: destroy the bowls yourself. Do not entrust all Athas to a blunderer like me."

"You will not blunder, Just-Plain Pavek; it's not in your nature. You will not question what I do or what I entrust to others. You will respect my judgment and you will do what I tell you to do. Tomorrow you will save Athas. Tonight you and your friends will be my guests. Your needs will be attended . . . and your wishes."

Lord Hamanu held out his hand. The golden medallion Pavek had refused yesterday rested in the scarred and callused palm of a born warrior.

Pavek wasn't tempted. "I'm not wise enough to wish, O Mighty King."

"You're wise enough. I would have lived a life much like yours, if I'd been as wise as you. But if you do not wish now, your wishes will never be heard."

He thought of Quraite and his wish that it be kept safe and secret, but he wouldn't take the gold medallion, not even for Quraite.

Hamanu smiled. "As you wish, Lord Pavek. As you wish." As he turned to Mahtra his aspect changed yet again, becoming that of a beautiful youth with one graceful arm extended toward her. She took it and they left the audience hall together.

TEN

For one night Pavek and his companions lived as if they were each the king of Urik. A score of slaves escorted them to a sumptuous room with a broad balcony that overlooked a garden as lush as any druid's grove. The walls were decorated with gold-leaf lattice. Music, played by musicians in galleries concealed by those lattices, floated on the breezes made by silk-fringed fans. The floors were cool marble polished until it shone like glass. Between the room and the balcony, there was a bathing pool, half in shadow, half in light. More slaves stood beside it. Armed with vials of amber oil, they promised to knead the aches out of the weariest man. Silk bedding in rainbow colors was piled in one of the corners while in the center of the room the slaves laid out a feast truly fit for a king.

Common foods had been prepared as no ordinary man had seen them before. The bread had been baked in fluted shapes then arranged on a platter so they resembled a bouquet of flowers. Cold sausage had been twisted and tied into a menagerie of parading wild animals. The uncommon foods had been prepared less fancifully. There was a bowl of fruit in varieties that Pavek had never seen before and Ruari, even with his greater druidic training, could not name. There were heaping plates of juicy meats, sliced thin and garnished with rare spices. But the feast's centerpiece was a silvered bowl filled with a fragrant beverage and with

185

colorless stones that were cold to the touch.

"Ice," a slave explained when the stone Pavek had been examining slipped through his numbed fingers. "Solid water."

Pavek picked the stone up and gingerly applied his tongue to the surface. He tasted water, wet and cold. There could be only one explanation for a stone that sweated water:

"Magic," he concluded, and returned the unnatural lump to the bowl.

The bowl's liquid contents, a blend of fruity flavors that were both tart and sweet, were more to Pavek's liking, but no amount of wonder or luxury could erase from his memory the images of Lord Hamanu's transformations. Ruari and Zvain were similarly affected. They ate, as boys and young men would always eat when their throats weren't cut, but without the energy they would have brought to such a meal had it been served in any other place, at any other time.

Orphanage templars learned what was important early in their lives. Pavek could sleep in just about any bed, or without one, and he could eat whatever was available, be it mealy bread, maggoty meat, or Lord Hamanu's rarest delicacies. He filled a platter with foods he recognized, then wandered out to the porch where the setting sun had turned the sky bloody red.

Zvain followed Pavek like a shadow. Since they'd left the audience chamber, Zvain had rubbed his cheek raw, doing far more damage than the Lion-King had done, at least on the surface. The boy's eyes were haunted, and he was clearly afraid to wander more than a few steps from Pavek's side. When Pavek sat on a bench to eat his meal, Zvain sat on the floor next to him. He leaned back, not against the bench, but against Pavek's leg and heaved a sigh that ended with a shudder.

Feeling more obligated than sympathetic, Pavek asked, "Do you want to talk?" and was relieved when the boy's reply was a sulky, sullen shrug.

Predictably, Ruari's misery took a noisier form. The half-elf joined them on the balcony, set his plate down, and paced an oval around Pavek's bench. Muttering curses under his breath, he seemed to want the attention Zvain didn't.

And when Pavek's neck began to ache from tracking Ruari's movements at his back, he relented and asked the necessary question:

"What's wrong?"

"I was scared," Ruari sputtered, as if he had betrayed himself earlier in the Lion-King's audience chamber. "I was so scared I couldn't move, I couldn't think."

Pavek set his plate beside Ruari's. "You were face-to-face with the Lion of Urik. Of course you were scared. He could kill you ten different ways—*all* ten different ways."

That was not the reassurance Ruari needed.

"I stood there. I just stood there and watched his hand—that horrible hand with those claws—as it swiped my staff. And then I fell down. I fell down, and I stayed down while you *argued* with him!"

"Be grateful you were on the floor. Fear makes me stupid enough to argue with a god."

Ruari's laughter rang false. "I'd rather be your kind of stupid than on my hands and knees like a crass animal, too scared to stand up. *Wind and fire!* She was laughing at me."

She. The only person to whom Ruari could be referring was Mahtra. But Mahtra hadn't laughed. She might have smiled; with that mask they didn't know what her face actually looked like, much less her expression. But she hadn't laughed aloud. Pavek was confused, wondering why, or how, the half-elf thought Mahtra had laughed at him; wondering why or how it mattered; confused until Zvain explained it all in a single, disgusted statement:

"You're getting mushy for her."

"Am not!" Ruari retorted with a vigor that convinced Pavek that Zvain knew exactly what he was talking about. "Wind and fire—she walked out of there with him." The long coppery hair whipped around to hide Ruari's face as he turned away from them. "How could she? Didn't she *see* anything?"

"Who knows what Mahtra sees, Ru?" Pavek said gently. "Except it's different. She's *new* and she's eleganta—"

"She walked off, arm-in-arm, with a monster—Hamanu's worse than Elabon Escrissar!"

"She walked off with *him,* too." Zvain pointed out, effectively pouring oil on Ruari's inflamed passions.

Ruari responded immediately by taking a swing at Zvain; Pavek caught the fist before it landed. If he'd had any doubts about what was eating at Ruari, they vanished the moment their eyes met. Pavek didn't want to argue, not over this. He certainly didn't want to defend the actions of either Mahtra or the Lion-King. What he wanted was to finish his meal, half-drown himself in the bathing pool, and then fall into a dreamless sleep.

But when Ruari roared a slur at him without hesitation, he roared right back, also without hesitation. Nothing they said made sense. It was tension and fear and exhaustion that neither of them could contain for another heartbeat. He couldn't stop it; didn't want to stop it because, like a two-day drunk, it felt good at the start.

They traded accusations and insults, backing each other across the balcony and to the brink of bloodshed. In any physical fight, Pavek would always have the advantage over a half-elf. Even if the half-elf struck first and struck low, Pavek's big fists and brawn could do more damage and do it quickly. Ruari tried to land a dirty punch, which Pavek expected. He seized the half-elf by the shirt, pinned him against the palace wall with one hand and took aim at a copper-skinned chin. But before he landed the punch, a shrieking annoyance leaped on his back.

"Stop it!" Zvain yelled, as frightened as he was angry. "Don't fight! Don't hurt each other."

Pavek caught his rage before it exploded at both youths. He looked from Ruari to his fist and willed his fingers straight. He could *hurt* Ruari—that's what he intended to do—but he'd kill a boy Zvain's size with one unlucky punch. Ruari's shirt came free and, wisely, Ruari retreated while Zvain slid slowly down Pavek's back until his feet touched the floor, his arms were around Pavek's ribs, and his face was pressed against Pavek's back.

"Don't fight," Zvain repeated. "Don't fight with each other. Please, don't make me take sides. Don't make me choose. I can't choose. Not between you."

Without a word, Pavek looped his arm back and urged the boy around. Ruari edged closer, keeping a wary eye on Pavek while he nudged Zvain above the elbow.

Still breathing heavily, Ruari said, "Nobody's asking you to choose," to the top of Zvain's head, but his eyes, when they met Pavek's, made the statement into a question.

It was one thing for Pavek to comfort a boy whose head didn't reach his armpit. It was another with Ruari who stood a head taller than him. Maybe that was the root of the problem between them, and the source of Ruari's unexpected attraction to Mahtra. The New Race woman was, perhaps, the only woman Ruari'd ever met who was tall enough to look him in the eye, and being neither elf nor half-elf, she touched none of Ruari's painful doubts about his heritage.

"Have you . . . *talked* to her?" Pavek asked, feeling awkward as Ruari's shrugged reply appeared. "She might—In the cavern, she felt *something* that made her control that power of hers. Hamanu's infinitesimal mercy, Ru, if she doesn't know how you feel . . ." He shrugged and stared into early twilight, unable to find the right words. This was more difficult than talking about Akashia.

"If she doesn't know," Zvain advised, fully recovered now and putting a manly distance between himself and Pavek again. "Then, don't tell her. Forget about it. Women are nothing but trouble, anyway."

He sounded so wise, so certain, so very young that Pavek had to struggle to keep from laughing.

Ruari lost the battle early, sputtering through lips that loosened into a grin. "Just wait a few years. Your time'll come."

"Never. No women for me. Too messy."

By then Pavek was also laughing, and the day's tension was finally broken. The feast looked more appetizing and the bathing pool became irresistible—once Pavek persuaded the slaves to share both the food and the water. Even the musicians emerged from hiding and, whatever Lord Hamanu had intended, for one evening honest people enjoyed innocent pleasures in his palace.

After he'd eaten and bathed, Pavek turned his weary body over to the slaves who, after sharing the feast, were that much more insistent on kneading the aches out of his muscles. The masseurs kept their promises only too well. Once his neck, back, and shoulders relaxed, Pavek fell asleep. He roused long enough to shake out some of the abundant silk bedding, then he was asleep again and remained that way until a loud knock awakened him. The room was midnight-dark and the only sounds were the groggy awakenings of Zvain, who'd curled up to sleep between Pavek and the wall, and Ruari, a short distance away.

With his pulse pounding, Pavek waited for the next sound, acutely conscious that he was half-naked and completely without a weapon. Last night he'd slipped so far into complacency that, although he could remember removing the sheath that held his prized metal knife along with his belt before he stepped into the bathing pool, he couldn't remember where he'd put it.

"Lord High Templar! Your presence is requested in the lower court."

Requested or required, Pavek didn't dawdle. He called the messenger into the room and ordered him to light all the lamps with the glowing taper he carried for that purpose. Slaves had cleared the remnants of the feast while he slept. Clean clothes in three sizes were piled on the table in place of food. A new staff, carved from Nibenese agafari wood and topped with a bronze lion-head, leaned against garments meant for a half-elf's slender frame. The gold medallion lay atop the pile intended for Pavek. Ruari pronounced himself satisfied with his gift, but once again Pavek left the medallion behind.

It was still pitch-dark when the messenger led them to the lower court, a cobblestone enclosure on the palace's perimeter. A maniple of twenty templars from the war bureau and their sergeant, a wiry red-haired human, were waiting. All twenty-one appeared to be veterans. Each wore piecemeal armor made from studded inix-leather. Vambraces covered their forearms and sturdy buskins, also studded, protected their feet, ankles, and calves. For weapons, they had obsidian-tipped spears and short composite swords that were edged with thin metal strips or knapped stone. Composite swords were common issue in the war bureau; like the templars who wielded them, they were tough and lethal.

Despite the metal sword hanging from his belt—an adjutant's weapon at the very least, if not a militant's—Pavek was in no way qualified to lead these men anywhere. He knew it, and they knew it. But orders were orders, and the sealed parchment orders the sergeant handed to Pavek said, after they were opened, that he was in charge.

"What have you been told?" he asked the sergeant, a grim-faced woman his equal in height.

"Great Lord, we've been told that you'll lead us underground and then to Codesh, where there's to be another maniple meeting us at midday. We're to follow your orders till sundown, then return to our barracks—if we're still alive."

The words on the parchment were different and included a warning from Hamanu to expect trouble in the cavern because he, the Lion of Urik, had decided not to send templars to claim the bowls. He preferred—in his words—to let Kakzim safeguard the simmering contagion until Pavek could destroy it completely. Hamanu's confidence that

Pavek would succeed was less than reassuring to a man who'd watched Elabon Escrissar die. Pavek crumpled the parchment in his fist and faced the sergeant again. "I can lead you to the cavern, but if there's fighting—and I expect there will be—I won't tell you how to do it."

"Great Lord, you might be a smart man," the sergeant said, giving Pavek a first, faint glimmer of approval.

"I've lived this long; I'd like to live longer. Were you told anything else? Anything about the bowls?"

"Bowls? What bowls?" the sergeant shot a look over her shoulder. Pavek didn't see which templar's eye she was trying to catch or the results of their silent conversation, but when she faced him again, the faint approval was gone. "Great Lord, we're waiting for one more, aren't we? Maybe she's got your answer."

Mahtra. In his mind's eye, Pavek could see Hamanu telling Mahtra how they were supposed to dispose of Kakzim's sludge. It was amusement again: Hamanu could resolve everything himself, but he was amused by the efforts of lesser mortals.

They didn't have long to wait. Mahtra entered the lower court from another doorway. As always, she wore the fringed, slashed garments typical of nightfolk. The sergeant sighed, and Pavek shrugged, then Mahtra handed Pavek another sealed scroll.

"My lord wrote his instructions out for you. He says you must be careful to do everything *exactly* as he's described. He says you wouldn't want to be responsible for any mistakes."

"Who's your lord?" the sergeant asked, apparently puzzled that her lord was someone other than Pavek, who occupied himself breaking the seal while Mahtra answered:

"Lord Hamanu. The Lion-King. He's the lord of all Urik."

Hamanu's instructions weren't complicated, but they were precise: flammable bitumen, naphtha, and balsam oil—leather sacks and sealed jars of which would be waiting for them at the elven market guardpost—had to be mixed thoroughly with the contents of each of Kakzim's bowls, then set afire with a slow match, which would also be waiting for them. The resulting blaze would reduce the sludge to harmless ash, but the three ingredients were almost as dangerous as the sludge. With bold, black strokes across the parchment, Hamanu warned Pavek to be careful and to stay upwind of the flames.

Pavek committed the writing to his memory before he met the consternated sergeant's eyes again. They were, after all, not merely templars, but templars from opposing bureaus, and the traditional disdain had to be observed.

"These instructions come from the Lion himself," Pavek said mildly. "He mentions bitumen, naphtha, and balsam oil—" The sergeant blanched, as any knowledgeable person would hearing those three names strung together. "The watch at the elven market gate holds them. We'll take them underground with us."

He'd spoken loudly enough for the maniple to overhear, and Pavek, in turn, heard their collective gasp. They were only twenty templars, twenty-two if they counted Pavek and the sergeant. There were hundreds of traders, mercenaries, and renegades of all stripes holed up in the elven market, every one of whom would risk his life for the incendiaries they were supposed to carry underground.

"Great Lord," the sergeant began after clearing her throat. "Respectfully—most respectfully—I urge you to leave your kinfolk behind. Wherever we go, whatever we do today, it will be no place for the unseasoned. Respectfully, Great Lord. Respectfully."

Pavek should have been insulted—beyond a doubt she included him among the unseasoned, respectfully or not— but mostly he was startled by her assumption that his motley companions were his family. Denials formed on his tongue; he swallowed them. Let her believe what she wanted: a man could do far worse.

"Respectfully heard, but they know more than you, and

they've earned the right to see this through."

"Great Lord, if there's fighting—"

"Don't worry about me or mine. Your only concern is keeping those bowls secure on their platforms until you've eliminated the opposition. Now—let's move out! We've got our work cut out for us if we're to catch that other maniple at midday in Codesh. I hope you're paid up with your fortune-seller. We're going to need a load of luck before the day's out."

The sergeant shot another glance behind her. This time Pavek saw it land on a young man in the last row of the maniple, another redhead. He called the man forward. The sergeant stiffened, and so did the rest of the maniple. Whatever was going on, they shared the secret. Pavek asked for the redhead's medallion. More grim and apprehensive glances were exchanged, especially between the two red-haired templars, but the young man removed the medallion and gave it to the high templar.

Lord Hamanu's leonine portrait was precisely carved, delicately painted, but that vague aura of ominous power that surrounded every legitimate medallion was missing. Without saying anything, Pavek flipped the ceramic over. As he expected, the reverse side of the medallion was smooth— the penalty for impersonating a templar was death; the penalty for wearing a fake medallion was ten gold pieces. The medallion Pavek held was fraudulent, but the mottled clay beads he could just about see beneath the "templar's" yellow tunic were genuine enough.

Underground, an earth cleric would be more useful than all the luck a fortune-seller could offer.

"When the fighting starts," Pavek advised, returning the medallion, "stay close to Zvain and Mahtra," he pointed them out, "because they'll be staying out of harm's way—as you should."

"Great Lord, you are indeed a smart man. We might all live to see the sun rise again."

Pavek grimaced and cocked his head toward the eastern

horizon, which had begun to lighten. "Not unless we get moving."

Corruption, laziness, and internecine rivalries notwithstanding, the men and women who served the Lion-King of Urik mostly followed their orders and followed them competently. The sergeant brought her augmented maniple through the predawn streets to the gates of the elven market without incident or delay. Three sewn-shut leather sacks were waiting for them. Their seams had been secured with pitch; each had been neatly labelled and branded with Lord Hamanu's personal seal. The sacks had been brought from the city warehouse by eight civil bureau templars, messengers and regulators in equal numbers, who remained at the market gates with orders to join the war bureau maniple when it was time to move the sacks again.

The elven market was quiet when a wedge-shaped formation of nearly thirty templars passed through the gate. It was much too quiet, and what sounds they could hear were almost certainly signals as they passed from one enforcer's territory to the next. There were silhouettes on every rooftop, eyes in every alley and doorway. But thirty templars were more trouble than the most ambitious enforcer wanted to buy, and there'd been no time for alliances. Observed, but not disturbed, they reached the squat, old building in its empty plaza as the lurid colors of sunrise stained the eastern sky.

The civil bureau templars would go no farther. Pavek took the sack of balsam oil onto his own shoulder while a pair of war bureau templars, both dwarves, took the other two. The sergeant opened the grated door and uttered a word in front of the bright blue-green warding, and it disappeared long enough for everyone to march through in a single file. With another word, she brought it back to life.

She sent two elves and a half-elf down the tunnel first, not to take advantage of their night vision, but to chant a barrage of minor spells meant to give them safe passage. Privately, Pavek was dismayed by the sergeant's tactics. He told himself it was only civil bureau prejudice against the war bureau's reliance on magic—a prejudice born in envy because the civil bureau had to justify every spell it cast and the war bureau didn't.

Still, he was relieved when one of the spell-chanters worked his way to the rear where the dull-eyed humans gathered, and reported that they'd gone too deep to pull anything through their medallions without creating an ethereal disturbance that could be easily detected by any Codeshite with a nose for magic.

The sergeant didn't hide her preferences. "If there's anyone at all in the damned cavern."

But the chanter saw things differently. "It will not matter where they are, Sergeant. The deeper we go, the harder we must pull, and the bigger the ethereal disturbance, which radiates like a sphere and will reach Codesh long before we do. It is also true, sergeant, that the harder we pull, the less we are receiving. I believe it will not be long before we receive nothing useful at all no matter how hard we pull. The Mighty Lord Hamanu's power does not seem to penetrate the rock beneath his city."

They conferred with the red-headed priest in templar's clothing. He couldn't account for the problems the chanters were having. In Urik, he and other earth-dedicated priests worked very quietly because Hamanu's power reached into their sanctuaries quite easily.

"The rock here must be different, Ediyua," he addressed the sergeant not by her rank, but by her name, confirming Pavek's suspicion that they were kin. "I could investigate, but it would take time, perhaps as much as a day."

Ediyua muttered a few oaths. In her opinion, they should return to the palace; the war bureau didn't like to fight without Hamanu backing them up, but Pavek was the great commander for this foray, and the final decision was his.

Hearing that the Lion-King's power wouldn't reach the reservoir cavern had shaken Pavek's confidence. He'd been so certain Hamanu was toying with them. Now it seemed the great king truly needed the help and skill of a ragtag handful of ordinary folk to thwart Kakzim's plan to poison the city's water. Pavek still considered himself and all of his companions to be pawns in a great game between Hamanu and the mad halfling, but the stakes had been raised to dizzying heights.

"The bowls," he said finally. "Destroying the bowls— that's the most important thing. If we go back to the palace without doing that, we'll be grease and cinders. The Lion's given orders that the bowls are to be burnt before we link up with the other maniple in Codesh at midday. And we're going to burn them, or die trying, because if we fail, the dying will be worse."

There was a grumble of agreement from the nearest templars. Even the sergeant nodded her head.

Pavek continued. "I was seen and recognized yesterday on the Codesh killing ground. Our enemy knows I'll be coming back, one way or another. He'll have guards in the cavern—workmen, too—but no magic except mind-bending. *He's* a mind-bender, I think. Tell everyone to be alert for thoughts that aren't their own. It's dark as a tomb in there. Keep your elves up front. Let them use their eyes. Forget spellcraft. There're twenty of you, Sergeant. If you can't defeat three times your number without pulling magic, Hamanu's infinitesimal mercy won't be enough to save you."

A globe of flickering witch-light magnified the sergeant's vexation at listening to a civil bureau regulator tell her how to prepare for a fight. But she gave the orders Pavek wanted to hear. All magic was stifled, and they finished their journey as Pavek recommended, keeping themselves low to the ground. He got a moment's satisfaction when another report filtered back to them stating that there were at least a score of Codeshites in the cavern, some working atop shining platforms, while the rest were both armed and armored.

Leaving the balsam oil with the two dwarves, Pavek followed the sergeant to the front of their column. As he'd done the previous day, he sneaked down the ramp and cautiously stole a peek across the reservoir. The scaffolds and bowls shone with their glamourous light, inciting awestruck gasps from his companions. Unlike the previous day, however, the cavern swarmed with activity. Workers were on the scaffolds and at their bases, hauling buckets up from the shore and adding who-knew-what to the simmering sludge. Beyond the workers stood a ring of guards—Pavek counted eighteen—all with their backs to the scaffolds and with their poleaxes ready.

Sometimes there was just no satisfaction in being right.

The sergeant swore and crawled back with him to the tunnel passage where they could confer. The plan they made was simple: Leaving the nontemplars behind with the sealed sacks; the rest of them would fan out along the shore and advance as far as possible before they were spotted by the dwarves among the Codeshites. Once they were seen, they'd charge and pray there were no archers hiding in the darkness. Even if there were, the plan wouldn't change.

Someone was sure to run for Codesh. Ruari and the redhaired priest had their orders to watch which way those runners went. Then, with Zvain and Mahtra's help, they were to carry the sacks to the scaffolds whatever way they could.

"With luck, we'll have those bowls burning before reinforcements arrive from the abattoir," Pavek concluded.

The war bureau templars commended themselves to Hamanu's infinitesimal mercy. Pavek embraced his friends. In the darkness it didn't matter, but his eyes were damp and useless when he joined the other templars on the shore.

* * * * *

Cerk sat in the rocks near the entrance to the tunnel leading back to the village. Among themselves in the forests, halflings weren't daunted by physical labor, but on the Tablelands, where the world was overflowing with big, heavy-footed folk, a clever halfling stayed out of the way whenever there was work to be done.

He'd earned his rest. Gathering all the bones for the scaffolds and the hides for the bowls had taxed his creativity to the limit. Simply getting everything into the cavern had been a challenge. The Codesh passage had collapsed sometime in the distant past. When Brother Kakzim had first found it, the twisting tunnel was barely large enough for a human and broad enough for a dwarf. There wasn't enough clearance to maneuver the long bones Cerk needed for the scaffolds. He'd hired work-crews every night for a week to clear away the debris before the longest bones could be manhandled into the cavern.

Brother Kakzim had raged and stormed. Elder brother wanted monuments of stone to support his *alabaster* brewing bowls. By the shade of the great BlackTree itself, Cerk could have kept those crews excavating for another year, and there wouldn't have been enough room to get the bowls Brother Kakzim wanted into the cavern—assuming he'd been able to find *any* alabaster bowls, much less the ten that elder brother swore he needed. Cerk had worked miracles to get enough hide to make the five wicker-frame bowls they did have.

A little appreciation would have been welcomed. Instead Brother Kakzim had assaulted Cerk both physically and mentally. The lash marks across Cerk's back had healed shut, but they were still sore and tender. In the end—at least before the end of Cerk's life—elder brother's madness had receded and reason prevailed. The contagion could be successfully brewed in the five bowls Cerk provided, and their scrap-heap origin could be disguised with a well-constructed glamour.

Cerk *still* didn't understand why the glamour had been necessary. It had taken every last golden coin in the Urik cache to create it: half to find a defiler willing to cast such a spell and the other half for the reagents. They'd gotten some of the gold back when they'd slain the defiler after he raised the glamour, but most of their money was gone, now. And for what? The workers who saw the illusion were the same folk who'd lashed bones together to form the scaffolds and stitched their fingers raw making the bowls. Cerk certainly wasn't impressed by it, and they weren't going to invite the sorcerer-king to the cavern to witness the spilling of the bowls, the destruction of his city.

The only other folk who'd seen the illusion were that scarred human, Paddock, and his companions. At least that's what Brother Kakzim had said yesterday when the foursome appeared in Codesh and headed like arrows for the old building that stood atop the tunnel. Paddock was the reason Cerk had spent the night underground, watching the men who were guarding the scaffolds.

When the do-nothing templars charged across the killing ground to rescue the scarred man and his companions, elder brother had had one of his fits. He'd bit his tongue and writhed on the floor like a spiked serpent. Cerk had feared Brother Kakzim would die on the spot—ending this whole ill-omened enterprise—but he hadn't. He'd gotten to his feet and wiped his face as if nothing strange had happened. Then he'd started giving orders. Elder brother wanted guards around the scaffolds and guards on the killing floor. He wanted more reagents added to the bowls, and he wanted them stirred constantly.

They had a night and a day to destroy Urik. They couldn't afford to wait the extra days until the contagion reached its peak strength, far beneath the conjoined moons. At least that's what Brother Kakzim swore, when he wasn't issuing orders or muttering oaths against the scarred man, Paddock, who, according to elder brother, was as relentless as a dragon. To Cerk, it seemed an unreasonable panic and the final proof that his mentor was irredeemably mad. Using the Unseen Way, Cerk had kenned the demon-dragon, Paddock, while he pounded on walls in the middle of the killing ground, and he'd found a mind that was remarkable only in its ordinariness.

Truly it was a tragedy—Cerk's own tragedy. Had he given

his oaths to Brother Kakzim, he would no longer consider himself bound by them. But he'd given his oath to the sacred BlackTree and his fate if he broke it would surely be worse than if he obeyed the orders of a madman. And so Cerk sat uncomfortably on the rocks, his mind empty except for the slowest curiosity about the lamp and how long its wick would burn before he had to refill the oil chamber.

Then Cerk heard a shout. He raised his head, but several moments elapsed before his thoughts crystallized into intelligence and he realized the guards he'd hired were under attack. Another moment passed before Cerk recognized the uniformly yellow-garbed attackers as templars from the city, and a third before he spotted a brawny, black-haired human with an ugly, scarred face in their midst.

Paddock!

Brother Kakzim wasn't mad—at least not where templar Paddock was concerned. The Codeshites were fighting for their lives, and they fought hard, but they were no match for the templars, who fought in pairs, one attacking, one defending, neither one taking an injury from the desperate Codeshites.

Cerk made one solid attempt to cloud the minds of the nearest templars. He sowed doubt, because it was easiest and most effective. One templar hesitated, and his Codeshite opponent struck him down as if he were a killing-ground beast. But the fallen templar's partner threw off Cerk's doubt. She finished off the Codeshite who'd struck down her partner with two strokes of her sword, then sidestepped and teamed herself with another pair. Another templar—Cerk didn't know which one—not only rejected the mind-bending doubt, but hurled it back.

The unknown templar's Unseen assault was the primitive defense of an untrained mind. Cerk thought he'd dodged it easily, yet it proved effective. His own doubts swelled. He saw no way to save the Codeshite guards or those who'd scrambled off the scaffolding to add confusion, not skill, to the fight. The bowls themselves were doomed, because Cerk did not doubt that Paddock had brought a way to destroy them.

Brother Kakzim would have another fit, but Brother Kakzim had to know, which meant that Cerk had to get to the surface. Grabbing the lantern—halfling eyes were no better than human eyes in the dark—Cerk darted through the rock debris and into the darkest shadow.

He ran as fast as he could, as far as he could. Then with his lungs burning and his feet so heavy his wobbly legs could scarcely lift them, Cerk slumped against the wall. The tunnel was quiet except for his own raspy breaths. He'd outrun the sounds of combat, and it seemed there was no one coming up behind him. A part of him cried out to stay where he was, to blow out the lamp and cower in the safe darkness.

But the darkness wasn't safe. Someone would follow him through the tunnel, be it templar or Codeshite, and whoever it was, it would be an enemy when they met. If there was safety, it lay with Brother Kakzim in their rooms above the killing ground.

The cavern was much closer to Urik than it was to Codesh. Cerk had a long way to go, running or walking. He started moving again, as fast as he could, as soon as he could.

ELEVEN

The faint light filtering through the roof of the little building on the killing ground was the sweetest light Cerk had seen, even though it meant he was no longer running from the templars but looking for Brother Kakzim. With that thought in his mind, the reasonably apprehensive halfling took the extra moments to refill his lamp from the oil cask inside the building and to replace the lamp on a shelf beside the door. He straightened his clothes and tidied his hair before he unlatched the door and strode onto the killing ground where, with any luck, no one would pay much attention to him.

Cerk *was* noticed, of course. Children were forbidden on the killing ground, and away from the forests, halflings were often mistaken for children—especially in Codesh where there were hundreds of children, but only two halflings, himself and Brother Kakzim. Most of the clansmen who warned him away from their butchering knew only that they'd found an old tunnel below the old building, but some of the clansmen knew exactly where he'd been—where he should still be—and why. Some of them had kin on what had become another killing ground.

Those folk were concerned by his unexpected appearance, Cerk could see that on their faces, and he could sense it in their surface thoughts. He didn't dare tell them what was happening underground lest he start a riot before he'd spoken to Brother Kakzim. So, Cerk walked by them, faithful to his sacred oath that placed his allegiance to the Black-Tree Brethren above all else. He was calm on the outside, but inwardly the young halfling suffered the first pangs of a moral nausea that he knew he'd have for a long, long time. Pangs that told him he was no longer young: Brother Kakzim's mad ambitions had changed the way he looked at himself and the world.

As he rounded the top of the stairs to the abattoir gallery and their rented rooms. Cerk could see Brother Kakzim sitting at a table, making calculations with an abacus, and inscribing the results on a slab of wet clay. Usually Cerk waited until elder brother finished whatever he was doing. There was nothing usual about today. He took a deep breath and interrupted before he crossed the threshold.

"Brother! Brother Kakzim—respectfully—"

Brother Kakzim swiveled slowly on his stool. His cowl was down on his shoulders. His face, with its scars and huge, mad eyes, surmounted by wild wisps of brown hair, was terrible to behold.

"What are you doing here?"

A mind-bender's rage accompanied the question. Cerk staggered backward. He struck his head hard against the doorjamb, hard enough to dispel the rage-driven assault and replace it with pain.

"Didn't I tell you to stay with the bowls?"

Cerk pushed himself away from the door, winced as a lock of hair caught in the rough plaster that framed the wood and pulled out at the roots. "Disaster, Brother Kakzim!" he exclaimed rapidly. "Templars! A score of them, at least—"

"Paddock?"

"Yes."

A change came over Brother Kakzim while the templar's name still hung in the air. For several moments, Brother Kakzim simply didn't move. Elder brother's eyes were open, as was his mouth. One hand was raised above his head, ready to emphasize a curse. The other rested on the table, as if he were rising to his feet. But he wasn't rising. He wasn't doing anything.

Then, while Cerk held his breath, the scars on Brother Kakzim's face darkened like the setting sun, and the weblike patches in them that never quite healed began to throb.

Cerk braced himself against the doorjamb, awaiting a mind-bending onslaught that did not come. He counted the hammer beats of his own heart: one . . . ten . . . twenty . . . He was getting light-headed; he had to breathe, had to blink his own eyes. In that time another change had happened. Brother Kakzim had lowered his arm. His eyes had become a set of rings, amber around black, white around amber: a sane man's eyes, such as Cerk had never seen above elder brother's scarred cheeks.

"How long?" Brother Kakzim asked calmly. Cerk didn't understand the question and couldn't provide an answer. Brother Kakzim elaborated, "How long before our nemesis and his companions find their way here?" His voice remained mild.

"I don't know, Brother. They were still fighting when I ran from the cavern. I ran when I could, but I had to stop to rest. I heard nothing behind me. Perhaps they won't come. Perhaps they won't find the passage and will return to Urik."

"Wishes and hopes, little brother." Brother Kakzim picked up the clay slabs he'd been inscribing and squeezed them into useless lumps that he hurled into the farthest corner, but those acts were the only outward signs of his distress. "Our nemesis will follow us. You may be sure of it. He is my bane, my curse. While he lives, I will pluck only failure from my branches. The omens were there, there, but I did not read them. Did you see his scar? How it tracks from his right eye to his mouth? His right eye, not his left. An omen, Cerk, an omen, plain as day, plain as the night I first saw him—"

He seems sane, but he is mad, Cerk thought carefully, in

the private part of his mind, which only the most powerful mind-bender could breach. Brother Kakzim has found a new realm of madness beyond ordinary madness.

"Have I told you about that night, little brother? I should have known him for my nemesis from that first moment. Elabon tried to kill him with a half-giant. A half-giant!" Brother Kakzim laughed, not hysterically as a madman might, but gently, as if at a private joke. "So much wasted time; so much time wasted. While he lives, nothing will go right for me. I must destroy him, if the BlackTree is to thrive. I must kill him. Not here. Not where he has roots. Cut off his roots! That's what we must do, little brother, cut off our nemesis at his roots!"

Cerk stood still while Brother Kakzim embraced him enthusiastically. This was better than mindless rage, better than being beaten, but it was still madness.

"Together we can do it, little brother. Gather our belongings. We must leave quickly—leave for the forest at once—after I've spoken to the others. We will fail, but we must not fail to try! Always try, little brother. Omens are not always what they seem!"

It is madness, Cerk thought in his private place. Pure madness, and I'm part of it. I can do nothing but follow him until we reach the forest—if we reach the forest. Then I will appeal to the Elder Brethren of the Tree. I'll spill my blood on the roots, and the BlackTree will release me from my oath.

He held his hand against his chest and squeezed the tiny scars above his heart, the closest thing to prayer that a BlackTree brother had.

"Don't be sad, little brother." Brother Kakzim suddenly seized Cerk's arms. "The only failure is the last failure. No other failure lasts! Gather our belongings while I talk to the others. We must be gone before the killing starts."

Grimly Cerk nodded his obedience. Brother Kakzim released him and walked out onto the open gallery where he picked up a leather mallet and struck the alarm gong.

"Hear me! Hear me, one and all. Codesh is betrayed!"

Cerk listened as the killing ground fell silent. Even the animals had succumbed to Brother Kakzim's mind-bending might. Then elder brother began his harangue against Urik and its templars generally, and the yellow-robed villains about to emerge onto the killing ground. It was truth and falsehood so tightly interwoven that Cerk, who'd been in the cavern when the attack began and knew all the truth there was to know was drawn toward the gallery with his fists clenched and his teeth bared. He stopped himself at the door and closed it.

The closed lacquered door and his own training gave Cerk the strength to resist Brother Kakzim's voice. No one else in the abattoir would be so lucky.

He was filling a second shoulder-sack when the room began to shake. It was as if the ground itself were shuddering, and even though he knew the Dragon had been slain, Cerk's first thoughts were that it had come to Codesh to consume them all.

The scrap of white-bark—the scratched lines and landmarks that had guided him to Urik a year ago and that he'd been about to stuff into the sack—floated from Cerk's fingers. He tried to walk, but a gut-level terror kept his feet glued where they stood, and he sank to his knees instead.

"Listen to them!" Brother Kakzim exclaimed as he shoved through the door. "Failed brilliance; brilliant failure. My voice freed their rage. Yellow will turn red!" He did a joyous dance on the quaking floor, never once losing his balance. "They're tearing down the gates, setting fire to the tower. They'll all die. I give every yellow-scum death to my nemesis! Let his spirit be weighed beneath the roots!"

Stunned, Cerk realized that the shuddering of the walls and floor was the result of mauls and poleaxes biting against the abattoir walls and the base of the watchtower where the templar detachment stood guard day and night. When he took a deep breath, he could smell smoke. His feet came unglued, and he bolted for the doorway where the scent was stronger. Dark tendrils filled the stairwell. He didn't want to be in Codesh when the templars emerged from the little building.

"We're trapped!"

"Not yet. Have you gathered everything?"

The maddest eyes in creation belonged to Brother Kakzim who'd loosed a riot beneath his own feet and didn't care. Cerk grabbed the sacks as they were on the table. He threw one over each shoulder.

"I gathered everything," he said from the doorway. "It's time to leave, elder brother. Truly, it's time to leave."

⋆   ⋆   ⋆   ⋆   ⋆

When Elabon Escrissar led his hired cohort against Quraite, there had been blood, death, and injury all around. There'd been honest heroism, too. Pavek had been an honest hero when he'd fought and when he'd invoked the Lion-King's aid, but he wasn't Quraite's only hero. Ruari knew he'd done less that day and risked less, too—but he'd been at Pavek's side at the right time to give Pavek the medallion and defend him while he used it. Ruari had been proud himself that day. He was proud of himself still.

But not for today's work.

Maybe there could be no heroics when your side was the stronger side from the start, when only your own mistakes could defeat you. The war bureau templars hadn't made any mistakes, and aside from one fleeting touch of Unseen doubt, there'd been no Codeshite heroics. Two templars had gone down. Another two were walking wounded. The red-haired sergeant collected medallions from the dead and put the wounded to work guarding their prisoners.

There were no wounded among the prisoners, only dull-eyed men and women who knew they were already slaves. Most of the dead Codeshites had died fighting, but a few had been wounded and got slit throats instead of bandages when the fighting was over.

Maybe they were the lucky ones.

Ruari wasn't sure. He'd brought the sack of balsam oil from the Urik passage and helped pour its fragrant contents into the five glamourous bowls. His mind said they were doing the right thing, the heroic thing, when they lit the purging fires. Kakzim and Elabon Escrissar had been cut from one cloth, and the Codeshites had earned their deaths as surely as the Nibenay mercenaries had earned theirs on the Quraite ramparts. Ruari's gut recalled the wounded prisoners, and as a whole, Ruari wasn't sure of anything except that he'd lost interest in heroes.

He'd have been happy to call it quits and return to Urik or, preferably, Quraite, but that wasn't going to happen. He and the priest had watched a lantern weave through the darkness at the start of the skirmish. They'd seen it disappear, and when the fighting was over they'd found a passage among the deep shadows. The wounded templars were heading home. The prisoners, their hands bound behind their backs with rope salvaged from the scaffolds, were headed for the obsidian pits. And Ruari was headed for Codesh, walking between Zvain and Mahtra, ahead of the templars and behind Pavek, the sergeant, and the priest.

They were on their way to meet another war bureau maniple. They were on their way to kill or capture Kakzim. Ruari should have been excited; instead he was nauseous— and grateful when Mahtra's cool hand wrapped around his.

The Codesh passage was much longer than the Urik passage. Caught in a grim, hopeless mood, the half-elf began to believe they were headed nowhere, that they were doomed to trudge through tight-fitting darkness forever. At last the moment came when he knew they were nearing Codesh, but it came with the faint scent of charred wood, charred meat, and brought no relief. Evidently, Ruari's companions caught the same aroma. Mahtra's grip on his hand became painful, forcing him to pull away, and Zvain whispered:

"He's burning Codesh to keep us away." The first words

Ruari had heard his young friend say since they left the elven market.

"No one would do that," the priest countered.

"He'd poison an entire city," Pavek said, "and more than a city. A mere village wouldn't stop him. *If* it's Kakzim. We don't know anything, except that we smell something burning. It could be something else. We're late, I think, the other maniple could have finished our work for us. We won't know until we get there." Pavek might have left his shiny gold medallion behind, but he *was* a high templar, and when he spoke, calmly and simply, no one argued with him.

The sergeant organized them quickly into a living chain, then gave the order to extinguish the lanterns. Ruari, his staff slung over his back where it struck his head or heel at every step, fell in with the rest. It was slow-going through the dark, smoky passage, but with hands linked in front and behind there was no panic. Taller than those ahead of him and endowed with half-keen half-elf vision, Ruari was the first to notice a brighter patch ahead and whispered as much to those around him. Ediyua called for a volunteer, and the first templar in the column went forward to investigate.

Ruari watched the templar's silhouette as he entered the faint light, then lost it when the man rounded the next bend in the passage. The volunteer shouted back to them that he could see an overhead opening, and screamed a heartbeat later. After giving them all an order to stay where they were, the sergeant drew her sword and crept forward. Mahtra, next in line behind Ruari, pulled her hand free for a moment, then gave it back to him. He heard several loud crunching sounds, as if she were chewing pebbles, and was about to tell her to be quiet when instead of a scream, the clash of weapons resounded through the tunnel.

Ediyua hadn't rounded the bend; Ruari could make out her silhouette and the silhouettes of her attackers, but it was someone else farther back in the column who shouted out the word, "Ambush!"

Panic filled the passage, thicker than the smoke. Discipline crumbled into pushing and shoving. Templars shouted, but no one shouted louder than Zvain:

"No! Mahtra, *no!*"

A tingling sensation passed from Mahtra's hand into Ruari's. It was power, though unlike anything he'd felt in his druidry. He surrendered to it, because he couldn't drive it out or fight it, and a peculiar numbness spiraled up from the hand Mahtra held. It ran across his shoulders, and down his other arm—into Pavek, all in the span of a single heartbeat. A second pulse, faster and stronger than the first, came a heartbeat later.

Time stood still in the darkness as power leapt out of every pore of Ruari's copper-colored skin. He felt a flash of lightning, without seeing it; felt a peal of thunder though his ears were deaf. He died, he was sure of that, and was reborn in panic.

The air was full of dust. Heavier particles rained around him like sifting sand. He didn't know what had happened, or where he was, until he heard a single phrase welling up behind him:

"Cave-in!"

Followed by the red-haired priest shouting, "I can't hold it!" from the front.

Other voices shouted out "Hamanu!" but there wasn't time or space to evoke the mighty sorcerer-king's aid.

Templars at the rear of the column surged forward, desperate to avoid one certain death, unmindful of the danger that lay ahead. Mahtra pushed Ruari, who pushed Pavek, who pushed the priest toward the dust-streaked light. Ruari stumbled against something that was not stone. His mind said the sergeant's body, and his feet refused to take the next necessary step. He lurched forward and would have gone down if Pavek hadn't yanked his arm hard enough to make the sinew snap. His foot came down where it had to, on something soft and silent. The next body was easier, the next easier still, and then he could see light streaming in from above.

Whatever Mahtra had done—Ruari assumed that she and her "protection" were responsible for the cave-in—it had destroyed the little building in the middle of the abattoir floor and any blue-green warding along with it. With Pavek leading, they emerged into a devastated area of the killing ground where stone, bone, and flesh had been reduced to fist-sized lumps. Smoke from the fires and dust from the cave-in made it difficult to see more than an arm's length, but they weren't alone, and they weren't among friends.

Ruari made certain Mahtra and Zvain were behind him, then unslung his staff as Codesh brawlers came out of the haze, poleaxes raised and swinging. He had no trouble blocking the blows—he was fast, and the wood of his new staff was stronger than any other wood he could name—but his body had to absorb the force of the heavy poleaxes. The force shocked his wrists, his elbows, his shoulders, and then his back, bone by bone, through his legs and into his feet before it dissipated in the ground. With each blocked blow, Ruari felt himself shrink, felt his own strength depleted.

There was no hope of landing a blow, not at that moment. He and the templars were surrounded. Those who were fighting could only defend—and pray that those who were evoking the Lion-King succeeded.

Desperate prayers seemed answered when two huge and slanting yellow eyes manifested in the haze. To a man, the Codeshites fell back, and the templars raised a chorus of requests for flaming swords, lightning bolts, enchantments, charms, and blessings. Ruari had all he'd ever want from the Lion of Urik already in his hands. He took advantage of the lull, striding forward to deliver a succession of quick thrusts and knocks with his staff's bronze finial. Three brawlers went down with bleeding heads before Ruari retreated to his original position; the last place he wanted to be was among the Codeshites when Lord Hamanu began granting spells.

The sulphur eyes narrowed to burning slits, focused on one man: Pavek, whose sword was already bloody and whose off-weapon hand held a plain, ceramic medallion.

A single, serpentine thread of radiant gold spun down from the Lion-King's eyes. It struck Pavek's hand with blinding light. When Ruari could see again, the hovering eyes were gone and Pavek was on his knees, doubled over, his sword discarded, clutching his off-weapon hand against his gut. The templars were horrified. They knew their master had abandoned them, though the Codeshites hadn't yet realized this and were still keeping their distance. That changed in a matter of heartbeats. The brawlers surged. Mahtra raced to Pavek's side; the burnished skin on her face and shoulders glowed as brightly as the Lion-King's eyes.

Her protection, Ruari thought. The force that had knocked him down in this same spot yesterday and collapsed the cavern passage behind them moments ago. *At least I won't feel the axe that kills me.*

But there was something else loose on the killing ground. Everyone felt it, Codeshites and templars alike. Everyone looked up in awe and fear, expecting the sorcerer-king to reappear. Everyone except Ruari, who knew what was happening, Pavek, who was making it happen, and Mahtra, whose eyes were glazed milky white, and whose peculiar magic would be their doom if he, Ruari, couldn't stop it.

He'd touched Mahtra once before when her skin was glowing; it had been the most unpleasant sensation of his life. But Pavek said she'd stopped herself because she felt him, Ruari, beside her.

If he could make her feel that again—?

It was all the hope Ruari had, and there was no time to think of anything better. He was beside her in one long-legged stride, had his arms around her and his lips close to her ear. The heat around her was excruciating. The charring flesh he smelled was undoubtedly his own.

"Mahtra! It's Ruari—don't do this! We're saved. I swear to you—Pavek's saved us."

Dust and grit swirled around them. The ground shuddered, but not because of Mahtra. Wrapped tight around Ruari's shoulders and waist, her magic was fading, her arms were cooling with every throb of her pulse. He could feel her breath through the mask, two gentle gusts against his neck. *Two* gusts. In the midst of chaos, Ruari wondered what the mask concealed, but the thought, for the instant that it lasted, was curiosity, not disgust. Then his attention was drawn into the swirling dust.

The land is guarded, that was the first axiom of druidry, which Ruari had learned in Telhami's grove. The axiom produced a paradox: if Athas was one land, there should be only one guardian and all druidry should flow from one source. Yet there were as many guardians as there were aspects of Athas, overlapping and infinite. The guardian of Quraite was an aspect of Athas. The guardian of Ruari's scrubland grove was an aspect of both Quraite and Athas.

And the guardian Pavek had raised through the packed dirt of the Codesh killing ground was an aspect like nothing Ruari had ever imagined.

It cleared the air inside the abattoir, sucking all the dust, the debris, the smoke, and even the flames into a semblance no taller than an elf, no burlier than a dwarf. But the ground shuddered when it took a ponderous step, and the air whistled when it slowly swung its arm. A Codesh brawler caught the force of its fist and flew in a great arc that ended on the other side of the wall, leaving her poleaxe behind. The semblance—it was *not* a guardian: guardians were real, but they had no substance; that was another axiom of druidry—armed itself with the axe and with its second swing took the heads of two more.

That sobered the Codeshite brawlers. The boldest among them attacked the semblance Pavek had summoned. They died for their bravery. The brightest surged toward Pavek, who had not risen from the ground. Ruari dived for his staff and regained his feet, ready to defend Pavek's life. The fighting was thrust and block, sweep and block, rhythm and reaction, as it had been before, with no time for thought until they'd beaten back the first Codeshite surge. Then there was time to breathe, time to notice who was standing and who had fallen.

Time to notice, through the now-clear air, the solid line of yellow-robed corpses hanged from the railing of their watchtower.

Until he had met Pavek, and for considerable time thereafter, Ruari would have cheered the hanging sight. He'd been conceived when his templar father had raped his elven mother, and he'd grown up believing the only good templar was a dead one. Even now he wouldn't want any of the men and women fighting beside him as friends, but he'd learned to see them as individuals within their yellow robes and understood their gasps and curses. He wasn't surprised when the war bureau survivors around raised their voices in an eerie, wailing war-cry, or that they pursued the Codeshites, who broke ranks and ran for the gate. What did surprise Ruari, though, was the four yellow-robed templars who stayed behind with him in a ring around Pavek, the red-haired priest, Mahtra, and Zvain.

The guardian semblance Pavek had raised was slow but relentless. Nothing the Codeshite brawlers did wounded it or sapped its strength. The best they could do against it was defend, as Ruari defended with his staff against their poleaxes—and with the same effect. Though formed from insubstantial dust and debris, the semblance put the strength of the land in each of its blows. Mortal sinews couldn't withstand such force for long. The brawlers went down, one by one, until the critical moment came when those who were left comprehended that they wouldn't win, couldn't win, and stopped trying. They broke ranks and fled toward the gate—which was apparently the only way off the killing ground and which was where the fighting between Codeshites and templars remained thick.

Ruari took two strides in pursuit, then stopped when the semblance collapsed into a dusty rubbish heap. Two of his four templar allies kept going, but two stayed behind, panting hard, but aware that they were in danger as long as they were in Codesh, as long as Pavek remained senseless and slumped in the dirt.

Pavek's eyes were open when Ruari crouched beside him, and he groaned when, with Mahtra's help, Ruari eased him onto his side. Blood soaked the front of the fine, linen clothes the Lion-King had given him. Blood was on his arms and on his hands. Ruari feared the worst.

The priest knelt and took Pavek's left hand gently between his own. "It's his hand," the priest said, turning Pavek's hand to show Ruari what had happened when the medallion burst apart. "He'll lose it, but he'll live, if I can stop the bleeding."

Looking down at bone, sinew, and tattered flesh, Ruari's fear became cold nausea. He knelt beside the priest as much from weakness as from the desire to help.

"There's power here—"

"The power he himself raised?" The priest refused Ruari's offer with a shake of his head. "It's too riled, too angry. I wouldn't try—if I were you."

The priest was right. Ruari had no affinity for Pavek's guardian. This was Urik, in all its aspects: Pavek's roots, not his. But the red-haired priest was no healer. The only help he could offer was taking the remains of the leather thong that had held Pavek's medallion around his neck and tying it tight around Pavek's wrist instead.

"Now we pray," the priest advised.

Pavek opened his eyes and levered himself up on his right elbow. "If you want to do something useful, find Kakzim, instead." Between his old scar and the pain he was trying to hide, Pavek's smile was nothing any sane man would want see. "The bastard must be around here someplace."

Zvain, who'd been watching everything, pale and silent from the start, needed no additional encouragement. He was off like an arrow for the gallery where they'd seen Kakzim yesterday. Mahtra headed after him, but Kakzim was just a name to Ruari, and Pavek had lost a dangerous amount of blood.

"Go with them," Pavek urged. "Take your staff. Keep them out of trouble."

"You need a healer—bad."

"Not that bad."

"You've lost a lot of blood, Pavek. And—And your hand—it's bad, Pavek. You need a *good* healer. Kashi—"

Pavek shook his head. "Kakzim. Get me Kakzim."

"You'll be here when we bounce his halfling rump down those stairs?"

"I'm not going anywhere."

Ruari turned away from Pavek. He looked into the priest's blue eyes, asking silent questions.

"There's nothing more to do here," the priest replied. "I'll stay with him. We're well out of harm's way, and these two will stay—" He cocked his head toward the two templars who'd remained with them. "If anyone gets the bright idea to finish what they started before the great king comes to render judgment."

"The Lion closed his eyes," Ruari snarled and surged to his feet. He found himself angry at the sorcerer-king, and disappointed as well. "He's not coming."

"He'll come," Pavek assured him. "I'll wager you, he'll be here before the fighting's over. You've got to find Kakzim first."

By the screaming, shouting, and clash of arms, the fighting remained fierce around the abattoir gate. Ruari couldn't be certain, but he thought there might be more templars—perhaps Nunk and his companions, perhaps the other war bureau maniple—outside the gate, keeping the brawlers on the killing ground until the war bureau fighters finished their retribution. He could be certain that Pavek was safer right now with two templars and a priest watching over him than Mahtra and Zvain were, searching the gallery for Kakzim without weapons or sense.

"I'll be back before the Lion gets here," Ruari assured the group closest to him before running to the gallery stairway, staff in hand.

Finding Mahtra and Zvain was no more difficult than listening for Zvain's inventive swearing from the top of the
charred but still serviceable stairway. Although the gallery
appeared deserted, Ruari set himself silently against a doorjamb where he could see not only his friends ransacking a
nearly empty room, but the rest of the gallery and killing
ground where two templars stood similar watch over Pavek
and the priest.

"Find anything?" Ruari asked, all innocence within the
shadows.

Mahtra said, "No," with equal innocence, but Zvain leapt
straight up and came down only a few shades darker than
Mahtra.

"You scared me!" Zvain complained once he'd stopped
sputtering curses.

Ruari countered with, "You'd be worse than scared if it
weren't me standing here," and could almost hear Pavek
saying the same thing. "You're damn fools, leaving the door
open and making so much noise."

"I was listening," Mahtra said. "I would've seen trouble
coming; I saw you. I would've protected—"

"What's to see? There's no one here!" Zvain interrupted.
"He's scarpered. Packed up and left. Cut and run. Got out
while the getting was still good—just like he did with deadheart Escrissar."

Ruari's spirits sank. Pavek *wanted* Kakzim; not catching
him was going to hurt Pavek more than losing his hand. "Is
there anything here? Pavek . . ."

"Nothing!" Zvain said, kicking over a stool for emphasis.
"Not a damn thing!"

"There's this—" Mahtra held out a chunk of what
appeared to be tree bark.

"Garbage!" Zvain kicked the stool again.

Ruari left his staff leaning against the doorjamb and took
Mahtra's offering. It *was* bark, though not from any tree that
grew on the Tablelands. Holding it, feeling its texture with
his fingers, he got a vision of countless trees and mountains

wrapped in smoke like the Smoking Crown Volcano . . . no, mountains wrapped in *clouds,* like nothing he'd seen before.

Any other time, he'd cherish the bark simply for the vision it gave his druid spirit, but there was no time, and the bark was more than bark. Someone had covered it with straight black lines and other, irregular shapes.

"Writing," he mused aloud.

That gave him Zvain's swift attention. The boy grabbed the bark out of his hands. "Naw," he drawled, "that's not writing. I know writing when I see it; I can read—and there're no words here."

"I know writing, too," Ruari insisted, although he was better at recognizing its many forms than in reading any one of them. "There's writing here, halfling writing, I'll wager. And other things—"

"That's a mountain," Mahtra said, tapping the bark with a long, red fingernail. "And that's a tree—like the ones I saw where you live."

"It's a map!" Zvain exalted, jumping up and throwing the bark scrap into the air. "Kakzim left us a map!"

Ruari snatched the bark while it was still well above Zvain's head and gave him a clout behind the ear as well. "Don't be a kank-brained fool. Kakzim's not going to gather up everything else and leave a *map* behind."

"What's a map?" Mahtra asked.

"Directions for finding a place you've never been," Ruari answered quickly, not wanting to be rude to her.

"Then maybe he left it behind because he doesn't need it anymore."

Ruari closed his hand over Mahtra's. She was seven, younger than Zvain. She not only didn't know what a map was, she didn't understand at all the way a man's mind worked. "It's garbage, like Zvain said, or it's a trap."

"A trap?" she asked, freeing herself and taking the scrap from his hand to examine it closely.

She didn't understand, and Ruari was still ransacking his mind, searching for better words, when they heard, first, a gong clattering loudly and, second, a roar that belittled it to a tinkling cymbal.

"*The Lion-King!*" Zvain said as they all turned toward the sound, toward Codesh's outer gate.

"Pyreen preserve and protect!" Ruari took the bark map, rolled it quickly, and pushed it all the way up inside his shirt hem. "Is there anything else? Anything?"

Zvain said, "Absolutely nothing," and Mahtra shook her head.

Ruari grabbed his staff and headed for the killing ground with the other two close behind him.

The first thing Ruari noticed was that the templars and Codeshites were still fighting near the gate. The second was that they'd moved Pavek out of the sun.

Pavek was sitting on the ground with his back against one of the massive tables where the Codeshites turned carcasses into meat. His head was tilted to one side; he seemed to be resting, maybe sleeping. His face was a gray shade of pale, but Ruari wasn't concerned until he was close enough to see that Pavek's mangled left hand was inside a bucket. Water was excellent for washing a wound and keeping it clean, but submerging that bad an open wound was a good way to bleed a man to death.

"Damn you!" he shouted and, grasping his staff by its base, swung its bronzed lion end at the three men standing by while Pavek slowly died.

The nearest templar raised his sword to parry the staff. The templar could have attacked, could have slain Ruari, who was fighting with his heart, not his head, and his heart was breaking; but the yellow-robed warrior didn't take the easy slash or thrust. He parried the staff, beat it aside, closing the distance between them until he could loft a sandal-shod kick into Ruari's midsection. Catching the staff with one hand as it flew through the air, he tried to catch Ruari with the other.

Ruari dodged, and landed hard, flat on the ground an arm's length from Pavek. Ignoring the pain in his own gut, the half-elf crawled forward. He plucked the frayed leather thong out of the dirt, then tried to lift Pavek's hand out of the bucket.

"My choice," Pavek said, his voice so weak Ruari read the words on his lips more than he heard them with his ears.

The priest held onto Zvain—barely. The burnished skin on Mahtra's shoulders was glowing again, and her bird's-egg eyes were open so wide they seemed likely to fall out of her face.

"What's happening?" she demanded.

"He's killing himself!" Ruari shouted. "He's bleeding himself to death!"

"The king is coming," the priest said, as if that were an explanation.

Pavek asked, "You couldn't find Kakzim?" before Ruari could challenge the priest.

"No, he's scarpered," the half-elf admitted, shaking his head and turning his empty palms up. All the disappointment he'd dreaded showed in Pavek's eyes just before he closed them with a shrug, as if the big man had stayed alive this long only because he'd hoped his friends would be successful. Taking a painful breath, Ruari finished: "He got away clean, again. Didn't leave anything behind."

"We found a map," Mahtra corrected. "Show him the map."

But Pavek raised his good hand and turned away. "No. No, I don't want to see it. Don't tell me about it. Just—Just get out of Codesh quickly. All three of you."

"Why?" Zvain, Mahtra, and Ruari demanded with a single voice.

Pavek looked up at the priest.

"Under necromancy, a dead man must tell the truth, but he can't reveal what he didn't know while he was alive."

"Necromancy?" Ruari said slowly, as the pieces began to fall into place. "Deadhearts? *Hamanu?*"

The templar who'd parried Ruari's staff nodded. "We kill our prisoners before we take them to the deadhearts. The dead don't suffer; they don't feel pain."

"They don't remember," the other templar corrected. "Everything stops when they die. They've got no present, no future; only the past."

"No."

"I can hope, Ru," Pavek said in his weak voice. "What good would I be anyway, Ru, without my right hand?"

"No," Ruari repeated, equally soft and weak.

"I raised a guardian, here—in Codesh, in *his* realm. He's not going to be happy, and he's not going to rest until he controls it or destroys it. I can't let him do that, and the only way I can stop him from trying . . . and succeeding is if I'm already a corpse when he finds me. It takes a druid to raise a guardian. The Lion-King's not a druid, Ru, and after I'm dead, I won't be either."

Another roar, louder than the first, warned them all that there wasn't much time.

"You can't raise it, Ru. I know that, and I know that you don't believe me when I tell you that—not truly—and that'll get you killed, if you don't get out of here . . . *now.*"

Pavek spoke the truth: Ruari didn't believe that he *couldn't* raise the Urikite guardian, and the Lion-King would use that belief. He'd die trying to raise the wrong guardian, or he'd die the moment he succeeded. He had to leave, and take Zvain and Mahtra with him, but he put his arms around Pavek instead.

"I won't forget you," he gasped, trying to remain a man, trying not to cry.

"Go home and plant a tree for me. A big, ugly lump of a tree. And carve my name in its bark."

The tears came, as many as Ruari had ever shed for someone else. Zvain wormed in between them, silently demanding his moment, and getting it, before Ruari pulled him to his feet.

"Wait—" Pavek called, and Ruari dared to hope he'd changed his mind, but Pavek only wanted to give him the coin pouch from his belt and his most prized possession: a small steel-bladed knife snug in its sheath.

"Some of the scum have run toward that far corner," one of the templars said, pointing where he meant. "There must be a way out. We'll go with you as far as the village walls."

The priest said he'd stay to the end, in case Pavek needed a nudge "to separate his spirit from his body before the Lion-King got too close." He said he wasn't worried about Hamanu, and that was a lie—but maybe he'd lost everything he cared about when red-haired Ediyua went down in the passage.

Ruari didn't say good-bye, just took hold of Mahtra and Zvain and started walking fast to catch up with the templars who'd already left. He didn't look back, either.

Not once.

Not until they were clear of the Codesh walls.

TWELVE

Pavek was gone.

Pavek was *dead*.

One of the many roars Ruari heard while trudging along the ring road to Farl might have marked the moment when the Lion-King found his high templar's pale corpse. Another might have marked the moment when deadheart spells animated Pavek's body one last time. The last roar, the loudest and longest that he and Mahtra and Zvain heard, could only have marked the king's frustration when he found that Pavek, Just-Plain Pavek, had outwitted him.

Ruari brushed a knuckle quickly beneath his eye, catching a tear before it leaked out, drying the telltale moisture with an equally quick touch to his pant leg. Life went forward, he told himself, repeating the words Telhami had used every time he bemoaned the violence and hatred that had brought him into an uncaring world. There was nothing to be gained by looking back.

He was half an elf, half a templar; nothing could alter that fact. Pavek hadn't taken his gold medallion, hadn't wanted what Hamanu wanted to give him, and Hamanu had punished him; nothing could alter that, either. A Urik templar's life, and death, belonged to Hamanu, Pavek had told Ruari that often enough.

Then Pavek raised a guardian spirit out of Urik, where no other druid would have dreamed to look for one. Pavek changed—tried to change—the lay of life in a sorcerer-king's domain, and Pavek had paid the price of folly.

Life went forward. Don't look back.

But Ruari did look back. He sneaked a peek over his shoulder every few moments. The skyline of Codesh was still there, crowned with a thin cloud of dust and smoke that grew thinner each time he looked.

"You come from Codesh?" an overseer called from one of the roadside fields, his slave scourge folded in his hand. "What's the uproar?"

"Damn butchers tried to slaughter their templars. Got rid of some of them, but Hamanu answered their call."

The overseer scratched his nose thoughtfully. "They killed a few templars, and the Great Lord himself came out for vengeance. That ought to put the fear into them. High time."

"High time," Ruari agreed, ending the conversation as they walked beyond the field.

"Get it right, Ruari, or you'll make folk suspicious. It's *Lord* Hamanu or *King* Hamanu or Great and Mighty Lord King Hamanu when you're talking to someone who's got a scourge in their hand!" Zvain objected once they were out of the overseer's hearing. "You can't talk about Hamanu as if you've met him!"

"But I have met him," Ruari complained. "He terrorized us, then he gave us gifts. He encouraged us, then he abandoned us. 'Hamanu answered their call'—that's the biggest lie I've ever told, Zvain: he closed his eyes!"

"Doesn't matter. I'm telling you, you can't talk about Lord Hamanu that way. Say it the way I told you, or folk are going to get suspicious and start asking questions."

Ruari shrugged. "All right. I'll try."

Zvain had lived in Urik all his life, while Mahtra had lived *under* it and Ruari had grown up nowhere near it. The three of them together didn't have half Pavek's experience or canniness, but Pavek was gone. Dead. And Zvain had suddenly become their font of wisdom where the city and its customs

were concerned. Ruari knew the responsibility weighed
heavily on Zvain's shoulders and the boy was staggering
under the load—

Wind and fire! They were all staggering, putting one foot
in front of the other because stopping meant thinking and
thinking meant Pavek. He'd known Pavek for a year, one
lousy year—and for most of that year they'd been at each
other's throats. . . . No, he'd been at Pavek's throat, trying to
rile him into a display of templar temper, trying to kill him
with kivet poison because . . . because?

On the dusty road to Farl, midway through the longest
afternoon of his life, Ruari couldn't remember why he'd
poisoned Pavek's dinner. But not so long ago he'd wanted
Pavek's death so badly it made him blind. Now he could
scarcely see for another reason and hurriedly sopped up
another tear before it betrayed him.

"What are we going to do when we get to Farl?" Mahtra
asked when another stretch of hot, dusty road had passed
beneath their feet. "Will we stay there? Overnight? Longer?
Where will we get our supper? How many coins do we
have?"

Ruari didn't know if Mahtra grieved at all. She couldn't
cry the way he and Zvain tried not to cry. Her eyes weren't
right for tears, she said, and the tone of her voice never varied, no matter how many questions she asked. Ruari didn't
care about anything, including Farl, which was where they
were headed. They were only going there because the two
templars who got them out of Codesh said they shouldn't
go back to Urik and the road to Farl was right there in front
of them when the templars said it. Without Mahtra's questions, Ruari wouldn't have given a single thought to where
they'd stay once they got to the village, or whether he ever
ate another meal.

Mahtra was living proof that life went forward and that
there was no use looking back. Her questions demanded
answers—his answers. If Zvain had become their wisdom,
Ruari discovered that he'd become their leader.

"We're poor," he said. "Not so poor that we'll starve right away, but—it's this way: I know the supplies we'd need to have to get back to Quraite: three riding kanks, at least seven water jugs, food for ten days, some other stuff, for safety's sake. That's what Kashi, Yohan, and I always had, but we had our own bugs, our own jugs, and Kashi did the buying when we needed food. I don't know how much going home will cost, or whether we have enough to get there."

"Couldn't you sell that?" Mahtra suggested, pointing at his staff.

Zvain offered a different idea before Ruari could answer. "I could—well—*lift* a bit. I got good at that." The boy dug deep in the wide hem of his shirt. He produced a little lion carved from rusty-red stone. "I lifted this right under Hamanu's nose!"

"*Lord* Hamanu," Ruari insisted, then, more seriously: "Wind and fire, Zvain—think of the trouble you could have gotten us into!"

"We'd be better off if I had," the boy replied, and there was nothing either one of them could say after that.

But nothing seemed to stanch Mahtra's questions. "Can I hold it? Keep it?"

"What for?" Ruari asked. "We get caught with something from Hamanu's palace and—" He mimed the drawing of a knife blade across his throat.

Mahtra took the figurine from Zvain's hand and held it up to her mask. "We won't get caught with it, if it's cinnabar."

Ruari cocked his head, asking a silent question of his own.

"I'll chew it up and swallow it," she replied. "If it's cinnabar. I can't tell through my mask. If it is, the more I swallow, the better I can protect myself. Lord Hamanu gave me plenty—" she patted a little pouch at her waist. "But, without Pavek, I don't think I can have too much cinnabar."

Zvain made disgusted, gagging noises, and Ruari's first

instinct was to do the same thing. But he couldn't act on his first instincts, not anymore, no more than Pavek had.

Ruari's throat tightened, but he beat back that instinct, too, and all the memories. He forced himself to think of the crunching sounds he'd heard before the power passed through him and the passage caved in. If they had to choose between selling the staff Hamanu had given him or the red lion Zvain had stolen, Ruari supposed they should keep the lion. He could fashion himself another staff, he had a good carving knife now, thanks to Pavek, but Mahtra's ability to transform the air around them into a mighty, sweeping fist was a better weapon.

"Keep it, then. Do whatever you do with it."

"If it's cinnabar."

He nodded. He'd taken ten strides, maybe twenty, without mourning Pavek. He'd strung his thoughts together and made a decision—the decision Pavek would have made, he hoped, and with that hope his defenses crumbled. The grief, the aching emptiness, overwhelmed him ten times, maybe twenty, stronger than before.

Unable to hide or halt the sudden flow of tears, Ruari sat down on the edge of the road. He wanted to be alone, but Zvain was beside him in an instant, leaning against his shoulder, dampening his sleeve. He wanted to be alone, but he put his arm around the human boy instead, thinking that was what Pavek would have done. If Mahtra had knelt or sat beside him, Ruari would have comforted her the same way, but she stood behind them, keeping watch.

"There's someone coming this way," she said finally. "Coming from Codesh."

With a sigh, Ruari got to his feet, hauling Zvain up as well. There was a solitary traveler on the road far behind them, and behind the traveler, a swath of green fields becoming the dusty yellow of the barrens. The ring road had curved toward Farl; Codesh had disappeared.

"Come on. We've got to keep walking."

"Where?"

The questions had started again.

"Where, after Farl? What are we going to do?"

He said nothing, nothing at all, and Zvain asked:

"Is it kanks and Quraite, or do we go somewhere else?"

It was easier for Ruari to get angry with Zvain's adolescent whine. "*Where else?*" Ruari shouted. "Where else could we go? Back to Urik? Do you think we could just set ourselves up in that templar-house? Damn it, Zvain, *think* first, before you open your mouth!"

Zvain's mouth worked soundlessly. His nostrils flared, his eyes overflowed, and, with an agonized wail, he spun on his heel and started back to Codesh at a blind, stumbling run. Ruari hesitated long enough to curse himself, then effortlessly made up the distance between them.

"I'm sorry—"

Zvain wriggled out of his grasp, but he was finished with running and merely stood, arms folded, head down, and jaw clenched in a sad, sullen sulk, just out of Ruari's reach.

"I said I was sorry. Wind and fire, I hurt inside, too. I want him here. I want this morning back; I'd make him take that damn gold medallion—"

"Was that why—?" Zvain's head came up. His cheeks were slick with tears.

"That's why Hamanu closed his eyes. Don't you remember, in that room with the black rock, Hamanu warned Pavek that if he didn't take the medallion, he wouldn't listen. He gave Pavek another chance to take it this morning; the medallion was sitting on top of his clothes. I saw Pavek leave it behind. Damn—" Ruari's voice broke.

"Not your fault," Zvain said quickly before his voice got lost in sobbing. He lunged at Ruari, giving the half-elf an embrace that hurt and dulled their other pain. "Not your fault, Ru. Not our fault."

Mahtra joined them, not to grieve, but to say: "The man behind us is getting closer. Shouldn't we be walking?"

The answer was yes, and just as the ring road curves had hidden Codesh, they brought Farl into view. Farl, a place where Ruari had never been, the first place he'd go *after* Pavek. And after Farl? He had to decide.

"I say we find ourselves kanks as soon as we get there, and head home—to Quraite."

"Whatever you say," Zvain agreed without enthusiasm.

But then, none of them had any enthusiasm. Ruari wasn't looking forward to returning to Quraite, to telling Kashi their misadventures, but he couldn't think of anywhere else to go.

"You have Kakzim's map," Mahtra reminded him, as if she'd heard Ruari's thoughts. "We could go to a place we've never been."

"The map's a trap," Ruari replied.

Zvain shot back: "Pavek didn't want to see it, didn't want to hear about it. Pavek thought it wasn't a trap. He thought it was worthwhile."

Pavek wasn't thinking; Pavek was dying! Ruari wanted to say, and didn't. He fished the map out of his shirt-hem instead and unrolled it as they walked. If the toothy shape near the right side of the bark scrap was a mountain . . . if the smudge above the shape was not a smudge, but smoke . . . then the mountain might be the Smoking Crown Volcano, and the circle in the lower right-hand corner might be Urik. A black line connected the circle and the mountain. The line continued leftward and upward in jagged segments, each separated with symbolic shapes: wavy lines that might be water, smaller mountains, smaller circles, and others Ruari couldn't immediately interpret. The black line ended at the base of a black tree, the only symbol that was the same color as the line and was, on the map, as large as the Smoking Crown.

And Pavek hadn't wanted to see the map, hadn't wanted to hear anything about it.

Because he didn't want to tell Hamanu where they'd gone?

It was possible. Pavek took risks. Today, he'd raised a guardian no druid dreamed existed, and he'd done it because it might keep them alive. A year ago, he'd surrendered himself into druid hands because getting rid of Laq was more important than his own life.

Go home and plant . . . a big, ugly lump of a tree. And carve my name into its bark.

"Later," Ruari said aloud, drawing concern from his companions, "we'll follow the map, somehow, wherever it takes us—all the way to that big black tree."

* * * * *

He'd fallen asleep in the wrong position, lying on a bed that was harder than dirt. Every joint in his body ached and complained when he yawned himself awake—

But he was awake.

Pavek knew he had awakened, knew, moreover, that he was alive. He remembered Codesh and sitting with his hand in a water bucket, hoping to die before Hamanu caught up with him. Those were his last memories, but he hadn't died. At least Pavek didn't remember dying, although the dead weren't supposed to remember—that was the whole reason he'd had his hand in the bucket: he hadn't wanted to be alive—feeling or remembering—when Hamanu found him.

Could he have died and been restored to life? Hamanu could transform life into death in countless ways, but as Pavek understood histories, legends, and dark rumors, the Lion-King could not transform death into life. A wise man wouldn't bet his life against a sorcerer-king's prowess. Pavek was willing to bet he hadn't died—

Though he'd almost be willing to bet that Hamanu hadn't found him. What Pavek saw when he opened his eyes seemed almost like Quraite: a one-room house with woven-wicker walls and a thatched roof. The door was shut, the window, open. From the very hard bed he could see leafy branches and cloudless sky.

Pavek thought about standing up, but first things first: there'd been a reason the last thing he remembered was his hand dangling in a bucket. It hadn't hurt then, despite the damage when the medallion burst apart, and still didn't. After taking a deep breath, Pavek lifted his left arm into the sunlight and, in complete amazement, rotated it front to back. Palm-side or knuckle-side, his mangled hand had been restored. Movement and sensation had been restored as well. Each finger bent obediently to touch the tip of his thumb.

He'd been healed before—several times at the templar infirmary and once in an unknown underground sanctuary—and had the scars to prove it. But there were no scars on Pavek's hand—at least not the scars he expected. Side-by-side comparison of his right hand with his left revealed a mind-boggling symmetry: every scar he'd ever gotten on his right hand was now duplicated on his left, and the left-hand scars he used to have were gone.

All healing was spellcraft of one sort or another, but this was spellcraft beyond Pavek's imagining. He rose from the bed, went to the window where the light was better—and his hands remained the same, *exactly* the same, but mirror images of each other.

Pavek was alive, restored, and wise enough not to waste time questioning good fortune. Setting both hands on the window ledge, he leaned out for a better examination of his surroundings. There were walls, not fields, beyond the tree he'd seen from the bed, masonry walls built from four rows of man-high stones. The sounds that came over those walls, though faint, were the sounds of a city, of Urik. Pavek knew the walls of Urik as well as anyone who'd ever spent a quinth of nights standing watch by moonlight. He knew how the city was put together, and he knew that the only place he could be was inside the palace, which meant Hamanu, which meant he *had* died.

It was just as well Pavek wasn't a gambling man.

There were sandals resting on the dirt floor beside the bed and clothes, fine linen garments like the ones he'd ruined in Codesh, hung on a peg by the improbably rustic door. Pavek wasn't surprised to find a gold high templar's medallion hanging beneath them. When he'd finished dressing and raking his hair with his fingers—he didn't need a bath or a shave, which said something about either the amount of time that had passed since Codesh or the quality of care he'd received since then—he stuck his head through the golden noose and opened the door.

"You're awake at last!"

The voice came from a human man, about his own age and stature, but better looking, a man who slapped his hands against his thighs as he stood up from a solid stone bench.

"How do you feel? How's the hand?"

Pavek held it out and flexed the fingers. "Good as new . . . good as the other one."

A smile twitched across the stranger's lips. Pavek sighed and dropped to one knee.

"A thousand thanks, Great Lord and Mighty King. I am not worthy of such miracles."

"Good—I had doubts you'd ever agree with me about anything."

Still on a bent knee, Pavek stared at his left hand and shook his head. "Great King, I am grateful, but I am, and will always be, a thick-headed oaf of a man."

"But an honest oaf, which is rare enough around here. I am not blind, Lord Pavek. I know what is done in my name. I am everything you imagine me to be, and more besides. Elabon Escrissar did amuse me; I had great hopes for him. I have no hope for an honest oaf, and an honorable one in the bargain. By my mercy, Lord Pavek—could you not at least have taken a *look* at that map?"

A man couldn't fall very far when he was already on his knee, which was fortunate for Pavek. "Did I die, Great King? I don't remember. Was I already dead? The red-haired priest—I never learned his name—he didn't . . . You didn't . . ."

"I didn't what, Lord Pavek? *Look at me!*"

In misery and fear, Pavek met the Lion-King's eyes.

"Do you truly think I must slay a man to unravel his memories? Do you think I *must* leave him a gibbering idiot? Look at your hand again, Lord Pavek: that is what I can do. Did you die? Does it matter? You're alive now—and as thick-headed as ever.

"A thousand years, Lord Pavek. A thousand years. I knew how to kill a man when I was younger than you. I've killed more than even I can count; *that* is the essence of boredom, Lord Pavek. Every death is the same; every life is different. Every hand is different."

Pavek swallowed hard, grinned anxiously, and said: "Mine aren't, Great King—not anymore."

Hamanu roared with laughter. His human disguise slipping further away with each unrestrained guffaw. The Lion-King grew taller, broader, becoming the black-maned, yellow-eyed tyrant of Urik's outer walls. He laughed until, like a lesser, mortal man, his ribs ached and, clutching at his side, he hobbled back to his bench.

The ground shuddered when his weight hit the stone.

"You amuse me, Lord Pavek. No, you didn't die. You came close, but that little priest wouldn't let you go. When I got there, he had hold of you by your mother's love, and nothing more. I gave him my thanks, Lord Pavek, and *he* had the wit to accept what I offered. Oh, between us, we could have yanked you back, if you'd already slipped away, but it wouldn't have been worth it. Believe me, I know."

While Pavek blinked, the leonine Hamanu vanished and a human one took his place. He was older than he'd seemed when Pavek walked through the wicker door: a man nearing the end of his prime, weathered and weary, with scars on his face and a touch of gray in his dark hair.

"I was born in there," this mortal Hamanu said. His voice was soft; Pavek had to stretch forward to hear it. "I took my first steps in the ancestor of that house when it stood a day's ride north of here, before the troll army swept through, destroying everything in its path—except me. I was in the

Scorcher's army. Later, much later, when the trolls were a memory—" Hamanu's plain brown eyes narrowed, and he seemed to be looking at a point behind Pavek's head, a point far-removed in place and time. His voice seemed to echo from that distant, imaginary place. "*I went to the Pristine Tower because trolls destroyed this house. I won the war I was made to fight; the war the others could not win.* Troll *means nothing to you*—" The king looked directly at Pavek again. "When the war was over and the dust, oh the dust, had settled, I rebuilt my house and I tried to bring back the wives and children the trolls had slain. They weren't the same."

A sense of loss, preserved for a millennium, filled the courtyard where they sat.

"I'm sorry. I never thought . . . never imagined. . . . We're taught you're a god: immortal, omnipotent, unchanging. I doubted, but . . ." Words fell off Pavek's tongue until he managed to choke them off with a groan.

"Did you? What did you doubt?" Another shimmering transformation, and the king was a beautiful youth. "My power? My eternity? Come—tell me your doubts. Let me reassure your faith."

Pavek remained where he was, mute and kneeling.

"Very well, doubt it all. Power has limits. Eternity has a beginning and an end. I was born no different than you. I have died many times—*Look at me, Lord Pavek!*"

Unable to disobey, Pavek straightened his back and neck. The human-seeming Hamanu was gone, replaced by the apparition who'd terrified them all in the audience chamber when he examined the stains on Ruari's staff. The long serpentine neck curved toward him. The whiplike tongue flashed out to touch the scar on his cheek. A blast of hot, reeking air followed the tongue.

"*See me as I truly am, Lord Pavek. Borys the Dragon is dead; Hamanu the Dragon is about to be born!*"

Another searing blast enveloped Pavek as he knelt, but, hot as it was, it wasn't enough to break the cold terror paralyzing his lungs.

"A thousand years I held back the changes. I hoarded every templar's spell; I kept Urik safe from change, Lord Pavek. Every mote of my magic is a grain of sand falling through the glass, marking the time until the change, when a dragon must be born. This shape you see is the sum of my changes: a thousand years more than a man, but ten thousand . . . twenty thousand lives less than a dragon. That incarnate fool, Kalak, would have sacrificed all the lives in his city to birth the dragon within him. I will not sacrifice Urik to any dragon. Urik is mine and I will protect it—but each day that I do nurtures the dragon within me, hastening the moment when it must be born."

The king stretched his long neck toward the bloody sun. His massive, fanged jaws opened and, expecting a mighty roar or a blast of fire, Pavek closed his eyes. But the only sound was a sibilant curse. When Pavek reopened his eyes, Hamanu in his most familiar leonine form had reappeared.

"You can appreciate my dilemma."

Pavek could understand that Urik was in danger either from its own sorcerer-king's transformation or from one of the other remaining sorcerer-kings, but true appreciation of the Lion-King's dilemma was beyond him. He nodded though, since anything else might provoke another transformation.

"Good, then you will be pleased and willing to tell me everything you know about this *thing* you raised, this druid *guardian,* this *aspect,* this *semblance* that formed in Codesh."

Pavek had been willing to bleed to death rather than respond to that request. He wished for Telhami's wisdom and remembered Telhami implying that she and Urik's king had once been more than friends.

"Great King, I can hardly tell you more than Telhami must have told you. I am a neophyte in the druid mysteries—no better than a third-rank regulator."

"Telhami said our cities were abominations. Gaping sores, she called them, where the natural order is inverted. She said that Urik obliterated the land from which it rose and swore no guardian could abide within my purview. I believed her then and all the years since, until you came back to Urik—not this time, but once before. Something stirred when you stood outside House Escrissar."

Once again, the blood drained from Pavek's face. Had all his memories been unraveled for his king's amusement? Every meager moment of triumph? Every defeat?

"*Yes, Lord Pavek,*" the Lion-King replied, his voice echoing in Pavek's ears, and between them as well. "*I know about House Escrissar.*" Then he smiled his cruel, perfect smile. "*I knew about it then; there was no need to probe deep into your past.*"

"Great King, what can I tell you that you don't already know?"

"How you raised a guardian that Telhami swore couldn't exist."

"Great King, I can't answer that. That first time outside House Escrissar, I didn't know what I'd done. In Codesh, I was desperate," Pavek didn't mention why. "And, suddenly—without my doing anything—the guardian was there."

"If despair is the proper incentive . . ." The Lion-King extended his claws. "Raise your guardian now."

Pavek, who had not yet risen from his knees, placed his identical palms flat on the ground. If despair were the necessary condition for druidry, he should have been able to raise ten guardians.

"Tell your guardian the Lion of Urik, the King of Mountain and Plain, requires assurance that it is not a pawn of my enemies."

In Codesh and last year, when they searched for Akashia outside the walls of House Escrissar, the guardian power had leapt into Pavek's body, but here, in the palace, in heart of Urik's heart, the land was empty—obliterated, exactly as Telhami had described it. The trees that shaded them were sterile sticks, engendered with Hamanu's magic and sustained in the same way. The stones in the walls were each a tomb for an aspect of a larger, long-vanished guardian.

Nothing Pavek did quickened the land: no druid magic, not even the simplest evocation of water, could be wrought where he knelt. He sat back on his heels.

"There's nothing," he muttered, omitting Hamanu's royal title. "Just *nothing*, as if there never was anything at all."

"Yet that night outside House Escrissar, something stirred, and in Codesh, you raised an invincible creature out of dust and offal."

Pavek nodded. "And now there's nothing. No guardian, no aspect, nothing at all. Druid magic should not work in Urik, Great King—yet I know it has, and not only for me. I don't understand; I must be doing something wrong. A thousand pardons, Great King. I am not Telhami; I don't have her wisdom or strength. Perhaps if I tried again, if I went back to House Escrissar—"

"Possibly," Hamanu agreed and frowned as well. The retribution Pavek feared seemed unlikely as the Lion-King scratched his chin thoughtfully with a sharp, black claw. "Telhami *could* get her spellcraft to work elsewhere in Urik, but never when I was nearby. Even so, she could work the lesser arts of druidry, never the great ones, never a guardian. It is a mystery you and I will unravel when you return to Urik."

Pavek sat still a moment, savoring the life he still had before asking: "When I return?"

"Kakzim lives. The Codeshites we interrogated said that Kakzim incited them to their rebellion, then left them to their fate. Some saw him and another halfling running away through the smoke. You will find them and bring them back, Lord Pavek. Justice is the responsibility of the high bureau, your responsibility."

"Did the Codeshites know where Kakzim might have gone?"

The Lion-King held out his hand. A knotted string appeared; it hung from a black claw's tip and held, within the knot, a few strands of pale blond hair. "A team of investigators searched what remained of their rented quarters.

They found this caught in the doorjamb. Hold it where the wind does not blow, and it will lead you to the halflings."

He took the string carefully, respectfully, but without quite concealing his skepticism. "How can you be certain? Hair is hair. My friends searched those quarters, too."

"And found that map you refused to look at." King Hamanu sighed heavily. "Mahtra has no hair. Both Ruari and Zvain have hair that's too dark, and all of them are too tall, unless Ruari was on his hands and knees when he hit his head. That is halfling hair, Pavek, and it will lead you to Kakzim. Guard it carefully. You begin your search tomorrow; kanks are waiting for you at Khelo. A double maniple from the war bureau awaits you there as well. The Codesh survivors volunteered; the others are solid veterans. We will make our own search for Urik's guardian when you return; you *will* return, Pavek, with Kakzim or proof of his death."

Orders had been given—orders the Lion-King had intended to give Pavek from the beginning, no doubt. Hamanu began to walk toward the wall and a door Pavek hadn't noticed before.

Acting on impulse, which had gotten him into trouble so often before, Pavek called out to him: "Great King—"

Lord Hamanu turned and showed an unfriendly face. "What don't you understand now, Lord Pavek?"

"My friends—Ruari, Zvain, and Mahtra—what happened to them?"

"If you spent half as much time thinking about yourself as you think about others, Pavek, you'd go farther in this world. Your friends escaped from Codesh before I arrived. They went to Farl. Five days ago, Ruari sold the staff I gave him to a herder; since then, I do not know. You know my dilemma, Pavek: magic hastens the dragon. I will not risk Urik to find any one man—not Kakzim, not a friend of yours. If it suits you, you may search for them after we've raised the guardian."

"It suits me, Great King," Pavek said to the great king's back.

★   ★   ★   ★   ★

With the purse Ruari had gotten from Pavek before he died, the silver he got in exchange for his staff, the handful of coins Zvain insisted he "found" beneath a pile of rubbish in a Farl alley, and the three silver coins Mahtra got he-didn't-ask-where, they had enough money to purchase three unimpressive kanks from the village pound and outfit them with shabby saddles, peeling harnesses, and other supplies of dubious quality.

Six days west of Farl, they were down to two kanks. Tempers were short, and they spent a part of each day arguing whether any of the landmarks they passed matched those on their white-bark map. If it weren't for Ruari's fundamentally sound sense of distance and direction, they'd have been hopelessly lost. Each time they set off in a direction the three of them eventually agreed was wrong, he'd been able to get them back to a place they recognized.

The sun was at its height in the heavens and there wasn't a sliver of shade anywhere—except in the lee of the same three boulders where they'd camped last night.

"I told you these rocks matched the three dots," Ruari grumbled as he dismounted. He hobbled the bug before offering a hand to either Mahtra or Zvain, who rode together on the other one.

"They're awfully small," Mahtra said.

"All right, they *don't* match the three dots—and we've followed Kakzim's damned map into the middle of nowhere. In case you haven't noticed, we're running out of land!" Ruari swung his arm from due north to due west where the horizon was a solid line of jagged peaks. "The circle is north of here, between us and those mountains, or it's not anywhere!"

"You don't have to shout," Zvain complained as he jumped down from the kank's saddle.

Mahtra tried to make peace. "We'll go north next. We always go two directions before we settle on one."

"At least two."

Ruari got the last word as he hobbled the second kank and let it go foraging. The surviving kanks were doing better than their riders. Bugs could eat just about anything that wasn't sand or rock; people were more particular. They'd run out of village food two days ago. Ruari didn't consider it a serious problem; he'd had little trouble hunting up a steady supply of bugs, grubs, and lizards—more than enough to keep the three of them healthy, but Zvain was fussy, and Mahtra truly seemed to become ill on the wriggly morsels. She'd sooner forage with the kanks—which she did, after Ruari rationed out their water.

It was midafternoon before they were remounted and headed north. Ruari wasn't as well-organized as Pavek, and certainly wasn't as effective getting Mahtra and Zvain moving; he owed Pavek an apology—

The half-elf closed his eyes and pounded a tight fist against his thigh. Pavek's name hadn't crossed his mind since sunrise. He was ashamed that he'd forgotten his friend for so many hours and was grieved by the memories, once they returned. The downward spiral between shame and grief hadn't ended when Mahtra and Zvain both called his name.

"Look—" Mahtra extended her long, white arm.

Wisps of smoke rose through the seared air. They could be mirages—the sun's pounding heat made everything shimmer by late afternoon. But the smoke didn't shimmer, and it wasn't long before they saw other signs of habitation. Zvain prodded their bug's antennae, urging it to greater speed; Ruari did the same thing—until he got his kank far enough ahead to force the other one to a halt.

"Not so fast! We don't know what's up there, who's up there, or if they're going to be friendly to the likes of us." Wind and fire, he was sounding more like Pavek every time he opened his mouth. "This could *still* be a trap. We go in slow, and we go in cautious. Stay close together. Keep your heads down and eyes open. That's what Yohan would say—"

Pavek, too, but by unspoken agreement, they didn't mention his name. "Understand?"

They both said they did, and probably with the best of intentions. But strangers weren't common in this faraway corner of the Tablelands. A handful of folk came out to meet them while they were still a fair distance from the settlement. They were mostly human or half-elves, like himself—which was no assurance of welcome, especially considering that every one of them was armed with knives, swords, *and* spears. Mahtra drew the most stares; that was to be expected, but Ruari drew a surprising number himself. He had Pavek's metal knife and a greenwood staff lashed to the kank's saddle where it wouldn't do him any good in a fight.

Still, their kanks could outrun all but the fastest elves. Ruari prodded his bug to a halt and let the strangers come to them.

"What brings you three to Ject?" one of the humans asked.

Before Ruari could voice a suitably cautious answer Zvain announced: "We followed a map!" and Mahtra added: "We're looking for two halflings, and a big black tree."

THIRTEEN

So much for keeping their heads down and their mouths shut.

Mahtra didn't know any better. She evidently thought when someone older asked her a question, she had to answer. But Zvain—? Ruari couldn't excuse his human friend for blurting out their secrets. Zvain knew the wisdom of discretion and outright deceit. He'd advised it often enough while they were still in Urik's purview. Once they were on the barrens, though, following that scrap of bark Ruari still devoutly believed was a trap, Zvain's common sense and wariness had evaporated.

The woman who'd asked them their business gave Mahtra and Zvain another eyeballing before returning her attention to Ruari. She was human and standing; he was half-elf and mounted on a kank's high saddle, yet she successfully looked down her nose at him, conveying a wealth of disdain in the arch of her brow.

"You look a tad underprepared for the mountains and the forests," she said dryly. "Do you even know where you are?"

Without hesitation, Ruari shook his head. Maybe there was more of Mahtra in him than he'd thought.

"Ject," she said.

He wasn't sure if that was her name, the name of the settlement, or a local insult—until he remembered someone had greeted them with the name as they rode up.

She grabbed his bug's antenna and got it moving forward. He could have seized the bug's mind with druidry, thwarting her intentions without twitching a muscle of his own. That would have been almost as stupid as mentioning the map or the halfling they were looking for. There was an aura around magicians of any stripe, an indefinable something that set druids, priests, defilers, and even templars slightly apart. Ruari didn't get that feeling from any of the strangers around him. He'd need a better reason than stubborn pride before he gave his own limited mastery away.

Ject was about Quraite's size, counting the buildings or people, but similarities ended there. Costly stone and wood were common here on the edge of the Tablelands. Ject's buildings looked as solid as Urik's walls, yet seemed as hastily thrown up as any wicker hut in Quraite. Striped and spotted hides from animals Ruari couldn't name cured on every wall. Skulls with horns and skulls with fangs hung above every door or window. Weapons, mostly spears and clubs, stood ready in racks outside the largest building. Taken with the hides and the skulls, they gave Ject the air of a community engaged in perpetual conflict.

And perhaps it was. The people of Ject had to eat, and there were no fields or gardens anywhere, just barrens and scrub plants up to the back walls of the outer ring of buildings. Ruari had heard tales of four-fingered giths who ate nothing but meat and the gladiators of Tyr who feasted on the flesh of those they defeated, but most folk required a more varied diet to remain healthy. If the Jectites were like most folk, they had to be getting their green foods and grain from somewhere else, possibly from a forest, if not from a field.

The human woman had mentioned mountains, which Ruari could see, and forests, which he could not. Beyond the mountains, there might be forests where the Jectites got their food, where the creatures whose hides and skulls were fastened to Jectite houses lived free, and where trees with bark smooth enough and pale enough to serve as parchment might grow.

For the first time since they'd left Codesh, Ruari thought they might have come to the right place. He wished Pavek were with them to savor the triumph—and to negotiate with the Jectites for the guide they'd need for the next step in the journey. But Pavek wasn't here. Ruari stared at the mountains, oblivious to everything else and waiting for the ache to subside.

By the time Ruari was himself again, they'd circled Ject's largest building and stopped in front of a warren of animal pens. Kanks, inixes, and such domestic animals were kept in one set of enclosures, while others held living examples of the beasts whose hides decorated the Jectite walls.

"Kirre," the human woman said when Ruari became enraptured by an eight-legged leonine captive.

The kirre had windswept horns to protect the back of its head as well as the more usual leonine teeth, a double allotment of claws, and wicked barbs protruding from its tail. Its fur was striped with black and a coppery hue that matched Ruari's skin and hair. Similar hides were curing on the front walls. Ruari imagined the strength it took to slay such a beast, the skill it took to capture one, but mostly he imagined the feel of its fur beneath his fingers and the throaty rumble of its purr.

"They're the kings of the forest ridge," the woman elaborated. "Are you so sure you want to climb up there looking for halflings and black trees?"

Ruari forgot to answer. As a half-elf, he had one unique trait he owed to neither of his parents: an affinity for wild animals, which his druidry complemented and enhanced. At that moment, deep in the throes of his own grief, he was especially vulnerable to the mournful glare in the kirre's eyes. Had he been alone, he would have been off his bug and reaching fearlessly inside the pen to scratch the cat's forehead.

But Ruari wasn't alone, and he wrenched his attention away. When he did the kirre threw itself against the walls of its pen and made an eerie sound, neither a growl nor a roar, that raised bumps all over Ruari's skin.

The woman gave him a contemptuous glance. "Half-elves," she muttered with a shake of her head. "You and your pets. Don't even think about cozying up to this one. She's bound for the games at Tyr. Turn her loose or tame her, and we'll send you instead."

Ruari's mortification turned to anger, though there was nothing he could do for himself or the kirre who was doomed to bloody death at a Tyrian gladiator's hand—and to be eaten thereafter. The thought sickened him and hardened him. Grabbing the nearly empty packs from behind the saddle, Ruari swung down from the bug's back and led the way toward the front of the large building.

In Quraite, he kept a passel of kivits, furry and playful predators about the size of the kirre's head. He kept them hidden in his grove where few ever witnessed the half-elven affection he lavished on them. When he returned to his grove, he'd still cherish them and care for them, but as he left the keening kirre behind, Ruari vowed that he'd return to Ject some day to bond with a kirre—and set one free, if he could.

The largest building in Ject turned out to be a tavern open to the sunset sky and vast enough to seat every resident, with benches to spare.

"We're traders and brokers," the woman explained. "And you've come at a slow time. Our stocks are down. Most of our rangers are out hunting. All our runners are out making deliveries and taking orders. If you're from the cities and you want something from the forest, we can get it. If you're from the forest and you want something from the cities, we can get that, too. There's nothing we can't provide, for the right price. But for ourselves—we stay here year round, and this is all we need."

She swept an arm around. Huge casks were piled in a pyramid against one wall. Long tables and benches filled the tavern's one room.

"What about you, my copper-skinned friend? What do you need? Supplies? You're looking a mite *empty.*"

She prodded the packs he had hanging down from his shoulder and, not accidentally, ran callused fingertips along his forearm. He'd have gotten smacked hard, on the hand and probably on the cheek, if he'd been so brazen with a Quraite woman, but when the tables were turned, Ruari was too astonished to do or say anything.

"A guide? I know my way around."

She headed for one of the tables and clearly intended that Ruari follow her. He paused before committing himself and turned back toward the open door.

Mahtra had her arm around a mul whose shoulders were so heavily muscled that his head seemed to rest on them, not his neck. The mul was twirling the long fringes of Mahtra's black gown through his thick fingers. She'd done the same thing in Farl the one night they stayed in that village, but no matter how many times Ruari told himself that Mahtra was *eleganta*, and that she could take care of herself better than he or Zvain, the sight made him uncomfortable.

What was it that Pavek had said to him the night Mahtra arrived in Quraite? *You're too pretty. You wouldn't survive a day on the streets of Urik.* Ruari was hoping he'd survive an evening in Ject. The woman beckoning him to the empty bench opposite her had already said she'd trade anything, anywhere for the right price. She was sending the kirre to Tyr, but she'd threatened to send him in its place. Ruari wondered where else she might send him for the right price and resolved that he'd drink nothing in this place, not even the water.

In the time it took him to reach that decision, Mahtra had disappeared with her mul. Zvain was nowhere to be seen; Ruari hadn't seen the boy since he'd first spotted the kirre. Climbing the walls of Elabon Escrissar's yellow-and-red house hadn't filled the half-elf with as much dread as the friendly folk of Ject had. He made his way to the empty bench and sat down across from the grinning woman, knowing he was on his own.

"Pleasure first; trade later. What'll it be?" she asked.

"Ale? Broy? The halflings make a blood-wine that's sweet as honey and kicks like a molting erdland."

Ruari whispered: "Ale." He couldn't stomach the thought—much less the sight—of the other two beverages, even if he wasn't going to drink them.

The woman snapped her fingers loudly and shouted for two mugs of something that didn't sound like ale. He felt betrayed, but said nothing. They stared at each other until the bucket-sized containers arrived in the fists of a weary, one-eyed dwarf. The human woman smacked her mug against his, sloshing some of the foamy brew onto the table, then she took a swig. Ruari pretended to do the same.

"So—you've got a map that shows the way to a black tree? Even with a map, there's a lot of treacherous country between here and there, especially for a lowlander like you. Kirres may be the kings of the ridge, but there're a lot of other ways to die up there. And the halflings themselves—"

Suddenly she was jabbering away in a language—Ruari supposed it was Halfling—that was full of chirps and clicks as well as singsong syllables.

"Didn't think so," she proclaimed and took another long pull at her mug. "Negotiating with halflings is a tricky pass, *if* you know their tongue—which you don't. You're going to need a guide, my coppery friend. And not just any guide, someone who knows the ridge well. Let me see your map, and I might be able to tell you who to hire."

It appeared that Mahtra and Zvain weren't the only ones who thought the map was real. Ruari decided he must look very young and very naive. Did she think he didn't remember the looks she'd given him while he was still astride the bug, or her threats? But even as his pride raised his hackles, he could fairly hear Pavek's voice at the base of his skull, telling him that some battles could be won without a fight. At least without an obvious fight.

He fumbled with his mug. "Would you?" he asked with a nervous smile. The smile was forced; the nervousness wasn't. There were no taverns in Quraite, and he'd learned his knavery from his elven cousins, who'd misled him many times before. "It's so hard to know who to trust. I guess I have to start somewhere—" The mug overturned, drenching him from the waist down in a sticky, golden brew— which was *not* anything Ruari had intended to do, though it worked to his advantage when the woman drained her own mug before demanding refills from the tapster.

After a certain point and a certain amount of ale, a human mind—or any other mind—became as suggestible as a kank's. Ruari had a lot to learn about mind-bending and druidry both, but he'd had a lot of experience lately with bugs. A few rays of sunlight still streaked the open sky above their table when Ruari caught his first predatory thought and wove it back into the woman's mind. The stars were bright from one roofbeam to the other and there were two empty pitchers between them on the table when Ruari figured he'd learned as much as he could.

She laid her head atop her folded arms when he stood up. The tapster caught his eye. Ruari joined him by the pyramid of casks.

"The lady—" He pointed to the woman whose name he hadn't learned. "Take care of her, please? She said she'd pay for everything."

"Mady?" the tapster replied with evident disbelief.

"On my honor, that's what she swore."

The tapster's eyes made the journey from Ruari to the woman and back again. " 'Tain't like her."

Ruari shrugged. "She said she wasn't feeling well. I guess the ale didn't agree with her."

"Aye—" the tapster agreed, rubbing his chin thoughtfully. "Maybe so. Didn't give you no problems now, did it?"

"Not at all," Ruari said and hurried out the door where he figured his problems would begin in earnest. "Zvain? Mahtra?" he whispered urgently into the darkness.

With what he'd learned from the woman, Mady, Ruari thought that a bit of druidry and his innate ability to follow the lay of the land could get them through the mountains and into the forest. He was less certain about the halflings. Mady had said the local halflings weren't cannibals, they merely sacrificed strangers to appease the forest spirits, and held celebration feasts afterward if the sacrifices had been accepted. It was too fine a distinction for him to swallow comfortably, but he'd deal with halflings when he had to, not before.

First, he had to find his friends and get out of Ject before Mady woke up.

"Mahtra? Zvain?"

The world was edged in elven silver as his eyes adjusted to the darkness. Ordinary colors vanished, replaced by the shimmering grays of starlight. Ruari could see the buildings with their hanging hides and skulls and brilliant candlelight seeping through cracked shutters. He could have seen anything moving from his feet to the farthest wall of the farthest building, but he couldn't see Mahtra or Zvain.

Growing anxious and fearing he might have to leave without them, Ruari started toward the pens where they'd left the kanks. The kirre started keening once it caught his scent. He almost missed someone calling his name.

"Ruari! Over here!"

It was Zvain, hiding behind a heap of empty casks between the animal pens and the tavern. Ruari dared to hope the shadow crouched beside Zvain was Mahtra, but that hope was dashed when he realized the shadow was standing and not crouched at all. Gray nightvision sometimes played tricks on a color-habituated mind. Ruari couldn't make sense out of what he saw: The stranger was a bit too tall and bulky to be a halfling. Its head was covered with wild hair that fell below its shoulders, so it couldn't be a hairless dwarf. He was about to decide Zvain had found another New Race individual when the stranger reached up to scratch its hair and pulled a dead animal off its bald scalp.

The stranger was a dwarf, a dwarf wearing a cap Ruari didn't want to see by the light of day.

"I solved all our problems, Ru," Zvain exalted, urging the dwarf forward. "This is Orekel. He says he can get us to the black tree."

It was true that Ruari's trousers were still damp and he smelled of sweat and ale, but the air around Orekel was almost certainly flammable. Ruari shook the dwarf's hand tentatively—and without inhaling—then retreated. Considering what he'd gone through to get free of Mady, Orekel was no improvement.

"We got it all figured, Orekel an' me," Zvain continued, unfazed by Ruari's silent displeasure. "All we have to do is give Orekel our kanks—he'll use them to settle his credit with the tapster in there, an' then he'll be our guide. It's a good deal, Ru—we can't take the bugs into the mountains anyway. Orekel's gone 'cross the mountains and into the forests a lot of times. You've got to hear the stories he tells! He says he can find anything up there—"

"Back up," Ruari interrupted. "You said we give him our kanks? How're we supposed to get home without our bugs?"

"Not a problem," Zvain said before turning to the dwarf. "You tell him, Orekel—"

"*Gold*," the dwarf said, grabbing Ruari's wrist and pulling on it hard enough to make the half-elf stoop. "That black tree—she's full of gold and silver, rubies and emeralds. The great halfling treasure! Can you see it, my friend?"

Everyone in Ject wanted to be Ruari's friend. "No," he grumbled, trying to free his wrist.

But a dwarf's fist wasn't lightly shed. Orekel pulled harder, and Ruari sank to one knee to keep his balance. They were more nearly face-to-face now. Ruari got light-headed from the fumes.

"Look ye up there." Orekel directed Ruari's attention to the mountains. "You see those two peaks that're almost alike. We go between them, my friend, and down into the forest. There's a path, a path right through the heart of the halflings' sacred ground, right up to the trunk of that big, black tree. Can you see it now? As much treasure as your arms can carry. Buy your kanks back with halfling gold. Buy a roc and fly home. Can you see it, son?"

"No." This time Ruari twisted his wrist as he jerked it up and out of Orekel's grasp. "If you know all this, what's kept you from getting rich yourself?"

"*Ru—*" Zvain hissed and gave Ruari a kick in the shin as well.

Orekel shuffled his ghastly cap from one hand to the other, giving a good impression of abject embarrassment. "Oh, I would go. I would've gone a thousand times and made myself as rich as the dragon. But I get tempted, you see, when I've got a bit of jingly at my belt. I get just a mite tempted and the wine, oh, she tastes so sweet. The next I know, I'm out here with a sore head and the tapster, he's got a claim on me. I regret my temptation. Lord, I do regret it. Never again, says I to myself each and every time, then along comes some jingly and it's all the same. I do see my flaws. I do see them, but they rear up and grab me every time. But you've come at just the right time, son. I'm sober as the day is long and not in so deep with the tapster that your bugs won't buy me out. We'd be partners, the three of us."

Ruari retreated another step. "Zvain," he said with more politeness than he felt or needed. "Would you come over here, please?"

Zvain hesitated, but took the necessary steps. "What? Did you make a better bargain with that *woman?*"

"Look at him. Get a whiff of him—if you dare. Your Orekel's a complete sot! I wouldn't give him a *dead* bug—"

The boy stood his ground. "Did you make a better bargain?"

"I learned some things. I could get us to those two mountains—"

"Did you learn how to speak Halfling? Did you know they're particularly fond of sacrificing half-elves?"

He didn't, and he hadn't, but: "That makes no difference. Wind and fire—I don't like this place at all. I'd rather be lost in the elven market than spend the night here where everybody wants to help us. Do you trust him with your life, Zvain? 'Cause that's what it's going to come down to—"

Ruari's tirade got cut short by the sound of a thunderclap on a dry, cloudless night. Zvain cursed, the dwarf dived for cover, swearing it wasn't his fault, while Ruari stared at one of the buildings where dust puffed through the upper story shutters.

"That white-skinned friend of yours?" Orekel asked from his hiding place.

"Yes," Ruari answered absently. He wondered what else could go wrong, and Pavek's voice at the base of his skull told him to quit wondering.

"Who'd she go with?"

"A mul. Big shoulders. Huge shoulders."

"Bewt. That's bad. You want to leave Ject *now*, son. Right now. Forget about her. It's late. I'm sorry, son, but Bewt— he's got a temper. You don't want to be in his way, not at all, son. We'll just leave the kanks here and tip-toe out the back. Son, *son*—are you listening, son?"

"Ruari?" Zvain added his urgent whisper. "Ruari— what're we gonna do?"

He didn't know—but he didn't have to make any decisions just yet. Mahtra had emerged from the building and was running toward them on Ject's solitary street, with her fringes flying. She didn't have Ruari's nightvision; he had to shout her name to let her know where they were. Other folk were coming onto the street, looking around, looking at Mahtra as she ran toward them.

Orekel was gibbering. "She—Her—She must've killed him."

That was a possibility; they'd better be running before the Jectites found the mul's body. It had come down to a choice Ruari was loathe to make: Orekel and tiptoeing into the mountains, or a kank-back retreat into the barrens. He was sure he was going to regret it later, but Ruari chose Orekel over the kanks because someone had unharnessed them.

Without the proper saddles, there was no way to ride or control the bugs.

An enraged mul—Bewt—stumbled onto the street. "Where is she?" he bellowed, looking left and right. Muls inherited their dwarven parent's strength, but their human parent's sight.

He turned to the dwarf. "Get us out of here, *quick*. Before he spots us."

Orekel cast a worried glance toward the tavern.

"Now—if you want to go to the black tree. Get going. I'll catch up." On level ground, a half-elf could literally run circles around a dwarf. "Keep an eye out for Mahtra; she's got ordinary eyes, and I've got something to do before I go."

"*Ru—!*"

"It should improve our chances," he said to Zvain. "Now *go!*"

After one last glance at the tavern, Zvain and Orekel shuffled off through the maze of animal pens. Ruari had Pavek's steel knife out when Mahtra came to a stop at his side.

"I told him I wouldn't remove my mask. I *told* him."

Ruari thought the words were an apology as well as an explanation. It was hard to tell with Mahtra; her tone of voice never varied no matter the circumstances. Bewt might not have understood the risk he was running when she warned him, but then, he shouldn't have tried to take off her mask, either.

"It's all right," Ruari assured Mahtra as he knelt down beside the kirre's pen and went to work on the knotted cha'thrang rope the Jectites used to secure the door. "Zvain's gone ahead—around there—did you see him? He was with a dwarf." The kirre came over to investigate. It touched his hand with a soft-furred paw. There was some rapport between them, curiosity mostly on the kirre's part. Even a half-elf druid needed time to bond with a creature of such size and ferocity—time they didn't have.

"Did you see them? Zvain and the dwarf? They headed

for the mountains. It would be better if you went after them. I don't know what the kirre's going to do when I get this pen open."

"I saw a shadow," Mahtra replied, eyeing the kirre with discomfort. "Ruari—hurry. They're coming. I'm sure they saw me run around the tavern. I'm sorry."

Ruari could hear the Jectites, too. He sawed furiously at the tough fiber. Without steel, he wouldn't have had a chance. "Just go. Follow the dwarf and Zvain. I'll catch up."

"All right," Mahtra said, and then she was gone, without a word of encouragement or hope.

But that was her way; Ruari understood the expressions playing across the kirre's tawny eyes better than he'd ever understand the New Race woman.

"Stand away from that pen, boy!" one of the Jectites shouted from a distance. "Call your friends back. You've got deeds to answer for."

Some of the Jectites split away and backtracked toward the front of the tavern, where the racks of spears stood outside the door. The rest, though, weren't coming closer. Ruari gave a sharp push on the knife and sliced through the last cha'thrang fibers. He held the door shut with his knee.

Beautiful kirre, Ruari advanced his thoughts cautiously into the cat's predatory mind. *Brave kirre. Wild kirre. Free kirre.* He recalled the forest vision he'd received from the white-bark map. The kirre's ears relaxed. Her eyes began to close, and a purr rumbled in her throat.

Those folk. Ruari transplanted his vision of the Jectite villagers into her mind, though a kirre's night vision was probably better than his own. He didn't know how she was captured, so he recalled the battle on Quraite's dirt rampart and transplanted the moments when he'd been most frightened and enraged. The images resounded in the kirre's memory. She echoed spears and nets and the unintelligible yapping of men. *Those folk.* Ruari repeated, then opened the door.

The kirre knocked Ruari down as she sprang free. He

scrambled to his feet while the Jectites screamed and the mighty cat roared. Running toward his own freedom, Ruari assuaged his budding guilt with the thought that whatever happened to the kirre, it was better than death in the Tyr arena. He could still hear her roars when he spotted Mahtra, her shoulders beacon-bright by starlight, running across the barrens beyond the village.

"Wind and fire—cover yourself up!" he advised when he caught up with her.

Zvain and the dwarf, Orekel, were panting from exhaustion, trying to maintain the pace she set, her legs as spindly as an erdlu's and likely just as strong.

"We can slow down." Ruari dropped his own pace to a walk, then stopped altogether when Orekel continued to wheeze. "They're too busy right now to come after us. Catch your breath. How far until we're under cover?"

The dwarf raised a trembling arm toward the mountains. Ruari suppressed a curse. Without kanks, they'd need luck to reach the foothills before sunrise and pursuit. If the villagers were going to chase them, they would be on the barrens long before then.

There were no trails, no places to hide. Ruari pushed his companions as hard as he dared, as hard as Orekel could be pushed. Slow and steady, that was the dwarven way. Even a dwarf as out-of-condition as the drunken Orekel could walk forever, but push him to a trot and he was blowing hard after a hundred paces. If he'd complained once, Ruari would have left him behind, but Orekel stayed game throughout the night.

* * * * *

Orekel sobered up, too, sweating out the wine and ale. When it came to their distant goal of Kakzim and the black tree, Ruari still didn't give the dwarf a gith's thumb of trust, but in simpler matters—like picking a path across the stone wash that abutted the mountains when Orekel's ankles were as much at risk as theirs—he was willing to let the dwarf have the lead.

The stone wash that they reached shortly before dawn was a nasty piece of ground. A fan-shape of stones ranging in size between mekillots and a halfling's fist spilled out of a gap between the mountains. There was no guessing how many stones there were, or how long it had taken to accumulate them all, but the footing was especially treacherous for long-legged folk like Ruari and Mahtra.

Ruari longed for the staff he'd left leaning against the Ject kank pen, but the rest of the gear they'd abandoned was no great loss. The important things: strips of leather for repairing their sandals, sealed jars of astringent salve they'd been carrying since they left Quraite, a set of firestones, a flint hand axe for firewood, and a handful of other useful objects were in the saddle packs he still had slung over his shoulder. The most important thing of all—not counting the whitebark map that was still in his sleeve and not as useful as the Jectites would have hoped—was Pavek's steel-blade knife, too precious for the sack. Ruari kept it secured in its sheath, and the sheath firmly attached to his belt. He'd use it to whittle himself a new staff out of the first straight sapling they saw, though by then, they'd probably be out of the mountains, where he'd have less need of it.

By midmorning, they'd picked their way across the stone wash, with no worse souvenirs than a collection of scraped ankles. But the worst lay ahead in the steep gap itself. Orekel said it would be safer, if not easier, if they'd had some rope to string between them as they negotiated the narrow ledges and nearly sheer cliff-faces. On the other hand, they could take the treacherous passages as slowly as they needed to: looking back toward Ject, they saw no dust plumes on the barrens.

Zvain had the most trouble climbing the gap. The human boy had the shortest reach, the weakest arms. He fell once when his legs simply couldn't stretch between one foothold and the next. It wasn't a serious fall—he skidded maybe two

or three times his own height down to a ledge that was wide
enough to stop and hold him. He and Orekel lifted him
using Mahtra's long black shawl as an improvised rope
between them. Zvain had a couple of nasty-looking scrapes,
but his confidence had taken the worst damage and, once
again, Ruari found himself wishing with all his heart that
Pavek were still alive and with them.

Even Orekel tried to cheer the shattered boy, offering the
loan of his lucky cap.

"This little ves kept me alive more than once, son," the
dwarf insisted with the shaggy fur hanging over his hands
instead of his ears. "The ves—they're canny little beasts.
Made me think I was somewhere I wasn't. Tried to lure me
right into their den. Gnaw me down to the bone, they
would've. But I got me this'un by the tail here. Squeezed it
so hard it had to show me where I was. Then I ate it for my
dinner and turned its skin into my lucky cap. But you're
looking like you need more luck today than me, so's you
wear it."

It was a sincere if inept attempt to get them moving
again, and it raised the dwarf a notch in Ruari's opinion; but
it did nothing for Zvain, who'd flattened his back against the
cliff and refused to take another step.

"Just leave me here. I've gone as far as I can."

Ruari and Orekel tried all manner of encouragement and
pleading, but it was Mahtra who found the magic words:

"If this is as far as he can go, why can't we do what he
wants and leave him here? The sun's coming around. It's
going to be as hot as the Sun's Fist against these rocks in a
little while. Why should we all die because he doesn't want
to move again?"

"She's right about the sun," Orekel said softly to Ruari,
though Zvain was between them and could easily hear every
word. "We got to get moving, son, or we'll fry."

They were already parched and achy from a lack of water,
which Ruari could remedy with druidry. The mountains
were livelier than the Sun's Fist. If they'd had a bucket, he

could have filled it several times over. Without a bucket, he was hoping they'd last until he found a natural depression in the rocks. Here on the ledge, he had nothing but his cupped hands to hold the water he conjured out of the air.

"Come on, Zvain," Ruari pleaded.

Mahtra walked ahead. "I'm leaving. Finding Kakzim's more important."

Orekel shrugged. "The lady's right, son. We can't stay here." He followed Mahtra.

"Zvain—?"

The boy turned slowly away from Ruari and took a halting step in Orekel's direction.

Ruari found his hollow rock near the top of the gap. On his knees with his eyes closed and his arms outstretched, he recited the druid mnemonics for the creation of water in the presence of air and stone. The guardian aspect of this place was sharp-edged like the cliffs, and heavy like the mountains themselves. Ruari couldn't hold it the first time, and his spell did not quicken. The recitation ended with the hollow as dry and empty as it had begun. Grimly, the half-elf withdrew Pavek's knife from its sheath and made a shallow gash along his forearm. With his blood as a spark, the spell quickened and water began to collect in the hollow.

When the water was flowing steadily, Ruari sat back on his heels, letting the others drink while he recovered from the strain of druidry in an unfamiliar place.

"Magician, eh?" Orekel asked.

"Druid." Ruari offered the correct name for his sort of spellcraft.

"Don't kill no plants, do you?"

"Wind and fire, no—I'm not a defiler, nor a preserver. I'm not a wizard at all. My power comes from the land itself, all the aspects of it."

"So long as you don't suck things down to ash. Can't go taking nobody into the forest who'd turn 'em into ash."

"Don't worry."

Zvain had finished drinking. Orekel drank next, with

Ruari's permission, then Ruari himself drank his fill. When he'd finished, water was still bubbling in the hollow, faster than they could drink it down. It spilled over the top and seeped across the soles of his sandals while Mahtra stood and stared.

"You better drink," Ruari advised. "I can't do that again until sundown, and we don't have anything to carry water in."

"Not while you're here. Will you walk ahead? I'll catch up."

The boy and the dwarf didn't need a second invitation, but Ruari stayed on the opposite side of the hollow, his fists propped against his hips.

"After all this time, Mahtra—after all we've been through —do you truly think we're going to laugh or run away screaming?"

"You might," she replied with that smooth honesty that left more questions than answers in Ruari's mind.

The half-elf shook his head and lowered his arms. "Have it your way, then," he said and started walking. He'd gone several paces when she called out:

"Wait!"

Ruari turned around as she lowered her hands from the back of her head, bringing the mask with them. The mask was a good idea, he decided immediately. Her face was so unusual, he couldn't keep from staring. Mahtra had no nose to speak of, just two dark curves matched against each other. She didn't have much of a chin, either, or lips. Her mouth was tiny—about the right size for those red beads she liked so much—and lined with teeth he could see from where he stood. Yet for all its strangeness, Mahtra's face wasn't deformed. With her eyes and skin, an ordinary human face would have been deformed. Mahtra's face was her own.

"Different," Ruari acknowledged aloud. "Maybe different enough to warrant a mask—but it's your face—the face that belongs to the rest of you."

"Ugly," she retorted, and he saw that her mouth did not shape her voice and words.

"No—Pavek's . . . " He sighed and began again. "Pavek *was* ugly."

"Akashia said no. She said he wasn't an ugly man."

Another sigh. "Kashi said that, did she?" It was too late to consider what Kashi might have meant. "What did she say about me?"

"Nothing. Nothing at all—but we weren't talking about you."

"Take your time," he said to Mahtra, rubbing his forearm, though that wasn't the part of him that hurt. "I'll wait just up here. We can let the other two get a bit ahead."

Ruari found himself a rock that gave Mahtra her privacy and him a good view of Zvain and Orekel as they continued up the gap. He took out Pavek's knife, and wondered whose black hair had been braided around the hilt. Not Kashi's. Not anyone Ruari had ever heard Pavek mention. Maybe they would have gotten their affections straightened out if they'd had the time; maybe not. One thing for certain: he'd made a fool of himself trying to capture Kashi's attention and affection when Pavek had already secured it.

Mahtra reappeared with her mask in place, and together they continued up the gap, easily catching up with Zvain and Orekel. The sun came around in the middle of the afternoon, baking their bodies into numb silence. The three lowlanders—who'd never seen a mountain up close, much less climbed one—thought the gap would never end, but it did as the sun was setting. As green faded to black, they got their first look at a verdant forest that stretched ahead of them as far as they could see.

For Ruari, the sight was a waking dream. Telhami's grove in Quraite remembered forests and offered the hope that a forest might return. This—this vastness that was everything the barren Tablelands had ceased to be, was Telhami's hopes fulfilled, Quraite's promise kept. He would have sat there staring at it all night, except the mountain cooled faster than the barrens did, and he was shivering before he knew it.

It wasn't long until they were huddled together against the rocks, trying to keep warm and not succeeding. Orekel said it was too dangerous to descend the mountain without sunlight to show them the way. There was nothing with which to build a fire and though Ruari's druidry could wring water and a bland but nutritious paste out of the cooling air, he knew no spell that would provide them with warmth.

Pavek might have known such a spell. Pavek claimed to have memorized as many of the spellcraft scrolls as he'd been able to read in the Urik city archives. But it seemed more likely that no one in the long history of the parched tablelands had bothered to formulate a spell for heat, so they took turns in the middle of their huddle. When dawn reached over the mountain crest, it found them stiff, sore, and still weary.

The descent into the forest was harder on their legs than yesterday's climb through the gap had been. Ruari discovered new muscles along his shins and across the tops of his feet. It would have been easier if his body had simply gone numb, but he felt every step from his heel to the base of his skull. He had no idea how the other three were doing; his world began and ended with the aches of his body.

When Orekel asked to see the map, Ruari dug it out of his sleeve without a second thought.

"Son, this here, this here's not a map, son."

"I never said it was," Ruari countered, smiling wearily and looking for something to sit on that wouldn't be impossible to get up from afterward.

"Son, we have a problem."

Ruari eased himself onto the trunk of a fallen tree. He wished he didn't hurt so much. The forest was a miraculous place—the promise every druid made in his grove fulfilled to the greatest imaginable measure. There were birds and insects to complement the trees, and gray-bottomed clouds in the distance bearing the promise of real, not magic-induced, rain. The land quivered and crawled with riotous life, more life in a handful of moist, crumbly dirt than in a day's walking across the barren Tablelands.

And Ruari couldn't appreciate it. Not only did he hurt too much, he wasn't here to immerse himself in druidry. He'd come to the forest to find a black tree, to find Kakzim and bring him to justice. For Pavek. All for Pavek, because it was Kakzim's fault that Pavek was dead. He'd take Kakzim's head back to Urik and hurl it at Hamanu's palace. Then he'd go home to Urik and plant a tree for his friend.

"Son—" Orekel tugged on his sleeve. "Son, I say *we* have a problem."

"You can't help us," Ruari said slowly. "That's the problem, isn't it? You can't find the black tree. All that talk in Ject about halfling treasure you hadn't brought out because you'd gotten 'tempted,' that was just wind in the air. You're no different than Mady: you thought we had a map we weren't smart enough to keep or follow."

Orekel removed his cap. "You put a mite too fine a point on things, son. The black tree, she's in this forest, and she's got treasure trove buried 'neath her roots. She's not two-day's walk from here, and that's a fact. But this here—" He held out the map. "Now, you don't rightly speak Halfling, so you're not likely to read it much either. So, you got to believe me, son, this here's not a map *to* the black tree; it's more a map to your place, I reckon, to Urik—that's where you come from, now, isn't it?"

Ruari tried to remember if he or Zvain or Mahtra had mentioned Urik since they'd met the dwarf, but his memory refused to cooperate. Maybe they had and Orekel was playing them for fools, or maybe he could read those marks, one of which spelled Urik. Either way, Ruari was too tired for deception.

"Around Urik, yes."

"Always best to be honest, son," Orekel advised, and suddenly his eyes seemed much sharper, his movements, crisper. "Now, maybe we can solve our problem—you being a druid and all—maybe you don't need a map to find the black tree. Like as not, you can just kneel down on the ground the way you did up on the crest and mumble a few words that'll show you the way."

Ruari said no with a shake of his head.

Zvain hobbled over. The boy looked at the tree trunk and—wiser than Ruari—chose not to sit down. "Sure you could, Ru. You've just got to try. Come on, Ru—try, please?"

He shook his head again; he'd already tried. As soon as Orekel had made the suggestion, Ruari had—almost without thinking—put his palms against the moss-covered bark and opened himself to the aspects of the forest. The blare of life would have overwhelmed him if he'd had the wit or will to resist it. Instead, it had flowed through him like water through a hollow log—in one side and out the other.

In the aftermath of that flow, Ruari considered it fortunate that he'd been numbed by aches and exhaustion. The guardian aspects of this forest weren't habituated to a druid's touch, weren't habituated and didn't seem to like it, not druidry in general, nor him in particular. For a moment, all the leaves had become open eyes and open mouths with teeth instead of edges.

That moment had passed once he raised his palms and consciously shut himself off from the forest's burgeoning vitality. Leaves were simply leaves again, but the sense that they were being watched persisted. For most of his life—even in his own grove, which was mostly brush and grass with a few sparse trees—Ruari had either been within walls or looking at a horizon that was at least a day's walk away. Here in the forest, he could touch the green-leafed horizon, and the forest, which had seemed like paradise before he sat down, had become a place of hidden menace.

He was afraid to cut himself a staff, lest he arouse something more hostile.

"Give it a try, son." Orekel urged. "What've we got to lose?"

"I'm too tired," Ruari replied, which was true. "Maybe later," which was a lie—but he didn't want to alarm the others.

"So, what do we do?" Zvain asked, backsliding into the whiny, selfish tone he used when he was tired, frightened, or both. "Sit here until you're rested?"

Orekel took Zvain's arm and gently spun him around. "Best to keep moving, son. Things that stay in one place too long attract an appetite."

"Move where?" Zvain persisted.

"Does it matter?" Mahtra asked. The climb down hadn't bothered her any more than the climb up, any more than anything ever seemed to bother her. If the New Races were made from something, someone else, then whatever Mahtra had been, it wasn't elven, or dwarven, or human. "We don't have a map anymore. One direction's as good as another if we don't know where we're going."

She offered her hand to Ruari, who accepted any help getting back on his feet. They hadn't wandered far when the lurking sense that they were being watched got worse, and not much farther beyond that when he felt the old, fallen leaves that covered the ground shift beneath his feet.

A heartbeat later, they were thrown against one another and hoisted off the ground in a net. Zvain screamed in terror; Orekel cursed, as if this had happened before, and—foolish as it was—Ruari felt better with his weight on the ropes, not his feet.

The sizzle of Mahtra's thunderclap power passed through Ruari not once, but twice. The sound was loud enough to detach a shower of leaves from their branches and make the net sway like a bead on a string. But it wasn't enough to send them crashing to the ground, and Mahtra's third blast was much weaker than the first two. The fourth was no more than a flash without the thunder.

Heartbeats later, they heard movement in the underbrush, and halflings appeared on the trail beneath them. Looking down, Ruari saw a score of halflings. None looked friendly, but the one who raised his spear and prodded the half-elf sharply in the flank had a truly frightening face, with weblike burn scars covering his cheeks and eyes as black and deep as night between the stars. He gave Ruari another poke between the ribs.

"The ugly man—Templar Paddock—where is he?"

FOURTEEN

"I've heard there's a hunters' village about a day's ride from here. They call it Ject. It's a way station for beasts on their way to the combat arenas of the cities. It's full of scoundrels, knaves, and charlatans of every stripe, some of whom'll lead a party across the mountains and into the halfling forests. It's a day's ride to the southeast, but we could hire a guide for an easier passage, if you think we should, Lord Pavek."

Unlike the ride from Quraite to Urik, there were no bells on the huge kank Lord Pavek rode, no excuse for not hearing Commandant Javed's statement, no excuse for not answering the implied question.

Still, under the guise of careful consideration, Pavek could take the time to shift his weight, easing strained joints and muscles. He'd been kank-back for the better part of three days, and the only parts of him that didn't hurt were the ones that had gone numb while the walls of Urik were still visible behind them.

Pavek thought he'd set a hard pace when he'd gotten himself, Mahtra, Ruari, and Zvain from Quraite to Urik in ten days. Since leaving Khelo shortly after his conversation with Lord Hamanu, Pavek had learned new things about the bugs'—and his own—endurance.

Together with Commandant Javed of Urik's war bureau, a double maniple of troops, and an equal number of slaves,

Pavek had pushed the war bureau's biggest, toughest bugs relentlessly, following the line he saw when he suspended the strands of ensorcelled halfling hair in the draft-free box he kept lashed to the back of his saddle.

And now, when they were almost on top of the mountains they'd been chasing since yesterday morning, the commandant was suggesting a two-day detour. More than two days: it would surely take longer to walk through the forest on the other side of the mountains than it would to ride to this Ject.

But Pavek had learned over the past few days not to trust Commandant Javed's statements at face value.

"Is that a recommendation, Commandant?" In that time, Pavek had learned the trick of answering Javed's questions with questions. It made him seem wiser than he was and *sometimes* kept him from falling into the commandant's traps.

"A fact, Lord Pavek," Javed said with a smile and no sign of the aches that plagued Pavek. "You're the man in charge. You make the decisions; I merely provide the facts. Do we veer southeast, or do we hold steady?"

A challenge. And another question, the same, but different.

Hamanu had said the templars in the double maniple were all volunteers, but the Lion hadn't said anything about the commandant, whether or not he was a willing participant in this barrens-trek or not; and, if he was, why? Those *facts* might have helped Pavek interpret Javed's smiles.

Commandant Javed had served Urik and the Lion-King for six decades, all of them illustrious. He was well past the age when most elves gave up their running on foot and sat quietly in the long sunset of their lives, but the only concession the commandant made to his old bones and old injuries was the kank he rode as if he'd been born in its saddle.

There were three rubies mounted in Javed's steel medallion, one for each time he'd been designated Hamanu's Champion, and two diamonds commemorating his exploits as Hero of Urik.

In his time, he'd commanded four-thousand man armies and led a handful into Raam to rescue a Urikite ambassador from the grand vizier's palace. As the Lion-King's most trusted commander, Javed had sailed dust-schooners on the Sea of Silt. He'd led an expedition across the very mountains and forests they faced today, and farther, to the fabled mountains of the Dragon's Crown at the edge of the world.

Among Pavek's cherished few memories of life before the orphanage was the day he'd stood on the King's Way, holding his mother's hand and watching the parade as the great Commandant Javed returned triumphant from a campaign against Gulg.

The farmers and druids of Quraite nowadays called Pavek a hero; Pavek reserved that honor for the black-skinned, black-haired elf riding beside him.

"A decision, Lord Pavek," the commandant urged. "A decision *now*, while the wheel can still turn freely." He gestured toward the outriding templars. "Timing is everything. Do not confuse a decision with an accident or lost opportunity, my lord."

Good advice. Excellent advice. So why wasn't Javed leading this expedition? Never mind that high templars outranked commandants: that only proved to Pavek that Commandant Javed had been more successful at holding on to his steel medallion than he himself had been at holding on to his regulator's ceramic one.

So why was Javed here at all? After conquering every challenge Urik's war bureau offered and successfully resisting a golden medallion, why was Commandant Javed headed into the halfling forest at a regulator's side, and looking to that regulator for orders?

"Now, Lord Pavek." The commandant smiled again, ivory teeth gleaming through the black gash in his weathered face.

Pavek turned from that face and looked straight ahead at the mountains.

"No guides," he said. "We've already got our guide." He thumped the box behind him and shot a sideways glance at the commandant, whose smile had faded to a less-than-approving frown. "When we brought the cavern poison to Lord Hamanu, he said we had time to destroy it because Ral didn't 'occlude' Guthay—whatever *that* means—for another thirteen days. Well, we got rid of the poison, but we didn't catch Kakzim. Maybe he's gone home in defeat and we can catch him anytime, but maybe he's got something else he can unleash when the moons 'occlude' four nights from now.

"If we go southeast and hire ourselves a guide, we're sure to lose at least two days getting back on the halfling's trail. Maybe more than two days, without kanks on the far side of the mountains. My rump would appreciate an easy passage, but not if I miss another chance to nab Kakzim."

The commandant's frown had deepened all the while Pavek explained the thin logic of his decision. He considered reversing himself, but the stubbornness that had kept him trapped in lower ranks of the civil bureau took hold of his neck and stiffened his resolve.

He faced Javed squarely, matching his scar-twisted smile against the elf's frown. "You wanted my decision, Commandant. Now you've got it: we hold steady, straight into those mountains ahead and the forest beyond. I want my hands on Kakzim's neck before the moons occlude."

"Good," the commandant said softly, almost as if he were speaking to himself, though his amber eyes were locked with Pavek's. "Better than I expected. Better than I'd hoped from the Hero of Quraite. Four days left from thirteen. Let's put on some speed, Lord Pavek. I could *walk* faster than this. We'll sleep tonight on the mountain crest. We'll sleep on the mountain, and we'll find your halfling before Ral marches across Guthay's face. My word on it, Lord Pavek."

*   *   *   *   *

Commandant Javed's word was as good as the steel he wore around his neck. Leaving behind the kanks, the slaves, and everything else that a templar couldn't carry on his back, the elf had had them sleeping on top of the mountain ridge one night and on the forest floor the next. They'd lost two templars in the process, one going up the mountains, the other coming down.

Carelessness, Javed had said both times, and refused to slacken the pace.

At the forest-side base of the mountains, the templars, including Pavek and Javed, paused to exchange the shirts they'd been wearing for long-sleeve tunics and leather armor that was fitted from neck to waist and divided into overlapping strips from there down to the middle of their thighs.

It was all part of the equipment Pavek had been given at the beginning of this journey, and he thought nothing of Javed's order until he touched the tunic's drab, tightly woven fabric.

"*Silk?*" he asked incredulously, fingering the alien fabric, which he'd associated with fawning nobles, simpering merchants, and women he couldn't afford.

"It's tougher than it looks," Javed answered, unperturbed. "Tougher than leather or even steel, in the right conditions. These halflings are fond of ambush. They lurk in these damned trees and spit arrows at you from their tiny bows; the bows are rather silly, but the poison will kill you. Leather can protect your vitals, elsewhere—" Javed smoothed the fabric on his arm. "Like as not, those halfling arrows will slide right off—but even if they don't, your own hide will split before the silk does, and the arrow will push the cloth right inside you."

"That's *protection?*" For all that the commandant had experience with the forest halflings on his side, Pavek began to remove his slippery tunic.

"Damn sure is. The barbs on the arrowheads don't catch your guts. Ease the silk out, and you ease the arrowhead out, too—with the poison still on it."

"Still on the arrow?"

Javed's enigmatic smile flickered at him. "Didn't believe it myself till I was fighting belgoi north of Balic. Watched a healer work an arrow clean out of a man's gut; silk was as good as new, and so was the man ten days later. Been a believer ever since. My advice, my lord, is to keep it on. We know your man's a poisoner."

*   *   *   *   *

The protection Mahtra's makers had given her against living creatures had no effect whatsoever on woven vine net. Unfortunately, she had exhausted herself against the halfling-made net before she realized that fact. She'd had nothing left when the halflings lowered them to the ground, and so she stood helpless, barely able to stay upright, when Kakzim had personally bound her wrists behind her back and taken her mask away.

Five days later, imprisoned beneath the great BlackTree, surrounded by dank, dark dirt, with Zvain and Orekel little more than voices in the blackness, she still shuddered at the memory.

That theft had been Kakzim's personal vengeance against her. He'd humiliated the others, too, especially Ruari. When the half-elf told Kakzim that Pavek was already dead, the former slave had reeled backward as if Ruari had landed a blow in a particularly vulnerable place, and then transferred all his vicious hatred from Pavek, who was beyond his reach, to Ruari, who had no defense.

Throughout their two-day-long, stumbling, starving walk through the mazelike forest, Kakzim had harried Ruari with taunts and petty but vicious physical attacks. The half-elf was badly bruised and bleeding from a score of cuts, and barely able to stand by the time they reached their destination: the BlackTree.

Nothing in her spiraling memory could have prepared Mahtra for her first sight of the halfling stronghold. The crude bark map they'd found in Codesh depicted a single tree as large as the Smoking Crown Volcano, which they'd ridden near on their way to the forest. But coming upon it suddenly in this arm's-length world of trees everywhere, the black tree seemed exactly as big as the volcano.

Ten of her standing with arms extended could not have encircled its trunk. Roots as big around as Orekel's dwarven torso breached the dim, moss-covered clearing around the tree's trunk before returning into the ground.

But it wasn't the black tree's trunk or roots that lingered in Mahtra's memory, sitting here in the darkness between those roots. It was the moment she'd raised her head, hoping to see the sky through branches as big around as a kank's body. There'd been no sky, only the soles of a deadman's feet.

She'd cried out. Kakzim had laughed, and—worse—the feet had moved, and Mahtra had realized that a living man, a halfling, hung above her, suspended from a mighty branch by a rope wound tight beneath his arms.

Worse still, the living, hanging halfling was not alone. There were other halflings dangling from other branches, more than she could easily count. Some of them were alive, like the halfling whose feet were directly above her head, but others were rotting corpses, barely recognizable.

Worst of all—the memory Mahtra could not escape even now in her prison beneath the tree—was the great drop of blood that had struck between her eyes as she stood, transfixed by the horror above her. With her hands bound behind her back, she hadn't been able to wipe the blood off, and her pleas for help, for mercy, brought only laughter from her captors.

Her skin was still wet when Kakzim ordered his fellow halflings to drive her, Zvain, and Orekel through a narrow hole between the roots. Prodded by sharp spears, they'd wriggled like serpents through the hole, a narrow tunnel, and—blindly at the end—tumbled into the dank, dirt pit that now imprisoned them.

Orekel had gone first; he'd hurt his leg falling several times his own height into the pit. Then Zvain, who'd landed on top of the dwarf, and finally her. She'd landed on them both.

They'd waited for Ruari, but she'd been the last to fall. Mahtra tried to remember if he'd wriggled down that tunnel behind her, but those memories were too confused. Perhaps he had, but the halflings had forced him into some other pit, down some other tunnel.

And maybe, she shuddered at the thought, they'd hung him in the tree.

That memory was all too clear. She'd been able to scrape the blood from her face, crawling on her belly down that tunnel, but there was nothing she could do for the blood in her memory.

It was daytime in the world above; she could tell because some light got in around the roots that wound around the sides of their prison. There was enough to see Zvain and Orekel, whose leg had swollen horribly since he fell. When night came, she could see nothing at all.

Night had come twice since they landed in the pit.

Food had come twice also, both times in the form of slops and rubbish thrown down the hole. It was vile and disgusting, but they were starving. Liquid seeped through the dirt walls of their prison. Mahtra's tongue tasted water, but her memory saw blood.

Orekel, who understood Halfling, said their captors were planning a big sacrifice when the little moon, Ral, passed in front of big Guthay. When he wasn't drunk with pain, he made plans for their escape:

Zvain was the smallest; he could climb up both their backs and through the hole to the tunnel. Then, using Mahtra's shawl, which Kakzim had left along with everything else save her mask and Ruari's knife, Zvain could hoist Mahtra to freedom. Her protection would do its work. They could find a rope—there was plenty of rope available—to get him out of the hole, find the treasure, and make good their escape before the halflings recovered from Mahtra's thunderclap.

That was Orekel's plan, when his ankle wasn't hurting so bad he couldn't think or talk. Maybe, if he'd been able to stand or she'd been confident her protection would work again, they might have tried it.

But Orekel couldn't stand and, though she'd chewed through and swallowed their last bit of cinnabar, the little lion that Zvain had stolen from the palace, Mahtra didn't think she'd ever be able to use the maker's protection again. Something was missing. There was now a dark place inside her, a place she'd never realized was lit until the flame went out.

And now there was no more talk of escape. Well into the third day of their captivity, their prison was quiet—except for Orekel's babbling and groans. She and Zvain had nothing left to say to each other.

Mahtra huddled by herself in the curve where the side became the bottom. She drew her knees up to her chest, rested her cheek on them, and wrapped her arms over her shins.

The spiral of her life had become a circle; she was back where she'd begun: in deep, silent darkness.

*   *   *   *   *

After his time in Telhami's grove, Pavek thought he'd be prepared for the forest, but there was little comparison between a meticulously nurtured grove and the wild profusion of a natural forest.

Instead of the guardian aspect that pulled a grove together with a single purpose, a single voice, the halfling forest was a battleground with every mote of life competing for its place on the land.

It was a place hostile to them as well—which was not entirely surprising. War bureau maniples did not go quietly, no matter where they went, though they were traveling light, at least as far as magic was concerned. Except for the medallions they all wore and the ensorcelled bit of halfling hair, Pavek knew of no Tablelands magic that they'd brought across the mountains into the forest. There were no defiling sorcerers with them, no priests, either—unless the forest sensed that templars borrowed spellcraft from the Lion-King or recognized Pavek's clumsy curiosity as the sign of a druid.

Even without magic, however, a living forest had reason to resent their intrusion. A double maniple of templars armed with broad-bladed, single-edged swords hacked a wide swathe through the undergrowth as they marched, still following the straight course set by the strands of blond hair Pavek now carried in a little pouch on the gold chain of his high templar's medallion.

It was the morning of the twelfth day and the start of their first full day in the forest. Last night, the two moons had been in the sky all night. They were both nearly full, and silvery little Ral was yapping toward golden Guthay's middle.

Pavek could remember other times when both moons had shown their full faces at the same time, but never when they'd been on the collision course of last night. It seemed to Pavek that Ral would crash against Guthay's trailing edge tonight or tomorrow night, which would be the significant thirteenth night. He mentioned his suspicions to the commandant once they'd broken camp and were marching through the forest again, and his concern that Ral would be destroyed.

"If Kakzim knew that the moons were going to crash—"

Commandant Javed cut him short with a withering look. "Hamanu won't let that happen. He slid little Ral right across the face of Guthay when I was a boy, and he'll do it again. Why do you think we're here with no magicians in our maniples and nothing more than a bit of halfling hair as our guide? Our king's not going to have any magic to spare for a few days, but the moons will survive."

Pavek bit his lip and held silent while he weighed what the

Lion-King had told him about how using magic now would destroy Urik. Easier to believe that no spells would be available until after the sorcerer-king had prevented catastrophe in the heavens than to think Hamanu had been serious about birthing dragons and the death of Urik.

Which thoughts made Pavek wonder why the Lion-King would have lied to him about such a matter, if the truth were so linked to this mission. That was not a question to ask Commandant Javed.

"I hadn't thought of it that way, Commandant," he said. "You're right. Of course."

"You're young yet. There's a lot to learn that never gets taught. You just have to put the pieces together yourself—remember that."

Pavek assured the older, wiser elf that he would, and their march through the forest continued. The sense that the forest itself was hostile to them grew steadily stronger until Javed and the maniple templars sensed it also.

"It's too damned quiet," Javed concluded. "Trees. I hate trees. The forest is an ambusher's paradise. They can put their scouts in the branches and tell their troops to lie low in the shade beneath them. Get out your hair, Lord Pavek; see if our halfling's tried to close a trap behind us."

It was the trees themselves that were looking down on them—at least that's what Pavek thought. The hair indicated it as well. Its line hadn't varied since they used it first at Khelo: Kakzim was still ahead of them.

But the two-time Hero of Urik took no chances. He tightened their formation, giving orders to every third templar: "Keep your eyes on the trees ahead of us, on either side, and especially behind. Anything moves, sing out. I'd sooner duck from wind and shadows than have halflings running up our rumps."

They did a lot of shadow dodging that morning, but they also got a heartbeat's warning before the first arrow flew at them. Trusting their silk tunics and leather armor, Commandant Javed ordered the maniples together in a tight circle. He commanded them to kneel, presenting smaller targets to the hidden archers and safeguarding their unprotected legs.

"Defend your face! That's where you're vulnerable," Javed shouted, taking his own advice when an arrow whizzed toward him. "But mark where the arrows are coming from. We'll take these forest-scum brigands when their quivers are empty."

The soft, smooth silk lived up to the commandant's claims, and the lightweight, slow-moving arrows failed to find targets time and again. One templar cried out when an arrow grazed her hand, and moments later she'd fallen unconscious. But she was their only casualty, and gradually the arrow flights came to a halt and the forest was silent.

"Mark where you saw 'em. Move out in pairs." This time the commandant gave his orders in a voice that wouldn't carry to the trees. "We don't have to catch them all, just one or two." Then he turned to Pavek and whispered: "You mark any, my lord?"

Pavek pointed to a crook halfway up one substantial tree where he'd spotted a shadowed silhouette against the branches.

Javed flashed his black-and-white smile. "Let's go catch us a halfling—"

But fickle fortune was against the heroes. Their quarry dropped down and hit the ground running. Javed's elven legs weren't what they'd been in his prime, and Pavek had never been much of a sprinter. The halfling went to ground in a stand of bramble bushes.

Other pairs were luckier. When the maniples reassembled near the body of the unconscious templar, they had captured four halflings, none of whom seemed to understand a word Commandant Javed said when he asked where their village was.

Intimidation was an art among templars. Pavek had been taught the basic skills in the orphanage. Being big, which Pavek had always been, and ugly, which he'd become early on life, Pavek had a natural advantage. The joke was that he was a born intimidator, but the truth was that Pavek didn't enjoy making other folk writhe in terror or anxiety. He was good at it because he hated it, and now that he held the highest rank imaginable, he intended never to professionally intimidate anyone again. He gave a hands-off gesture and stepped aside to allow the commandant to finish what he'd begun.

"You're lying," Javed told the captives who knelt before him. He looked aside to Pavek and began speaking above heads that rose no higher than his thigh. "My name is Commandant Javed of Urik, and I give you my word as a commandant that we're searching for one man, one male halfling with blond hair and slave scars on his face. He committed crimes in Urik, and he will answer for them. No one else need fear us. We won't harm you or your families or your homes if you give us the criminal we've come for. You will help us—understand that. Dead or alive, one of you will guide us to your homes. Now, which one of you will it be?"

The commandant's voice had been calm and steady throughout his short speech. By simply watching him or listening to the tone of his voice, it would have been difficult for the halflings to know that he was talking to them, or for them to realize the threatening promise he'd made—if they truly didn't understand the words he'd uttered. And that was the impression the captives strove to convey: none of them volunteered to be the templars' guide.

From the side, Pavek knew what was coming next. He'd seen two of the halflings flinch when Javed implied the necromancy for which the templarates were infamous. A third had lowered his eyes when the commandant asked for a volunteer. Although necromancy would be more difficult without borrowed spellcraft, Pavek trusted that Javed wouldn't have made the threat if he didn't have the means to carry it through. He also trusted that one of the other templars would have seen the halflings' reaction and would report them to the commandant. Pointing out an enemy who'd shot poisoned arrows at him didn't trouble him, but condemning a man to death and worse because he wouldn't betray his home and family wasn't something Pavek could do.

As Ruari had told him when they'd argued in Escrissar's garden, he had a convenient conscience.

And not long to wait. The maniple templars had caught all four halflings reacting to Javed's speech. The commandant grabbed the lone woman in the group, not—Pavek assumed—strictly because of her sex, but because she had huddled close by one of the men. When templars of any rank, from any bureau, wanted fast intimidation results, they turned their attention to the smaller, weaker partner in a pair, if a pair was available.

While one templar held the woman from behind and another pressed his composite sword's blade against her pulsing throat, Commandant Javed removed a scroll from his pack. He broke the heavy black seal and began to read the mnemonics of the same necromantic spell Pavek had expected the Lion-King to use on him at Codesh. Midway through the invocation, the sword-wielding templar pricked the halfling's skin with the blade's razor-sharp teeth.

The woman gave no more reaction to the pain and the trickling of her own warm, red blood than she had to the commandant's speech, but the sight was too much for the halfling she'd huddled against. He sprang to his feet.

"Spare her, and I'll lead you to our village," he said in the plain language of the Urik streets.

His halfling companions, including the woman whose life he was trying to save, sputtered epithets in their clicking, screeching language. The woman got another nick in her throat; the other two halflings got savage blows from the hilts of templar weapons. Templars did not tolerate in others those treacherous, divisive behaviors they practiced to perfection among themselves.

"And the scarred, blond-haired halfling?" Javed asked.

The traitor wrung his hands. "I know of no such man."

Javed's long arm swung out to clout the halfling. He staggered and tripped over his indignant companions.

"We know he came this way!" the commandant thundered. "I will have the truth, from your mouth or *hers!*" He shook the scroll he still held in his right hand and began again to read the mnemonics.

With a hand held over his bleeding mouth, the halfling scrambled toward Commandant Javed. "Great One," he cried, "there is no such man. I swear it."

"What do you think, Lord Pavek? Is he telling the truth?"

Eyes turned toward Pavek, who scratched the bristly growth on his chin before asking: "Which way to your village?"

Eager to respond to a question he could answer, the halfling pointed in the direction they'd already been headed, but regarding his truthfulness, Pavek could only scratch his chin a second time. Halflings were rare in Urik, unheard of in the templarate. He could count the number he knew by name on the fingers of one hand, and save his thumb for Kakzim. As far as he was concerned, halfling faces were inscrutable. The male halfling in front of him could have been Zvain's age, his own age, or venerable like Javed; he could have been telling the absolute truth, or lying through his remaining teeth.

The only certainty was that Pavek held lives on the tip of his tongue. He looked at Javed; the commandant's shadowed face was as inscrutable as the halfling's. In the end, Pavek relied more on hope than logic.

"I believe him about his village. As for the other—" following the commandant's lead, Pavek didn't say Kakzim's name aloud "—men of no account frequently don't know the answers to important questions." Fate knew, he, himself, dwelt in ignorance most of the time. "We'll talk to the elders when we get there."

Javed bowed his head. "Your will, Lord Pavek." He crumpled the scroll he'd been reading, and it vanished in a flare of silvery light.

The village to which their halfling captive led them wasn't far away. If they'd been on the barrens instead of deep in a forest, the templars would have spotted it from the ambush sight. Of course, without the forest, there would have been no ambush, and no halfling houses, either. The halflings lived in a circle of huge, spreading trees around a shaded, moss-covered clearing. Some of their homes had been carved out of the trees' trunks so long ago the bark had healed around them. Others were perched in their branches like nests. The homes seemed both alive and ancient, and all of them were too small for even a dwarf's comfort.

Tiny, feral faces—halfling children—peeked out of moss-framed windows, but the men and women of the community had gathered in the clearing, with weapons ready. A duet of Halfling singsong passed between the templars' captives and the anxious villagers. One of the templars translated:

"Our fellows said they had no choice; we would have killed them and gotten the information from their corpses. The old fellows in the center, they speak for the village and they wanted to know why we've come, what we're looking for."

Commandant Javed nodded. Speaking clearly in the Urikite dialect, confident the elders could understand, he said, "We've tracked a renegade halfling to this village, a blond man with Urik slave scars on his cheeks. If they surrender him at once, and if they provide us with an antidote for the poison they used on our comrade, we will depart immediately. Otherwise we'll destroy this village and everyone here, one by one. Children first."

When the elders protested in a passable dialect that there was neither an antidote nor a blond, scarred halfling, Commandant Javed turned to Pavek.

"My lord?" he asked, cold as a man's voice could be.

Pavek set down the sword he'd held ready since the ambush began. He dug out his bit of ensorcelled hair and let it spin freely, as much to give the halfling elders addi-

tional time to consider their folly—they might be superb
fighters for their size, but they didn't stand a chance against
Javed's maniples. For the first time, the hair pointed in a different direction, almost perpendicular to the path they'd
been following since Khelo. The halflings who'd watched
this subtle bit of Tablelands magic seemed impressed, but
did not recant.

Their elders repeated that there was no antidote for the
poison the halflings smeared on their arrowheads. The templar woman would die without awakening. And there was
no blond-haired halfling with Urikite slave-scars on his
cheeks in this village or anywhere else. Didn't the templars
know that halflings would sooner die than surrender their
freedom?

Faced with such intransigence, there was nothing Pavek
could do to save them or their village. He met the commandant's eyes and nodded. Javed barked orders to his maniples:

The first were to stand with swords drawn, guarding the
armed adults and venerable elders already gathered in the
clearing. The second would collect flaming brands from the
halfling hearths and set fire to the tree homes—and be prepared to snare the halfling children as they fled their burning shelters.

When a human templar seized the first halfling child as it
bolted, hair and clothes aflame, toward its parents, the
armed halflings surged against their enemies in a desperate
attempt to save their children.

But the templars had their orders; the carnage was pro-
ceeding to its inevitable, one-sided conclusion, but just as
blood began to flow:

STOP!

It was a frantic, mind-bending assault against them all,
templar and halfling alike, and the Unseen, unheard shout
was, in its way, louder than the shrill halfling screams or the
crackling flames. It echoed in Pavek's mind, and was
enough to make him retreat from the dirty work of slaying

halflings. He was not alone in his retreat: though most of the templars brought their swords down toward their victims without hesitation, some did not, and even the halflings' resistance seemed to falter.

Paddock! Another Unseen shout, accompanied this time by an image Pavek recognized as his own face. *Make them stop, Paddock. I'll give you what you want!*

A second face loomed in Pavek's mind, a face covered with shiny, weblike scars, a face surrounded by tangled wisps of dark brown hair, a face he didn't recognize until its eyes absorbed his attention.

Eyes like black, bottomless pits, eyes of infinite hate and madness.

Kakzim's eyes.

"Stand down!" Pavek shouted. "Javed! Commandant! Give the order to stand down. Now!"

For a moment he wasn't certain the order would be obeyed, but Javed pulled his sword-stroke before it sliced a halfling's head from its shoulders, and once their commandant stood down, the other templars followed.

A halfling came out of the underbrush bordering the village—from the direction the ensorcelled hair had foretold. His hair was blond and his face dark, but he wasn't Kakzim, and the marks covering his face were not slave-scars, but bloody bruises.

Leaning on a crutch, favoring a bandaged leg and an arm that was bound up beneath his ribs, he made slow progress toward the cautiously waiting templars. As he approached, Pavek realized the bruises, while not fresh, were a long way from being healed. His right eye was swollen completely shut; the left was crowned with a festering scab.

Whoever had beaten the halfling—and in Pavek's experienced opinion, several fists and clubs had been involved—they'd known what they were doing. Though he wasn't near dying, it would be a long time before the man could move easily again, if he ever did.

"Paddock," the battered halfling said through puffy lips

once he reached the edge of the clearing.

"Pavek," Pavek corrected and waited without saying anything more.

"My name is Cerk," the halfling said, then added something in Halfling. "I've told them this is my fault. They were protecting me. I am to blame; this is the BlackTree's judgment. They've told you the truth: there is no antidote for our poison, and they know no one whose hair is blond and whose cheeks bear the scars of Urik's slaves. If you'd asked them about Kakzim—"

Heads came up among the village halflings, even among the four they'd held captive since the ambush. Kakzim's name was known here, and to judge by the expressions on the halfling faces when they heard the name, both feared and hated. A flurry of clicks, whistles and musical syllables passed among the halflings.

"They're cursing a black tree, my lord, Commandant," said the templar who'd translated the conversations earlier. "I don't think it's a place."

"It is a place and a brotherhood," Cerk explained. "They were my home, but they belong to Kakzim now. He is mad."

"We know that," Pavek said impatiently, when Cerk seemed to consider madness a sufficient explanation. "Where can we find him? Where's this black tree? You said you'd give us what we want."

"What *you* want, Pavek. He fears you as he fears nothing else; he knew you would come. You are the only one who can stop him—"

There was another outburst of Halfling. Their templar began to translate, but Cerk held up his hand and the man fell silent.

"The BlackTree has been the center of my people's lives since we came to this forest many, many generations ago. It holds the knowledge of our past in its roots. We would sooner die than deliver it to outsiders—dragon-spawned templars, especially. But Kakzim has already taken the BlackTree from us. You, Pavek, are our last hope."

Pavek thought hard and fast before speaking. "This knowledge it holds in its roots—you mean the knowledge to make poisons like Laq and that sludge Kakzim was going to pour into our water? Our king said if those bowls had been emptied, everyone in Urik and beyond would die. Is that the knowledge you're trying to protect?"

"It is only a very small part of the knowledge the Black-Tree has preserved," Cerk countered, then added softly and sadly: "But it is the knowledge Brother Kakzim absorbed and seeks to expand, now that he's usurped the Brethren to his own purposes."

"You helped him," Pavek voiced the conclusion as it formed in his mind. "You helped him in Urik, helped him return to the forest. Then he turned on you—"

Cerk nodded, a movement that made him stiffen with pain. "We came back to the Brethren. I recanted my vows; I denounced what we had done. I called on the elders to do what must be done—but while they sought a consensus, Kakzim split the Brethren and turned one half against the other. Brother Kakzim has a mighty voice; no one can resist it now. There is no one left but you, Pavek. Your friends said you were dead in Codesh, but they hadn't seen your corpse. I should have known that you weren't dead, were coming. That you weren't far behind, Pavek."

"Lord Pavek," Commandant Javed corrected. His sword remained unsheathed as he approached. "Speaking of a mighty voice, this one's spinning a pretty tale. The hair points to him. I think we've found our halfling, don't you, my lord? Let's settle this now." He raised his sword for a decapitating strike.

Pavek restrained Javed's arm. "He's not Kakzim, Commandant. We'll let him take us to this tree—"

"Only you, Pavek—"

"See!" the commandant sputtered. "What did I tell you?"

"Your men won't be able to resist Kakzim," Cerk said without a trace of fear or doubt. "*You* won't be able to resist him. Or, if you do, he'll string you up with the others, slit your veins, and feed your blood to the BlackTree to placate it and consolidate his dominance over it."

It had the sound of an unpleasant death worthy of Hamanu himself, and an equally worthy, unpleasant ambition. For those reasons alone, although there were others, Pavek was inclined to believe the battered little man—but not to agree to his terms.

"We'll take our chances together. You'll lead us there. And, Cerk, *what others?* What friends of mine have you been talking to?"

"Hamanu's mercy!" Javed erupted before Cerk could answer. "With him leading us, we'll need two days to get anywhere."

"Then we'll still be there in time, Commandant," Pavek snarled, surprising himself and Javed with his vehemence. "Now, Cerk, again—*what others?*"

"The others—I don't know their names. The ones that were with you on the killing ground. They followed us— same as you did—we assumed you were with them, but obviously we were wrong. Kakzim was waiting for them when they crossed the mountains. He brought them to the BlackTree. I don't know what time you're thinking of, Pavek, but there's no time for your friends. I'm certain Kakzim will sacrifice them tonight when the moons converge: the blood of Urik to atone for his failures in Urik. I heard him say so many, many times. He'd hoped it would be your blood, of course, but he still needs to make a sacrifice and the best time will be tonight."

"Tomorrow night!" Pavek protested. "The thirteenth night. I have the Lion-King's word—"

"Tonight," Cerk insisted. "Halflings have forgotten more than the dragons will ever know. Hamanu's calculations are founded in myth; ours in fact: The convergence will be tonight. We're too late for them, but Kakzim will be drunk and bloated. Tomorrow will be a good time to confront him—"

"*Tonight!* We'll get there tonight, if I have to carry you. Start walking!"

FIFTEEN

Another night, another day in shades of darkness beneath the black tree. Orekel's ankle had swelled up to the size of a cabra fruit. It was hot—not warm—to the touch; Mahtra had heard Zvain say so more than once. And painful. The dwarf couldn't move without moaning, couldn't move much at all. Zvain took Orekel's share of the slops the halflings dumped into their pit and carried it to him in his hands. The boy collected water from the ground seeps the same way.

His behavior made no sense to Mahtra. The dwarf didn't need food or water; he needed relief from his suffering. She didn't understand suffering. Father and Mika had died, but they'd died quickly. They hadn't suffered. Pavek had taken longer to die, but not as long as Orekel was taking. She'd asked Zvain, "What is wrong with the dwarf that he hasn't died?"

Zvain had gotten angry at her. He'd called her the names the street children had shouted when she'd walked from the templar quarter to the cavern in what seemed, now, to have been another life. Mahtra was hurt by the names, but not the way Orekel was hurt. She didn't die; she just crouched in the little place she'd claimed as her own.

Darkness thickened again; another night was coming. Mahtra thought it was the fourth night. She'd lost track of days and nights while she sat outside House Escrissar because they were the same while she lived them and fell one on top of the other in her memory. She didn't want to lose track of days again; it seemed somehow important to know how long she stayed in a particular place, even if the only events to remember were Orekel's groans and the slops falling from above.

Still thinking about time, Mahtra tried to make four marks that would help her keep the days and nights in order. The roots that intruded into their prison seemed an ideal place to carve her counting lines, but they were too tough for her fingernails; she broke two trying. Her nails were the color of cinnabar and tasted faintly of the bright red stone. She scratched along the dirt floor, searching for the broken-off pieces and had found one when she heard scratching sounds through the dirt beside her.

"Zvain—?" she whispered.

"*Shsssh!*" came the whispered reply. "I can hear it."

An animal digging through the dirt, drawn, perhaps, by the sounds she'd made? A large animal? An animal like the one Ruari had freed on the other side of the mountains? Fear tremors shook Mahtra's hands, nothing more. No warmth rising from the burnished marks on her skin, no heaviness in her arms, her legs, or her eyes. She'd chewed and swallowed all her cinnabar, but that wasn't enough. She didn't know what was missing, but cinnabar wasn't enough. If Ruari's beast burst into their prison, she'd have no protection.

Clumps of loosened dirt fell around Mahtra. Scrambling on her hands and knees, she retreated to the far side of their prison, closer to Zvain and Orekel. The dwarf was unaware of the changes, but Zvain was tense and trembling, too. They clutched each other's hand.

"You can't go *boom*, can you?" he asked.

"No—I chewed up all my cinnabar, but something's missing."

"Damn!" the boy swore softly, and said other things besides. Father wouldn't have approved, or Pavek, but they were the words Mahtra would have used herself, if she'd remembered them.

Then there was light, so bright and painful that she couldn't see. Closing her eyes was no improvement. Her eyelids couldn't keep out the light after so much time in darkness. Mahtra warded the light with her hands, finally restoring the darkness with the pressure of her forearm against her closed eyes.

But she wanted desperately to see.

There were halfling voices, halfling words, halfling hands all around her, pulling her away from the wall, pushing her toward the agonizing light. She stumbled and needed her hands to catch herself as she fell. Her eyes opened—no choice of hers—and the light was less painful.

Halflings had scratched sideways into their prison!

For a heartbeat, Mahtra held the hope that they'd been rescued. Then she heard Kakzim's voice.

"Hurry up! The convergence begins before sundown! Hurry!"

Mahtra didn't know what a convergence was, but she didn't think she'd like it.

With halflings pushing and shoving, she crawled through the sideways hole, emerging into a tunnel that was high enough for the halflings to stand comfortably, but nowhere near high enough for Mahtra. Crawling was demeaning and not fast enough to satisfy the halflings, who harried her with sharpened sticks. She walked stooped over, like the old slave-woman at House Escrissar, and stopped when they thrust their sticks toward her face.

Zvain came out of the prison after her. Being not much bigger than the halflings themselves, the human youth could, and did, put up a fight that got him nowhere except beaten with sharp sticks and bound with ropes around his wrists and neck. Mahtra saw these things because the tunnel where she sat waiting had its own light: countless bright and flickering specks. The specks moved, gathering themselves into little worms that streaked up one side of the tunnel, across, and down the other where they broke apart and disappeared. The specks were white, but the little worms could be any color, or several colors and changing colors.

There'd been worms in the reservoir cavern, even worms that glowed faintly in the dark, but nothing like these fast-moving, fast-changing creatures that seemed to be made from light itself. Watching them, Mahtra forgot the prison she'd just left, forgot Zvain, forgot the halflings with their sticks—nothing mattered except touching a worm. . . .

"*Ack!*" a halfling shouted in its own language, and struck Mahtra's knuckles with its stick.

She pulled her hand back to her hard-lipped mouth.

"Behave yourself! The halfling knowledge isn't to be touched by corrupt mongrels like you." Kakzim sneered. "Your protection doesn't work in the dark, does it, Mahtra?"

With her stinging hand still pressed against her mouth, Mahtra gave a wide-eyed nod, which was a lie—one of the very few that she'd ever told, but one for which she thought Father would forgive her. Pavek certainly would, or Ruari or Zvain. She could almost hear the three of them telling her not to let Kakzim know that she'd felt a spark inside when the halfling struck her hand.

Or that Kakzim himself had told her something she hadn't known before: darkness *did* stifle her protection, but she needed only a very little light to make it work again. A daily walk between the templar quarter and the elven market had been enough, so that she'd never suspected light was as important as cinnabar, but the little worms she mustn't touch were almost bright enough themselves.

The halflings were sealing their prison, leaving Orekel alone inside it, and that made Zvain frantic. He fought again, screaming that he and the dwarf couldn't be separated, and got beaten again. The two humans Mahtra knew best, Zvain and Pavek, were each inclined to risk themselves for others, regardless of the consequences. It was very brave, she supposed, but also very foolish. Wherever they were going—now that the halflings were making them move forward again—the dwarf was better off where he was.

As for Ruari—Mahtra hoped, as the halflings prodded her through another tight passage, that Ruari was with Pavek and Father in the place where people went after they died.

But Ruari was still alive.

They came out into another prison chamber, similar to the one they'd left, except it was open to the sky and afternoon bright, and the first thing she saw was Ruari's long, lean body hanging down from rope tied around his wrists. The second was the shallow movements of his ribs.

Still, alive wasn't necessarily better. The rope that held Ruari suspended from a bark-covered pole—a broken tree limb—lying across the pit opening had obviously been adjusted to a particularly cruel and precise height. Ruari's toes barely touched the stump below him. He could balance, but couldn't relieve the strain on his back and arms.

Mahtra called his name. His head, which had fallen forward against his chest, didn't move. Zvain did more than call; he bolted away from his guards and threw himself at Ruari's legs. He either had not remembered or didn't care that his own hands were tied and the slightest jostle would upset Ruari's delicate balance atop the stump.

Ruari swung free. He made a sound that should have been a scream but was a hoarse gasp instead. The muscles of his upper body knotted in spasms Mahtra could feel in her own back and shoulders.

"Go ahead. Cut him down," Kakzim said, handing a knife to another halfling who attacked the knots at the end of Ruari's rope.

Mahtra had last seen the knife the halfling used when it was attached to Ruari's belt and first seen it attached to Pavek's. Now it belonged to Kakzim, who reclaimed it once Ruari's weight was sufficient to fray through the rope. Mahtra had a half-heartbeat to remind herself that no good came from owning things, before Ruari landed in the bottom of the pit: a twitching, groaning collection of arms and legs that couldn't hope to stand on its own.

A second halfling untied Zvain's wrists.

"Get him up, you two," Kakzim barked at Mahtra and Zvain.

It seemed unspeakably cruel to seize Ruari by the wrists and ankles, to drag him to the opening where they'd entered the pit and manhandle him through the tight passage, but Zvain and Mahtra had no choice in the matter. The halflings were eager to put their sharp sticks to use and, no matter what they did to him, it would have been worse if they'd forced the barely conscious Ruari to move on his own. Like Orekel, the half-elf was oblivious to everything that wasn't pain. He didn't recognize them by sight or sound, though he knew Kakzim's voice and cringed whenever he heard it.

Mahtra had guessed where they were headed and what Ruari's part in the "convergence" would be when the passage through which they were dragging Ruari began to slope upward to the surface. The thought that he would hang from the black tree until he died and rotted disturbed her, although she saw no alternatives. She'd seen people slay other people—the nightmare image of Father's crushed skull was never out of memory's reach—but she didn't know how to kill, didn't want to learn, not even to end Ruari's suffering.

She was strong enough to carry him in her arms, and she picked him up once they stood outside without asking permission or waiting to be told. The cinnabar she'd swallowed quickened as soon as the sunset light struck her face. She could make a *boom,* as Zvain called her protection. She and the boy might be able to run far enough and fast enough to escape the halflings, but not if she were carrying Ruari. They'd have to leave the half-elf behind, the dwarf, too—and then there'd be a chance that Zvain wouldn't come with her.

Mahtra didn't need Zvain or anyone else since Father had died. She could escape on her own—and would, she decided, before she let the halflings drive her underground again or hang her in the tree. But those things weren't happening right now and something altogether different might happen before they did, so she decided to wait before making her own escape.

A horde of halflings stood waiting beneath the black tree's branches. They chanted phrases Mahtra didn't understand when she appeared with Ruari draped across her arms, and repeated them as she followed Kakzim to a long, flat stone set in the ground like a bed or table.

"Put him down," Kakzim said, and she obeyed, then retreated, also obediently.

Kakzim shouted something in Halfling, and the chanting stopped. Everything was quiet while the blood-colored sun shot rays of blood-colored sunset through the leaves of the black tree. Kakzim used the metal-bladed knife to make a pair of shallow gashes along the inside of Ruari's shins, just above his ankles. There was a groove in the flat stone, unnoticeable in the shallow light until it began to fill with Ruari's blood and channel it to the moss-covered ground. When the first red drops struck the moss, the chanting resumed and somewhere someone began beating a deep-voiced drum.

The drum beat slowly at first, while halflings wound more rope around Ruari's chest, beneath his armpits. It began to beat faster when one of the halflings climbed into the tree with the rope's free end tied loosely around his waist. After weaving carefully through the main limbs, the halfling shinnied out along one of the thickest branches, then looped his end of the rope over the branch and dropped it to the ground.

"Grab it and pull," Kakzim ordered, his voice almost lost in the shrill chanting of the other halflings. "Both of you! *Now!*"

"No!" Zvain shouted back. "I won't. You can kill me, but you can't make me do that!"

The halflings guarding them had exchanged their sharpened prods for stone-tipped spears once they were above ground, and Zvain's arms bloodied fast, batting the tips away as he tried to stand his ground. Though most of the halflings aimed at his flanks and thighs, trying to make him walk, one thrust high, putting a gouge just above the boy's left eye.

Between Zvain's shriek and the blood that flowed thick and fast down his face, it was impossible to measure his injury, except that it wasn't what Kakzim wanted. The one-time slave screamed at his halflings, disciples—and one of them, perhaps the one who'd thrust high, threw his spear aside and dropped to one knee with his hands pressed over his eyes and ears. As he swayed from side to side, oblivious to the world, blood began to trickle from his nostrils. And all the while, Kakzim stood, tense, with his fists clenched, his eyes closed and the scars on his face throbbing in rhythm with the solitary drum.

"*Mahtra*," Zvain pleaded, staring at her with his un-bloodied eye while he kept both hands pressed over the other.

Blood no longer trickled from the halfling's nostrils; it poured out of him in a steady stream. He'd fallen on his side, already unconscious.

"Yes, Mahtra," Kakzim purred. He turned from the dead halfling. "Take up the rope and *pull*."

Mahtra was angry and frightened by the blood and dying. She was hot inside and could feel her arms starting to stiffen. The cloudy membranes in the corners of her eyes fluttered as she considered if this was the right moment to loose her protection.

"Do something!" both Zvain and Kakzim shouted at the same time.

The drum beat faster and so did Mahtra's heart, yet her thoughts whirled faster still. She had a lifetime to look from Zvain to Ruari and finally to Kakzim. There was nothing she could do for the half-elf or the human, but she would not leave this place while the scarred halfling lived. Her protection was not a fatal magic; she'd have to kill him with her hands.

Her hands were strong enough to lift Ruari. They were surely strong enough to snap a halfling's neck. Mahtra could imagine flesh, sinew, and bone giving way beneath her hands as she took her first stride toward Kakzim.

You will die, she thought, her eyes fixed on his. I will kill you.

Mahtra struck a wall midway through her second stride, an invisible wall, an Unseen wall of determination that was stronger and more focused than her own. It had no words, only images—images of a white-skinned woman taking the rope and pulling it, hand over hand, until Ruari was high in the black tree. The image was irresistible. Mahtra turned away from Kakzim. She took the rope and gave it a powerful yank; Ruari's shoulders rose from stone slab. His head fell back with a moan. His long coppery hair shone like fire in the sun's last light.

They would all die. They would all be sacrificed to the black tree: the sacred BlackTree, the stronghold of halfling knowledge. Their blood would seep down to the deepest roots where it would erase the stigma of failure and disgrace. Paddock—

Her hands faltered. The rope slipped. She could see the familiar face with its jagged scar from eye to lip. His name was not Paddock; his name was Pavek. *Pavek!* And he would not approve of what she was doing—

A fist of Unseen wind struck Mahtra's thoughts, shattering them and leaving her empty-minded until other thoughts filled the void: It was not fitting that BlackTree refused to hear Kakzim's prayers, refused to acknowledge his domination. He'd committed no crimes, made no errors. He'd been undone by the very mongrels and misfits he'd sworn to eliminate, which was surely proof of the honor and validity of his intentions.

Pavek would have been the perfect sacrifice, but Pavek had escaped. Kakzim would offer three sacrifices in Pavek's place—Ruari first, then Zvain, then Mahtra herself—all three offered while the two moons shone with one light. Their blood would nurture the BlackTree's roots, and all of Kakzim's minor errors would be forgiven, forgotten. The BlackTree would accept him as the rightful heir of halfling knowledge.

She tied the rope off with the others already knotted at the base of the BlackTree's huge trunk, then she looked at Zvain. His turn would come next, when the overlapping moons were visible above the treetops. Her turn would come at midnight, when Ral was centered within Guthay's orb. She would walk freely to the stone, made by halflings and unmade the same way.

Made by halflings?

Mahtra recaptured her thoughts, broke the wall, and beat back the Unseen fist. Made by halflings—the voices in the darkness at the beginning of her memory were halfling voices. The makers who had made a mistake and cast her out of their lives with no more than red beads and a mask, those makers were *halflings*. Now another halfling, the same halfling who had slaughtered Father, had cast her out of her own thoughts, and . . .

She remembered what she'd done while Kakzim controlled her mind and those memories tore through her conscience. She raised her head, hoping the images were a dream, knowing they weren't. That was Ruari hanging above her head. That was Ruari's blood seeping into the dark moss, and she was the one who'd hung him.

Mahtra couldn't cry, but she could scream. She turned her head toward Kakzim when she screamed and nailed him with a look as venomous and mad as he'd ever given the world. Thunder brewed inside her as all the cinnabar she'd swallowed in the darkness quickened. The last thing she saw before the cloudy membrane slid over her eyes was Kakzim running toward her with his arm raised and the metal knife in his hand.

He *might* succeed in unmaking her, but that would come too late. Mahtra extended her arms, as if to embrace a lover, and surrendered herself to what the halflings had given her, confident that her thunder would kill.

★   ★   ★   ★   ★

Pavek had carried their guide almost from the start of their headlong march through the forest. He believed too late for halfling legs might be just in time for longer human legs, if they stormed through the forest like a thirst-crazed mekillot, never slowing, never weaving right or left. The little fellow on Pavek's shoulders had collected a few more bruises dodging branches on a maze of trails not made by anyone of Pavek's extended height, but Cerk hadn't complained, simply grabbed fistfuls of Pavek's hair and shouted out "right" or "left" at the appropriate time.

The twin moons had risen before the sun completely set. Between them, they shed sufficient light through the leaves to keep the trail visible to Pavek's dim, human eyes; but it was a strange light, filled with ghosts and shimmering wisps and luminous eyes in slanting pairs and foreboding isolation. The novice druid's skin crawled as Cerk guided him through the haunted trees, but he never hesitated, not until a solitary clap of thunder rolled through the moonlit forest.

"Mahtra!" Pavek shouted.

"The white-skinned woman is still alive," Cerk agreed.

Thinking he no longer needed a guide, Pavek came to a stiff-legged halt and tried to lift Cerk down, but the halfling clung to him, insisting:

"You won't find it without me, even now. We must all stay together!"

Pavek turned to Javed, who'd halted beside him, as the other templars had come to a stop behind them. With his nighttime skin and elven eyes, the commandant was little more than a moonlit ghost himself.

"You heard him, Commandant."

"Do you think you could ever outrun *me,* my lord?" Ivory teeth made a smile beneath glassy eyes.

"Javed—" Pavek dug the toe of his sandal into the loose debris that covered the forest floor. "I plan to outrun death itself."

He filled his lungs and pushed off with all the strength in his body. The elven commandant fell behind for two paces, then he was back at Pavek's side, grinning broadly, running effortlessly.

"Lean into your strides, Pavek, put your head down and *breathe!*"

Pavek hadn't the wherewithal to answer, but he took the lessons to heart as Cerk shouted another "Veer left!" in his ear.

He saw hearthfires flickering in the near-distance. He'd heard nothing louder than Cerk or the pounding of his own feet since the thunder rolled over them, but silence didn't reassure him. Mahtra's protection was a potent weapon. She could have felled a score of halflings, but they wouldn't stay down for long. Pavek fingered the knotted leather looped over the top of his scabbard and drew his sword as he and Javed led their templars into a clearing that was larger than the whole halfling settlement, quiet as a tomb and almost as dark at its heart.

"Spread out. Keep your wits and swords ready!" Javed shouted his orders before he stopped running.

In pairs, as always, the men and women of the war bureau did as they were told.

"Mahtra! Mahtra, where are you?" Pavek set Cerk down without protest and spun on his heels as he called her name again: "Mahtra!"

"Pavek?" Her familiar, faintly inflected voice came from the black center of the clearing. "Pavek!"

He heard her coming toward him before her pale skin appeared in the moonlit. Javed took a brand from the nearest hearth. Her mask was gone. Another time, her face would have astonished him—he would have made a rude fool of himself gaping and staring. Tonight, he blinked once and saw the blood on Mahtra's neck, shoulder, and arm instead; her own blood, from her stiff, uncertain movements. Then he noticed the bodies. There were bodies everywhere: halflings on the ground, felled by thunder and just starting to move; halflings overhead, dangling from the branches of the biggest tree Pavek had ever seen, halflings whom Mahtra might have stunned, halflings who'd died long ago, and—scattered in the torchlight—bodies that weren't halflings, including a lean, lanky half-elf he recognized between two heartbeats.

"Cut him down," Mahtra pleaded before Pavek could say a word.

"Hamanu's mercy," Pavek's voice was soft, his lungs were empty, and his heart. "Cut him down." He couldn't breathe. His sword slipped through his fingers. "Zvain?" he whispered, starting another sweep of the bodies in the tree and those on the ground, looking for a halfling who wasn't a halfling.

"Alive," Mahtra said. "Hurt. Cut him down?"

All of which confirmed Pavek's dire guess that Ruari was neither hurt, nor alive. His mouth worked silently; the commandant gave the order. Two templars ran where the hanging ropes led, into the dark, toward the great tree's trunk. Their obsidian swords sang as they hacked through the ropes. Bodies fell like heavy, reeking rain, Ruari's among them, completely limp . . . deadweight . . . *dead*.

Pavek started toward his friend's lifeless body; the emptiness beneath his ribs had become an ache.

Mahtra stopped him. "Kakzim's gone. He grabbed me; he was touching me when the thunder happened. Another mistake. He got away."

"Which way?" Rage banished Pavek's grief and got his blood flowing again. "*Which way, Mahtra?*"

"I don't know. He got away before I could see again."

Pavek swore. His rage was fading without a target; grief threatened. "Couldn't you hear something?" he demanded harshly, more harshly than Mahtra deserved.

Her neck twisted, bringing one ear down to her bloody shoulder: her best impression of misery and apology. "A sound, maybe—over there?" She pointed with her bloody arm.

A sound, that was all the help Mahtra could give him; it would have to be enough. Retrieving his sword, Pavek jogged into the moonlit forest. Javed called him a fool. Cerk warned him his chase was futile and doomed. He could live with doom and futility—anything was better than facing Ruari's corpse.

Kakzim left no trail. There was a path, but it petered out on the bank of a little brook. Kakzim could have crossed the water or followed it upstream or down—if he'd come this way at all. The chase was futile and doomed, and Pavek knew himself for a fool.

A sweating, overheated fool.

The forest was cooler than the Tablelands, but not by much, and its moist air had glued Pavek's silk shirt to his skin. He knelt on the bank, his sword at his side, and plunged his head beneath the surface, as he would have done after a day's work in Telhami's grove. The forest spoke to him while he drank, an undisciplined babble, each rock and tree, every drop of water and every creature larger than a worm trumpeting its own existence: wild life at its purest, without a druid to teach it a communal song.

Pavek raised his dripping head. The moons had risen above the treetops. Javed was right: little Ral was slipping, silently and safely, across Guthay's larger sphere. Silver light mixed with gold. He could feel it on his face, not unlike the sensations a yellow-robe templar felt when Hamanu's sulphur eyes loomed overhead and magic quickened the air.

Insight fell upon him. Templars reached to Hamanu for their magic. Druids reached to the guardian aspects of the land for their magic. Kakzim had wanted the power of two moons when he aimed to poison Urik or sacrifice Ruari. It was a useless parade of insights: Magicians reached for magic to work their magic. Different magicians reached to different sources. A magician reached to the source that worked for him, and magic happened.

Anyone could reach, but if a man grabbed and held on with all his strength, all his will, magic might happen. And if you were already a doomed fool, you might as well reach for the moons, and the sparkling stars, too.

Pavek reached with his hands and his thoughts. He drew the silver-gold moonlight into himself and used it to summon the voices of the forest. When he held them all— moons and voices together—and his head seemed likely to burst from the strain, he shaped a single image.

Kakzim.

Kakzim with slave-scars, Kakzim without them. Black-eyed Kakzim, hate-eyed Kakzim. Kakzim who had come this way.

Who had seen Kakzim pass? What had felt him?

Pavek heard a shadow fall on the far side of the brook, felt a whisper: *This way. This way.* A child-sized footprint floated on the water, reflecting the silver-gold moonlight. Not daring to look away, Pavek found his sword by touch alone, returned it to its scabbard, and forded the brook. More footprints greeted him on the far side. Branches glimmered where the halfling had brushed against them. The forest creatures whose minds he had touched echoed Kakzim's image according to their natures. Something large and predatory shot back its own potent image—*food*—warning Pavek that with or without magic, he was not the only hunter in the forest.

He wasn't a fast runner, even measured against other humans, but Pavek was steady and endowed with all the endurance and stamina the templar orphanage could beat into a youngster's bones. One of his strides equalled two of Kakzim's, and one stride at a time, Pavek narrowed the gap between himself and his quarry.

The moment finally came when merely human ears heard movement up ahead and merely human eyes spied a halfling's silhouette between the trees. Releasing the forest voices and the silver-gold magical moonlight, Pavek drew his sword. Still and silent, he planned his moves carefully, borrowing every trick Ruari had ever shown him. But physical stealth wasn't enough.

Kakzim struck first with a mind-bender's might. The halfling's initial strike stripped Pavek of his confidence, but that wasn't a significant loss: Pavek truly believed he was an ugly, clumsy, dung-skulled oaf—and unlucky, besides. Relieved of those burdens, Pavek was alert and centered behind his sword as he approached the trees where Kakzim lurked. Next, Kakzim sent his mind-bending thoughts after Pavek's bravery and courage, which was a waste of the halfling's time. Pavek had never been a brave man, and his courage was the same as a tree's when it stood through a storm.

"You are an honest man!" Kakzim muttered in disgust, but loud enough for Pavek to hear the halfling judge him as Hamanu had judged him. "You have no illusions."

And with that, Kakzim shrouded himself in an illusion of his own. Instead of bringing his sword down on a halfling's unprotected neck, Pavek found himself suddenly nose-to-nose with an enemy who wore Elabon Escrissar's gold-enameled black mask and took the stance of a Codesh brawler with a poleaxe braced in both hands.

It was a poor illusion, in certain respects. Pavek could see moonlight through the mask and did not believe, for one heartbeat, that he faced either Escrissar or a butcher. It was, however, an effective illusion because he couldn't see Kakzim, and he didn't see the knife Kakzim wielded against him, even when it sliced across his left thigh. Reeling backward in pain and shock, Pavek instinctively slashed the illusionary Escrissar from the left shoulder to the right hip and was stunned when he met no resistance.

Pavek's leather armor and even the silk of his shirt would protect his body from the knife he *thought* Kakzim was using against him, but no man could survive for long, taking real wounds from a weapon he couldn't see.

A real weapon, Pavek reminded himself. Kakzim could lose himself in an illusion, but the knife remained real, fixed in the real grip of the halfling's arm, limited by a halfling's reach, a halfling's skill. He'd taken a wound in his thigh because it was exposed, but also because it was Kakzim's easiest target. Pavek kept his arms and the sword in constant motion, warding against the attacks he thought a halfling might choose, while he, himself, looked for a knife-sized flaw in the illusion.

Kakzim chuckled; Pavek slashed at the sound. The halfling wasn't a fighter, not with steel. Kakzim sent illusion after illusion into Pavek's mind. Some were people the halfling must have plucked out of Pavek's memory, others were total strangers. All of them had weapons and all of them withered in the barren soil of Pavek's imagination.

All except one—

One dark-eyed woman returned, no matter how many times Pavek sent her image away. Her name was Sian. She had hair like midnight and a luscious smile. She'd never met a man she didn't love; never met a man she didn't love more than she loved her tagalong son. Pavek couldn't fight the memory of his own mother, couldn't look for a knife in *her* hand.

Kakzim had found his weakness. He took another gouge along his left leg. It was painful, but not yet disabling. The halfling's weapon was a small knife, but, then again, in human terms, any halfling weapon would seem small.

Pavek gritted his teeth against the pain. Once again, he reasoned his way past his long-dead mother—and became aware of another Unseen presence in his mind. It was furtive, but not small. It faded from a glancing thought, and with Kakzim reconstructing Sian's image, Pavek couldn't afford a second outward thought: the first alone cost him another gash—this one on his right shin, and deep enough to affect his balance.

Pavek dropped his weaving defense to attack the place Kakzim might have been. He heard a gasp his mother had never made, and then something heavy, sharp and strong came down on his shoulder, slicing through his leather armor, snagging the silk, without tearing it.

Not a halfling, Pavek's mind reached *that* certainty with

the speed of lightning. No halfling had the power, the sheer weight, to drive him to his knees. And, to his knowledge, nothing could strike a man so many times as he went down. The beast had twice as many legs as it needed and a tufted tail with wickedly curved spikes protruding through the shaggy hair. Fortunately, the spikes curved toward the tail's tip and were sharp on their inner edge, else Pavek would have lost an eye, at the very least, as the beast sank down on its too-many-feet between himself and Kakzim.

It was the Unseen predatory presence he'd felt moments ago and, quite probably, the predator that had responded to his *Kakzim*-image with *food*. Ears flicking constantly, it flooded the minds of its prey with a simple but powerful mind-bending attack. Pavek knew this, because it considered him prey. It considered Kakzim prey, as well, because the halfling had shed his illusions. Beads of sweat bloomed on Kakzim's forehead as he absorbed the beast's assault, trying—no doubt—to dominate it and turn it against Pavek.

If he'd been a clever man, Pavek would have used his few precious moments to slay the beast and Kakzim, too, but he was awed by its power, its lethal beauty. Hamanu styled himself the Lion of Urik, though no one in Urik had ever seen a lion. This many-legged creature could be Hamanu's lion. It had almost as many ways to kill its prey: if mind-bending wasn't enough, it had eight clawed feet, an abundance of teeth, a pair of horns, and the spikes on its tail.

Pavek was lucky to be alive, and he should kill it while he had the chance, but lethal as it was, it was beautiful, too, with irregular stripes across its long back, its tail, and down each leg. Magical silver-gold moonlight limned each muscular curve of its body as it fought Kakzim for dominance. The dark stripes were tipped with starlight; the lighter, tawny stripes, with fire.

Though he knew what he should do, Pavek found himself thinking of Ruari, instead. It was so easy to imagine the two of them together, Ruari on his knees, scratching all the itchy places that were sure to collect around those horns and ears.

So easy, and so breathtakingly sad that the half-elf would never touch, never see—

The lion made a sound deep in its throat, the first sound it had made. Pavek sensed its concentration had faltered. He feared Kakzim had won. Then, in his mind's eye, Pavek saw Ruari as he'd not seen him before: angular and flat-nosed, coppery hair and coppery skin coming together around slit-pupiled coppery eyes.

Ruari? Pavek was no mind-bender, but after enduring so many of Kakzim's Unseen assaults, he had a notion of how to channel his thoughts to the lion. *Ruari—? Is that you?* Telhami, after all, persisted as a green sprite in her grove. Perhaps on this magic-heavy night, Ruari had found a refuge in the mind of a lion.

But before the lion could answer, Kakzim lunged forward and thrust his knife between its ribs, high above its front legs. The lion leapt aside and yowled. Pavek saw—and recognized instantly—the knife sticking out of a tawny stripe. It was his knife, the knife he'd given to Ruari in Codesh, the knife whose hilt he'd wrapped with a lock of his mother's midnight hair.

Faster than thought and with a scream of his own, Pavek took his sword-hilt in both hands. He easily dodged the lion's thrashing tail and committed everything to a sweeping crosswise slash with his sword.

Kakzim's body toppled forward; his head came to rest where the wounded lion had stood a heartbeat earlier. The lion was already gone into the forest, roaring its anger and agony, taking Pavek's knife with it. Pavek called his friend's name, but Ruari's spirit had not come to rest in the great cat, and soon the forest was quiet again.

He cried for his knife as he hadn't yet cried for Ruari and had never cried for Sian. Then Pavek picked up Kakzim's gory head by a tuft of hair. He remembered the four of them—him, Mahtra, Zvain and Ruari—first returning to Urik; it seemed a lifetime ago. Zvain had wished for honor and glory; he'd wanted to throw Kakzim's head at Hamanu's feet.

If Zvain lived, he, at least, could have a wish come true.

But the strength of purpose that had sustained Pavek since morning finally failed him. Walking slowly with Kakzim's head in one hand and his sword back in its scabbard, Pavek slowly retraced his way to the black tree. Ral slid free of Guthay; the forest remained bright, but the silver-gold light came to a sudden end.

★　★　★　★　★

Dawn was coming, the fainter stars had already vanished for the day, and Pavek's injured legs hurt with every plodding step he took. By the time got back to the brook where he'd reached for moonlight magic, Pavek didn't know quite where he was, and really didn't care. He stumbled on the wet stones and went down. The cool water felt good on his wounds. He didn't want to stand again; couldn't have, if he'd tried. Pavek barely had the strength left to heave Kakzim's head onto the far bank where someone could find it. For himself, all he wanted to do was put his head down and sleep.

"Hamanu's infinitesimal mercy! You caught him? You killed him!"

Pavek didn't recognize the voice—didn't see anyone at all until Javed laughed and pulled him out of the water. Mahtra was waiting on the bank, too. Her mask was in its accustomed place and her shawl was expertly wound around her shoulder.

"Lord Javed is very good at bandaging; he'll take good care of your legs," she confided to Pavek.

With one arm bound against her, Mahtra remained as strong as many men, and had no trouble propping Pavek's weary body against a tree. The commandant—whom she called Lord Javed, as she'd once called Elabon Escrissar Lord Elabon—stood nearby tearing strips of silk into bandages. Everyone said the Hero of Urik took good care of his men, and apparently that was no myth. He unslung a roll of soft black leather and surveyed an assortment of salves and potions that any healer would be proud to own.

Mahtra must have seen Pavek staring. "Don't worry," she reassured him. "My lord is very wise, like Father. He's been everywhere—even to the tower where I was made. There's nothing he doesn't know."

Pavek was too weary to say anything except the first words that came into his mind: "You've made a good choice, Mahtra. He'll take good care of you."

"I know."

The commandant had already taken care of almost everything. While Javed cleaned and bandaged Pavek's three wounds, he carefully explained everything that he'd done while Pavek was chasing Kakzim through the forest—and in Lord Pavek's name, of course. The corpses had been respectfully laid out beneath the black tree; they awaited the proper burial rites, which the halfling, Cerk, would perform with the assistance of the Brethren who'd sworn their loyalty to him. Javed had personally examined all the wounded before sending them to the halfling village for rest, food, and other care. Those halflings who'd refused to swear to Cerk had been sent to the village, also—under the watchful eyes and sharper swords of Javed's maniples. And once Lord Pavek's wounds were bound up, they'd be going back to the village. There was a litter waiting, with two strong dwarves to carry it, if Lord Pavek didn't think he could walk that far.

Pavek nodded. He listened to everything the commandant said, but he didn't really hear any of it. His legs had been numb before Javed bandaged them, and they felt no different now. He needed help standing, and if it weren't for Javed's arm under his, he'd have fallen several times along the path from the brook to the black tree. He'd had the presence of mind to make certain Kakzim's head wasn't left behind. Beyond that, whatever Javed said, wherever Javed took him, however he got there, it was all the same to Pavek.

The sky was glowing when, with the commandant steadying his every step, Pavek walked beneath the black tree again. The moss-covered clearing was quiet—

"Pavek!"

Zvain ran toward him. There was a big bandage around his forehead, covering one eye, but he ran too well to have been seriously injured. Pavek opened his arms and let the boy try to catch him as he fell.

EPILOGUE

In waking dreams, Pavek remembered being helped to an improvised bed. Someone apologized, saying there wasn't a single piece of linen anywhere large enough to cover him from head to foot. He remembered laughing and then falling asleep. He remembered sunlight and food and more apologies because, wounded though he was, he'd have to sleep under the stars; the houses were too small. He remembered wondering where he was, and then sleeping some more.

The sun was at its height when his eyes opened again, clear-headed and ready to deal with the man who'd awakened him.

"Do you think you'll live, Lord Pavek?" Commandant Javed asked with his usual cryptic smile.

Pavek shoved himself up on one elbow. Every muscle ached and every ache brought back a memory. By the time he was sitting, he'd recalled it all: from putting on a silk shirt to Mahtra carrying Kakzim's head in a silk shirt sleeve. There was a day and a night's worth of dreamless heartbeats between him and those memories.

"If I'm not dead now—"

"Your life was never in danger," the veteran elf assured him quickly. "A few nicks and scratches, a bit more running than you're used to—" He grinned again. "But you'll mend."

"I'll mend," Pavek agreed, closing his eyes briefly, thinking about faces he'd never see again. "I'll mend."

When he opened his eyes, Mahtra stood behind Javed. Her shoulder wasn't bandaged; there were no scabs or scars. He wondered if he *had* dreamed.

"The child heals quickly," Javed confided in a whisper. "Remarkable. I've never met anyone like her."

Pavek nodded. It was a relief, a guilt-ridden relief, to know he didn't have to think about what would happen to her. He was going to need every thought he had to get himself pointed at the future again.

"It's time for another decision, my lord," Javed said, and Pavek groaned—only half in jest. "We've done what we came to do. There are two maniples camped out in the trees here, cramped, hungry, and itching to get home. There are two men bound to bed and not likely to get up for another week. And there's you. You can head for home now—I judge your legs are equal to the mountains, if we take them a bit slower than we did the last time. Or you can stay here, heal up some more, and come home a bit later. You understand, my lord, you're in charge still, and there's no one leaving here without your say-so."

"Two injured men?" Pavek mused aloud. Of everything Javed had said, those were the words that stuck in his mind. They'd lost a templar to halfling poison, but she wasn't a man. "Zvain—?" he asked anxiously. In his memory, the boy had looked lively enough beneath his bandage—at least before Pavek had fallen on him, whenever, wherever that had happened—if it weren't another dream.

Javed grimaced. "Not him. I'd forgotten him—or tried to. He's fine. Says he'll do whatever you do: stay or leave."

"Who's injured then? I don't remember," Pavek scratched his head, as if knowledge seeped through his scalp.

"A noisy dwarf from Ject—you remember Ject, the village south of here on the far side of the mountains? And that half-elf friend—"

"—Ruari? Ruari's alive?" Pavek caught himself reaching for Javed's hands. "He didn't die on Kakzim's tree?"

"No," Mahtra said, cocking her head. "I *told* you. You heard me, Lord Javed, didn't you? I told him first thing, as you were pulling him out of the water." She turned back to Pavek. "You didn't pay any attention!"

"I didn't hear." Pavek hid his face behind his hands, unsure if he would laugh or cry, and did neither as the emotions shattered against each other. He uncovered his face. "How is he? Where is he?"

Javed put a hand on Pavek's shoulder, holding him down with very little effort.

"Where he is, is over there—" A black arm reached toward the other side of the halfling village where another improvised bed held another tall man, a copper-haired man whose copper hair was the only unbandaged part of him. "How he is, is surviving, mending bit by bit. They damn near killed him, those BlackTree halflings. If it had been up to me, I'd've slain the lot of them—even for a half-breed bastard. But, I've taken your measure, my lord, and I didn't think you'd *approve*. If I was wrong, Lord Pavek—?"

Another smile, which Pavek gamely returned. "No, you've measured me right, Commandant, and you have my leave to take the maniples back to Urik. I choose to stay here, with my friends."

The commandant nodded. An elf could always appreciate the notion of friendship, even if he didn't appreciate the friends. "Your permission, my lord, I'll take the head with me, as proof of what we've accomplished. Somehow, I think it might be a while before you and your friends wander back to Urik. If you listen to that dwarf, you'll waste the rest of your life looking for halfling treasure!"

Not treasure, Pavek thought, but a lion and a knife . . .

He said good-bye to them later that afternoon. Then, with Zvain on one side and a talkative dwarf named Orekel bending his ear on the other, Pavek took up vigil at Ruari's side.